To So Few

Hunter

Books by Cap Parlier:

—

Anod series
The Phoenix Seduction (1995)
Anod's Seduction (2004) [reprint of The Phoenix Seduction]
Anod's Redemption (2004)

—

Sacrifice (2000)
The Clarity of Hindsight (2016)
Apocalypse Endeavor (2019)

—

To So Few series
To So Few – In the Beginning (2014)
To So Few – The Prelude (2014)
To So Few – Explosion (2015)
To So Few – The Trial (2016)
To So Few – The Verdict (2017)
To So Few – Frustration (2018)
To So Few – Deflection (2019)
To So Few – Hunter (2020)

—

and with **Kevin E. Ready:**
TWA 800 – Accident or Incident? (1998)

—

Coming soon from Cap Parlier, To So Few – Struggle, the ninth book of the series novel of flight and a warrior's life.

—

These and other great books available from Saint Gaudens Press
Post Office Box 405
Solvang, CA 93463-0405
URL: http://www.saintgaudenspress.com
Visit Cap Parlier's Web Site at: http://www.parlier.com

To So Few

Hunter

by
Cap Parlier

SAINT GAUDENS PRESS
Phoenix, Arizona & Santa Barbara, California

Saint Gaudens Press
Post Office Box 405
Solvang, CA 93464-0405

Http://www.SaintGaudensPress.com

Saint Gaudens, Saint Gaudens Press
and the Winged Liberty colophon
are trademarks of Saint Gaudens Press

Print edition ISBN: 978-0-943039-53-4
eBook edition ISBN: 978-0-943039-54-1
Library of Congress Catalog Number - 2020932246

Printed in the United States of America

The TO SO FEW series books are works of fiction. Any reference to real people, objects, events, organizations, or locales is intended only to give the fiction a sense of reality and authenticity. Other names, characters and incidents are the products of the author's imagination and bear no relationship to past events, or persons living or deceased.

Dedication

—

This volume of the To Fo Few series is
dedicated to my paternal/maternal ancestors and family members
who have served this Grand Republic under arms
since before we gained our independence
from Great Britain.

—

Acknowledgement

—

Once again, my profound gratitude goes to John Richard for his critical and constructive review of the manuscript. He constantly challenges me to do better and to tell a more compelling story. His interest in history always stimulates me to dig deeper into the extraordinary details I have tried to capture in this volume, the prior books, and as inspiration for future stories.

Jeanne remains my steadfast and irreplaceable partner in life. Her support and care sustain my writing. I cannot imagine life without her.

The editors and staff at Saint Gaudens Press continue to amaze me, offering invaluable support and assistance along with incomparable skill and attention to detail.

—

Prologue

—

War enveloped the entire planet for the second time in a generation and the aftermath of the devastating Japanese surprise attack on allied armed forces in the Pacific region. The cascade of nations aligning with the Allies, primarily the Soviet Union, Great Britain and the United States, and with the Axis: Germany, Japan, and Italy, progressed quickly as nations chose sides. The Germans and Italians occupied virtually all of Europe, other than the neutral countries (Switzerland, Sweden and Portugal) and had a very friendly relationship with Franco's fascist Spain. The Japanese occupied nearly the entirety of East Asia and the Western Pacific, and with the surprise attack on the United States armed forces at Oahu, Hawaii, the Japanese Imperial Navy demonstrated its supremacy in the Pacific Ocean.

The *Wehrmacht*, the armed forces of Nazi Germany, were literally at the gates of Moscow. The Red Army hung by a fragile threat, aided by the brutal cold of winter in Russia, but they were still on the field of battle. The Germans had transitioned from West to East in June 1941, which ended The Blitz nightly bombing campaign of England, and brought the British time to replenish, refurbish and gain strength. The fight across the English Channel was far from over, but emphatically did not have the intensity and desperation of the Battle of Britain during the summer of 1940, and the raw brutality of The Blitz. The Royal Navy was making begrudgingly slow progress against the life-threatening violence of the German U-boat submarine menace, but they still did not have the upper hand, even with the assistance of the United States Navy, covering the Western Atlantic to the Icelandic meridian. Yet, any progress was good.

The vital supplies under the landmark Lend-Lease Act had begun flowing to the British, and now the Soviet Union and China, and helped stimulate the rapid expansion and conversion of the industrial capacity of the United States for war. Mobilization of the American economy jumped exponentially with the attack on Pearl Harbor. Men and women from all walks of life volunteered for service—the nation needed them.

Prime Minister Winston Leonard Spencer Churchill, CH, TD, Member of Parliament for Epping, and President of the United States Franklin Delano Roosevelt had evolved an extraordinary friendship and unprecedented private channel for their communications over the last several years that enabled the president to take considerable political risk in the American effort to sustain the British against the German onslaught.

Young American volunteer fighter pilot Flying Officer Brian Arthur 'Hunter' Drummond, CBE, MC, DFC, transitioned to become a teacher and leader within the Royal Air Force's No.71 'Eagle' Squadron. Brian Drummond stood out physically among his brethren, standing 6 feet, 2 inches, with an athletic, 185-pound body, a distinctively chiseled, unblemished face, light brown, wavy hair, blue-grey eyes, and a fair complexion. He looked younger than he was at 20 years of age. His 19 aerial victories and his unofficial designation as a triple ace had come with a price, having had four aircraft shot out from under him and having been wounded twice—the last time nearly taking his life. Brian and Charlotte Grace (Palmer) Drummond, GC, née Tamerlin, had married after Christmas last year, and their firstborn, a son named Ian Malcolm Drummond, had been brought into a wartime world the following June. Charlotte was a strikingly attractive, 27-year-old, relatively tall woman with porcelain skin, prematurely gray hair, blue-gray eyes, and distinctively fine features. She was a strong, independent and confident person, who ran the now 385-acre, Standing Oak Farm, outside Winchester, Hampshire. The farm had been in the Tamerlin family for more than two centuries when Charlotte inherited the property. Brian used some of his substantial inheritance from his parents' estate to help Charlotte double the size of her original farm. Charlotte was also the humble recipient of the George Cross – the highest civilian award for heroic action – for risking and nearly losing her own life to pull the unconscious Brian from her farm pond and out from under the tangle of the sinking parachute.

Brian's closest brother-in-arms, Flying Officer Jonathan Andrew Xavier 'Harness' Kensington of Newcastle, had been Brian's classmate during their pre-war flight training and fortuitously gained assignment to the same squadron, No.609 Squadron, seven weeks after Brian. Jonathan cut quite the figure of virile British manhood – curly blond hair, ice-blue eyes, and half a foot shorter and 20 pounds lighter than his buddy, but also an accomplished Spitfire pilot. Jonathan held the distinction of being one of the few 'line' fighter pilots to fly captured enemy aircraft with the exploitation team at the Royal Aeronautical Establishment, Farnborough. Like Brian, Jonathan married his longtime girlfriend, Linda (Mason) Kensington, at the family estate of Carlingon Castle, outside Newcastle.

Brian's benefactor and protector in the Royal Air Force – Air Commodore John Henry Randolph Spencer, CMG, DFC – had been Great War squadron mates with American volunteer, fighter pilot and ace Malcolm Bainbridge. Malcolm had been Brian's flight instructor since the young man had been nine years old and died nearly two years ago in a tragic aircraft accident. John was now 44 years old, of moderate stature – 5 feet 9 inches tall and 155 pounds at his last check – green eyes, and dark brown hair, streaked with grey, now limited to a laurel band just above his ears. He luckily managed to marry the beautiful, outgoing, and eight years younger Mary Elizabeth Ann Spencer née Armstrong 13 years ago. John's commitment, energy and expertise garnered him a promotion and assignment as Chief Controller, No.11 Group, at Uxbridge, the air defenders of Southeast England, who had borne the brunt of the German air assault during the summer of 1940. Although he did not and never would brandish his family connection, John Spencer was also a nephew of Prime Minister Churchill, to whom he had introduced Brian before the war and after the American's arrival in England.

Squadron Leader Lord Jeremy Robert Kenneth 'Mud' Morrison, now the commanding officer of No.32 Squadron and the younger brother of the 8th Duke of Cottingstone, had been Brian Drummond's first RAF flight instructor and had become friends with the American. Mud remained a fun-loving, fast-living, fighter pilot who repeatedly crossed paths with Hunter and Harness. He loathed to use his courtesy title or his brother's peerage in any social occasion, and often proclaimed he was just another fighter pilot.

Trevor Thomas Andersen graduated from Cambridge University with a degree in European history in 1926, and he already had a job. During his college years, he attracted the attention of an influential man, Director of Naval Intelligence Vice Admiral Sir Geoffrey Ian 'Jumper' Pike, KCB, DSC. Trevor's frankly rather ordinary, Aryan appearance with longish light brown hair, blue eyes, and medium build attracted little notice. Trevor's fluency in French, German and Polish, along with the unusual ability to quickly switch to one of several dialects, made him nearly ideal for intelligence fieldwork. After several apprenticeship missions, Trevor was given a code name – 'Diamond.' He also picked up several alias *personae*, including that of Robert Henry Stone Johnston, a leather goods salesman. After the formation of the Special Operations Executive (SOE) – tasked by Churchill to set German-occupied Europe ablaze – Andersen transferred from the Admiralty to SOE. Trevor had carried out numerous missions into occupied Europe, including a successful mission to capture a German Enigma coding device and an unsuccessful mission to capture or kill German General Erwin Rommel.

And so, here begins our story.

———

Chapter 1

People sleep peaceably in their beds at night
only because rough men stand ready
to do violence on their behalf.

--George Orwell

Monday, 8.December.1941
Pan American Airways Pacific Clipper
32° 46' South – 172° 02' East
08:30 hours

Captain Robert 'Bob' Ford kept his eyes and attention scanning the instrument panel in front of him. The massive Boeing Model 314 flying boat, in this instance aircraft registration number NC18609 and known as Pacific Clipper, cruised at 8,000 feet pressure altitude, heading south-southeast. They were between solid cloud layers with no visible horizon or sight of the ocean below them. The ride comfort remained smooth and easy for the 12 passengers and 10 crewmembers on board. Four hours ago, the aircraft had lifted off smoothly from the water near Noumea, New Caledonia, on the 5th and last leg of their scheduled flight from Treasure Island in San Francisco Bay, to Auckland, New Zealand, that had begun five days earlier. The crew looked forward to a few day's downtime in picturesque New Zealand.

"Skipper?"

"Yeah, John," Bob said to Radioman John Poindexter over the intercom.

"I've got a hot one."

"Let's see it," the aircraft commander responded, to acknowledge for the crew that John would be off the intercom for a few seconds, so John could plug his headset into the auxiliary communications jack near the captain's seat. The whole flight deck crew looked at the radioman and the piece of paper he carried. John handed the paper to Bob, and then plugged in his headset.

SECRET

Date: *12/8/41 in flight*
From: *HQ Miami*
Text:
Do not respond Stop Radio silence in flight Stop Serious situation Hawaii Stop Hold Auckland Stop Contact naval attache NZ immediately upon arrival Auckland Stop Contact hq asap thereafter
END

SECRET

"What do you think it means, Skipper?"

"What the words say."

"Well," Poindexter replied, "I do not know, either, but whatever it is, it is not good." He handed the message to First Officer and Copilot John Henry Mack. After reading the message, Mack shook his head and handed the message back to Poindexter.

Bob Ford glanced over his shoulder to confirm that the whole flight deck crew was looking at him. "Look, guys," he began over the flight deck intercom, "the message says something has happened in Hawaii, and we are to hold at Auckland. First and foremost, we've got passengers to deliver to Auckland. Let's focus on the task at hand. We'll sort this out once we get to Auckland. There is no purpose served with speculation. We'll learn more when we get to the station. We must maintain radio silence, so we will likely hear no more until we arrive in New Zealand."

Their employer and the owner of the aircraft—Pan American Airways, Inc.—formed in 1927, with the merger of three smaller air service companies, and adopted the Pan Am moniker and logo. The company had worked with Boeing to produce the much longer-range Model 314 and initiated Pacific region air service just a few years prior. They now provided commercial air transport and airmail service to Tokyo, Hong Kong, Manila, and of course, New Zealand and Australia. The airline had grown to be a significant provider of air service throughout the Caribbean, Central and South America, as well as Western Europe, and now the Pacific and Asia.

———

Monday, 8.December.1941
United States Consulate General
23 Customs Street East
Auckland, North Island
Dominion of New Zealand
11:30 hours

The Pacific Clipper had arrived 15 minutes late from the planned schedule. The remainder of the flight leg from New Caledonia had been thankfully uneventful . . . except for the unusual message. The aircraft was moored at its assigned buoy and the tender platform secured to the aircraft. Captain Ford left First Officer Mack in charge of the refueling, resupply, and off-loading of the massive flying boat. Bob took Second Officer/Navigator Roderick Nicholas 'Rod' Brown with him to the Consulate. The city remained strikingly calm and ordinary, other than a larger than expected number of military uniforms among the pedestrians of the city.

An armed U.S. Marine security guard sat at the Consulate lobby counter. "May I help you, sir?" he asked.

"I have a message," Ford said, holding the paper, "to see the naval attaché."

"To my knowledge, sir, Captain Morehouse is in Wellington."

"How about the Consul General?"

"He is in Wellington, as well, for a meeting with the ambassador."

"Then, who is in charge here?" asked Bob Ford.

"The duty consular officer is Assistant Commercial Attaché Jillian."

"May I speak to him, please?"

"Please take a seat. I will call him. Your name, sir?"

"Ford, Bob Ford. I am the captain of the Pan Am Pacific Clipper that landed in the bay an hour ago."

Ford and Brown did as suggested, and sat together in two of a dozen chairs. There was nothing to indicate anything unusual or untoward.

Five minutes later, a middle-aged man dressed in a light blue, seersucker suit appeared in the lobby. "Mister Ford?" he said, as he extended his right hand, "I'm Commercial Attaché Isaac Jillian. How may I be of service?"

Ford and Brown stood and shook hands with Jillian. Several other apparent civilians sat in the lobby waiting for something. "Is there a more private place we can talk?"

Jillian did not answer and only nodded his head. He gestured for the two visitors to follow him. A small meeting room adjacent to the lobby served as that location. Jillian closed the door and gestured for the visitors to sit. He further gestured for Captain Ford to proceed.

"I am the captain of the Pan American Pacific Clipper. We arrived here an hour ago, and we received this message in flight from New Caledonia," Bob handed the message to Jillian. When Jillian looked up, he continued, "We are trying to figure out what is going on and what we are supposed to do with that," he said and pointed at the message still in Jillian's hand.

"Captain Morehouse, the naval attaché, is due to arrive later this afternoon. We do not know the purpose of his visit, but your message suggests he is coming to talk to you. The situation in Hawaii is indeed quite serious, I'm afraid. The Japanese Navy attacked Pearl Harbor . . . well, actually, all of Oahu . . . all U.S. forces."

"Dear God!" exclaimed Ford. "Damage? Have they invaded?"

"We do not know. We are trying to figure things out as well. Washington appears to be rather preoccupied, as I'm sure you can appreciate. Captain Morehouse will likely have more information, but there are no messages or instructions for you or your flight that I'm aware of. You may be here for a while."

"Are we at war?"

"I cannot give you any more information than I already have," Jillian answered.

Bob Ford tried to digest what Jillian had just told them. "When is Captain Morehouse supposed to arrive?"

"He is due here at four this afternoon . . . unless he encounters any delays en route. He is driving up here from Wellington. It is about an eight-hour drive."

"Can I signal New York?"

"We have no public communications means in the Consulate," Jillian answered. "The public telegraph office is several blocks away. I'm afraid we have no means to clarify the situation for you."

"Thank you, Mister Jillian. We'll go check on our aircraft and crew. We will brief our passengers on what you have told us so far. However, I suspect many of them will make their way here for information and assistance. We have fulfilled our mission, and delivered our passengers and mail, and now we are faced with what next. Perhaps our station chief will have some instructions from headquarters. We'll be back at four to talk to Captain Morehouse."

"Very well," Isaac said. "I'll leave a message to that effect for Captain Morehouse."

"Thank you." Ford and Brown stood, shook hands with Jillian, and departed.

Once outside the Consulate and walking toward the Pan Am office near the service dock, Brown observed, "That was a bust."

"Yeah," Bob said. "We are apparently at war, although we have no confirmation of that. Without Hawaii, we cannot make it back to California." They walked in silence for nearly a block. "Let's check in and get the crew fed. At least we have hotel rooms, so we might as well check in. As Jillian said, we may be here for a while. God only knows for how long. We may be stranded here for the duration of the war." Both of them withdrew to their thoughts and mental images as they walked.

———

Wednesday, 10.December.1941
RAF North Weald
Saffron Walden, Essex, England
United Kingdom
14:10 hours

The cold rain froze into a sheet of ice on everything—buildings, roads, grass, anything exposed to the rain. Despite the abysmal conditions, No.71 Squadron remained on alert, which left the pilots continuously chewing on what they could perceive as happening with the newspapers and radio media speculating in the light of very little hard information. The expressed opinions of the American pilots progressively became more agitated and consistent. Brian felt the same, but did not engage in the wild speculation, based on predominantly emotion rather than facts. The Americans were unanimous in their desire to return to the United States and join the inevitable fight against the Japanese. As the British leader of 'B' Flight and Red Section, Flight Lieutenant Charles Gordon 'Whitey' Whittington chose to stay out of the multiple conversations that continued to boil in the dry, warm interior of the squadron alert building.

Squadron Leader Stanley Thomas 'Tug' Meares, DFC, remained in his office beyond the volatile words until the red alert phone on the raised desk of Squadron Operations Clerk Corporal James 'Jimmy' Harris rang, terminating all the conversations instantly. Jimmy listened and said, "Standby, please, sir." He covered the mouthpiece of the telephone handset and said in a louder than normal voice, "Skipper, Group on red." Jimmy kept the mouthpiece covered and put the earpiece to his left ear. Satisfied the commander had lifted his handset, Harris returned his handset to the cradle. The room remained silent in anticipation of any indication regarding the conversation. Several minutes passed. Several of the pilots began to fidget, but no one spoke.

Tug Meares appeared at the doorway to his office. "Gentlemen, if I may have your attention," he said, although he already had every man's keen and silent attention. "I have been called to Group for an unspecified meeting of squadron commanders. Since we cannot fly, I will have to utilize the railway, and thus will be away for the remainder of the day. Before I release you blokes, I want to note a couple of items. I have heard most of your arguments for transfer, and I cannot dispute a single one. I fully appreciate your sentiments, interests and opinions. However, until the Air Ministry and Fighter Command make a decision, we remain a vital fighter squadron in service to the Crown. I want that fact to remain immovably at the forefront of your conscious thought. To be distracted . . . distracted by anything around us . . . is a recipe for getting yourself killed. Let us not forget that reality." He paused. No one spoke or even moved. "Second, I must go to Uxbridge for this meeting, I shall take the opportunity to discuss the matter of transfer with Air Vice Marshal Leigh-Mallory." The statement generated a rumbling in the room and several clapping of hands. "I cannot promise anything, but perhaps I can turn up some additional relevant information."

"Thanks, Skipper," Pilot Officer Arnold Samuel 'Salt' Morton interjected.

Meares simply nodded his head. "Off the record and unofficially, I will offer a suggestion that you contact your brethren at One-Twenty-One and One-Thirty-Three Squadrons to agree on a delegation of representatives from all three American volunteer squadrons to meet with the American ambassador in London, if you are able to gain an appointment and meet with him. I will also caution all of you, he may not choose to meet with you, but it is worth a try, it seems to me."

Several of the pilots voiced their approval of and support for Tug's suggestion.

Meares raised his right hand for silence. "While I am absent, Whitey will be in charge. I remind each of you that we will be expected to return to Available status tomorrow morning at sunrise. I will also note that the Met Office forecast for tomorrow is not favorable, but that does not preclude our duty. Am I clear?"

"Yes sir," came the resounding chorus of responses.

The room remained quiet as Meares donned his overcoat, gloves, and peaked cover. When Tug departed on his journey to No.11 Group headquarters, Whitey stood and said, "We are released, gentlemen. You lads have a lot to discuss, none of which I am a party to here. You can remain here, or you can carry on in the Officer's Mess bar. Do not forget Tug's admonition, we are back on duty tomorrow morning at dawn. Have a good night." Again, the American pilots held their words until Whitey Whittington allowed Jimmy Harris to precede him and closed the door behind them both. Whitey opened the door immediately. "Make sure to switch off the lights and secure the fire when you are finished."

"Wilco," Flight Lieutenant Chesley Gordon 'Pete' Peterson responded with the aviator's contraction of 'Will Comply.' Pete stood, stepped back, and faced his squadron mates. "Who wants to represent our position?" No one answered or volunteered.

"We all should go," Pilot Officer Joshua David 'Frog' Forcier offered.

Peterson smiled. "I don't think that would be appreciated . . . a bunch of us flooding the embassy. We need one or two from each of the three Eagle squadrons."

"Has anyone talked to the guys in 121 and 133 Squadrons?" asked Salt Morton.

"I've got a couple of buddies in 121," said Pilot Officer Robert Charles 'Sweet' Sweeny, Jr., "but I've not talked to them or anyone else about transferring to the Army Air Forces."

"You and Hunter are the two senior Americans in our squadron," observed Pilot Officer Paul James 'Dusty' Langford. "I'd suggest the two of you represent us."

"I'm good with that," Pete answered. "How about you, Hunter?"

"Sure. I guess so," Brian said. "I'm not so good at such things, but I can do it."

"You're the most decorated in all three squadrons, and you are our ace," Dusty added.

Brian waved his hand dismissively and did not say anything else.

"OK, then," Pete said. "I'll contact the senior American in the other two squadrons and we'll get this set up as soon as possible."

"You know what we want," added Salt. "Let's just do it."

"We have a plan," Dusty added

They nodded, affirmed, cheered, and clapped as they stood. Sweet spread the coals in the wood-fueled space heater. They switched off the lights, secured the building, and headed to the Officer's Mess in the persistent freezing drizzle.

———

Thursday, 11.December.1941
Headquarters, No.11 Group
Uxbridge, Middlesex, England
United Kingdom
10:00 hours

Tug had decided to remain in Uxbridge after the late afternoon meeting, when he was given an appointment time of this morning for his requested private meeting with Air Officer Commanding-in-Chief, No.11 Group, Air Vice Marshal Trafford Leigh-Mallory, CB, DSO. The Group commander had too much on his plate yesterday afternoon. Meares took advantage of his extra time at Group headquarters for other squadron business, not least of which was thwarting the transfer and relocation of the squadron to RAF Kirton, Kirton-in-Lindsey, North Lincolnshire, for reduced operational tempo and rest. He knew it had taken the first American volunteer fighter squadron far too long to be considered ready for combat, and they did not want to rest. They were full of anger and determination, and they needed to focus that energy on the enemy.

"The commander will see you now, sir," announced the marshal's personal secretary.

Squadron Leader Meares marched into the commander's spacious office and saluted. "Thank you for taking the time for me, sir."

Leigh-Mallory gestured for Tug to sit on the couch, while he sat in the overstuffed chair directly opposite Meares. "What's on your mind?"

"First, thank you for your support of my request not to transfer the squadron to 12 Group and Kirton. That is not what these lads need at the moment. They are charged up and need to point their rage at the enemy, not take a rest break in the north." Leigh-Mallory simply nodded his head and did not answer. "Since the Japanese attacks that began a few days ago, the Americans have been consumed by the surprise attack on their naval base at Pearl Harbor and the American government's declaration of war on the Japanese."

"We are fighting Germany and her Axis allies."

"Yes sir. They are well aware of that, but they want to join their countrymen now that the United States is in this war."

"What are you or they proposing?"

"They would like to transfer to the American Army Air Forces as soon as possible."

"Easily said, Tug, not so easily done. That process will take diplomatic and military negotiations that have not begun. It is not as simple as giving them transport home. Further, I suspect the Germans will not be far behind their Japanese colleagues in declaring war on the United States. If that happens, the U.S. will begin building up their forces in Europe and specifically here. Having a command structure here will make their transfer far easier and quicker. The world situation is not clear, especially with respect to events in Asia and the Pacific still evolving. Please convey to your pilots that I have heard their request. I will raise the issue as soon as possible with Fighter Command, the Chief of the Air Staff, and the Air Minister. There may well be other factors involved that neither of us is aware of at the moment. I urge you to tell them I understand their sentiment and request. I actually support their request. For now, we must ask them to be patient and allow events to play out, but we must not jump too quickly."

"Yes sir. That is easily done. I must also inform you that they have requested an audience with the American ambassador for the same purpose."

"When?"

"I was informed last night that they have an appointment this morning, in fact, just about this time."

"They have every right to open the question with their ambassador. He should certainly be aware of their desire to join their country's armed forces in this war. I cannot imagine that we would discourage such initiatives; however, I must caution against over-zealous action that might complicate our operations and their position in the eventual transfer."

"I'm not sure I understand your point there, sir."

"I have had several frank conversations with General Arnold, the chief of the U.S. Army Air Forces. He is keenly aware of the difficulty we had getting your pilots to work together as a team, as a front-line fighter squadron, and more importantly, within our air defense system. Regression in performance would not be appreciated or looked upon kindly by me . . . or the Air Ministry. We have a job to do, and they are part of the task before us. They must do their assigned missions to the best of their ability until arrangements can be made. I believe their transfer is inevitable, but proper preparations must be completed first."

"Yes sir. Thank you for the explanation. I will probably not share the details, but I think the message is clear, and I will inform them carefully. If I may ask since they will undoubtedly ask me, when can the proper arrangements be made?"

Leigh-Mallory grinned and chuckled. "They are a persistent bunch, aren't they?"

"Yes sir, they are."

"The honest answer is the timing is too difficult to predict at the moment. However, my guess would be several months, perhaps even half a year."

"Thank you, sir."

"Thank you for bringing this matter to me, Tug. Now, I am already late for my next meeting. Please keep me informed as the situation with your pilots evolves. I will do the same, as I am able."

"Yes sir. Thank you for your time." Meares stood and saluted, as Leigh-Mallory passed him, leaving his office before Tug.

—

Thursday, 11.December.1941
Embassy of the United States of America
No.1 Grosvenor Square
Mayfair, London, England
United Kingdom
10:30 hours

The telephone calls to their sister squadrons and the embassy were frank, productive, and realistic. No.133 Squadron was based at RAF Eglinton, County Londonderry, Northern Ireland. No.121 was located at RAF Kirton, Kirton-in-Lindsey, North Lincolnshire, England. Both agreed to send two senior American volunteer pilots. However, when Pete called the U.S. Embassy in London to get an appointment, he was shocked that Ambassador Winant agreed to meet with them the next day, which in turn precluded the representatives from the other two squadrons from joining. Both of the more distant squadrons delegated to Peterson and Drummond to represent them as well. They all shared the same objective.

Pete and Brian checked in at the lobby, and were confirmed to be on the ambassador's guest list for their appointment. A junior aide, who did not introduce himself, escorted the two RAF officers to the top floor, corner office, overlooking the trees of Grosvenor Square that were now leafless in winter inactivity.

The ambassador stepped around his desk and toward both officers as they entered. "Welcome, gentlemen. I am Gil Winant," he said, extending his right hand first to Pete, and then to Brian. John Gilbert 'Gil' Winant had been the three-term governor of New Hampshire when President Roosevelt nominated him to replace the former ambassador Joseph Kennedy. Winant took up his post in February of last year while The Blitz was still devastating London and other major cities in Great

Britain. He served as the representative of the United States and the president, to the Court of St. James's. Winant gestured toward the facing couches with a low table as long as the couches between them. "Would you care for some coffee . . . or tea, if you wish?"

"No, thank you, sir," the two pilots said in unison.

"It's fresh Columbian coffee ground in San Francisco. Very good, actually."

"Neither one of us are coffee drinkers, Mister Ambassador," Pete responded and glanced at Brian. "Thank you, though."

"Very well. How may I be of service?"

"Thank you, sir, for meeting with us so quickly. We had hoped to have two representatives from our two sister squadrons, but they are based in the Midlands and Northern Ireland, and could not make it in time. So, they delegated their representation to Brian and me." Winant nodded his head. "We have listened and read the press reports of the attack on Pearl Harbor as well as the president's speech to Congress. The United States is now at war with Japan." Again, the Ambassador nodded. "All of us, to the man, chose to come here and help the British in defending the last bastion of freedom in Europe because we had skills the British needed."

"And, if I may interrupt you here, I will tell you preemptively that Germany and Italy have declared war on the United States, and we will likely reciprocate later today in Washington. I understand the extraordinary sacrifice and contribution each of you has made to the defense of freedom. The president is keenly aware as well. If I have been properly informed," Winant said and looked to Brian, "you have met the president."

"Yes sir, I have . . . in the Oval Office," Brian responded.

"You are also the highest-scoring American ace behind Eddie Rickenbacker from the Great War."

"And, he was awarded the Medal of Honor," added Pete.

"Yes, he did."

"I don't like to talk about that stuff, Mister Ambassador. I am just a guy who loves to fly, and I have been blessed to fly some of the best fighters in the world."

"You are also one of the most decorated pilots we have."

"Which is partly why we are here," Pete interjected. The ambassador's puzzled expression prompted him to continue. "We are three squadrons of experienced combat fighter pilots, Mister Ambassador. We are Americans, and our nation is at war with Japan. We need to join our comrades in defeating Japan."

"The sentiment is certainly understandable," Winant answered. "What do you think I can do to help that process?"

"Our squadron commander met with the chief of 11 Group this morning to request our transfer to the Army Air Forces. We know that we must work through the military chain of command, which we are doing. We do not yet know the outcome of that meeting, but we were encouraged to convey our request to you as the most senior American representative in England."

"I am that. I have no authority in military matters, and at the moment the most senior American military officer in Great Britain is Admiral 'Bob' Ghormley, who is the Special Naval Observer to Great Britain. He is an observer and has no command authority. The best I can be in this instance is a messenger. With your consent, I will enthusiastically pass along your request to the State Department and via State to the War Department."

"We respect your counsel, Mister Ambassador, and to that end, perhaps the conveyance of our collective request through the Royal Air Force would be better than passing our request directly, recognizing that the implied message of a request outside the military chain of command would not be well received by the generals."

Ambassador Winant nodded his head in agreement. "Very wise. So, I shall pass along the information to inform our leadership that I am aware of your request to the Air Ministry rather than intervene on your behalf."

Pete looked at Brian. "Do you agree?"

"Yes," Brian succinctly answered.

"We truly appreciate your willingness to meet with us, to hear our initiative, and to assist us in achieving our desire to transfer to the Army Air Forces as soon as possible."

"You are most welcome. Is there anything else I can do for you?"

"No sir. Thank you for listening," Pete said. Brian followed Peterson in standing, shaking hands with the ambassador, and departing his office. Neither of them spoke until they were outside and headed to Bond Street Underground Station for the Central Line to Epping and the return to RAF North Weald. "What did you think?" Pete asked.

"I thought it went very well. He seems to understand our situation rather well."

"My thoughts exactly. We need to compare notes with Tug. Hopefully, he'll be back by the time we arrive."

"Yeah. We can go from there. He left his door open for us . . . depending upon how things play out."

They boarded the train and headed back to base.

—

Thursday, 11.December.1941
Office of the Coordinator of Information
National Institutes of Health Building
2430 E Street Northwest
Washington, District of Columbia
United States of America
08:15 hours

Fatigue was verging upon exhaustion for the Coordinator of Information (COI) Colonel William Joseph 'Bill' Donovan, also known by various popular monikers—Big Bill and Wild Bill, among more colorful references and the code reference designator of '109.' Bill had not slept in four days, which brought back vivid memories from 23 years ago, when he led the 1st Battalion, 165th Regiment, 42nd Infantry Division, and could only find sleep in 5, 10 or 20-minute segments in combat. He was not as young as he was in those days when he was awarded the Medal of Honor, Distinguish Service Cross, Distinguish Service Medal, Silver Star, and three Purple Hearts. Bill felt the added burden of being only five months into his tenure as the chief of the president's fledgling strategic intelligence service. He had spent the last four days between the White House, the newly formed COI Research & Analysis Section, and his office. They were struggling to absorb the mountain of information coming to them, and then forming an accurate as possible picture of what was happening. Bill kept his growing focus on the future rather than trying to digest the past. There would be congressional, military, and civilian commissions to study the facts of what happened four days ago. The COI did not need to waste limited time and capacity on what happened. The president wanted and needed to know what was going to occur next and what might happen in the weeks, months and years ahead.

Colonel Gonzalo Edward 'Ned' Buxton knocked and did not wait for a response to enter Donovan's corner office on the Ground Floor of the Center Building. Ned had been Donovan's COI deputy from day one. He had commanded 2nd Battalion, 328th Infantry Regiment, 82nd Infantry Division, during the Great War, and had known Bill Donovan since their service together on the Western Front. Medal of Honor recipient Sergeant Alvin Cullum York carried out his combat exploits as part of Buxton's battalion. Both Buxton and Donovan were plank-holders, founding members of the American Legion that traced its genesis to a celebratory dinner at the Allied Officers' Club, Rue Faubourg, St. Honore, Paris, France, on the evening of 16.February.1919. Buxton handed the red, candy-striped folder to Donovan. "This just came in."

TOP SECRET - PERSONAL

```
ZZZZ/1138AOH427/XX-XX-XX/143576/HGLLEFAN/628/ZZZZ
MOST SECRET - EYES ONLY COI
DATE 41 12 11 1511 HOURS
FM NP6
TO 109 106
CC 17F
SUBJ ARCADIA
BREAK
SENDER TO ARRIVE WITH PRINCIPAL FOR SUBJECT
CONFERENCE BREAK NO SUPPORT REQUIRED OR
NECESSARY BREAK NP6 WITH 17F REQUEST PRIVATE
MEETING WITH 109 AND 106 CIRCA 19411222 ASAP
UPON ARRIVAL BREAK EXPECT INITIAL TOPICS
CURRENT STATUS SPECIAL OPERATIONS JOINT CONDUCT
SPECIAL COMMUNICATIONS AND SUPPORT FOR ARCADIA
END
MOST SECRET - EYES ONLY COI
ZZZZ/1138AOH427/XX-XX-XX/143576/HGLLEFAN/628/ZZZZ
```

TOP SECRET - PERSONAL

"Wow! Hot off the press," Bill said.

"Quite so."

"OK. This is from Jumper," Donovan observed, referring to the designation NP6 for Director Naval Intelligence (DNI), Naval Intelligence Division (NID), Royal Navy, Vice Admiral Sir Geoffrey Ian 'Jumper' Pike, KCB, DSC, who had received his moniker during heroic action aboard HMS *Spitfire* during the famous naval engagement of the Battle of Jutland and became DNI in 1939, before the war in Europe began. "Who is '17F'?"

"That designator does not appear in my book. Do you want me to query Jumper?"

"No, no, not necessary. They will be here in a week. If his identity was essential to our discussions, Jumper would have informed us. So, they are coming with Churchill and the chiefs for the joint planning conference. The British contingent plans to arrive on the 22nd and be here for a month."

"We'll be ready," Ned offered.

Donovan looked up from his papers with a puzzled expression on his face. "We have an awful lot to do for the conference."

"I have faith, Bill."

"As do I, but we must be realists. Based on what they are proposing for our agenda, I suspect they are apprehensive about the maturity of the COI, given that we are now at war and only five months old. We have so many irons in the fire. They want to know what to expect from us, and I imagine they are grappling with how they might help us get up on step."

"Is there anything out of the ordinary you need us to prepare for?"

Bill laughed hard. "Everything!"

"That's a lot."

"You got that right in spades. My most immediate concern is getting up to date information to the president. We were caught nearly blind in the Pacific. I'm focused on getting us caught up and ahead of the intelligence for the president. To be blunt, Ned, you're going to have to handle the organizational, personnel, and fundamental operations matters. I think Jumper included you, knowing that I am going to be consumed by the current situation."

"Do you want me to handle the meeting?"

"No. We need to do it together. I've not heard from 'C,'" Bill said, referring to Colonel Stewart Graham Menzies, DSO, MC, also known as 'C' in honor of the original Director-General of the Secret Intelligence Service (MI6). "So, I assume Jumper is representing 'C' on this trip. Until we hear otherwise, we should assume that Jumper will be speaking for the British intelligence services *in toto*. I suspect the discussions we shall have with Jumper in coincidence with the ARCADIA conference will set the tone for future collaboration."

"Got it."

Donovan leafed through a stack of papers in the tray on the left side of his desk. He found the paper he wanted and handed it to Ned. "I received this from Cordell earlier this morning at my daily briefing with the president." Secretary of State Cordell Hull had served as the nation's chief diplomat since the very beginning of President Roosevelt's administration.

MR. CHARGE D'AFFAIRES:

The Government of the United States having violated in the most flagrant manner and in ever increasing measure all rules of neutrality in favor of the adversaries of Germany and having continually been guilty of the most severe provocations toward Germany ever since the outbreak of the European war, provoked by the British declaration of war against Germany on September 3, 1939, has finally resorted to open military acts of aggression.

On September 11, 1941, the President of the United States publicly declared that he had ordered the American Navy and Air Force

to shoot on sight at any German war vessel.
In his speech of October 27, 1941, he once
more expressly affirmed that this order was
in Force. Acting under this order, vessels
of the American Navy, since early September
1941, have systematically attacked German
naval forces. Thus, American destroyers, as
for instance the Greer, the Kearney and the
Reuben James, have opened fire on German
submarines according to plan. The Secretary
of the American Navy, Mr. Knox, himself
confirmed that American destroyers attacked
German submarines.

Furthermore, the naval forces of
the United States, under order of their
Government and contrary to international
law have treated and seized German merchant
vessels on the high seas as enemy ships.

The German Government therefore
establishes the following facts:

Although Germany on her part has strictly
adhered to the rules of international law
in her relations with the United States
during every period of the present war,
the Government of the United States from
initial violations of neutrality has finally
proceeded to open acts of war against
Germany. The Government of the United States
has thereby virtually created a state of war.

The German Government, consequently,
discontinues diplomatic relations with the
United States of America and declares that
under these circumstances brought about by
President Roosevelt Germany too, as from
today, considers herself as being in a state
of war with the United States of America.
Accept, Mr. Charge d'Affaires, the expression
of my high consideration.
December 11, 1941.
RIBBENTROP

"So, it's official," Ned observed.

"No, not yet. Congress anticipated the German action. They are passing the declaration of war resolution on Germany, as we speak . . . and on the Italians. The president expects to sign the instruments of war later today."

"Not a particular surprise."

"No, it's not, is it? I suppose the only aspect of a surprise might be why it took Germany four days to join their Japanese ally. But, regardless, the stage is now set. Based on my earlier discussions with the British, I think we should anticipate a strong and persuasive argument from them for a Germany first strategy."

"Makes sense, actually."

"Other than the Japanese attacked us. The Germans didn't. But, yes, that is my opinion, in that Germany and Hitler seem to be the lynchpin in the Axis machine." Donovan thought for a moment, and Buxton did not intrude into his chief's contemplation. "Things have been busy since Sunday, but they are going to get much busier for us once Churchill arrives."

Buxton handed the German message back to Donovan. "The Prime Minister will not be happy about the sinking of the *Repulse* and *Prince of Wales* early yesterday morning either, but the Germans played directly to Churchill's advocacy."

"Yes, they did. The loss of those two battleships . . . without air cover, I must add . . . may well be the death knell for battleships and the dawn of the supremacy of the aircraft carrier. They will mourn the loss, but are far more concerned and focused on the threat to Singapore, Australia, and New Zealand. With the invasion of the Malay Peninsula and Siam, the Japanese will most likely press their action in the Philippines to eliminate the last of our outposts in the Western Pacific and consolidate their domination of the Dutch East Indies, and if they accomplish that, they will gain vast essential resources, and the bases they need to isolate and consume Australia and New Zealand. It is impossible to avoid what all that would mean to Burma and India. To that end, His Majesty's Government has already petitioned the War Department and the White House to assume control of the AVG," Donovan said, referring to the American Volunteer Group, known as the Flying Tigers, as the press has dubbed them, "to support the defense of Burma and India."

"I can't imagine we would agree to that," Ned mused.

"Me either, but in these times, anything is possible. At any rate, that is an operational issue, not an intelligence matter. The president secretly authorized the AVG and the recruitment of active duty military pilots, so I cannot see anyone else making that decision other than the president. He promised those squadrons to China, not India."

"Oh, I just heard from 'Bill' Eddy—a message from Cairo this morning." Donovan gestured for Ned to get to the point. "He's ready to go and has a tentative transport date of next week. I confirmed with the Department of the Navy that he will be transferred to COI tomorrow, which is the last hurdle."

"Interesting juxtaposition, don't you think?" Donovan stated a rhetorical question. Lieutenant Colonel William Alfred 'Bill' Eddy, USMC, left academia as the clouds of war gathered and joined naval intelligence. He held a PhD in English from Princeton University, and grew up speaking English and Arabic with comfortable fluency. Eddy had been posted as the naval attaché in Cairo. He agreed to join the COI as the organization's chief of station in Tangiers. "He is going to be the naval attaché in a country with no navy or naval assets."

Buxton chuckled, and then said, "It is a bit of a stretch, but he is ideally suited for this assignment."

"I agree. I first met him a year ago. I was impressed then. My admiration has grown with each subsequent month. He knows precisely what has to be done and what is likely to be coming his way."

"If you are convinced, he is the correct person for the job, then we need to get him in place. Bob Murphy knows him, talked with him numerous times, and concurs with the assignment." U.S. *Chargé d'Affaires* to Vichy France Robert Daniel 'Bob' Murphy had been in his post since the so-called Free Zone was established.

"I know. I've talked with Bob more than a few times about the situation and about Bill's assignment. I think they will work well together in getting the source network established and making the necessary connections with French generals and admirals. This will be our first big test, Ned. We cannot fail or misstep. The chiefs . . . and the president will be watching closely to see what we can contribute."

"Do you think North Africa is going to be our first operation?"

"To be frank and candid, I have no idea. The strategy, and tactical objectives and decisions, will be made and agreed to over the next few weeks. I just know there is no way on God's little green earth that we and the British can gather up, equip, train, and deploy sufficient military forces to carry out a successful invasion of Continental Europe in one or two years. We have only just begun our industrial mobilization. The only displacement operation in all of the Nazi-occupied territories seems to be North Africa."

"Well then, I think we have the correct people."

"Agreed, but we need more people like Bill Eddy."

"And, we will find them, Bill."

"Yes, of that I have faith. However, we must also justify our existence. More people, powerful people, than not, want us to fail and disappear."

"The double-edged sword."

"Yep . . . cuts both ways, but this is our lot in life, and we must not fail. The president needs us to be successful, and the people, although they will not realize it for many years."

"I know you've got a scheduled meeting, so I'd better get out of your way."

"Yeah, I'm already a few minutes late for departure, but I know James can make it up en route." James Freeman had been Donovan's skilled and accomplished driver in Washington for several years now. "I've got a meeting with Intrepid this afternoon at his office to adjust operations at Camp 'X' in the light of recent events." Camp 'X' was a remote, isolated, training facility located between Whitby and Oshawa in Ontario, Canada, and had only just begun operations on the day before the attack at Pearl Harbor. The site was known by many designations; the British Special Operations Executive (SOE) referred to it as Special Training School 103 (STS 103), the Royal Canadian Mounted Police (RCMP) called S 25-1-1, and the Canadian military labeled it Project-J. This was the site that would train offensive clandestine agents of the Allied nations who would fulfill Churchill's objective of setting Nazi-occupied Europe ablaze until liberation arrived.

Ned Buxton saluted. "Do you want to retain the TS-PERSONAL?"

"No," Donovan responded and handed the classified message back to Buxton, so the Archive Section could properly secure the message. Donovan stood, placed a few selected papers in his leather briefcase, and grabbed his bag.

Buxton quickly looked out one of the windows. "Looks like Freeman is waiting for you."

"I'm sure. He's never late. So, I'm off. Hold down the fort, Ned. See you Monday."

"Safe journey, Bill."

With that, Bill Donovan departed. Ned Buxton switched off the lights and closed the door.

———

Thursday, 11.December.1941
Headquarters, Fighter Command
Bentley Priory
Stanmore, Middlesex, England
United Kingdom
14:30 hours

Tug Meares felt like he had inadvertently been sucked into a whirlpool when an immaculately uniformed sergeant stopped him. Leigh-Mallory had not wasted time raising the question of the status of all three American volunteer squadrons. The Air Officer Commanding-in-Chief of Fighter Command wanted to meet post-haste with the AOCinC No.11 Group and the designated representative for all three of the American volunteer fighter squadrons. The No.11 Group commander wanted the No.71 Squadron commander with him for the automobile ride across the northern suburbs of London.

They discussed the pluses and minuses to the proposed transfer, and Meares learned the potential of a transfer had been discussed with American commanders, but only in a very general sense. Leigh-Mallory knew of but could not disclose the pending ARCADIA conference or any one of many topics to be discuss between Chief of the Air Staff Air Chief Marshal Sir Charles Frederick Algernon Portal, KCB, DSO & Bar, MC, and Chief U.S. Army Air Forces Lieutenant General Henry Harley 'Hap' Arnold, USA [USMA 1907]. One of those topics was the potential transfer of the American volunteer pilots.

The two air force officers arrived at Fighter Command a quarter of an hour before their scheduled meeting and were shown into the commander's conference room. They waited in silence with a cup of tea each. Air Officer Commanding-in-Chief Fighter Command Air Marshal Sir William Sholto Douglas, KCB, MC, DFC, entered the room spot on time. No other officers or personnel joined the three officers. Douglas gestured for Leigh-Mallory and Meares to sit, which they did on the same side of the table to Douglas's left and the senior officer closest to him.

"We'll get to the transfer question last, but first, at Leigh-Mallory's request, we will address the pending relocation and transfer of your squadron. As I understand the situation," Sir William said looking directly at Meares, "your squadron is slated to move to Kirton and transfer to 12 Group for rest and training, as we have done for every squadron since The Battle," he said with particular emphasis, "and the German abandonment of daylight bombing and fighter operations. So, let me hear it, why do your pilots not want to have their rest cycle?"

"To state the reason succinctly and frankly, they feel they fought long and hard to gain sufficient respect for them to carry out combat operations rather than action-less patrols."

"Patrols are combat operations, Meares."

"Yes sir. I am only trying to convey the mood of my pilots. They felt they have been relegated to what they call dog-and-pony shows and prohibited from meaningful combat operations for far too long."

"Because they were too individualist and not operating as a team . . . as a fighter squadron. We could not allow them to engage in cross-Channel operations until we had confidence they would perform properly."

"I understand that, sir. I do believe each and every one of the American pilots appreciates their probationary duration and the reasons why. But they have since proven themselves as worthy as any fighter squadron in the Air Force, and they feel the need to continue proving themselves worthy."

"Admirable sentiment, however, there is a reason for these rest periods that perhaps they do not sufficiently comprehend. During The Battle, we demonstrated in painfully graphic terms what happens to fighter squadrons that have been kept on the line too long. In those tenuous days, we came dreadfully close to dissipation, exhaustion and the point of collapse. We cannot and will not allow that state to return." Douglas looked to Leigh-Mallory. "You have rejected this request but thought it prudent to raise it to me."

"Yes sir. Simply put, number 71 squadron is like all the other squadrons of Fighter Command and as such should comply with Command rest policy."

Douglas nodded his head and lapsed into contemplation. "With respect," he said, looking at Leigh-Mallory, "they endured their protracted probationary period and, in fact, have proven themselves to be part of the air defense team. I think if I had been with them through those uncertain days, I would probably feel the same, as I think you would as well. Let's see if we can find a compromise." Douglas shifted his gaze to Meares. "How about this? Let us transfer your squadron to Martlesham, still in 11 Group, but slightly farther from the current RODEO operations." RODEO was the code name given to low-level, fighter sweep operations across the English Channel. "We should lower the tempo of operations for the squadron during their rest cycle, but not curtail their involvement altogether. The pilots should have longer and more frequent furlough periods to accomplish the rest objectives." Douglas held Meares' eyes, as if he was waiting for a response.

Tug picked up the gesture. "I think that should work, sir."

Douglas then looked to Leigh-Mallory. "I can agree to that compromise," Leigh-Mallory responded.

"Very well then, make it so. Now, let's jump to the transfer question." Meares opened his mouth to speak but stopped instantly when the chief of Fighter Command held up his hand to stop. "Let me state clearly that the Chief, the Minister, and I have discussed this matter with General Arnold and other senior leaders in the American air force. I believe it safe to say that the transfer of the three American volunteer squadrons will occur. It is only a matter of time, based upon previous discussions. I can assure your pilots the issue will be raised as soon as appropriate in our joint coordination with our American colleagues. Now with that said, I cannot offer more."

"That should be sufficient, sir."

Douglas grinned at Meares, and then his face went devoid of expression as he looked to Leigh-Mallory. "Right then, have we dispensed with the issues?"

Leigh-Mallory looked at Tug Meares. "Yes sir. Thank you for your time, sir," Tug responded.

"Excellent. Now, before we adjourn, as the commander of . . . of this august unit, I want you to leave here with one very clear overriding axiom, this squadron, your squadron, is just one unit among 67 of His Majesty's fighter squadrons in this command. They are not a pack of prima donnas. They will be judged by their performance. While these details are sorted out over the next few months, they must remain focused on their assignments. Their desire to leave us cannot be a distraction. They have grown into valuable, respected members of Fighter Command. They must remain so until the transfer can be properly completed. Do I make myself clear, Squadron Leader Meares?"

"Yes sir, you do . . . quite clear. I will ensure my pilots know and remember their place."

"Thank you, Tug. Now, if you both will excuse me, I have a command to tend to here." Douglas did not wait for a response and departed the conference room.

Leigh-Mallory's automobile and driver were waiting outside in the large gravel driveway. Before they left the warmth of Bentley Priory, Leigh-Mallory stopped and turned to Meares. "We will drop you off for your journey back to North Weald. Do you prefer Rail or Underground?"

"Underground is easier, but Rail is closer."

"Don't worry about that. We will drop you off at Harrow Station—the terminus of the Bakerloo Line."

"That should work just fine. Thank you, sir."

They exited the building, settled in the passenger compartment of the staff car, and the senior officer instructed the driver accordingly. Once they reached the asphalt roadway and less movement noise, Leigh-Mallory spoke. "I trust you are satisfied."

"Yes sir. Thank you for your time and interest."

"My presence was not necessary, but Air Marshal Douglas wanted me to be a party to the conversation. I do believe his words of caution at the conclusion are the most salient. Your principal task will be keeping your pilots focused on their flying and avoid the distraction of this transfer question. I cannot tell you more, but between you and me, we should have a workable agreement and timetable by the end of next month. From that point, the Americans should have a clear path."

"That will be helpful. They are good men, great pilots. They deserve our support."

"Of that, I have no doubt. They shall receive the recognition they deserve in due course, but they simply cannot be distracted by their inevitable frustration with the pace of the methodical process that will eventually be established for the transfer."

"I shall do my best to keep their eyes on the ball."

"I am certain you will. You've done a magnificent job gaining coherence with that lot."

"Thank you, sir."

The driver expertly navigated the repaired streets of North London.

"One more thing while I've got you as a captive audience," Leigh-Mallory said. Meares listened. "You and Whitey have performed well in a difficult assignment. You will be well taken care of when the transfer occurs. I urge you and Whitey not to worry about your future."

"Thank you, sir. I will privately convey that point to Flight Lieutenant Whittington."

They reached Harrow Station. Meares thanked Leigh-Mallory for his support and the ride to the Underground Station. The car departed. Tug obtained his ticket, waited in the subway car for the departure time, which occurred on schedule. He took the Bakerloo Line to Oxford Circus Station, changed to the Central Line, and went to the terminus at Epping. Tug tried to find a taxi and eventually jumped onto a passing air force truck returning to North Weald after the evening meal. It had been an exhausting couple of days. He did not want to answer the inevitable questions from his pilots. Tug found a base staff car, went back out into town, stopped at the closest pub, ate a simple cheese sandwich, drank a pint of beer, and returned to welcome sleep.

—

Thursday, 11.December.1941
Oval Office
The White House
Washington, District of Columbia
United States of America
15:00 hours

Earlier in the morning, Washington time, the governments of Germany and Italy joined their Imperial Japanese ally and declared war against the United States. Congress, with the encouragement of the president, wasted no time in matching the Germans and Italians.

"Mister President," Hopkins announced as he entered the Oval Office, "the courier from Capitol Hill arrived with both declarations."

President Roosevelt extended his right hand into which Hopkins placed the two folders. Franklin placed the folders on his desk. He examined the contents of the first folder, and then the second. They were Senate Joint Resolutions 119 and 120—the formal Declarations of War against Germany and Italy, respectfully. With no ceremony and considerable solemnity, President Franklin Roosevelt ascribed his signature to both documents. He blotted his signatures, closed both folders, and pushed both of them across the desk to his principal aide. "The world is officially in the second global war in a generation. History will likely not look kindly on what is to become of us."

Hopkins did not respond, picked up both folders, and departed the office. The world was at war.

—

Chapter 2

The struggle against power is
the struggle of memory against forgetting.
-- Milan Kundera

Saturday, 13.December.1941
HMS Duke of York
55° 58' 22" North – 4° 44' 49" East
River Clyde Anchorage
Greenock, Renfrewshire, Scotland
United Kingdom
09:45 hours

The Prime Minister stood on the flag bridge of the modern battleship with the First Sea Lord Admiral of the Fleet Sir Alfred Dudley Pickman Rogers 'Dudley' Pound, GCVO, GCB, GBE, as they weighed anchor and the colors were shifted. The magnificent warship moved slowly out the River Clyde Estuary toward the west, then turned south. As the estuary widened, the battleship increased speed slightly but remained slow enough to maneuver through the anti-submarine defenses past Great Cumbrae and Little Cumbrae islands into the Firth of Clyde. Several destroyers were clearly visible working anti-submarine search patterns.

"The anti-submarine procedures never cease to amaze me," Churchill proclaimed.

"After the tragedy and embarrassment of the *Royal Oak* in '39, we had to devise an elaborate combination of defensive measures to prevent any recurrence. Every major harbor or port, and several minor ports have defensive provisions that require careful maneuvers for entry and departure. The demands upon ship handling are considerable and definitely not trivial."

"I am fascinated every time I witness the process. My compliments to the captain."

"I will pass along your words, Prime Minister. We will clear the Isle of Arran and the last of the countermeasures in less than an hour. We will increase our speed for our transit and head out into the Atlantic. We should be in open ocean by mid-afternoon. The Met Office forecast for our transit is better than expected, especially for this time of year, so our transit should take nine days."

"Thank you, Sir Dudley. By the way, in case you have not heard, the United States officially declared war on Germany and Italy. So, the stage is set, and the ARCADIA conference is all the more important."

"We are ready, Prime Minister. We all are."

"I know, but I am more worried about the Americans. We have been planning for this day much longer than they have. We must walk a very fine line to bring them along without seeming arrogant or professorial."

"We will manage."

Churchill laughed softly. "I am not worried about you or the other chiefs. I am worried about me."

"We have faith in you, sir."

"I do get carried away from time to time."

This time Admiral Pound chuckled. "I do believe the proper response is no comment."

Churchill nodded his head and smiled. "The entire world is once again at war. We'll begin our final preparation later this afternoon, once we are out to sea and up to speed. These upcoming meetings with our American colleagues will perhaps be the most crucial to date and may well prove to be the pivotal milestone on our journey to victory." Churchill began to pace on the flag bridge as his attention turned from the scenery of their departure to his thoughts about what lay ahead. He turned to look directly at Admiral Pound with a serious expression on his face and concern in his eyes. "I have tried subtly to gauge President Roosevelt's thinking and opinions. I do believe he is amenable to the Germany first strategy, but we must be cautious not to overplay our hand. While we have been in this war longer, we will all be dependent upon American industrial capacity, and in time, they will field more men under arms than we could ever hope to achieve." The prime minister paced silently again. "I think we can both understand and appreciate the potential American position of focusing their might on Imperial Japan, but if I read Franklin's words correctly, the Americans will attempt to find a reasonable balance between satisfying our Germany first proposal, while applying maximum pressure on the Japanese. The hard part for all of us will be finding the correct balance."

"I presume that process will be the prime topic of discussion over the next few days," said Sir Dudley.

Churchill smiled. "Yes, it most assuredly will, and more importantly, we must all be on the same sheet of music. They may well be looking for any division or weakness in our arguments to lessen their two-front campaign initiative. The Pacific will largely be a naval war. We must do our best to support the Pacific theater of operations without diminishing our sight of the target."

"And where do you suppose we will find the naval forces to join the Americans in the Pacific?"

"First Sea Lord, I acknowledge that we are stretched quite thin at the moment. Our task is to define the proper strategy to focus our available resources to chip away at the Italian and German positions to free up resources that we can shift to the Pacific."

"Easier said than done, Prime Minister."

"Of that, there is no dispute, First Sea Lord." Churchill gazed outside. Without taking his sight off what lay ahead of the ship's bow, Winston said, "We must find the path forward. We have a few days to accomplish that task before we dock at Norfolk, Virginia. We are headed northwest, and we're increasing speed. I've got to get through my morning Dispatch Box before lunch."

"Yes sir. We will join you in the flag wardroom for lunch. Good luck."

"Thank you, First Sea Lord."

Admiral Pound left the bridge to the ladderway below. The prime minister walked through the aft access hatch to the flag stateroom, where his duty administrative assistant, Principal Private Secretary John Miller Martin, waited for his return. Churchill poured himself a short brandy and went to the desk, where they jumped into the paperwork.

—

Saturday, 13.December.1941
Residence
The White House
Washington, District of Columbia
United States of America
08:30 hours

"Thank you for joining me for breakfast, Mister Attorney General," President Roosevelt said, as Attorney General Francis Beverley 'Frank' Biddle entered the residence. Biddle had replaced Robert Houghwout 'Bob' Jackson in August 1941, when Jackson was confirmed and had taken his seat as an associate justice on the U.S. Supreme Court. Frank was also a distant cousin of Tony Biddle, who served as ambassador to the governments in exile in London.

"Good morning, Mister President," Biddle said, as he took the proffered chair opposite the president across the comparatively large, rectangular, mobile, dining table. "Thank you for the invitation."

"You said it was urgent, and I have a full calendar today."

The duty stewards served the president and attorney general their selected meals and departed closing the door behind them.

"With the ARCADIA Conference looming, I know everyone's attention will be on the British and our combined planning for joint operations, as right it should be. However, I thought I should get the news to you directly and swiftly. You may recall a visit and briefing at Hyde Park by FBI Director Hoover and Special Agent-in-Charge E. J. Connelly."

"Yes, I do . . . vividly."

"I am pleased to report the conclusion of our prosecution in federal court in the Southern District of New York of those arrested in New York. We collected 19 guilty pleas and achieved convictions for the remaining 14 perpetrators. Sentencing for all of the spies is scheduled for the 2nd of January. The British have convicted and sentenced a half dozen more spies linked to this network. The FBI agents involved were masterful in their interrogation of the spies, and from that work, we feel it safe to say the Duquesne Spy Ring is no more."

"Congratulations, Frank. Please convey my deepest and sincerest gratitude to all those involved in the investigation, apprehension, and prosecution of these spies. Churchill and MI5 will be pleased that we finally broke down this spy ring." Roosevelt lapsed into thought as he ate a few bites of his Eggs Benedict and sausage links. "If I may ask, what about the Sebold fellow . . . if I got his name correct?"

"Yes, William Sebold is his Anglicized name. Thank you for asking. He is quite well, under constant protection, and continues to help us with German agents. I must also confess, Mister President, the warrantless wiretap surveillance you authorized a year and a half ago was instrumental, vital, for the investigation and prosecution of this case. Humbly, I must add, the authority you granted us nearly two years ago continues to yield essential information for the pursuit of other German and Italian agents in our country."

"We took a risk a year and a half ago, Frank, as you should know from your in-briefing with Bob Jackson. The war and the pending war powers act in Congress will alter the legal basis of the warrantless surveillance program."

"Quite so. The Office of Legal Counsel has passed judgment on the act on the table before Congress. I can take a deep breath once the war powers act is passed and signed into law."

"Thank goodness for small blessings. But, between you and me, Frank, my concern for this particular power is not today or tomorrow, but rather what happens with this authority and especially Edgar when the war is concluded. I have a dreadful suspicion that J. Edgar Hoover will not so willingly abandon the extraordinary tool he has in his toolbox. The potential for abuse is excessive. Weaning him off that authority at war's end will not be so easy; however, it will be critical to the future of the republic."

"We must win the war first," answered Frank Biddle. "One step at a time."

"Indeed. One fight at a time. Until that day arrives, I believe we are both convinced this authority is an essential element for the prosecution of this war."

Biddle nodded his head and changed the subject. "You have not mentioned any Department of Justice involvement in the ARCADIA Conference, but we stand ready to assist in any manner necessary."

"Thank you, Frank. I think this will be, if not solely, a military planning affair. However, I can assure you that we will call upon you and Justice if any legal matters arise."

"Thank you, Mister President. Justice stands ready to assist as you wish."

Roosevelt nodded his head in acknowledgment. They both continued on their breakfast in silence. Biddle informed the president on several ongoing criminal investigations and prosecutions of national or White House interest . . . in summary only. When they finished their breakfast, the president excused himself to move onto his official agenda for the day. As Biddle stood, Harry Hopkins knocked and entered. Salutations were exchanged, and Biddle accompanied Hopkins as he pushed the president's wheelchair to the residence elevator. The attorney general left at the Ground Floor. The president and Hopkins went to the West Wing and the Oval Office, while Biddle returned to the Department of Justice building a few blocks down Pennsylvania Avenue in the Federal Triangle area.

———

Sunday, 14.December.1941
RAF Martlesham Heath
Woodbridge, Suffolk, England
United Kingdom

No.71 Squadron landed at the aerodrome at mid-afternoon and took up residence at the same operations building they had departed six months ago. The pilots quickly adjusted to their new, old base and settled in. Since they had operated from Martlesham so recently, they did not need any orientation or training flights. Their dispersal hut was two buildings down from their last hut, yet, it was exactly the same as their previous green clapboard building.

"Here we are, lads. Have a seat, while I check in with Group and get our orders," Tug Meares announced and did not wait for any acknowledgments. He disappeared into his office and closed the door.

"Why did they send us back here?" asked Frog Forcier, as the Green Section pilots sat in open chairs in the corner opposite the squadron commander's office.

"Because Group, Fighter Command, and the Air Ministry want us here," Brian answered.

"Yeah, and what the hell are you yakking about Frog?" Dusty Langford protested. "You weren't even with the squadron the last time we were here."

"OK, but haven't all the guys said moving south was where the action is?"

"Yes, that is what they've said," Dusty responded.

"Orders are orders," added Brian. "Get used to it. Fighter Command undoubtedly has many reasons for moving us here, and this place is better than Kirton-in-Lindsey. We do not need to understand how or why our orders are decided. Our task is to do the best we can to fulfill the orders and accomplish the mission."

"But, aren't we farther away from France?"

"Yes, we are," Whitey proclaimed from a few chairs away. "Hunter is correct. Based on experience, we were moved here to rest and sharpen up. The war is far from over, and there is more than enough fight still ahead to satisfy your apparent bloodlust, Frog. Getting shot at is not fun no matter how you cut it."

"I'm not bloodthirsty!" Forcier objected strongly.

"It sure sounds like it," replied Whitey with a calm, measured tone.

Brian held up his left hand in front of Frog that stopped the Green Section, Left Wing pilot. "There is no point in arguing about this," he declared. "The skipper is in there," he said, moving his hand and extending his index finger, pointing to the office, "getting our instructions from Group—Eleven Group, the same group we have been in since November of last year. Fighter Command wants us to rest and recharge. So, let's not look a gift horse in the mouth."

Frog nodded his head and remained silent. No one else spoke or even moved. Forcier stood and went outside despite the particularly chilly afternoon air. Several others joined him.

Dusty Langford leaned toward Hunter and whispered, "He'll get over it."

Brian nodded his concurrence, leaned his chair back against the wall, and closed his eyes. *Feelings remain particularly tense and agitated since the 7th of December—just one week ago. Everyone seems to be consumed about fighting and demanding transfer to the Army Air Forces. Patience is not a word with which many of us find affinity. If we are going to have some slow ops or downtime, I'd rather be with Charlotte and Ian. Who knows what any of this . . . ?*

The skipper's door open and stopped his thoughts. Tug Meares stepped out, looked at the faces in the dispersal hut, and said, "Where are the others?"

"Outside," responded Jimmy Harris.

"Would you be so kind to recall them, so I do not have to repeat myself?"

"Yes sir." Harris jumped off his stool behind his tall desk, opened the door, looked, and then stepped outside, closing the door behind him.

Tug remained quiet, smiled briefly a few times, and crossed his arms.

The door opened. The three pilots returned to their chairs without words. Harris closed the door to retain the warmth from the coal-stove heater.

"We have been placed on reduced duty status for a week. Two sections will remain at Available status, while the other two sections are granted a two-day pass. Well, actually, it will be more than two days since the first group can depart immediately." Meares paused, perhaps expecting some cheers. Surprisingly, none came. He looked at Brian. "Since you are unfortunately in 'A' Flight, your section will take leave second with Blue Section." Meares looked at Whitey Whittington. "'B' Flight, you are released ahead of normal time. I remind each of you that you must return and be ready for duty by noon Wednesday." Several yes-sir responses were heard, as the 'B' Flight pilots stood. Those who had not yet doffed their flight gear did so and hung their kit on each respective wall peg. Squadron Leader Meares waited for the 'B' Flight pilots to disappear, and then looked at each of the remaining pilots. "We are released for the rest of the day." Tug looked at Harris. "Group has already marked the squadron as Unavailable today." Harris nodded his acknowledgment that he had nothing more to do, other than secure the dispersal hut for the night. Looking back at the pilots, Meares added, "Report back to the Hut by dawn tomorrow morning." Several pilots stood.

"Excuse me, Skipper," Brian said. "For planning purposes, when will our pass commence?" Everyone stopped and turned to their commander.

"Good question, Hunter. I meant to state that. We will get the same extra time as 'B' Flight, so our pass will commence Wednesday afternoon and last until noon Saturday."

"Thank you, sir."

"Any other queries?" Various negative gestures and utterances came on top of each other. Squadron Leader Meares also gestured for the remaining pilots to skedaddle, and then returned to his office.

The five remaining pilots climbed into the covered bed of the RAF truck. Brian felt a bit off being the youngest among the pilots, and yet being one of the most senior officers by rank.

Frog Forcier leaned toward Hunter. "I'm sorry I got carried away," he said, just barely audible over the sounds of the moving truck.

"No problem, Frog. We all understand. Just tone it down a little in the future. None of us, including the skipper, control our orders."

"Was I wrong?"

"No . . . not wrong. I just think it is wasted emotion. We have enough to focus our energies when the undercarriage locks up into the wheel wells." Brian continued a little louder, so all four of the other pilots could hear him. "Concentrate on your flying. Forget about what happens in London or Uxbridge . . . or on the other side of the world."

"OK," Frog responded with resignation.

When they arrived, they scattered—a couple heading into London. Brian laid down still in his uniform on his made bed for a short nap.

———

The darkness of his room told him the nap had been longer than expected. Brian checked the luminous dial of his aviator's wristwatch. Ten minutes remained for the evening meal in the Officer's Mess dining room. There were not many officers dining in, so there was plenty of food available.

After dinner, Brian went to one of the telephone booths for the pilots' use. He waited patiently as the various operators made the necessary connection via their switchboards.

"Winchester 4-3-7-9," Charlotte's soft voice finally answered.

'Go ahead, sir," the initiating operator announced.

"It's me, sweetheart."

"Is everything OK?" his wife asked with genuine concern.

"It sure will be in a few days."

The pause suggested Charlotte was searching her memory as if she might have forgotten about some engagement she was supposed to attend. "What happens in a few days?"

"I will wrap my eager arms around you."

Charlotte squealed a little. "Do tell."

"They moved us. I will have to tell you where later. I called to hear your voice."

"That's so sweet."

"It's the truth. I miss you so much. And, I shall arrive on the late train Wednesday night."

"What time? The 11-15 from London?"

"Yes, if everything is working on time with the Underground and Railway."

"Very well. There probably won't be any taxis at that hour. I'll come pick you up."

"Is that OK?"

"Of course, it is, you ninny. Edith will stay with Ian." Edith Hanscom had been Ian's nanny since just less than two months after their son's birth.

"I have so much to tell you about the last week."

"I cannot say I am eager to hear how all this has affected you and your colleagues. The news from the Pacific and Asia is just dreadful. I imagine we have only heard a small portion on the wireless or in the newspapers."

"Yes, very terrible. I cannot say more over a telephone line. So, let me say, I love you, and I will see you Wednesday night."

"I can't wait," Charlotte squealed.

"If you do not hear from me, everything is going to plan, and I will see you in a couple of days."

"I love you," she said and waited for Brian to hang up.

"I love you very much, Charlotte," Brian responded and hung up the handset. He sat in the telephone booth for a minute or so, as his mind's eye saw the vision of Charlotte Grace waiting on the railway platform as his train came to a stop in Winchester. He had not seen her or felt her soft strength in two months. Their reunion was long overdue. Brian eventually left the telephone booth for the Officer's Mess bar for a pint of beer with a few of the other pilots, none from No.71 Squadron.

—

Monday, 15.December.1941
Hotel Victoria
Princes Street and Waterloo Quadrant
Auckland, North Island
Dominion of New Zealand
15:45 hours

The entire Pacific Clipper crew gathered in the small ground floor conference room, as Captain Ford had requested. The consulate staff had been exceptionally sympathetic and helpful, especially Naval Attaché Captain Bradley Morehouse, who kept them informed as information came in. The extent of the Japanese attack at Hawaii and throughout the Western Pacific region staggered the comprehension of everyone. The damage done to the U.S. Pacific Fleet defied the imagination, and luckily the carriers had been at sea during the attack. The United States, Great Britain, and the British Commonwealth were formally at war with Imperial Japan and the German Empire. They had been waiting for the week since the attack, as the company vacillated on what action to take on their status. The decision had arrived an hour ago.

"OK, guys," Ford began, "we finally have a decision. Our first task is defined. Tomorrow, we fly back to Noumea, New Caledonia, to retrieve the Pan Am employees and close the office. From there, we will take them to Gladstone, Australia." He paused. No one spoke or even twitched. "That's the easy part."

"OK, Skipper," said Poindexter. "I'll bite. What's the hard part?"

Ford looked down at the table, then connected with the anticipatory eyes of each crewmember, including the pursers. "Our instructions are simple and direct. Headquarters has given us the choice. One, we can remain in Australia for the duration of the war, and at some point, when we can safely journey back across the Pacific, fly back to the States. Or, two, we can make our way back to New York . . . going west . . . the long way around."

"We have no stations . . . anywhere west of Australia," observed Poindexter.

"Well, actually," Rod Brown interjected, "Japan, China, and the Philippines are west of the Gladstone Station in Australia. Hell, even Japan is west of most of Australia."

Ford held his right hand with a stop gesture. He waited for everyone to look back at him. "We now know the Japanese have invaded the Malaya Peninsula and are headed toward Singapore. They have also invaded Siam and the Philippines. According to Captain Morehouse, the naval attaché here, the Army is really strapped and outnumbered on Luzon. The British have more than their hands full in Malaya and Hong Kong. We cannot go north or east. Further, the window of opportunity to the west is rapidly closing. Even if we decide to make the west transit attempt, we have some logistical obstacles to surmount before the Japanese close the window. Unfortunately, our employees north of us cannot be recovered. We can save the Noumea personnel before the Japanese get there; thus, our return to Noumea. Mack, Rod, and I did a quick map study to see if it is even possible to make it back to the States. Rod, why don't you do the honors?"

The crew's navigator took the baton. "We have laid out a potential route across the south side of the Dutch East Indies. That will be the most dangerous part since we will be the closest to the war at those points. Assuming we get through those stops, we will cross India, the Middle East, and Africa before we cross the Atlantic."

"We have already ordered large auxiliary fuel tanks that are being constructed in Gladstone," Ford added, "where they will be installed and checked for operation, to give us the necessary fuel reserves for a couple of the longer legs, if we decide to make the journey."

"Once we get to Brazil," Brown continued, "we will finally have functional Pan Am stations to help us get the rest of the way back to New York."

"How long will this take?" asked Chief Purser Barney Sawicki.

"We have not done sufficient planning," answered Rod Brown. "Based on what we've done so far, I'd guess it will take us about three to four weeks to accomplish. Unfortunately, we have no way to prepare for or anticipate the problems we may encounter en route. We have no wheels. We have to find appropriate, qualified, water landing sites that enable us to land, and more importantly, take off with full fuel and supplies."

"Are we going to be able to get supplies?"

"We don't know," Ford jumped in. "We are also prohibited from contacting potential waypoints due to war communications restrictions. We are going to be on our own, and we will have to wing it as best we can. We could get stranded at any point due to any number of reasons, not least of which might be not finding sufficient fuel, water, and food, or being arrested, or having the aircraft impounded."

"Or, shot down," muttered John Mack.

Ford ignored the clear and obvious potential, negative outcome. "The provisional route we have laid out gives us manageable legs, reasonable potential sources for fuel and supplies, and most importantly, minimal war risk. This is not to say that we will not have exposure. The entire world is now at war. Anything might and can happen, and worse, we have no way to anticipate what may await us at any one of the dozen or so necessary waypoints. Yet, I think it is safe to say that we will have multiple points where we may have to adjust or alter our route. It will just be us. Any questions?"

"We don't know enough to ask questions," mumbled Sawicki.

"This is not going to be easy. There are no assurances, but this is our only option to get back home in the foreseeable future, and we have a rather limited window to execute this plan. If the Japanese," Ford paused to consider his words, "well, let's just say, we have several critical legs that could terminate the plan with no options remaining. As a consequence, headquarters authorized me to offer the option to each of you individually, first, to remain in Australia . . . probably for the duration of the war. If we cannot gather a minimum volunteer crew, the decision will be made *de facto*." Ford paused to allow for any crewmember to speak up. None of them did so. "You will continue to be paid, although the means to accomplish that payroll has not been established yet. They insisted that I emphasize that attempting the return flight must be entirely and completely voluntary. Understood?" Bob Ford looked at each crewmember and received an affirmative head nod. "OK. Each of you does not have to make a final decision until we reach Gladstone. A consular officer will meet us when we arrive, and we expect he will provide whatever governmental assistance we need." Ford looked around the table one more time. "Now, let's go enjoy a worthy dinner and get a good night's sleep. Tomorrow is going to be a long and challenging day."

———

Tuesday, 16.December.1941
Residence
The White House
Washington, District of Columbia
United States of America
08:25 hours

The president was not quite ready and dressed for his day when the duty secret service lead agent announced the early arrival of Coordinator of Information Colonel William Joseph 'Bill' Donovan for yet another off-the-book meeting before the day's chockablock full agenda. Roosevelt waved for the agent to show Donovan into the residence dining room while he finished tying his necktie and donning his light grey suit jacket.

The agent pushed the president's wheelchair from the bedroom to the dining room. Donovan stood just inside the door dressed in a lawyer's dark blue suit, white shirt, and silver and blue striped necktie. The two leaders nodded to each other.

"Good morning, Mister President," proclaimed Donovan.

"Is it, Bill? I've not yet looked out the window."

"Well, it is cold with snow on the ground, but the sky is comparatively clear with scattered small cumulous clouds and brilliant sun."

"Well, then, you must be correct; it is a good morning. Anyway, please be seated. I am certain the chef has prepared an exquisite breakfast as he always does." The president nodded to the chief steward. The chief and his two assistants efficiently served both leaders their breakfast and departed, closing the door behind them. "We are expecting the British to arrive on the 18th and the ARCADIA Conference to begin that afternoon . . . assuming they don't get delayed or diverted en route."

"They should be OK as long as the sea state does not slow them down into the U-boat speed range."

"We shall pray for them."

"Indeed!"

"So, what little news tidbits do you have for me this morning?" asked the president.

"We have confirmation the Japanese Combined Fleet has made ports in the Home Islands, and the victory celebrations are surprisingly subdued. We suspect Yamamoto did not want to appear to be gloating with their success."

"Wise, but no factor. By the way, if you are not aware, I have opened discussions with General Marshall and Admiral Stark to consider carrying out a demonstrative raid on the Home Islands as soon as humanly feasible to accomplish."

"I will talk to the chief of staff to see what we can do to help."

"Please do. What about the West Coast?" the president asked.

"So far, we see no signs of any major operation against the West Coast or anywhere in North America. However, spot actions by Japanese submarines are possible. The Navy and Coast Guard have quickly reassessed and reinforced their anti-submarine defenses at all West Coast harbors and ports. We must be prepared to deal with limited local actions."

"Do you think the Army, Navy, and Coast Guard are prepared?"

"Yes sir, I do."

Roosevelt nodded his head. "What else?"

"The situation in China is deteriorating rapidly for the British in Hong Kong. The garrison forces may be able to hold on for another week or two. No reinforcement or relief is possible. The AVG is moving into China . . . to Kunming, I do believe. We have several agents working to prepare the ground for their arrival. The British opened a concerted theater initiative to subsume the AVG for the defense of Burma and India."

"Your opinion, Bill?" the president interjected.

Bill Donovan thought about the president's query. The American Volunteer Group (AVG) had been proposed in November 1940, by its commander, Major Claire Lee Chennault, and created and sanctioned by the president in secret without the consent of Congress in February 1941. One hundred Curtiss P-40B Warhawk fighters were diverted to the AVG under the Lend-Lease Program in March. The aircraft and associated equipment began to arrive at Rangoon in the summer, along with 300 American volunteer pilots recruited from U.S. military aviation units by Chennault with presidential authority. "There are only three heavy squadrons, hardly enough to support either the British or the Chinese. I believe Chennault will provide support as he is able while training and preparing for the move into China, but he intends to move all three squadrons within the next few weeks."

"So, they should not be diverted to support the British in Burma?" asked the president.

"My opinion, no, they should not. The British have viable air assets in theater, albeit stretched thin and insufficient in an offensive manner. The Chinese Air Force is collapsing due to poor training and obsolete equipment in the face of determined Japanese offensive operations. The need is greater in China."

"Can those three squadrons make a difference?"

"Again, my opinion only, yes. Chennault is a clever, experienced commander who has a rather ingenious plan to amplify his limited assets."

Roosevelt nodded his head in agreement. "What's next?"

"Air bombardment of numerous sites in the Philippines continues unabated. We have confirmed the transport of several front-line Japanese divisions. We cannot be certain of their objective, but our assessment is the land invasion of the Philippine Islands appears to be inevitable."

"That is MacArthur's assessment as well. He has requested substantial reinforcements to defend the islands." Roosevelt did not wait for the obvious question. "Based on last night's discussion, reinforcement is not possible for a host of reasons."

"Then, success is unlikely," Donovan spoke with solemnity.

Roosevelt glanced at his wristwatch and at the wall clock to confirm the time. "I do not have much time left, Bill. Give me what you can in five minutes."

"Certainly, Mister President." Donovan thought for a moment, then continued, "The British situation in North Africa is tenuous. They are stretched dreadfully thin with Churchill's diversion of ground and air assets from Egypt to Greece and the Balkans. The British have insufficient reserves and have thinned the Home Forces to bolster North Africa in the light of the reduced threat to England. That brings me to a little but most interesting assessment from our Russia desk. One of our analysts happens to be a petroleum engineer recruited from Standard Oil. The German oil sources contain higher than normal amounts of paraffin, which means their lubricants most likely retain that paraffin. During normal operations, this reality is of no consequence, except in very specialized refinements and uses. However, in cold weather, the paraffin solidifies and becomes rather gummy. This simple fact may well slow down the German advance, affecting trucks, armor, and aircraft. I am informed that there is no easy solution. This fact also emphasizes a strategic objective to deny Germany access to new oil supplies that might easily remedy this operational problem. We have seen signs the cold weather is substantially reducing the German offensive potential during the winter months."

"Have you validated this assessment with MI6?"

"Not yet."

"Please do so as soon as possible. This information will be useful in our discussions with the British at the upcoming conference."

"Yes sir . . . without delay."

"Now, I really must go." Roosevelt pushed himself back from the table. Donovan stood. The president began to wheel himself toward the door.

"May I assist, Mister President?"

"By all means, Bill, if you have the time."

As the door opened, one of the two duty Secret Service agents moved to replace Donovan, who shook his head, stopping the replacement. The four men boarded the modest elevator. The president did not look at Donovan and said, "Well done, Bill. I look forward to your development of this information."

"Thank you, Mister President. We will report as soon as we are able."

No further words were spoken as they made their way to the Oval Office. Secretary of the Treasury Henry Morgenthau, Jr., who had also held his office since the beginning of the Roosevelt administration, waited patiently outside the president's office. He stood and followed them into the Oval Office. The two Secret Service agents remained in the anteroom. Donovan thanked the president for his time and departed.

———

Thursday, 18.December.1941
Standing Oak Farm
Winchester, Hampshire, England
United Kingdom
09:45 hours

They had consummated their reunion late last night and managed a few hours of sleep before the morning chores. The crew had been fed, the cows and goats had been milked, and the chicken's eggs collected. The milk had been prepared for delivery, and the crew departed for the dairy processing plants in Winchester. Edith had taken Ian upstairs for playtime.

After they washed up, Charlotte said, "So, is it time to talk?"

"I think so," Brian responded. "My inclination is to go to our bench."

"Then, this must be serious."

"Well, I suppose so, but it is too cold for the bench. So, the fireplace chairs will have to suffice."

Charlotte did not respond and walked to the two overstuffed chairs, partially facing each other and the fireplace. They sat with a cup of tea each.

"So, what is so serious?" asked Charlotte.

"Serious was your word, not mine. My only point was a lot has happened since I was last here and last saw you. Much of the news I could not talk about on the telephone or write in a letter. I find peace at the bench," Brian said, referring to the large, birch bench Charlotte had installed under the old oak tree by the pond made famous by her rescue of him a year and a half ago, for which she had been awarded the George Cross by The King for her selfless heroism.

Charlotte did not react and held Brian's eyes. She took a sip of tea, waiting for her husband to continue.

"First and easiest, Group moved us back to Martlesham for recuperation, thus my presence here. As I said last night, I'll have to leave early Saturday morning to make it back by noon." Brian paused for a response. None came. "Since the Japanese attack on Pearl Harbor and the United States entry to the war, we initiated a request for transfer to the U.S. Army Air Forces." Charlotte gasped. Brian held up his hand. "Squadron Leader Meares met with Group and Fighter Command toward that end. Pete Petersen and I met with the ambassador in London. Our request has been made."

"Oh, Brian, please tell me you are not going back to the States, and then to the Pacific to fight the Japanese."

"We have only requested the transfer of all three American volunteer squadrons. We have no idea what will happen. We have been told to be patient for arrangements to be made with the Army Air Forces."

"When?" she interjected impatiently.

"We don't know. The best we have is a suggestion that the process will likely take months to accomplish."

"Do you really want to do this? . . . to leave Ian and me?"

"Charlotte, please. That is way too far ahead. While going to the Pacific is certainly possible, it is also just as likely that we could be transferred to U.S. forces here. Surely, the U.S. will send substantial forces here, in addition to the Pacific, to defeat the Germans."

"The Japanese attacked America, not the Germans."

"Well, that is not entirely true. A German submarine sank the *Reuben James* destroyer in late October; 96 American sailors died. The president even talked about it . . . rattlesnakes of the Atlantic. Remember?"

"You know what I mean," Charlotte said with palpable frustration.

Brian nodded and looked into the fire as much to avoid Charlotte's eyes as to gain time to think. "Yes, I know what you mean. I just wanted you to know what has happened beyond what shows up in the press."

"Why don't you stay here? Don't transfer? I'm sure John Spencer can help."

"I would be lying if I tried to claim that I have not considered that potential."

"I only see you every couple of months as it is. That is better than the years it would be if you transferred to the Pacific."

"The best I can or should do at this stage is urge patience and diligence," Brian responded. "As I often have to caution our newer pilots, we must not worry about that which we do not control. No decisions are pending or imminent. We will continue to discuss things as we learn more facts."

This time, it was Charlotte's turn to think about what had been said, except she held Brian's eyes. "I certainly understand why you wanted to use the bench," she said as if there was only one bench in the entire world that mattered to them. "I have to trust your judgment, Hunter."

Brian laughed heartily at the break in the tension. "Callsign . . . ay!"

Charlotte smiled broadly and nodded her head. "Appropriate touch, don't you think?"

"Quite so," Brian chuckled. "We will have a lot of surprises and obstacles to deal with as a family before this war is over. We will discuss them and deal with them as they come."

The sound of footsteps descending the stairs announced the approach of Edith Hanscom. She cradled Ian in her arms, who was whining and fidgeting in apparent protest. "I held him off as long as he would tolerate, Mum. He is hungry. Would you like to feed him, or should I?"

"I will, Edith. Thank you," she said as she unbuttoned her flannel shirt and extracted her left breast. "My breasts are telling me it is past feeding time." Charlotte supported Ian's head and neck as she accepted their son from Hanscom. Charlotte settled Ian in the crook of her left arm, and the infant promptly found her nipple and began suckling. Once satisfied their son was properly engaged, Charlotte gestured for Hanscom to sit with them, then looked at Brian. "Edith has been an absolute godsend," she announced. "I cannot imagine how I might have handled the caring for Ian as well as tending the farm. I know generations of women have done it over millennia, but I just can't imagine how."

"Thank you, Mum," Edith responded with humility.

"Yes," Brian added, "I am most grateful as well, since I am not here to help."

"Thank you, Mister Drummond. I am honored to be of assistance. You are a glorious couple, and Ian is an adorable child."

"Is there anything we can do to make your service with us any more comfortable?" Brian asked.

"You both have been most generous with me, Mister Drummond. I cannot think of anything. Thank you so much for asking."

Charlotte switched Ian to her right breast and smiled at her husband. They were indeed blessed. The sound of the farm's delivery truck on the driveway gravel announced the return of the farm crew. Brian rose to begin preparing sandwiches for everyone. Edith joined him to assist. Life on the farm continued.

—

Thursday, 18.December.1941
HMS Duke of York
49° 15' North – 47° 35' West
11:30 hours

The last of their preparations while en route to the United States had gone well so far. Prime Minister Churchill was surprisingly content with the efforts of the Defense Committee—the three service ministers and the three service chiefs. For all those months and years, he had nurtured his relationship with the president and prepared the ground for this crucial first joint planning conference, the crescendo moment was nearly upon them. The United States – British Staff Conversations of nearly one year ago had been constrained to discussing and working out operational military matters to ensure their actions were coordinated and not in any conflict. The ARCADIA Conference would be the very first time the two governments and military staffs could address the strategic approach and objectives in the prosecution of the war ahead of them.

Winston remained grateful the day of their true joint collaboration had finally arrived, to begin in a few days.

The knock on the flag stateroom hatch diverted his attention from the report before him to the entry of his duty private secretary John Miller Martin. "Excuse me, Prime Minister. You asked for a positional update, and the captain has informed me, just now, the sea state continues to be higher than forecast. The destroyers cannot keep up against the higher than expected swells, and we have slowed again. The navigator's revised arrival time is now the 22nd. The captain indicated we should arrive at Hampton Roads at dawn on Monday and dock at Naval Station Norfolk a few hours later. We have confirmatory messages from Washington that transportation arrangements have been amended accordingly, which means we shall arrive in the District of Columbia just after noon. You will be residing with the president at the White House residence. All of the other lodging arrangements have been confirmed."

"Thank you, John. Please send a simple acknowledgment message to the White House."

"Yes sir. Right away. Before I tend to this task, you did not have anyone scheduled to join you for luncheon. Do you have any wishes?"

"Only if you would be so kind to join me, John. Let us make this a working lunch. Please ensure a couple of the stenographers are properly fed before lunch. I have not made as much progress with the Dispatch Box as I thought."

"As you wish, Prime Minister." Martin departed.

Winston returned to the shipping report before him.

14:30 hours

Per their planned agenda, the Defense Committee gathered in the Flag Wardroom for the appointed meeting. The Defense Committee included:

The service ministers:

-- First Lord of the Admiralty Albert Victor 'AV' Alexander, CH, PC, Member of Parliament for Sheffield, Hillsborough Division, Labour Party member;

-- Secretary of State for War Henry David Reginald 'David' Margesson, MC, PC, Member of Parliament for Rugby, Conservative Party member;

-- Secretary of State for Air Sir Archibald Henry Macdonald 'Archie' Sinclair, 4th Baronet of Ulbster, CMG, PC, Member of Parliament for Caithness and Sutherland, Liberal Party member; and,

the service chiefs of staff:

-- First Sea Lord Admiral of the Fleet Sir Dudley Pound—Chief of Staff of the Royal Navy;

-- Field Marshal Sir John Greer 'Jack' Dill, KCB, CMG, DSO—Chief of the Imperial General Staff (CIGS); and,

-- Air Chief Marshal Sir Charles Frederick Algernon Portal, KCB, DSO & Bar, MC—Chief of the Air Staff.

The usual complement of staff officers and aides were missing for this specific meeting. The prime minister specifically requested ULTRA access-list personnel only to enable the frankest discussions of the proposed strategic session before they would make their presentations to their American counterparts.

Before Churchill entered the wardroom from his stateroom, he stopped and faced John Martin. "This is a special session. Please ensure the guards are posted with strict instructions that we are not to be disturbed by anyone. To you, I will add the exception, if we receive an urgent message from the King or President Roosevelt."

"Absolutely, sir. I will make it so. I shall remain close by in case you might need me to assist."

Churchill nodded his head, opened the hatch, and stepped into the Flag Wardroom. The assembled group stood. The prime minister gestured for everyone to sit as he took his seat at the head of the table. Both entry hatches were closed.

"I would like to say a few words before we get to the meat of the matter." No one objected or spoke. "Just a reminder to restate the obvious, the conference we shall enter into with the Americans is a military strategy negotiation. This is not a diplomatic exchange. We have one primary, overriding objective in this conference—Germany first. The Americans will hold a very strong and powerful urge to focus their might on the Japanese, and rightly so. I think we can all understand and appreciate their natural inclination. We must be soft, subtle, gentle, sophisticated, and refined in our arguments. We expect to have numerous sessions jointly with our counterparts. Yet, perhaps more importantly and significantly, we will likely have individual private sessions with our respective leaders. I have done my level best to coordinate with the president before and after the 7th of December. I believe the President is inclined to support the Germany first strategy; however, he has withheld his commitment until the conclusion of our joint discussions. Based on my communications with the president, I think we agree that General Marshal is supportive. Admiral Stark is not aligned and will likely argue vociferously for an American focus on Japan, to leave us to deal with Germany. General Arnold has so far presented a neutral position with respect to the dominance of one strategy or the other. We must not appear too attentive to Stark's emphasis. I will also note that Secretary Knox is more closely aligned, based on my discussions with Big Bill Donovan and their personal relationship, than Admiral Stark." Churchill looked at the first sea lord directly. "You will have the most direct access, Sir

Dudley. We will be dependent upon your discussions with Stark to represent his opinions on strategy."

"Yes sir," Sir Dudley interjected. "I will listen intently and probe gently to understand Admiral Stark's position and arguments."

Churchill nodded his head. "The president will not likely intercede with his military chiefs." Winston paused and looked down at the table with nothing in front of him. "One more important element regarding our primary objective, we must not overplay our vulnerabilities. First, the president well knows the essentials by our voluminous message of one year ago. We do not want them to see us as weaker than they already know. We must not hide from our vulnerabilities; just not allow them to become the principal argument against the Germany first strategy. Second, they have plenty of reminders from our Lend-Lease requests alone. We do not need to restate them or emphasize them. Third, the stark reality for us and the underlayment of our strategic war proposal . . . our limits in manpower and industrial capacity are translated into time. I believe to my soul that with Lend-Lease supply support, our ultimate victory over Germany is simply a matter of time. We need American military assets to shorten the time."

"That might be overstated a bit," said David Margesson. "We are stretched to our bloody limit. We have insufficient forces in any of the multiple theaters of operations in which we are engaged. If the Germans should manage to subdue the Soviets, they will surely turn their military might back upon the Home Islands and us. If that should happen, we will have no choice but to sacrifice one or more of our colonies or territorial holdings."

Churchill smiled at Margesson. "Reality is acknowledged, David. My only point in this vein is the emphasis on time. The Americans must be convinced that Germany is the lynchpin. Further, once Germany is defeated, the Americans must believe we will redeploy our forces to support the defeat of Japan."

"That sell is fairly easy," David added, "but the trick will be convincing the Americans to split their forces with sufficient strength sent to Europe to achieve a Germany first strategy."

"Therein lies the rub, now, doesn't it?" the prime minister said. Several heads nodded in concurrence. "I think we all know this is a very fine line I am asking you to walk, and worse, we do not have much leverage beyond our knowledge of the battlefield and our adversaries. For now, let us assume we are successful. The next step will be turning General Marshall's penchant for a direct assault on the Continent to end the war as soon as possible to a more reasonable approach."

"That particular task may be more straight-forward," offered Sir John Dill. "We have Marshall's inclination and the Soviet's second front demand on one hand, and logistics on the other. The key will be convincing the Americans of the intelligence we have from ULTRA, and from MI6 and SOE field agents regarding the German order of battle in Western Europe and specifically occupied France. If we achieve that task, then the logistics becomes problematic—supplies, harbor facilities, transport lift capacity, landing craft and such. We must land with overwhelming force or," Sir John left a poignant silent pause, "face stalemate or annihilation."

"Passchendaele," David Margesson mumbled from bitter memory. The Great War battle of Flanders Fields dominated British military thinking—half of a million casualties on each side rendered the battle a meat grinder of human lives.

"Precisely!" exclaimed Churchill with an unusual vehemence in his voice. "We cannot tolerate such an event or even the possibility of that dreadful carnage. It will take time to build up, train and prepare sufficient forces to assault the Continent directly." Churchill paused for thought. "With the assumption that we can convince the Americans of the Germany first strategy, are we now in unanimous agreement that Vichy French North Africa should be our first joint objective. We must attack the soft underbelly of Europe, not the hardened top shell."

Sir John cleared his throat. "As discussed, two days ago, the chiefs reviewed the Northwest Africa invasion plans we have developed. We are in agreement," he paused to look at and received a confirmatory head nod from Sir Dudley and Sir Charles, "this is our best shot at the soft underbelly and will place the Germans and Italians in an obvious vice. As we squeeze them, it will be up to the Navy and Air Force to finish them off as they attempt to flee the vice."

"Now, we must convince our American cousins of the wisdom of this approach. To that end, I would like to discuss our presentation tomorrow morning. I will attempt to be the naysayer as each of you presents our argument for the Germany first strategy and the Africa campaign approach. We need to clear the what-next plan to support the underbelly advance. I will leave you to it," the prime minister announced and stood. The others stood as well. The ministers and senior officers departed via the passageway hatch, while the prime minister used the other hatchway to return to his stateroom and paperwork.

———

Thursday, 18.December.1941
Oval Office
The White House
Washington, District of Columbia
United States of America
10:10 hours

As Bill Donovan entered the Oval Office, Harry Hopkins stood at the president's left shoulder behind the so-called Hoover Desk. "Good morning, Mister President, and good morning to you, Harry."

"Thank you for joining us at such short notice. I have a bill to sign that I wanted you to witness."

"Yes sir. I am at your service."

President Roosevelt thumped the folder in front of him. "This is the War Powers Act of 1941." Donovan nodded his head and stood in front of the president's desk. Roosevelt affixed his signature to the legislation. Hopkins used the crescent blotter to dry the signature, closed the folder, and pushed it to the left. The president's principal aide placed another folder in front of the president and opened it. "This is an executive order formally establishing the censorship office to control information exchange during wartime that we will discuss shortly." Roosevelt signed his name, and Hopkins again blotted it dry. Harry closed the folder, placed both folders under his left arm, and then wheeled the president around the desk to his usual position between the facing long couches. The president gestured for Donovan to sit, which the coordinator of information did, closest to the president on the couch to his right. Hopkins departed with the newly approved documents.

President Roosevelt went immediately beyond any pleasantries to the business at hand. "In accordance with the legislation I just signed into law, you are directed to coordinate with the new censorship office and other intelligence agencies of the government to carry out international intelligence surveillance and also coordinate with the FBI to prosecute intelligence source leads involving foreign sources."

"That is a rather slippery slope, Mister President."

"Yes, it is. In confidence, I will inform you that 18 months ago, I authorized the attorney general and FBI director to carry out warrantless wiretap surveillance as part of our counterintelligence program. As a direct consequence, we collapsed a major German spy and espionage network."

"I am aware of the Sebold case, but I was not aware of your wiretap authorization."

"It remains highly classified and I trust you will respect that fact. I tell you this because I am now approving your psychological warfare proposal, and I want you to utilize all available sources of intelligence to focus that program."

"Yes sir. We are ready, Mister President. I trust Attorney General Biddle and Director Hoover are comparably supportive of this initiative."

Roosevelt chuckled softly. "Attorney General Biddle, yes, he has endorsed your psychological warfare proposal. As you well know, Director Hoover does not play well with others. He is aware of my directive to you, and he has his orders. I urge you to coordinate closely with Frank Biddle to engage and harness Edgar. This is too important. I would prefer you work things out with Frank and Edgar. We have common enemies. We need all the tools we have at hand to vanquish our adversaries."

"The lance has been lifted."

"Thank you, Bill. I look forward to great and grand accomplishments from you and your organization."

"Thank you, Mister President."

Roosevelt nodded his head. "To change the subject while I have you, we received a confirmatory message from Churchill. They expect to arrive in DC Monday afternoon. I do not anticipate any direct involvement by the COI, but I will need your latest assessments."

"Certainly, sir. Ned or I will be available at any time you need us. If I may," Donovan paused for Roosevelt's consent nod, "we have confirmed the paraffin discussion we had a few days ago. We queried several disassociated, independent, petroleum engineers. The oil sources the Germans are using are contributing to the difficulties we are reporting from frontline German armor and infantry units. The Russian winter is not being kind to the Germans. After our disclosure to MI6, they confirmed our assessment just this morning."

"Excellent work, Bill. My compliments to the analyst and his team. It's about time the Germans face some adversity. Who would have thought something as simple as oil composition could stop a powerful army?"

"The Germans are hardly finished in this fight, but the paraffin content appears to have slowed them down and bought the Red Army time to gain strength. I will also add that field reports indicate the Germans were ill-prepared or unprepared for cold-weather combat. They lack cold-weather clothing for their troops and normal cold-weather equipment. They are also expending precious fuel reserves to heat the equipment and keep the paraffin liquid. Now, we must hope it is enough."

—

Saturday, 20.December.1941
RAF Martlesham Heath
Woodbridge, Suffolk, England
United Kingdom
12:10 hours

Brian was the last of the 'A' Flight pilots to return from their extended pass, arriving just in time. The snow and ice storm the previous day had not affected rail travel; however, it had severely affected roadway movement from the railway station to the airbase. The air force shuttle truck had moved slowly but safely through the slippery streets.

The pilots greeted the Green Section leader as he entered the No.71 Squadron Dispersal Hut and closed the door behind him to retain the warmth of the interior.

Squadron Leader Meares appeared at his office door. "Welcome back, Hunter. You are out of uniform," he announced.

Brian quickly scanned his service uniform and hat. He could not see anything out of order other than he was not wearing his service ribbons under his pilot's wings, which was allowed and his choice to do, to avoid the attention they brought. Brian looked back to Meares with a puzzled expression.

"Attention to orders," Tug said, causing everyone in the hut to stand. "The Air Minister, on behalf of The King and His Majesty's Government, takes pleasure in promoting Brian Arthur Drummond to the rank of flight lieutenant." Cheers erupted, along with applause, and slaps on Brian's back.

"Party time tonight," several of the pilots shouted out.

Meares raised both hands for quiet. He waited. As they settled down, Meares added, "The Met Office forecast more snow later this afternoon, and the existing ground cover is not likely to clear for several days. Base Operations has closed the aerodrome and reported the base inoperative. Now that we have everyone back, we are released for the day. I will check with Base Ops early tomorrow morning to determine our status, and I will post our status on the message board in the Mess before morning meal. If the Met Office is correct, we will have no operations tomorrow, either." Meares turned to look at Corporal Harris. "I have already reported the squadron as Unavailable." *I could have stayed with Charlotte and Ian*, Brian thought.

"Yes sir," Harris responded. "The transport lorry is outside."

"Let's not keep the driver waiting on his appointed rounds," Tug commanded. The pilots moved slowly to the truck. "Hunter, a word, please."

Brian faced the flow and joined Meares.

"Here is your warrant," Tug said, handing Brian the single piece of paper that was his promotion warrant. "You will note the effective date is actually the 18th, while we were on pass."

"Thank you, sir."

"Well deserved, I must say. Congratulations. Now, let's blow this pop stand, as you American brothers like to say on occasion." Corporal Harris would be the last person to depart and would secure the Dispersal Hut.

———

Chapter 3

Democracy arose from men thinking
that if they are equal in any respect
they are equal in all respects.

-- Aristotle

Monday, 22.December.1941
Office of the Coordinator of Information
National Institutes of Health Building
2430 E Street Northwest
Washington, District of Columbia
United States of America
16:40 hours

Bill Donovan knew the hectic would soon become more intense. The British contingent for the ARCADIA joint planning conference was due to arrive at any moment. The COI was as prepared to support the conference as they could be, and the president had given him all positive signs that he was satisfied with the daily morning briefings. There would be surprises in such events, but that reality was normal.

The knock at the door broke Donovan's concentration on the latest field report in front of him. Before he could respond, Ned Buxton entered and closed the door behind him. "We just received word from the gate, Jumper is here." They had roughly five minutes or so before reaching the center, headquarters building. "I also got word from Bill Eddy. All of his transport arrangements have finally been settled. He departs for Tangiers a couple of days after Christmas. He expects to be up and running within a week or so, just after New Year's Day."

"Excellent. While we do not yet have a peg in the ground," Donovan said, "I suspect, and perhaps even believe, the British will be successful in convincing the president, and perhaps even the joint chiefs, to take on offensive action in Europe, or more likely in North Africa, as soon as practicable. Eddy will not have much time. My last conversation with Bill satisfied my concerns. He has a very clear vision and will be working under the premise that the first major Allied offensive operations may well be through his domain."

"Right. I sure hope so. It is likely to be our first major test as well," Ned added.

"Precisely. We've got the best man. We'll stand up to the test."

"I have faith, Bill. Now, I'd better get to the front door to welcome our guests." Buxton did not wait for consent. The process did not take long.

The familiar face and form in a Royal Navy vice admiral's winter uniform appeared. Buxton announced their guests and closed the door behind him.

Donovan stepped forward to greet his guests, extending his right hand. "Welcome back to Washington, Sir Geoffrey."

"Thank you very much, Bill. May I introduce my personal assistant Lieutenant Commander Fleming?"

Donovan shook hands with a very British appearing, 30-ish, trim, modest height man in Royal Navy Volunteer Reserve winter uniform with distinctive zigzag sleeve stripes. As they learned, Admiral Pike had recruited Ian Lancaster Fleming in May, with his service beginning in August 1939, having seen traits that proved quite useful to intelligence operations. Fleming had been at Pike's right hand from the beginning of the war. Bill looked at Jumper. "How long has he been with you?"

"So, you are '17F'? I'm surprised I have not met you before," Donovan observed.

"Yes, he is," responded Pike immediately. "I keep him very busy."

"Well, nonetheless, I am pleased to make your acquaintance." Donovan gestured to the overstuffed, leather chairs and couch surrounding a coffee table. They sat, and Ned served coffee for the four of them. Pike and Fleming took to the couch. Buxton and Donovan sat in the single facing chairs.

Admiral Pike jumped right to it. "We docked at Norfolk this morning and arrived at Anacostia an hour or so ago."

"I trust your transit was uneventful," Bill said.

"Yes, delightfully uneventful. The *Duke of York* is an amazing battleship. However, the North Atlantic was stormier than forecast, and the sea state was higher than expected, which slowed the destroyers and as a consequence, delayed our arrival."

"I am sure . . . but, not invulnerable," observed Donovan referring to the British battleship.

Expression vanished from Pike's face. "Yes, well, we are still assessing the loss of *Prince of Wales* and *Repulse*, but the evidence we have so far strongly suggests the lack of viable air cover proved fatal."

"A lesson I hope and trust we shall all learn well."

"We have only to do our best and add in a few prayers. I have a few quick items to dispatch." Donovan nodded his head. "First, if you have not heard already, MI6 confirmed your analyst's report on paraffin in the source oil the Germans are using. They are indeed suffering inordinate immobilization of their armor, lorries, and aircraft. As a result, they have been forced to expend even more precious fuel for heaters . . . when they have heaters, and worse for them, they abandoned otherwise serviceable vehicles when they could not use heaters or ran out of expendable fuel."

"Thank you, Sir Geoffrey. I will pass along your confirmation."

"We have it from reliable sources that the Germans are deploying their Type IX U-boats to the eastern and southern coast of the United States to intercept merchant shipping before convoys are formed."

"I will get that information to the Navy this evening."

"They already have it . . . Navy to Navy after all," Pike said and smiled. "We believe the U-boat offensive on your coasts will be significant and should not be underestimated."

"Understood," Bill responded and nodded to Ned, as if to say, take a note.

"Perhaps even more significant to the future, again from reliable sources, three days ago, Hitler dismissed 37 field marshals and generals on the eastern front, including Guderian, for Christ's sake, and he took direct command of the armed forces. He is clearly unhappy with the stagnation of his BARBAROSSA campaign."

"Their best armor general," Donovan mused, referring to *Generaloberst* Heinz Wilhelm Guderian, the leader of the *Blitzkrieg* stab to the French coast during the Battle of France.

"One and the same, and arguably the best armor general of our time. This information does not end their invasion, but it portends a likely downturn for the German Army in Russia. Our Soviet friends are encouraged by the information. By the way, the Red Army is focusing on heaters behind German lines in the field as an indicator of their vulnerability. This moment in history may well prove to be the turning point. Dismissing the generals *en mass* may well prove to be equivalent to Stalin's induced purges of his generals before the war in Europe broke out."

"The generals do not control the weather. These are the first positive signs we've seen against Army Group Center since the invasion began last June."

"Our opinion as well. Now, unless you have other items . . . ," Pike paused. Donovan shook his head in the negative, since he was content to listen. "How is your COI growth progressing?"

Donovan showed no reflexive reaction whatsoever. "Quite well, if I do say so. Why do you ask, Sir Geoffrey?"

"To be frank, you are at war now. Your organization is barely five months old, and you are now faced with the demands of war information."

"I appreciate your concern, Sir Geoffrey," Bill Donovan responded with a calm, dispassionate tone. "We are gathering up some of the nation's best minds in the full array of fields necessary for strategic intelligence. We are deploying field agents and operatives as we speak. From our earlier discussions in London, Bill Eddy is leaving in a few days to take up his post in Tangiers to be prepared should our governments decide on North Africa for our first major joint operation."

"Fine man Eddy."

"Yes sir, he is. He has impeccable credentials and a worthy temperament for the assignment. We have men like Bill Eddy already with us, and we are actively seeking others who can hit the ground running just like Eddy. I will not claim we are a mature intelligence agency. You and Stewart Menzies have been most generous with me, in trying to educate me, and I have tried to learn the lessons as quickly as I could. I am not sure what your expectations are of the COI, Sir Geoffrey. Clearly, there is something, or perhaps a list of somethings, that causes you concern. If you have constructive criticism to offer, we are all ears. We have much to learn."

Pike shook his head. "No, no, Bill. It is not that at all. As you have done with the paraffin discovery, you are already producing valuable intelligence for both of us. In the spirit of cooperation, we want to continue to help you mature the COI as quickly as possible. To that end, I would like to offer you the intermittent services of young Ian Fleming here," Pike said, gesturing to his assistant, "to assist you, as you may require. He has been intimately involved in our intelligence work and would be useful counsel to you in addition to Intrepid."

William Samuel Stephenson, code-named Intrepid, had been Prime Minister Churchill's personal choice for a variety of intelligence, special operations, and liaison activities in the United States since the early days of the Churchill premiership. Stephenson quickly established an office in the International Building, Rockefeller Center, Manhattan, New York City, under the cover of the British Passport Control Office.

"That said," Jumper Pike continued, "I must confess that Commander Fleming remains a valuable aide. I am unable to establish him here as Intrepid is in New York. If you agree, a couple of months of temporary duty is manageable."

"Once again, that is most generous, Sir Geoffrey. We shall eagerly welcome your munificent offer."

"If a little more time would be beneficial, we should talk as soon as you see the need. To be frank, I have other pending tasks for Commander Fleming."

The four men concluded their initial discussion. They adjourned to allow the visitors to complete the process of settling into their lodging. They would reconvene in a couple of hours at Bill Donovan's Georgetown residence for cocktails, dinner, and more social conversation.

———

Wednesday, 24.December.1941
Residence balcony
The White House
Washington, District of Columbia
United States of America
21:15 hours

Dressed for the cold, night air with blankets to help, Franklin Roosevelt and Winston Churchill had moved to the balcony overlooking the Mall. The national Christmas tree festively decorated and illuminated with copious lights stood with the Washington Monument behind the tree. The obelisk monument was only sparsely illuminated by the city lights and a few spotty floodlights. The president's two, duty Secret Service agents stood well back from the two leaders.

"What a glorious scene," Churchill pronounced.

"Yes, it is, so peaceful in a troubled world."

"I am so honored to be here on this Christmas Eve to enjoy the magnificent holiday of salvation and redemption."

Roosevelt looked at Churchill, who was sitting in a provided chair next to his wheelchair. "I am honored that you agreed to stay with me in the White House."

"Such a historic residence and especially the Lincoln bedroom. You are most generous, Franklin. You are blessed to be able to celebrate the birth of Jesus of Nazareth. We are not so fortunate, as the Nawzee minions still linger about and remind us from time to time."

"We discussed the wisdom of lighting the tree and the city. We decided the risk was low and the symbolism incalculable after the events of two weeks ago."

"A wise choice, I must say. I am so glad you are able to show such defiance to the darkness of evil." Winston paused. They both stared off to the holiday scene. "If I may, Franklin, I shall take this quiet moment to inform you that I have taken the decision to move General Dill to a new post as Chief of the British Staff Mission to the United States. We will station him here in Washington with his vital assignment of ensuring the utmost coordination between the two military staffs and chiefs."

"A most generous move, I must say. I have been quite impressed by Jack—a good listener, perceptive thinker, and articulate spokesman."

"My assessment as well, which is why I think we need him here rather than his most important post in London."

"I look forward to working with Field Marshal Dill to achieve victory. Who will replace him as chief of staff?"

"General Sir Alan Brooke," Churchill answered matter-of-factly.

General Sir Alan Francis Brooke, KCB, DSO & Bar, was currently serving as Commander-in-Chief Home Forces since the beginning of the massive aerial battle in the sky above Southeast England and the pinnacle of Nazi Germany's invasion threat. His charge was and remained the land defense of the Home Islands.

"Is General Brooke here?"

"Yes. I anticipated this change before we departed from Scotland. The reassignment will be effective tomorrow. I might also add that General Sir Bernard Paget will succeed Sir Alan as commander of Home Forces.

"To change the subject, the situation on the Malay Peninsula continues to deteriorate. Singapore is in jeopardy. The Hong Kong garrison is likely to surrender to overwhelming force tomorrow. We are unable to reinforce or supplement our colonial forces, so I am afraid the clouds will continue to darken in Asia."

"You are not alone, I'm afraid, Winston. Our Marine detachment on Wake Island also surrendered also to overwhelming Japanese forces after a brief but valiant fight. As you know, a large Japanese force landed at various sites within the Philippines, and General MacArthur signaled that he has ordered a fighting retreat to the fortress on Corregidor Island at the mouth of Manila Bay. Amidst the gloomy news, we have one positive sign."

Churchill smiled. "Do tell."

"Three days after the Japanese attack, the America First Committee disbanded and dissolved itself. Pearl Harbor has united this country like none of us ever could. I can . . ."

"Oh my goodness, Franklin," Churchill interrupted the president. Please do not sell your courageous and monumental efforts to educate and inform the American people as well as Congress. Consider where we were two years ago. Your fireside chats, as well as your risky decisions to sustain us that culminated in the Lend-Lease Act, are your accomplishments, Franklin. Your words sustained and encouraged me, the free people of the world, and I respectfully submit were instrumental in changing the course of a swiftly moving river of isolationism. You did those things, Franklin, no one else. History shall record your heroic and Herculean efforts to sustain us in the fight against the Germans were uniquely selfless and indeed noble in the highest order. Respectfully, I do not believe anyone else other than you could have done what you have done."

Roosevelt smiled broadly and nodded to his guest. "Coming from the man who led and encouraged his nation through her darkest hours that is a fine tribute. 'We shall never surrender.' Masterful words of extraordinary leadership, Winston! Now, I shall unabashedly entice you to retire to the warmth of the interior with a snifter of brandy. I'm afraid I am gaining a bit of a chill."

"Say no more," Churchill declared and rose to push the president's wheelchair, but one of the Secret Service agents beat him to the handles of the wheelchair. They moved together to the living room of the residence and were handed a healthy portion of brandy. As they enjoyed the warmth of the amber elixir, they shared familial stories centered upon the national service of their children. They laughed and enjoyed each other's company for another hour before retiring for the night.

—

Sunday, 28.December.1941
Lincoln bedroom
The White House
Washington, District of Columbia
United States of America
08:45 hours

Winston Churchill completed his morning bath and walked out of the bathroom with his valet Frank Sawyers following with a large, white, White House towel. His skin was still wet and quite pink from the warmth of the hot bath.

Franklin Roosevelt, dressed in a light grey suit with a solid medium blue tie on a crisp white shirt, entered the room, being wheeled by the duty Secret Service agent. On seeing Churchill naked, the agent stopped. Roosevelt averted his eyes, threw up his left hand to cover his eyes, and exclaimed, "Please excuse me, Winston! I am terribly sorry to have intruded."

Churchill waved off Sawyers, who was attempting to cover the prime minister and turned to squarely face Roosevelt. "You see, Mister President, I have nothing to conceal from you and everything is in plain view between us."

Roosevelt collected his composure and overcame his sense of propriety to look directly at Churchill. "Well, Winston, thank you for your candor and frankness."

"What brings you to my bedchamber, my friend?"

"I understand you are preparing to leave for Ottawa for your speech to the Canadian Parliament."

"Correct."

"I wanted to wish you good luck, or as they say on Broadway, break a leg."

Churchill laughed heartily. "Thank you very much."

"For household planning purposes and for clarity, you leave today by train for Ottawa and are scheduled to give your speech to Parliament on the 30th. Correct?"

"That is correct."

"By your current plan, you will take the return train on the evening of the 31st to arrive in Washington on the morning of the 1st—New Year's Day."

"Correct. I can return earlier if you wish," Churchill said without movement or gesture.

"Not necessary, Winston. I just need to inform Eleanor, since I caught 'what for' in not sharing your agenda with her or her office."

Churchill chuckled. "We both share that burden and obligation."

This time Roosevelt laughed softly. "Very well, then. Again, good luck on your trip and with your speech. I shall be listening."

"Thank you very much, Mister President."

Roosevelt gestured for the agent to push him out. By this time, Winston was nearly dry. Sawyers assisted him in completing the process and dressing for the day's journey north.

———

Thursday, 1.January.1942
Oval Office
The White House
Washington, District of Columbia
United States of America
14:45 hours

Prime Minister Churchill had just returned from Ottawa, Canada, and his speech to the Canadian Parliament on Tuesday. President Roosevelt was alone in the Oval Office, reading one of the multitudinous pieces of correspondence that came to him every single day.

"Happy New Year, Franklin," Churchill said boldly, as he entered the Oval Office.

Roosevelt gestured to the couches, as he abandoned his reading and wheeled himself to his usual spot between the facing couches. "Happy New Year to you, Winston," Roosevelt said and stopped his wheelchair. "I suspect it will not be so happy, but there is always hope."

"Indeed."

"Congratulations on another exemplary speech. I listened with sagacious interest and outright awe. I confess to my juvenile exuberance at your chicken neck comment. Genius, I say, genius!"

"Thank you, Franklin. Language and public speaking are lessons I learned from my father . . . one of many valuable lessons."

"You vastly exceeded Lord Randolph, if my most humble opinion matters," Franklin pronounced with a broad smile illuminating his face.

"Thank you, again, Franklin."

Roosevelt wheeled himself backward a short distance to the front of the all-American Hoover desk. He turned and retrieved a single sheet of paper, wheeled himself back to his position, and then extended his hand and paper to Churchill. "This is the official print version of the declaration we agreed to last week."

A Joint Declaration
by

The United States, the United Kingdom, the Union of Soviet Socialist Republics, China, Australia, Belgium, Canada, Costa Rica, Cuba, Czechoslovakia, Dominican Republic, El Salvador, Greece, Guatemala, Haiti, Honduras, India, Luxembourg, Netherlands, New Zealand, Nicaragua, Norway, Panama, Poland, South Africa, Yugoslavia

The Governments signatory hereto,

Having subscribed to a common program of purposes and principles embodied in the Joint Declaration of the President of the United States of America and the Prime Minister of the United Kingdom of Great Britain and Northern Ireland dated August 14, 1941, known as the Atlantic Charter.

Being convinced that complete victory over their enemies is essential to defend life, liberty, independence and religious freedom, and to preserve human rights and justice in their own lands as well as in other lands, and that they are now engaged in a common struggle against savage and brutal forces seeking to subjugate the world,

DECLARE:

(1) Each Government pledges itself to employ its full resources, military or economic, against those members of the Tripartite Pact and its adherents with which such government is at war.

(2) Each Government pledges itself to cooperate with the Governments signatory hereto and not to make a separate armistice or peace with the enemies.

The foregoing declaration may be adhered to by other nations which are, or which may be, rendering material assistance and contributions in the struggle for victory over Hitlerism.

Done at Washington
January First, 1942

"That is as we agreed to last week," Churchill declared.

"So, His Majesty's Government agrees to the public release of the declaration?"

"Yes," the prime minister replied, "most emphatically."

"Excellent. Then, so be it."

"May I retain this copy?"

"By all means."

Churchill sought a new topic. "My chiefs inform me the joint conference is proceeding swimmingly well."

"That is what I understand, as well."

"We have a lot of planning and work to do in preparation for Operation BOLERO. Trying to find billeting, accommodations, and training grounds for more than one million men in just over a year will certainly challenge our Home Secretary. We will be provisionally ready to accept the initial contingent by the first of May, I am told."

"Excellent," Roosevelt responded. "Marshall has told me that orders will be issued shortly for various Army units to complete preparations for redeployment. Plus, as General Arnold has reminded me that you already have several squadrons of American fighter pilots with you."

"Yes, we do. I know Air Chief Marshal Douglas and General Arnold have had preliminary discussions about the transfer of our American eagle squadrons once you have sufficient command structure in place to assume leadership of those squadrons."

"That should be late spring or summer according to our air force chief," the president added.

"We shall be ready."

"At a more personal level on this topic, have I been informed correctly that you know our highest scoring ace among that bunch?"

Churchill smiled broadly. "I most assuredly do—Flight Lieutenant Brian Drummond. I am told he goes by the combat callsign Hunter. I met him the first time before the war began, and he was newly arrived in England. He is a very impressive young man, of which you should be rightly proud."

"I have met him as well. We are indeed proud of him and what he has accomplished so far. We have a war bond drive campaign being planned for later this year. We should showcase his achievements as inspiration for all Americans."

Churchill nodded his head in agreement. "Most appropriate, it seems to me." Churchill paused and stared at the snowy scene outside. "The chiefs also inform me the initial operational plan integration has gone surprisingly well." Roosevelt nodded. "Rather than develop separate or parallel plans, I have advised the British chiefs to join with your chiefs to generate joint plans that we can both execute."

"We are agreed."

"Excellent. I wanted to take a moment to convey my opinion to you, and if necessary, discuss any differences we may have, so that we may properly represent our joint position." Roosevelt again nodded his head. "I believe we are in complete agreement on the overarching strategy of Germany first."

"We are."

"In that, I must state to you personally my deepest and sincerest gratitude for that commitment, especially in the shadow of the horrific tragedy you suffered in the Pacific."

"Thank you for your kind words." Roosevelt held up his hand for a moment. Churchill did not intrude. "Yes, as we have discussed, I think Germany first is the correct strategy. However, I want it clearly understood that this strategy does not preclude or delay our operations against the Japanese in the Pacific and Asia. There will be constant and inevitable pressure on resources."

"Quite understandable, Franklin. As long as we can continue to talk on a frank, candid, and private level, we can resolve whatever differences arise. In that spirit, I must say, I am encouraged by the extensive mutual cooperation of our military staffs. They have agreed on the two principal initiatives. My apprehension about ROUNDUP is jumping too quickly into placing Allied forces on the Continent facing the direct assault of substantial Nawzee forces. While I heartily support the planning and fully advocate for our actions to relieve pressure on the Soviets, I am extraordinarily cautious about taking on a continental endeavor with inadequate forces."

Roosevelt rubbed his chin and looked off toward the portrait of Abraham Lincoln on the office wall. "The Red Army desperately needs help. We have been discussing their near imminent collapse for six months. While they have finally shown signs of stiffening their defenses, they are a very long way from gaining the upper hand. We have opened discussions with the Kremlin to expand Lend-Lease support to the Soviet Union, although we are several months away from a suitable agreement. They need us to draw off German ground and air forces in front of them . . . to enable them to take the offensive." Roosevelt lapsed into contemplation, again. Churchill chose not to interfere with the president's thoughts. "None of us wants another Passchendaele, Winston; but, war is not without risk, and sometimes, victory comes to those willing to risk. We must find a successful balance."

Churchill leaned forward and held Roosevelt's eyes. "Therein lays my singular greatest worry, Franklin. Passchendaele was a brutal, horrible, meat grinder that chewed up a generation of our young men. We cannot afford a repeat of that debacle."

"I certainly understand and agree. None of us wants that risk. Unfortunately for those of us in leadership positions, we cannot allow ourselves to be paralyzed by that fear. War is a risk by definition."

"I can agree with that. I just advocate between us that we must have ample forces to overwhelm the local German forces to secure a beachhead of sufficient size to allow the logistics footprint to rapidly grow and carry us all the way to Berlin. Anything short of that magnitude of ROUNDUP operation will have an unacceptable risk of failure . . . or even worse . . . stalemate. That was Passchendaele."

Operation ROUNDUP was an early American plan to make a direct assault on Northern France in the belief that U.S. forces would make the decisive difference and lead to the early demise of Germany. ROUNDUP was tentatively planned for execution in the spring of 1943.

"Then, I deduce you are not a fan or supporter of SLEDGEHAMMER, either?"

As British resistance to ROUNDUP stiffened, the American Army planning staff developed operations plan SLEDGEHAMMER as an alternative to or subset of ROUNDUP. Less ambitious, SLEDGEHAMMER was intended to create a lodgment on the Continent on the Cherbourg Peninsula or near Brest. The objective would be to hold the region until a full-scale invasion could be established. Both ROUNDUP and SLEDGEHAMMER were intended to help the Soviets and draw off German forces in Russia.

Churchill chuckled softly. "No, I am not . . . for the same reasons. It is a reasonable objective to obtain a lodgment on the Continent for future operations; however, we will not likely be successful against the Germans. They are too good and too strong, and they presently have the advantage of holding the ground."

"I appreciate your candor, Winston. I cannot disagree with or dispute your assessment, so we must continue to talk frankly as the chiefs evolve these plans. I remain quite concerned about sustaining the Soviets. We must find a way to help them hold off the Germans and grind them down." Churchill nodded his acknowledgment. "Then, what are your thoughts about GYMNAST?"

"We have had a similar plan we called ACROBAT, to create a western front to assist the 8th Army by placing Rommel's *Afrikakorps* in a vice from which they cannot escape. GYMNAST is a much better plan, especially since it is a joint plan. Brigadier Eisenhower's briefing on the plan sketch impressed me. I have confidence he and his staff will deliver a good working plan for us to build on. We are weakening Rommel's forces. While we have hard fighting ahead, I believe we will eventually take the offensive. GYMNAST will assist that eventual offensive and contribute to Rommel's defeat in North Africa."

Operations plan GYMNAST grew from British resistance to Operation ROUNDUP and involved landing sufficient forces on the coast of French Northwest Africa, facing territorial Vichy French forces rather than hardened German armed forces. Since it was seen as less ambitious than ROUNDUP, the tentative execution date was pegged in October or November of 1942. Operations plan ACROBAT predated GYMNAST and entailed landing sufficient forces near Tripoli to draw off the *Afrikakorps* and aid the British 8ᵗʰ Army to the east.

"That seems a bit optimistic, given the current situation."

"Perhaps so. Nonetheless, I have faith, together, we shall defeat the Nawzees in North Africa. Beyond that inevitable victory, I wanted to float a conceptual idea with you in private . . . to give you time to think about my proposal." Roosevelt nodded. "I think we are far more likely to find success by attacking the soft underbelly of Europe rather than take the risk of a direct frontal assault on the hard shell Nawzee stronghold along the Channel coast. Given their occupation, they will maintain the ability to move more forces, more rapidly than we could ever do with the constraints of amphibious operations."

"Your proposal sounds reasonable for now. We need a lot more blocks to be placed firmly for us to have a foundation."

"Agreed. Thank you for listening, Franklin. We have a basis for our future intercourse."

"Yes, we do."

Churchill smiled. "The Combined Joint Chiefs of Staff have done exceptionally well so far. I commend their progress."

"Likewise. I am pleased and quite comfortable with the progress of our talks and plans."

"On that note, I intend to avail myself of Ed Stettinius's generous offer of his villa in Pompano Beach, Florida, along with General Marshall's munificent contribution of his personal transport aircraft for my conveyance. I'm going to take a few days to relax before heading back to the war."

"When do you intend to leave?"

"On Monday the fifth. I'll be enjoying the sun and beach for five days. I expect to return to Washington by train to close out the joint conference, and then head back to England on the 15ᵗʰ of this month."

"I'll hold down the fort while you are gone."

"Hold down the fort?" Churchill asked with genuine curiosity.

"A uniquely American western phrase meaning to manage things."

"Ah, yes, the Wild West."

"Exactly."

Winston excused himself to take a nap before supper and headed up to the Lincoln Bedroom for his rest.

———

Friday, 2.January.1942
Oval Office
The White House
Washington, District of Columbia
United States of America
14:00 hours

"While we await Big Bill's arrival," Churchill said, "I think it prudent to update and close-out one of our earlier topics." Franklin nodded his consent. "You will recall our concern that MAGIC may have been compromised via the Soviets nearly a year ago." Again, Franklin nodded his head. "We have seen no indications whatsoever that the Japanese reacted to the information. Have you?"

"No . . . not to my knowledge. The experts have difficulty from time to time, as the enemy changes their core sequence, but they have recovered productivity every time, so far."

"We have the same difficulty with ULTRA. So, I think we can declare the scare of that message closed."

"Excellent. It was too close for my comfort."

"Mine as well, but we seem to have dodged a bullet. I also believe it is time to integrate ULTRA and MAGIC," the prime minister proclaimed.

"What do you have in mind?"

"First, an exchange of specialists seems warranted. Second, we need the means to share product . . . perhaps a top-level code used only for the shared product. Third, we need the means to analyze . . ." A knock at the door stopped their conversation.

Grace Tully knocked again and entered. She had ably replaced Franklin Roosevelt's long-time private secretary Missy LeHand, who suffered a major, incapacitating stroke in June 1941, at 42 years of age. Grace had been Missy's assistant since Roosevelt's election. She announced the arrival of Coordinator of Information Bill Donovan. The president looked at the prime minister, who nodded his consent, and Franklin gestured for Grace to send him in.

"Good afternoon, Mister President," Bill Donovan said, as he entered the Oval Office, and did not wait for more than a head nod response. "Great to see you, again, Prime Minister." Churchill sat on the couch farthest from the contoured door, while the president sat in his characteristic wheelchair between the two couches.

"Likewise, Big Bill," Churchill responded.

Donovan sat directly opposite Churchill. "I came as quickly as I could," Donovan continued, looking at the president. "What do we have?"

"Thank you for your prompt response, Bill. The prime minister and I were discussing a rather ominous matter, and we agreed we should take advantage of your insight."

"Yes sir."

"We have discovered indications the Nazi menace is turning their unique malevolence to innocent people of the Jewish faith in their occupied territories. Mister Churchill generously shared special intelligence."

Churchill handed the first of two pieces of paper to Donovan.

MOST SECRET - ULTRA

```
HIGH SECRET
DATE: 31 JULY 1941
TO: CHIEF RSHA
FROM: RGR
FINAL SOLUTION
BREAK
AS A SUPPLEMENT TO THE TASK WHICH WAS ENTRUSTED
TO YOU IN THE DECREE DATED 24 JANUARY 1939 TO
SOLVE THE JEWISH QUESTION BY EMIGRATION AND
EVACUATION IN THE MOST FAVOURABLE WAY POSSIBLE
GIVEN PRESENT CONDITIONS I HEREWITH COMMISSION
YOU TO CARRY OUT ALL NECESSARY PREPARATIONS
WITH REGARD TO ORGANIZATIONAL SUBSTANTIVE AND
FINANCIAL VIEWPOINTS FOR A TOTAL SOLUTION OF
THE JEWISH QUESTION IN THE GERMAN SPHERE OF
INFLUENCE IN EUROPE BREAK INSOFAR AS OTHER
COMPETENCIES OF OTHER CENTRAL ORGANIZATIONS
ARE AFFECTED THESE ARE TO BE INVOLVED BREAK I
FURTHER COMMISSION YOU TO SUBMIT TO ME PROMPTLY
AN OVERALL PLAN SHOWING THE PRELIMINARY
ORGANIZATIONAL SUBSTANTIVE AND FINANCIAL
MEASURES FOR THE EXECUTION OF THE INTENDED
FINAL SOLUTION OF THE JEWISH QUESTION BREAK
BREAK HAIL VICTORY BREAK HAIL HITLER END
HIGH SECRET
DECIPHERED: 9 SEPTEMBER 1941
```

MOST SECRET - ULTRA

Donovan returned the message to Churchill and looked from the prime minister to the president.

Churchill began, "As noted, it took us over a month to decipher this one." Winston held up the message. "We have found clues from just after the German invasion of the Soviet Union that the Nawzees were headed to the attainment of rather sinister objectives. I do believe we have discussed those clues last August." Roosevelt nodded his agreement. "Those messages were just hints. This one," he said, holding up the message, again, "confirms a concerted, purposeful organization at the highest levels of Nawzeedom. They intend to unleash the efficiency of German industrial precision to achieve their vile purposes."

"It appears, Bill," Roosevelt interjected, "they aim to exterminate European Jews on an industrial scale."

Donovan nodded his head a few times. "All of the information we have, so far, validates that assessment. They started in Germany even before the Enabling Act and the various Hereditary Acts. As you know," Donovan said, looking to both leaders, "they opened *Konzentrationslager Dachau*, just north of Munich, a concentration camp for 'undesirables,'" Donovan said and added gestured air quotes. "German Jews were among those confined along with journalists, political opponents, homosexuals, degenerates and such. When they occupied Poland, they segregated parts of all major cities with barriers and armed guards, and moved Jews into those areas. They call them ghettos. At first, the Germans claimed it is for simple medical quarantine reasons . . . and temporary. Our sources in Poland indicate, and I do believe Colonel Menzies at MI6, and we agree, the confinement provisions are neither temporary nor innocent."

"His Majesty's Government agrees," added Churchill.

"What or who is RGR?" asked Roosevelt.

"Göring."

Donovan said, "In German, *Reichsmarschall des Großdeutschen Reiches*, RGR, or Empire Marshall of the Greater German Empire. This is a message directly from Göring to Heydrich—the chief of the German Empire Main Security Office . . . among other titles. It is noteworthy that Fat Hermann did not even copy Himmler. This message also explains the special action group message we discussed last August at Placentia Bay."

"Quite so," Churchill added.

"The Final Solution of the Jewish Question," commented Roosevelt in a barely audible voice.

"Yes."

"Rather ominous," Roosevelt said.

"Most emphatically, yes, quite ominous indeed," added Churchill. "Then, this one," he said, holding up the second sheet of paper, "we just deciphered before we boarded *Duke of York*." The prime minister handed the message to the president.

MOST SECRET - ULTRA

```
SECRET
DATE: 10 DECEMBER 1941
TO: RGR
FROM: CHIEF RSHA
FINAL SOLUTION
BREAK
PURSUANT TO YOUR MESSAGE OF 31 JULY 1941 AND
OUR DISCUSSION OF 20 NOVEMBER 1941 EXECUTION
CONFERENCE SET FOR 20 JANUARY 1942 BREAK
TESTS OF MEANS SUCCESSFUL BREAK EXPECT FULL
IMPLEMENTATION NO LATER THAN 20 FEBRUARY 1942
ALL SITES BREAK BREAK HAIL VICTORY BREAK HAIL
HITLER END
SECRET
DECIPHERED: 12 DECEMBER 1941
```

MOST SECRET - ULTRA

Roosevelt held the message out to Donovan, who retrieved it and read it, and then returned it to Churchill. "What does all this mean?" the president asked.

"We cannot know precisely, however, based on our acquired knowledge, we believe this means the damnable Nawzees have proven their chosen method of extermination, and they are ready to execute the agreed to plan for their attempt," he said with uncharacteristic solemnity, "to eradicate the Jewish people in the occupied territories. As we discussed last August, the damnable SS has deployed special operations units behind the army in the Baltics, the Ukraine, and Western Russia, which we now believe is an extension of this policy. Their vile intentions are not confined to Poland or Germany."

"Do we know where this conference is going to be held?" Roosevelt asked.

"No," Churchill answered with solemnity. "If we did, or we find out before the event, I would urge an all-out, concentrated bombing raid." The three men remained silent, lost in thought, for a couple of minutes. "We are trying to discover the location."

"Do you have anything to add?" the president asked his coordinator of information.

"We are collaborating with MI6 to query our respective sources in Berlin," responded Donovan. "As of this morning, unless the prime minister has heard anything more recent . . ." Bill paused. Winston shook his head in the negative. "None of our sources is even aware of the conference, set aside knows the location."

"This conference is most likely a by-invitation-only affair," Churchill added, "and, even at that, the invitation was most likely conveyed verbally and directly, rather than by messenger, intermediary, or missive. We'll keep looking."

"As will we," Bill added. "I will also report that we have it, upon reliable sources, the German chemical company I.G. Farben has received several large orders for a cyanide-based insecticide known by the trade name Zyklon B. We have not yet confirmed the supposition that a special unit of the SS has received the first shipment of stock material."

"That is their chosen 'means' mentioned in the second message?" Roosevelt asked.

"It appears so, but I must caution that we have not confirmed that aspect," answered Donovan.

Churchill adjusted the topic. "I have one potential action to suggest."

"Let's have it," Roosevelt said with a tinge of impatience.

"Heydrich is a pompous, arrogant, son of a bitch," Churchill said, inducing laughter in both of the Americans. "As the Nawzee Empire Protector of Bohemia and Moravia, in addition to his myriad other duties, he has been consistently quite cavalier with his movement through Prague. He travels in an open, convertible, Mercedes with the top down in decent weather. He has only a driver and bodyguard, and no escort security entourage. Our information has established that he travels on schedule by the same route every day he is in Prague."

"Assassination," interjected Bill Donovan.

"Yes, precisely."

"That is a dangerous proposition and perhaps unwanted precedent," the president commented.

"These are desperate times, Franklin. The Blond Beast—the Butcher of Prague—is the head of the snake. SOE has several dozen Czech agents that would be perfect for such a mission. This will not be the first and will not be the last such opportunity for these dark activities in this war."

"There will undoubtedly be reprisals," Roosevelt contributed, "part of setting Europe ablaze."

"Yes. There will be reprisals . . . an unfortunate and unavoidable collateral consequence. Regardless, the elimination of Heydrich will send a very clear message to the people of the occupied countries . . . and to the Nawzees. We are coming for them."

"Clear messages are important. In the spirit of comparable candor, we have initiated planning for a carrier-based bombing raid on Mainland Japan. I have not yet received confirmation that the mission is do-able, but the military chiefs have a positive impression."

"Excellent, Franklin. When?"

"My request was as soon as possible. If such an operation is feasible with our precious few aircraft carriers, we are looking at early springtime."

"If you agree, we should shoot for a springtime attack on Heydrich."

Roosevelt looked directly at Bill Donovan. "Are you agreed with the proposed operation?"

"Absolutely, Mister President," Bill responded with strength.

"Very well, then. Good luck to you, Winston."

"And, to you, Franklin."

—

Tuesday, 6.January.1942
Pan American Airways Pacific Clipper
40° 30' North – 73° 55' West
06:25 hours

The crew of the bedraggled Pacific Clipper flying boat saw the New Jersey and New York coastline in the clear, cold air of early morning twilight. The accumulated oil stains and dirt gave the aircraft a very tired and worn appearance for the last couple of weeks that none of them particularly cared about in the grander scheme of things. Euphoria animated the entire crew as they alternated gazing out the portals. The entire crew occupied the flight deck with the recognition they were nearly done with their epic journey fraught with adversity, challenges, and successes.

"Municipal Tower, this is Pacific Clipper, inbound from Auckland, New Zealand, 20 miles south at 5,000 feet for landing at the Marine Terminal."

"Aircraft calling New York Municipal Tower, say again your call sign," the tower controller radioed.

"This is Pacific Clipper for landing."

"Roger, Pacific Clipper, hold at your present position and altitude."

"Wilco, Tower."

Captain Ford switched to the intercom. "Roger, mark our hold point. Mack, let's make right turns, your side, five-mile legs."

John Mack banked the large flying boat to the right. When he had reversed course and leveled the wings, he punched the clock and checked the airspeed indicator. Two and a half minutes at their loiter speed would give him five-mile legs.

"Got it, Skipper," acknowledged Rod Brown.

They orbited at the mouth of New York Harbor in silence, other than the radio traffic of other aircraft on approach to and landing at New York Municipal Airport. Bob Ford reached the limit of his patience. "Tower, this is Pacific Clipper, what seems to be the problem?"

The tower controller did not hesitate. "We have no record of your flight or aircraft. We are at war. Continue to hold at your present position."

"For how long?"

"Pacific Clipper, you should have two pursuit planes intercepting you in the next few minutes, to validate your identity. We will give you instructions once they have reported."

"Standing by."

They continued their orbit, until John Mack said over the intercom, "I've got two P-40 fighters closing fast off the starboard rear quarter."

"Let's stay steady while they check us out," Bob said.

The flight deck crew took quick turns looking out the starboard side portholes to see the fighters closing on them. The two fighters split, one on each side. Ford observed the left fighter that was now abreast of the cockpit. The pilot was clearly checking the aircraft markings. His leather helmet, dark goggles and oxygen mask covered the fighter pilot's entire head and face. Ford saluted. The fighter pilot kept his eyes on the flying boat and did not react for a minute or two. Eventually, the pilot held up a gloved left hand and extended his thumb, and then saluted with his left hand before he banked hard to the left and departed with his wingman.

"We've come thirty bloody fucking thousand miles over the last three weeks," came the voice of First Engineer Homans 'Swede' Roth over the intercom, "to be stuck in this damnable orbit. Are they going to let us land or not?"

"The nation is at war, Swede. What would you expect them to do when a strange aircraft shows up unexpectedly?"

Roth had quite a long pause, and then said, "Well, there is that."

The crew listened to the drone of the engines, synchronized propellers, and radio control chatter for several more minutes.

"Pacific Clipper, this is Municipal Tower. You have been positively identified. You've certainly come a long way. The northwest landing area is clear. Wind is seven knots from zero nine five. You are cleared to land. Welcome home."

"Pacific Clipper, cleared to land. Thank you. It's great to be home . . . finally."

The large flying boat turned up the Hudson River, banked over Harlem, and set down on the water south of Riker's Island. They shut down all four engines and secured the aircraft, as the ground support crew tied up the aircraft.

"Let's straighten up, guys. Juan Trippe himself is on the pier to welcome us home."

The Pacific Clipper and her crew's long journey home were finally over.

Their extraordinary effort became the grist of legend. History recorded their epic flight home and their exemplary ingenuity solving the planning, logistical, and negotiating difficulties during every leg of their trial. It was a magnificent story in and of itself.

——

Tuesday, 6.January.1942
RAF Martlesham Heath
Woodbridge, Suffolk, England
United Kingdom
14:45 hours

Launching an entire fighter squadron these days to watch over a 13-ship convoy northbound through the North Sea with four destroyers in escort seemed particularly unusual after the Battle of Britain and six months after the German invasion of the Soviet Union. But here they were, each section taking a corner of the ship formation below them. Tug's Blue Section orbited 5,000 feet higher on the far side of the convoy from Hunter's Green Section ahead of the convoy. Whitey's Red Section took the high position behind Green Section, while Pete's Yellow Section had the other low position catty-corner from Green Section.

Brian quickly scanned the sky around them. Dusty and Frog maintained perfect positions standing off behind and below each wing of Hunter's Spitfire Mark V fighter, humming along and barely above the maximum endurance airspeed. *Something has to be very special in the hold of at least one of those ships.* Neither Control nor any of the squadron's pilots called out any even remotely suspicious. *This is not going to sit well with the more eager of the lads among us. This is a whole lot better than getting shot at, and it is still flying. Flying is flying.* Brian remembered the desperate days of July 1940, when convoy escort was not so boring and far more deadly. He maintained his continuous scanning of the sky around them, his aircraft's instrument panel, the convoy below them, and his wingmen. Convoy escort missions were indeed boring, for all of them, but Brian knew there were important reasons for these missions. Nonetheless, they were still boring, no matter how anyone tried to package them. As Brian scanned, he noted, *we are approaching our bingo fuel level. Something will have to give pretty soon to make it back to base.*

"Eagle Leader, this is Cowslip calling," came the voice of the duty sector controller for the North Weald Sector.

"Cowslip, this is Eagle, go ahead."

"Grinder is inbound from the west-northwest of your current position. You should be near bingo fuel. You are released to return to base."

"Roger, Cowslip. We have Grinder in sight. We are bingo. Eagle, Eagle Leader, RTB."

Brian banked smoothly to the left, allowing his wingmen to adjust their positions as they turned for the rendezvous with Blue Section, and headed for home base. Tug maneuvered the squadron around small cumulous clouds as they approached Martlesham. Tug directed the squadron into sections in trail for landing straight ahead. They were cleared to land and did so as sections in fine form. Dusty and Frog followed their leader to the assigned parking positions. Brian switched off his electrical equipment, closed the throttle, and shut off the fuel to the big Merlin engine in front of him.

As the propeller came to a stop, Crew Chief Corporal Henry Joyce Jacobs was on the left-wing root when Brian slid his canopy back. Jacobs opened the small access door and said, "Any squawks, sir?"

"None, Henry. She was a charmer, as always," Brian responded, as he unstrapped and disconnected from his aircraft. "Just low on petrol. We used all we had."

"We will fill her up and give her a good check."

"Thanks, Henry."

Dusty and Frog joined Brian as they walked back to the intelligence hut and took their turn for the mission debriefing. As they completed, they returned to Dispersal Hut, removed their flight gear, and hung their flight equipment on the assigned wall pegs.

Salt Morton and his Red Section compatriot Henry Carl 'Buddy' Courtland from Bridgeport, Connecticut, jumped right into it. "Those damn convoy escort missions are the most boring in the world."

"You got that right," Salt contributed.

"I think Frog had it right three weeks back. We're being punished for requesting transfer."

Frog learned enough to avoid joining the discussion. Brian tried to ignore the yammering.

The rants of the less experienced squadron pilots carried on unabated as if they expected some different outcome. Tug Meares chose not to intervene and to allow his pilots to vent some of their frustration.

As he often did when he wanted to disengage from meaningless conversation, Brian leaned his straight-back, wooden chair against the wall and closed his eyes. Most of the pilots recognized the obvious sign and respected the signal.

One of the newer pilots in the squadron, Yellow Section, Right Wing, Pilot Officer Michael Raines 'Sloppy' Butterfield from Seattle, Washington, decided to ignore the sign. "Hunter, you're always the one talking us down.

Why aren't you giving us your opinion?" Sloppy paused, awaiting a response that did not come. None of the others chose to intercede. Butterfield clapped his hands loudly. "Hunter!" he shouted. "Wake up. We need your wisdom." Again, no one spoke, and Brian held his position and kept his eyes closed. "Hunter!" Sloppy shouted, once more.

Brian lowered his chair and stood up straight, almost as if he intended to fight. Several muffled gasps were heard. "You know how I feel about such bullshit. You do not need me to repeat myself. Keep flapping your gums, if it makes you feel better, but I don't have to listen to it." Brian did not wait for a response and decided to take a walk in the cold winter air. *I'm getting very tired of that crap.*

———

Chapter 4

The tyranny of a multitude is a multiplied tyranny.
-- Edmund Burke

Wednesday, 7.January.1942
Cap's Place seafood restaurant
2980 Northeast 31ˢᵗ Avenue
Lighthouse Point, Pompano, Broward County, Florida
United States of America
13:10 hours

The comparatively remote erstwhile Prohibition-era speak-easy had morphed into a destination seafood restaurant of some acclaim that had come highly recommended by his short holiday host—Ed Stettinius. Reformed rumrunner Captain Eugene Theodore 'Cap' Knight had created the facility in 1928, thus the popular name of the establishment. Cap's Place was a natural choice for the planned meeting.

Winston Churchill had arrived ten minutes early, 20 minutes ago. His impatience was beginning to mount as he waited. He had not seen Lady Castlerosse—Jessie Doris Delevingne—since their last rendezvous at Maxine Elliott's Cote d'Azur villa Chateau de l'Horizon in 1936. Doris had married Valentine Edward Charles Browne, 6ᵗʰ Viscount Castlerosse, in May 1928. Social gossip of the pre-war years had it that Doris and Valentine had divorced in 1938, after a tumultuous marriage. Part of his impatience rested upon the paucity of information regarding why she had requested this meeting.

The door opened, and Doris walked in like a ray of brilliant sunlight. Winston stood. She was still attractive and radiant as he remembered her. The door closed as Doris stepped toward Churchill. They touched cheeks in the European manner, and then Doris gently grasped his cheeks with both hands and kissed him on the lips.

Still holding his cheeks, Delevingne softly said, "Thank you for seeing me, Winston." Doris released his head. Churchill nodded his acknowledgment. "I have not seen you since you became first lord and now prime minister, so congratulations on your accomplishment."

"Thank you, but it is more of a curse than an accomplishment." Winston stepped to the side and gestured to the table set for two with a simple mixed green salad and a nice, poured Chardonnay. They sat. "To what do I owe this pleasure?"

"Directly to the point, as always."

Churchill smiled. "My apologies. That was a bit brash. My life has changed dramatically in the last two years, and I find myself more impatient these days."

"So, has mine?"

"How have you been? What have you been up to since we were last together?"

Delevingne took a bite of her salad and a sip of her wine. "As you probably know," she began, "Val and I divorced in 1938." Winston nodded his head in agreement. "When the Germans attacked us, I left for safety. I was alone and so scared. I have remained in New York for the last year and a half . . . well, except for a few months last summer in Hollywood."

"It was not an easy time for any of us, and my dear Doris, I doubt you were ever alone."

Doris ignored Winston's comment. "And now, the United States is at war as well," the countess added. Winston waited patiently without expression, giving her time to compose what she wanted to say. "I want to go home."

"To England?"

"Yes, to England, you ninny."

"You are safer here, Doris. The Germans may once again turn their wrath upon us if they are able to subdue the Soviets. We still get occasional air raids, even after The Blitz ended last May, and we command the skies, now. The German U-boats remain a palpable threat to our supply lifeline. My point is, as I said, you are safer here."

"I don't want to be safer. I want to be at home. I'm not happy here. I want to go home and go back to the way things were."

Winston smiled softly as he held her eyes. "Doris, my dear, London is not the city it was when you left. I'm afraid we shall never return to the way things were, and any semblance of normalcy is a long way off. We must first vanquish the bloody Hun . . . excuse my profanity."

This time, Doris Delevingne looked into Winston's eyes, as she thought about what she wanted to say. She shook her head. "I have tried everything. I thought long and hard about bothering you with my problems, but I have tried everything. I have tried booking ships, airplanes, and even tramp steamers. Everything is either restricted or booked solid, moving military personnel to Europe . . . to England."

"You are asking for my assistance?" asked Winston smiling at her.

Delevingne tilted her head slightly to the right and smiled back at him in her most demure, seductive manner. "Yes, my darling Winston, I am."

"You are just as persuasive as you have always been."

"So, you will help me?"

"Yes, Doris. I will make some discreet inquiries and see what I can arrange."

"I can ask for no more," she said and took a sip of her wine.

"I will need your personal contact information, Doris." Lady Castlerosse had thought ahead. She reached into her purse, extracted a folded note card, and handed the prepared, handwritten note containing all of her contact information to the prime minister. Churchill smiled. "You knew how this was going to go, didn't you?" Doris lowered and tilted her head slightly, and again smiled in a very familiar fashion. "I will likely not be able to contact you directly. However, my personal representative in Manhattan is a very good and dear friend, Bill Stephenson. If I am able to secure passage for you, it will likely be Bill who will contact you directly and ensure you have no difficulties."

Delevingne clapped her hands together softly in a jubilant, almost prayer-like manner. She stood, went to his side of the table, leaned over, showing just enough cleavage, and kissed Churchill passionately. "Thank you so very much, my dearest Winston. You have always been so special to me." Doris returned to her seat rather than press her luck.

"Don't count your chickens before they hatch," Churchill cautioned.

"How provincial," she giggled.

As they leisurely enjoyed the remainder of their meal, they reminisced about their shared experience on the French Riviera before the war and the ensuing events in their lives since those peaceful days. Each of them wanted to talk about the other, which amounted to an intriguing *tête-à-tête* among intimate friends that only they shared.

When their meal was complete, Doris Delevingne excused herself, kissed Winston on the cheeks, and was ushered out the back exit and driven to the Pompano railroad station for her return to New York City, as she awaited the outcome of her appeal. Churchill waited a handful of minutes, then departed through the main restaurant. The full house of patrons stood, applauded, and cheered loudly as the prime minister made his way through the tables. Several people were bold enough to pat Churchill on the back of his shoulders. Winston smiled broadly, nodded his head, waved to the crowd of customers, and repeatedly held his 'V' for victory hand gesture high, instigating more vigorous cheers. He thrived on such affirmation, and the moment served as a worthy bookend to the very personal meeting.

———

Thursday, 15. January. 1942
British Overseas Airways Berwick
39° 15' 20" North – 76° 34' 30" West
Baltimore Harbor
Baltimore, Maryland
United States of America
08:30 hours

"Welcome aboard, Prime Minister," said Captain John Cecil Kelly-Rogers, standing on the aircraft's port sponson.

"Thank you, Captain," Churchill responded and extended his right hand to the aircraft's commanding pilot.

Kelly-Rogers gestured for the prime minister to precede him through the port sponson hatch. Once inside the Boeing Model 314 flying boat, registration number G-AGCA and known more popularly as Berwick, the Captain informed Churchill, "Our flight time to Bermuda will be about four and a half hours. Once we level off at our cruising altitude of 11,000 feet, I will set aside our company regulations and invite you to the flight deck, if you would like to have a feel for the aircraft."

Churchill beamed with anticipation. "I would be honored, Captain."

Kelly-Rogers excused himself and proceeded to the flight deck to prepare for takeoff.

The prime minister settled into his first-class seat and buckled his seat belt. John Martin and Lieutenant General Sir Hastings Lionel 'Pug' Ismay, KCB, DSO, buckled into the rear-facing seats across a narrow, fixed table between the two rows of seats. Ismay held a variety of concurrent positions that, in sum, made him the principal military assistant and liaison to the prime minister. Churchill sat in silence, staring out the porthole at the water and the cityscape beyond. Ismay and Martin recognized the expression, and respected their chief's contemplation.

The engines started one after the other until all four were humming at fast idle and the aircraft moved slowly forward. The flight crew presumably completed their takeoff checklist and received their takeoff clearance. The engines advanced smoothly to the full roar of takeoff power, and the aircraft picked up speed, kicking up saltwater spray. The spray outside the porthole dropped away. The frequency of hull bumps increased rapidly, as the aircraft's speed increased until one last bump marked their takeoff. The next leg of their journey home had begun.

They climbed steadily and smoothly into the cold winter air as they headed east into the rising Sun. The Chesapeake Bay and DelMarVa Peninsula passed beneath them. Seemingly within minutes, they were over the Atlantic Ocean.

Churchill shifted his gaze from the exterior to Ismay. "We had a successful conference," the prime minister pronounced.

"I do believe so, Prime Minister," the general responded.

Churchill nodded his head a few times, and then continued, "We achieved our primary objective . . . that being Germany first."

"Yes, we did," Ismay responded, "but, I would urge caution and vigilance. There should be no doubt the Americans are strongly focused upon Japan, and rightly so. Yes, they did agree to Germany first; however, as I read between the lines of their contributions, they intend to undertake a two-ocean prosecution of the war."

"Yes, yes, and as you say, quite understandable. The Pacific will be primarily a naval war, while Europe will be predominately land and air combat. If any nation can carry out a two-ocean war, it is the United States. Pearl Harbor has galvanized American public opinion and focus. I have felt that dramatic shift myself. Just a few days ago, I had lunch at a local restaurant during my short holiday break. The cheers were profound and heartfelt . . . deeply emotional. The world changed a month ago with the Japanese strategic mistake.

"Further, we agreed to the first, joint, major combat operations in the European Theater. Most notable, Operation BOLERO—the massive build-up of American armed forces in England, for what will inevitably be the cross-Channel assault to end Nawzee tyranny; and Operation SLEDGEHAMMER, which you recognize I am not a proponent, for the large-scale attack on occupied France to fulfill our commitment to Uncle Joe and the Soviets. We need to relieve pressure on the Reds, but the last thing we can tolerate or endure is another Passchendaele," Churchill said, referring to the devastating, meat-grinder battle in Northwest Belgium that consumed so much of British and Allied manhood in the fruitless stalemate.

"Hear, hear. None of us want that . . . including the Americans."

"Unfortunately," Churchill continued, "their ambition and desire to help sustain the Soviets are seriously coloring their judgment regarding a direct assault against the Germans, who are now deeply entrenched along the entire coastline of occupied France."

"Perhaps so, Prime Minister," Ismay responded, "but I would be remiss if I did not highlight the presentations and planning of Brigadier Eisenhower. He seems to have a keen appreciation for joint operations and measured action within our logistical capacity."

Churchill nodded his head in agreement. "Yes, Pug, but he is a junior general, who follows his orders, and General Marshall was quite demonstrative in expressing the American Army's position and, from my discussions with President Roosevelt, those views of the President, as well." They sat in silence for several minutes with the drone of the aircraft's engines and the rush of the airstream just beyond the aircraft's skin. Churchill looked back to Ismay. "I was most encouraged by Eisenhower's concept for GYMNAST"—the operation plan for the Allied invasion of Northwest Africa, leading to the link-up with the British 8th Army, "as an alternative to SLEDGEHAMMER."

"I think the Chiefs unanimously favored GYMNAST, as the first joint step," added Ismay.

"The difficulty will be convincing the Americans to take that more modest step."

"Operation RUTTER will tell us a lot about the complexity and difficulty of a cross-Channel endeavor against the Germans."

"Quite right, Pug, indeed it will. Planning is proceeding nicely. Lord Mountbatten should be ready to execute the plan by mid-Spring."

Commodore Lord Louis Francis Albert Victor Nicholas 'Dickey' Mountbatten, GCVO, became Chief of Combined Operations the previous October, and had been charged with planning and conducting a modest, demonstrative raid on the Channel coast of German-occupied France— Operation RUTTER. The raid had been tentatively planned for late spring or early summer when weather should be more favorable for such an operation. The operation had gained support from the American military chiefs to test the Germans and offer at least a gesture to Stalin for a second, western front.

"That is my understanding, as well."

Captain Kelly-Rogers appeared in their compartment, next to the prime minister's seat. "Please excuse my intrusion, Prime Minister."

"Yes, yes," Churchill said, waving his hand dismissively.

"We are level in cruise flight over the Atlantic Ocean, on course for Bermuda. If you would like to experience the cockpit of this magnificent machine, now would be a good opportunity. We are in calm, cloudless skies."

Churchill smiled. "Lovely. I will enjoy the opportunity, Captain." He nodded his head to Ismay and Martin, unbuckled his seat belt, and then stood and looked to Captain Kelly-Rogers. "Lead on, Captain."

Kelly-Rogers turned and led the prime minister into the galley and the circular ladderway up to the flight deck. The aircraft commander introduced the prime minister to his duty flight crew as well as the second officer navigator, engineer and radio operator. With introductions and greetings complete, Kelly-Rogers gestured to the open pilot's seat on the left of the flight deck. Churchill carefully maneuvered himself into the seat. Kelly-Rogers stood just to the right side of the seat and oriented Winston to the controls and instruments, and then invited the prime minister to perform a few gentle, modest turns to feel the aircraft's responsiveness. Churchill asked several cogent questions regarding the aircraft's performance like range, speed, service ceiling, lift capacity and such. They even managed to take a commemorative photograph of the occasion. Winston spent just over 30 minutes in the pilot's seat before extricating himself, thanking Kelly-Rogers and the flight crew, and returning to his seat. At that moment, Churchill decided to continue his journey to England on the Berwick rather than debark at Bermuda to join his military chiefs and staff aboard the *Duke of York*. This was a much better means of travel and would take far less time to complete.

———

Saturday, 17.January.1942
Cabinet War Rooms
New Public Offices
Whitehall, London, England
United Kingdom
18:00 hours

The heartfelt, enthusiastic cheers and applause greeted the prime minister as he entered the underground conference room. The full War Cabinet, along with the cabinet secretariat and military support staffs, nearly filled the room. The defense ministers and military chiefs would have been invited to join the debriefing; however, they were still en route aboard HMS *Duke of York*, crossing the Atlantic Ocean.

As had become his public practice, Churchill held up his 'V' for victory gesture, as he made his way to the center chair. He shook hands with Secretary to the War Cabinet Sir Edward Ettingdene Bridges, KCB, MC, and then gestured for everyone to sit. Bridges had held his position since 1938.

Sir Edward said in a firm voice, "Please secure the door. The Cabinet will come to order." The cacophony of the full conference died out swiftly. "Thank you all for attending this special meeting of the War Cabinet. Let the record show, the full membership of the War Cabinet is present. The sole agenda item for this special meeting is to receive the prime minister's ARCADIA Conference report. The floor is yours, Prime Minister."

"Thank you, Sir Edward, and thank you all for your warm welcome home. I shall diverge slightly from my report since news from the field is certainly related and impactful on our accomplishments at the ARCADIA Conference. First, General MacArthur has withdrawn American forces in the Philippine Territory to the island fortress of Corregidor. President Roosevelt informed me that reinforcement of the Philippine garrison is not possible. The collapse of the American resistance in the Philippines appears imminent. Hong Kong has fallen. The situation on the Malay Peninsula continues to deteriorate, and General Percival's forces are withdrawing toward Singapore in the face of the overwhelming Japanese force. Just this afternoon, upon my return to No.10, I was informed for the first time by the War Department that General Percival disclosed the major defense guns installed for coastal protection are incapable of turning to face the enemy advancing toward the island. Rommel and his *Afrikakorps* are showing signs of taking the offensive in Cyrenaica with General Auchinleck on the defensive and demanding reinforcement. My point is, we will likely have darker days ahead. We must gird ourselves against further disappointment and anguish.

"On the positive side," Churchill continued, "the Red Army has stiffened outside Moscow and has begun to gain back ground lost to the Germans at the gates of the capital city. This brings me to the ARCADIA Conference.

"First and foremost, my time with President Roosevelt on both professional and personal bases has reinforced my assessment of the American leader. I am confident we are aligned to the best possible level. President Roosevelt agreed with and affirmed for the government the Germany first strategy. The combined joint chiefs of staff accepted that strategic approach. The chiefs carried out a spirited exchange regarding how to prosecute that strategy. A substantial faction of the American military wants a direct assault on the Continent to give Stalin a second, western front to draw off German forces in front of him, and to shorten the war to the greatest extent possible. We argued, I believe successfully, that the logistics of building up sufficient personnel, equipment, and supplies to carry out an invasion of occupied France will not support a cross-Channel invasion in the near term. I will note here that it is my personal opinion, which I expressed to the president, it will take one to two years to build up sufficient forces to conduct a cross-Channel invasion, and advance with force to Berlin and victory. Some generals, and I will leave it at that, advocate for a beachhead in France to hold as a base for future operations. The leading site for which they advocate in that scenario is Cherbourg. The reality of such a notion is the Germans will not allow us time and opportunity to prepare sufficient defenses to maintain such a beachhead, even if it could be initially gained. At the end of the day, we agreed to proceed with planning for our first major joint operation to be executed against Vichy French Northwest Africa, to assist the 8th Army and to create a base to assault the soft underbelly of Europe. To support the strategy, we agreed to Operation BOLERO, which is the movement of and build-up of American armed forces in this country. We must direct the home secretary to closely coordinate with the military ministries to provide appropriate quarters and training grounds in accordance with Operation BOLERO. Further, we jointly directed Lord Mountbatten and the Combined Operations group to plan and execute short strike raids on the French coast as soon as possible. These plans will be discussed and approved by the War Cabinet. To conclude my summary remarks, I believe, and I think the chiefs will affirm, that we accomplished all that we set out to achieve with the joint strategy conference in Washington. One overriding reality was solidified and reinforced with steel that despite the darker days ahead, we shall go forth together toward ultimate victory."

Silence remained until the Cabinet recognized that the prime minister's report was completed. Deputy Prime Minister Clement Richard Attlee, Member of Parliament for Limehouse, and Leader of the Labour Party cleared his throat and said, "Thank you, Prime Minister, and on behalf of the War Cabinet, welcome home and well done." The others applauded politely.

"Thank you, Clement. We have considerable hard work, pain, and agony ahead. Nonetheless, the only action we have presently on the table is direction to the home secretary to provide for Operation BOLERO."

"That seems a bit rash, Prime Minister," Attlee replied. "Shouldn't we have some understanding of what that directive means and what it will cost His Majesty's Government?"

Churchill glanced with a stern expression to his right, and to his deputy and principal political adversary in peaceful times. "I do not see that we have many choices. We need American forces and supplies to beat the Germans. We need them here. Further, Lend-Lease will give us considerable resources to build the facilities necessary to support BOLERO."

"Lend-Lease cannot buy or acquire land."

"True, but that is our part of the challenge."

"How many men?" asked Minister of Labour & National Service Ernest Bevin, Member of Parliament for Wandsworth Central and leading Labour Party member.

"The initial, agreed-to, working assessment is one million men and associated equipment and supplies."

"One million men!"

"Yes, Ernie. That is the current estimated peak level. However, we may well pass upwards of two million men through this country once we initiate the final assault," Churchill reported rather matter-of-factly.

"That is a lot of men to accommodate," Attlee added.

"An impossible number," observed Bevin.

"Many things were impossible when the war began, but we have found a way. We will . . . we must find a way with this matter. The reality is we have no choice. England is the only free land available for the build-up of the necessary invasion forces and materiel. Further, we do not have much time to prepare this country. To that end, I ask for the War Cabinet's concurrence to task the home secretary with the fulfillment of the BOLERO facilities requirements."

"How much time?" asked Attlee.

"By the initial BOLERO plan set in motion during the ARCADIA Conference, the first major combat units will begin to arrive in April or May. It will take one to two years to achieve peak deployment." Churchill paused to look at each War Cabinet member in the eyes. "Are we in agreement?"

Silence filled the room for several seconds until Attlee cleared his throat and said, "You are asking us to sanction the issuance of a blank check. May I suggest a workable compromise here?" The prime minister nodded his reluctant agreement. "I think we can support instructing the home secretary to quickly study the BOLERO plan and present to the War Cabinet a preliminary implementation plan to achieve the BOLERO requirements."

"We need action, Clement, not studies."

"I appreciate your sense of urgency, Winston. However, we need to see the means and resources necessary to adequately satisfy the needs."

"I could agree to two weeks to present the fulfillment plan to the Cabinet," the prime minister responded.

"That is not much time for such a massive undertaking," Bevin said.

"Yet," Attlee contributed, "I agree with the prime minister. We do not have much choice to prosecute this war, and time is of the essence."

"Very well, let's see what Henry can produce in two weeks," conceded Ernie Bevin.

Henry was Home Secretary Herbert Stanley 'Henry' Morrison, PC, Member of Parliament for Hackney South, and another Labour Party member, who had held his ministry position since October 1940.

"All in favor?" queried the cabinet secretary. All seven members of the War Cabinet raised a hand.

Churchill turned to Bridges. "Sir Edward, please record the unanimous decision of the War Cabinet and so inform the home secretary."

The sole agenda item was closed. The special meeting was adjourned. Several MPs remained to chat with the prime minister about various peripheral matters, now that he was back in the chair. Churchill extricated himself, stopped by his small underground office to see the stack of paper awaiting his review and action, and then climbed the stairs to his reinforced temporary residence while No.10 was being repaired and restored.

———

Saturday, 17. January. 1942
No.10 Annexe
New Public Offices
Whitehall, London, England
United Kingdom
21:10 hours

The small initial family dinner upon his return home included Winston's wife, Clementine, and their youngest child and daughter Mary in her quasi-Army uniform of the Auxiliary Territorial Service (ATS) with the initials appearing on the cap badge.

Mary joined the Women's Voluntary Services for Civil Defence in 1939 and served on a 3.7-inch anti-aircraft gun crew positioned in London at Hyde

Park during the Battle of Britain. She transferred to the ATS last year, still serving on an anti-aircraft gun crew.

The dinner conversation centered upon Winston's impressions of early wartime America, especially in contrast with life in London. Yet, Winston's mood had darkened.

"Something seems to be bothering you, dear," Clementine observed.

Winston looked down at the empty, used dinner plate. "I feel the Black Dog licking at my heels. He showed up before I left America."

"Oh Papa," 19-year-old Mary said. The whole family recognized Winston's reference to looming depression that came to him from time to time and occasionally reached incapacitating levels.

"You had a very successful meeting with Roosevelt and the Americans from the sounds of it," Clementine said. "What could possibly be dragging you down?"

Winston slightly and briefly grinned. "Yes, the meeting with the Americans went quite well, better than expected, actually. However, the war news is near-universally dark. At least during the terrible days of the great air battle, we fought above our land, in our sky. What will come, what lays ahead, will not be so favorable. I do not need to drag you down with me, but I need you to know that the Black Dog is here, Clemmie."

Mary stood and went to her father. She wrapped her arms around his chest and kissed the top of his bald head.

Winston patted their daughter's arms on his chest in a gesture of gratitude. The affection of his family helped and often truncated the visits of the Black Dog. "Let it suffice to say, the war news is not positive . . . anywhere."

"We are not under imminent threat of invasion," Clementine stated. Mary released her embrace, stood up, and took to the task of rubbing his shoulders with multiple kisses to his head.

"True, but that may well be temporary if the Red Army does not find the means soon to beat back the Germans. They are simply too close to the edge of the abyss. Even during those dark days after the fall of France, I did not feel like this. We have lost Hong Kong, and we are on the verge . . ." Winston stopped for several seconds. "I must stop. My recounting of our situation may help you understand better, but it is also what has beckoned the Black Dog. Please forgive me."

"Perhaps we should take a few days at Chequers, or even Chartwell like we did last May," suggested Clementine. "The challenge of painting a winter scene might well be the distraction and stimulation you need to shoo away the Black Dog."

"Excellent suggestion, Clemmie, but I just returned from nearly a month away and far too much happening in the world. I just have to deal with this episode."

"What can I do to help?" asked Mary as she continued to massage her father's shoulders.

"My dear darling Mary, what you are doing is a good start. It feels so good." Churchill paused. Clemmie moved her chair closer and gently grasped Winston's hand. "While you are working, Mary, we have not heard about your duties."

Mary laughed softly. "To be honest, Papa, since the Battle of Britain and the Blitz ended, it has gotten rather boring. We still do incessant drills to keep our procedures sharp. But, we have not fired a shot in anger since last May."

"That sounds an awful lot like a good thing . . . better than being in constant combat," Winston said softly without conviction.

"Yes, I suppose so. But, my precious father, I need to feel I am doing my part to win the war."

"We are each doing our part, Mary, and each part is vital to the war effort. There are chaotic days ahead, of that I am certain. We are very proud of you, Mary." Winston paused and looked up at his youngest daughter. "May I ask you, how do the other women of the Auxiliary Territorial Service you serve with feel about this lull in action?"

"Interesting query, Papa," answered Mary. "Some of them are grateful for nothing to shoot at or shooting at them. Others feel just like me."

"Well, my darling Mary, at least you are stationed in London rather than like your brother."

The Churchills' second child and only son Major Randolph Frederick Edward Spencer-Churchill, Member of Parliament for Preston, had been serving on the staff of the General Headquarters Middle East in Cairo, Egypt, since early 1941.

"I'd rather be where the action is."

Clementine gasped. Winston chuckled softly. "You are definitely your father's daughter."

"Yes, I am and proud of that fact."

"Don't get too ambitious, Mary. We have already lost one child. We do not want to lose another," Clementine said with stern commitment, referring to the tragic death of their fourth child, Marigold Frances Churchill, from septicemia at not quite three years of age in 1921.

"Listen to your mother, Mary. She is a wise and caring matriarch."

"I do, Papa, all the time, but we are at war, and the country needs me like it does Randolph and you."

"I will not argue, Mary," said Churchill. "I understand, respect, and I am rightly proud of your sense of service to the Kingdom. You have already sacrificed so much due to my service. As your mother so precisely stated, we cannot bear to lose another child."

Frustrated that she was not making headway, Mary dismissively said, "I have duty early in the morning." She moved around the table to face her father and mother. "If you will excuse me, I really must be on my way."

They wished each other goodnight. Once Mary departed the building, Clementine suggested, and Winston agreed to make it an uncharacteristic early night as well.

—

Sunday, 18. January. 1942
American Eagle Club
No. 28 Charing Cross Road
Covent Garden, London, England
United Kingdom
18:45 hours

Nearly half of the No.71 Squadron pilots had decided to take the train into London for some genuine American cuisine. The Club had opened and been dedicated the Queen Consort Elizabeth not quite a year ago to offer a little touch of home for American citizens serving in England with British and Canadian forces. The public facility was not restricted or closed, yet, it was focused a small touch of America in England. The five pilots, including Hunter, headed up the stairway to the cafeteria floor of the four-story building.

"Ah, the sweet smell of hamburgers," declared Pilot Officer Bradley Thomas 'Hick' Hickerson of Macon, Georgia.

"You got that right," Salt affirmed. "A nice juicy burger is going to taste a lot better than those damn cheese sandwiches they serve us in the Mess."

The grill and dining room on the 2nd floor was busier than Brian remembered on any of his prior visits—not quite full but close. The pilots made their way through the crowd to the order line. Before they reached the line, a young, clearly intoxicated, young man dressed in an American Army uniform with a single chevron on his sleeves shouted from a couple of yards away, "What the hell are these weak-assed, fucking Limeys doing in the American Eagle Club?"

Frog began to turn to face the belligerent drunk soldier but stopped when Brian grabbed his left wrist. Brian's left wingman looked over his shoulder at Brian, who simply shook head for Frog to ignore the antagonist.

"You assholes don't belong in here," the man pressed on.

Then, another soldier with sergeant's chevrons stepped in front of the PFC. They heard the sergeant speak in a firm, commanding voice. "You have no clue who those officers are." The PFC looked rather surprised and demurely shook his head. "They are all Eagle Squadron pilots. They are Americans. And worse, the one with the two broader stripes on his sleeves," the sergeant said, gesturing with his thumb over his left shoulder, "is the third-highest scoring ace in the whole of the Royal Air Force. So, Private, you will apologize for your coarse rudeness and show these Americans the respect they deserve."

The five RAF officers turned to face their antagonist and waited.

The PFC looked directly at Brian and said, "I am terribly sorry, sir. I didn't know."

Brian nodded his head in acknowledgment, then looked at the sergeant. "Thank you, sergeant."

"It is my honor, sir. Thank you for your service in defense of freedom." The sergeant looked over his shoulder at the stunned PFC and said more to the soldier than to Brian. "We all owe you an enormous debt of gratitude."

"Thank you, sergeant. I hope you have a great evening. Enjoy."

Brian turned to the line, and the others followed.

Frog stood behind Brian. He leaned forward and whispered into Brian's right ear, "That was interesting."

Brian only shook his head. Frog did not press his thought. No further words passed between the Eagle pilots. They collected their hamburgers, French fries, and ice-cold bottles of Coca-Cola. They found an empty table at the back of the dining hall.

Sweet waited until each of them had taken a few bites or two to open the conversation. "Do you know that sergeant, Hunter?"

"No, actually, I don't. I've never seen him before."

"He sure knew you," Sweet added.

"Who doesn't know the ace of aces!" interjected Hick with enthusiasm.

"Yeah, baby," Frog said.

"True," Salt contributed, "but, if that PFC is what we are going to have to deal with as our countrymen fill this country, I am not too keen on the notion."

Sweet nodded his head and observed, "Eventually, we will be in the uniforms of Army officers, and PFC's will show us the respect we deserve."

"One thing for certain," Brian commented, "that young man should stay away from alcohol."

They all laughed, and then enjoyed a few more bites. The Americana meal felt good and tasted great.

Salt swallowed his mouthful and took a good drink of his Coke. He silently belched from the carbonation. Salt looked directly at Brian and asked, "Do you think they are really going to transfer us to the Army Air Forces?"

"None of us are in the circles of power," Hunter answered, "so, we have no way to know for sure. That said, yes, I think they will transfer us as soon as the Army is here to accept us."

"The Army is here," interjected Frog. "This room is filled with mostly soldiers and a few sailors. The Army is here," Frog repeated.

Brian stared at Frog for several seconds, and then looked back at Salt. "I don't see many pilot's wings in this lot."

"Good point," admitted Frog. "Do not pass Go. Do not collect $200," Frog quoted from the popular board game Monopoly.

"Brian . . ." They heard from behind Hunter. Brian looked over his shoulder to see the familiar form of Lieutenant Draper Laurence Kauffman, USN [USNA 1933], now attired in the winter uniform of the U.S. Navy rather than his Royal Navy Volunteer Reserve uniform in which he had been dressed the last time the two met.

Brian stood and turned to his advancing friend. "This is quite a change," Brian said, gesturing to the new uniform.

"Yeah, I'm leaving."

"Hey guys, allow me to introduce Lieutenant Draper Kauffman, bomb disposal expert *extraordinaire*." Gesturing to the group who were now standing as well, Brian continued, "These are all Eagle Squadron pilots. Salt Morton, Hick Hickerson, Frog Forcier, and Sweet Sweeney."

"Great to meet you guys." They all shook hands.

"So, what changed besides the uniform?" Brian asked.

They all sat. Kauffman joined them, sitting across the table from Brian. Draper answered, "Short answer . . . Pearl Harbor. It seems my explosives work over here got me noticed and recalled. In fact, I leave tomorrow morning. They are flying me directly to Pearl Harbor to deal with some nasty fusing the Japanese used in the attack. They have a bunch of unexploded ordnance. Damn things have already killed a half dozen more men."

"Damn!" Salt exclaimed.

"How do you do it?" asked Hick.

Kauffman smiled, swallowed his bite, and sipped his Coke. "The same way you blokes climb into those confined cockpits and launch off to let bad guys shoot at you."

They all laughed.

"*Touché*," Sweet responded with his best French accent.

Brian wanted to give Draper a little opportunity to finish his meal while it was warm since the pilots had mostly already finished. "Draper joined the American Volunteer Ambulance Corps in France in February 1940, for the same reasons we all joined the RAF. He was actually captured by the Germans in June, in the final days of the Battle of France. The Germans released him in August. He made his way to England, joined the Royal Navy Volunteer Reserve, as a mine disposal expert. The Blitz expanded his work substantially dealing with all those unexploded bombs."

"Nasty business," Nick said.

"War is hell," Kauffman quoted General Sherman.

"Seems we are behind you, Draper," continued Brian, to give Kauffman more of a break to finish his meal. "We have requested a transfer to the Army Air Forces, but as you can see," he said, gesturing to his uniform, "we are still awaiting transfer. Also seems more Americans are showing up in London. We all want to join the fight against the Japanese."

"The Germans are still in this thing, although they appear to be focused on the Soviets," Draper said and took the last bite of his hamburger.

"Oh, we still have Germans shooting at us when we head into France."

"I'm sure, just as we still have bombs to be defused leftover from The Blitz."

"We're going to Shepherd's Pub to toss a pint or two. Would you like to join us?" Brian asked.

"I would love to do so. Thanks for the invite, but respectfully, I must decline. I've got a pre-dawn call to begin my odyssey to Pearl Harbor."

"We've got a pass and hotel rooms for the night," added Brian.

They followed Kauffman as he stood. Frog and Hick shook hands with the Navy lieutenant and excused themselves to bus the plates and utensils for the group. Brian and the others wished Kauffman good luck on his journey and in his new assignment. They walked out of the building together and split at the dark street. The Eagle pilots were off to their favorite public house for some evening libation.

———

Tuesday, 27.January.1942
Office of the Coordinator of Information
National Institutes of Health Building
2430 E Street Northwest
Washington, District of Columbia
United States of America
16:40 hours

Bill Donovan and Ned Buxton sat in the plush chairs of the former's office. As was their practice at the end of a conventional workday, they met to confer about the day's activities, although neither of them finished their work until well into the evening.

"Have you read it all?" asked Ned, referring to the unreleased copy of the Roberts Commission Report.

Soon after the Pearl Harbor attack, President Roosevelt commissioned a group to study the facts associated with the Japanese attack on U.S. armed forces stationed on Oahu, Territory of Hawaii, and centered on the large naval base at Pearl Harbor. U.S. Supreme Court Associate Justice Owen Josephus Roberts led a group of two admirals and two generals to collect, analyze, and present the facts related to the attack.

"Yes, the whole thing, word for word. I am told the report will be presented to Congress tomorrow. I got our copies from the president."

"What do you think?"

"At the bottom line, they want someone to blame, and Admiral Kimmel and General Short are the designated scapegoats."

Admiral Husband Edward Kimmel, USN [USNA 1904], had been promoted and assumed command of the U.S. Pacific Fleet in February 1941. Lieutenant General Walter Campbell Short, USA, had assumed command of the U.S. Army's Hawaii Department, at Schofield Barracks on Oahu, in February 1941, as well.

"Frankly, I was far more interested in what was not reported in the document," Donovan declared.

"Intelligence?"

"Exactly. The report documents some of the alert message traffic in an attempt to show that Oahu was warned. And yet, we know the underlying intelligence was scattered all over the place. To be blunt about it, we failed the president and the nation."

"That's pretty harsh, Bill. We were only four months old."

"True, but I hold us to a much higher standard. The Commission illuminated Japanese spies and our fragmented counter-intelligence work. I think it is pretty clear there was no concerted counter-intelligence program to protect the island or military facilities. The Commission was surprisingly frank about the success of Japanese intelligence prior to the attack. We were not mentioned."

"I noticed that as well," Buxton added.

"We were lucky. Under my vision of COI and what I believe the president expects of COI, we failed miserably, and not even the president has mentioned that failure."

"What are they going to do with this?" Buxton asked, holding up the Report summary.

"First, this is not a charging document. However, it does not reflect kindly upon Kimmel and Short. The Commission cleared everyone above Kimmel and Short. They have both been relieved of command, which is punishment itself, likely the end of their careers. I suspect there will be a military investigation and quite possibly charges for at least dereliction of duty."

Donovan's deputy considered Bill's words. "What do you propose we do with this?" Ned asked.

"First and foremost, this must never happen again. We had the clues and failed to connect the dots. The Pacific Fleet was asleep that lazy Sunday morning. The Army had early warning radar operating that morning, detected the inbound raid, and failed to take defensive action. As the report states, they had sufficient personnel to operate the radar network 24-hours a day but were only operating for three hours each morning."

"Of that, we are all agreed."

"Second, our job is to collect, assemble, analyze, and present the intelligence. It is my opinion that various agencies of the government had sufficient information to know the Japanese intended to attack various U.S., British and Dutch locations, including the Hawaiian Islands. We had a few radio cuts on the Japanese fleet that could only have one purpose, given the other intelligence. We failed, Ned. Yet, that's not what the Roberts Report established. Hell, we are not even mentioned in the Report. So, the government wants to fry two good, competent officers, because the intelligence apparatus failed."

"Bill," Buxton said with some frustration, "surely you recognize the resistance we face in just the collection task alone. The damn FBI won't even talk to us unless they want something, let alone share the information they collect. The State Department is only one notch better than the FBI. The Army and Navy are not particularly . . . how shall we say . . . generous."

"All true," Donovan replied with calm, quiet solemnity. "We must win the trust and engagement of the other agencies and the operational folks. In fact, I think the operational guys will be the key. The intelligence bureaus will be overcome when the operational guys rely on our information. The target data for the president's special mission to bomb the Japanese Home Islands may well be our first opportunity. We can help with target data. Depending upon how the planning plays out and what they decide, GYMNAST will likely be the second. Now that I think of it, did I mention my lunch with Louis Mountbatten last week?"

"No, you didn't. Chief of Combined Operations?" asked Buxton.

"Yes. We had a private lunch last week before he headed back across the pond. The closest operation is a commando raid, masked as a small-scale probe, to go after the electronics of the German Würzburg and Freya radar units operating at a small coastal chateau near Bruneval, just north of Le Havre. Operation BITING, the Bruneval raid, is planned for the middle of next month. The second is a larger scale raid against the coastal defenses at Dieppe in July."

"Have they asked for our assistance?"

"No, they've got what they need at least for the Bruneval raid. Photoreconnaissance has pinpointed the radar units they are going after, and they know enough about the units for their precision. It sounds like they have a well-thought-out plan to capture the electronics and destroy the units before extraction. Churchill suggested, perhaps more strongly recommended, that they include our Special Operations section. I agreed to provide a small group of observers to go along."

"Does the same apply to the planned Dieppe raid?"

"That is a little different. It goes under the reference of Operation RUTTER, a division-size challenge to the coastal defenses at Dieppe, to test the Germans and gather information for future planning. The Rangers will have a small unit involved. We will work with MI6, SOE, and Mountbatten's planners to refine the intelligence for the operation. The combined joint chiefs reviewed both sets of plans, adjusted accordingly, and sanctioned the plans, including our involvement. My point in bringing these small-scale operations up is they are watching us. They want to see what we can contribute to the success of conventional military operations."

"We have our work cut out for us as if we didn't already know that," Ned chuckled.

"Quite right, my friend."

"Do you want to distribute the Roberts Report?"

Donovan thought for a moment. "I don't know how useful it will be for our work since we are or should be concentrating on the future rather than what is behind us. I would make the department heads aware of the report and make it available for anyone to review at the archive section."

"Very well. Let me get to it," Buxton said, stood and departed.

———

Monday, 2.February.1942
Office of the Director of Naval Intelligence
The Admiralty
Whitehall, London, England
United Kingdom
14:30 hours

When First Lord Alexander and First Sea Lord Admiral Pound entered Admiral Pike's office, Jumper rose and met them at his small conference table. Pike waited for his assistant to close the door, and they were all seated at the table. "As we discussed last week, we had several disassociated indications the Germans were going to attempt a breakout of the *Scharnhorst* and her task force from their confinement at Brest. Station X received three messages sent a few days ago and deciphered a few hours ago that confirm they are going to press the Channel sometime in the next two weeks."

Pike pushed the folder with both messages to the First Lord.

MOST SECRET - ULTRA

```
SECRET
DATE: 29 JANUARY 1942
TO: NAVAL COMMAND WEST AIR FLEET 3
FROM: ARMED FORCES HEADQUARTERS
OPERATION CERBERUS
BREAK
THE LEADER HAS PERSONALLY APPROVED AND ORDERED
THE EXECUTION OF OPERATION CERBERUS AS SOON
AS TASK FORCE CERBERUS IS READY BUT NO LATER
THAN 15 FEBRUARY BREAK STRICT RADIO SILENCE TO
BE MAINTAINED TO MINIMIZE EXPOSURE BREAK GOOD
FORTUNE TO ALL BREAK BREAK HAIL VICTORY BREAK
HAIL HITLER
END
SECRET
DECIPHERED: 2 FEBRUARY 1942
```

MOST SECRET - ULTRA

Alexander read the second message.

MOST SECRET - ULTRA

```
SECRET
DATE: 29 JANUARY 1942
TO: AIR FLEET 3
FROM: AIR FORCE HEADQUARTERS
OPERATION THUNDERBOLT
BREAK
AF3 ORDERED TO DEPLOY ALL AVAILABLE COMBAT
FORCES TO SUPPORT OPERATION CERBERUS PER
APPROVED PLAN BREAK DIRECT COORDINATION WITH
NAVAL COMMAND WEST TO ENSURE MAXIMUM PROTECTION
TO TASK FORCE CERBERUS BREAK STRICT RADIO
```

```
SILENCE REQUIRED TO MINIMIZE EXPOSURE BREAK
BREAK HAIL VICTORY BREAK HAIL HITLER
END
SECRET
DECIPHERED: 2 FEBRUARY 1942
```

MOST SECRET - ULTRA

The first lord passed the first two messages to Admiral Pound, and then picked up the third and last message from the folder.

MOST SECRET - ULTRA

```
SECRET
DATE: 30 JANUARY 1942
TO: NAVAL COMMAND WEST FATHERLAND COASTAL
COMMAND
FROM: NAVY HEADQUARTERS
OPERATION CERBERUS
BREAK
ALL E BOAT CHANNEL UNITS UNDER YOUR COMMAND ARE
ORDERED TO FULL ALERT BREAK EACH BOAT MUST BE
MAINTAINED AT FULL ARMAMENT AND FULL FUEL FOR
THE DURATION OF THIS ORDER BREAK ALL PERSONNEL
LEAVE TERMINATED UNTIL OPERATION COMPLETION OR
TERMINATION BREAK BREAK HAIL VICTORY BREAK HAIL
HITLER
END
SECRET
DECIPHERED: 2 FEBRUARY 1942
```

MOST SECRET - ULTRA

The first lord waited for Admiral Pound to finish reading. "The third message is the keystone, isn't it?" Alexander asked.

"Yes sir," Pike responded. "Together with the other two, we are certain they are going to press the Channel sometime in the next two weeks."

"So, it will be up to the Air Force and us to stop them," the first sea lord said matter-of-factly, after reading the third message.

"Are we ready to do so?" A.V. asked.

"Yes sir. We meet with the Air Ministry every day to discuss the latest intelligence. I do not know, yet, whether the Air Force has these messages.

However, if not, they will soon. Bomber Command continues to maintain the pressure on Brest. The latest photoreconnaissance from yesterday afternoon gave us no indications their move is imminent. The big ships still have their elaborate camouflage netting on them."

"The prime minister told the War Cabinet we must stop them and end this scourge," Alexander added. "Is there any other way?"

"We considered a surface attack like the Force 'H' action at Mers-el-Kébir two years ago, but we abandon the notion when the Air Force could not give us sufficient air cover for the surface units."

"Understood."

"We are keeping our surveillance and patrol operations at normal levels," Pound reaffirmed. "We have heightened the alert level among the passive units like Chain Home. The Air Force has also repositioned fighter and bomber units closer to the Channel to reduce reaction time when they do pull the trigger."

First Lord Alexander looked back to Jumper Pike. "Please see to it that the Air Ministry has or receives this latest intelligence."

"I will see to it personally, as soon as we conclude here."

"I think we are done unless you have anything else for us," A.V. said.

Admiral Pike stood, signaling the conclusion. The three men shook hands and departed. Alexander and Pound turned right, and Pike went left to leave the Admiralty and walk across Whitehall to the Air Ministry building.

—

Chapter 5

The bold are always lucky.

-- Danish proverb

Wednesday, 11.February.1942
RAF Martlesham Heath
Woodbridge, Suffolk, England
United Kingdom
16:35 hours

"**W**e have been at Readiness or Standby every daylight hour for the last three days," protested Salt Morton.

"Is that supposed to be a news flash?" Dusty Langford challenged his compatriot. "We've all been in here on the edge."

"This is exhausting staying here tight as a stretched rubber band."

Langford laughed. "You have no idea, Salt. There are only four of us who served during the great air battle. We were like this for weeks at a time. Yes, it is very exhausting, but part of our job is to deal with it. Plus, as we've been briefed each morning for the last couple of days, we are on alert for those German battleships making a run for it through the Channel to reach Germany."

"I wish they would at least let us fly," contributed Sloppy. "Even patrol racetrack patterns would be better than this perpetual waiting."

"Then, you would be complaining about the boring mission," Dusty responded. "If you are not comfortable with the waiting of our alert status, then do something to get your mind off it—read a book, play checkers or chess, knit a shawl for your momma. Do anything you wish to get your mind off the wait."

"If they do launch us on the mission we're briefed for," Whitey added, "it is likely to be a rather nasty affair. Those ships have a lot of anti-aircraft guns in a comparatively small space. There are going to be a lot of bullets and shells in the air around us as we are trying to do our job."

Brian nodded his head in agreement. He had just leaned his chair back and closed his eyes when Tug Meares joined them from his office.

"OK, lads," Meares announced, "a couple of things before we are released." No one spoke in any form. "First, just to follow up on our earlier briefing, the airfield remains largely unserviceable—still not dry. Base ops has marked our clear dry line with small orange flags. The dryline will confine us to single aircraft takeoff procedures. I will be orbiting overhead at 2500 feet at max endurance to save fuel for the join up. Second, I just talked to Group. They have no indication that anything has changed. So, tomorrow will likely be another alert day."

"Oh, great," interjected Salt.

"So, you expect us to be at Available status at dawn tomorrow?" asked Buddy.

"I was going to get to that before I was interrupted," Tug responded with detectable annoyance. "When I am done here, we will be released for the evening. Well, truth be told, Group has already released us, but I am not done." Several of the pilots chuckled. "We are confined to base again tonight. While the bar in the Mess will be open, I caution each of you to not overindulge. Yes, we must be back here with the whole lot of you and report Available at dawn tomorrow. The Met Office has forecast broken and overcast clouds tomorrow for most of Southeast England and the Channel, so we will have a somewhat complicated situation if we have to launch on this mission tomorrow. Any questions?" No one spoke up or even twitched. "One last item . . . I am not going to intercede in your grumbling about conditions . . . as long as your griping does not interfere with our mission. However, the less experienced among us can learn a lot from the more experienced pilots. Listen, pay attention, and learn—it will make you a better pilot. Our task is killing Germans, full stop. The air ministry will use us as a proper tool to that end, but they will not be wasteful. I urge you more impatient blokes to sharpen up your fortitude. Understood?"

"Yes sir," came the chorus of responses.

"Very well, then. We are released. Corporal Harris, if you would be so kind to secure the building upon our departure. We'll see you in the morning."

"As you command, sir," Harris responded.

The pilots began shuffling to hang up their flight equipment and make their way to the door. The transport truck stood outside to carry them to the mess. Brian was one of the last to leave. *I'll try to call Charlotte after the evening meal . . . well maybe after a pint with the lads.*

—

Wednesday, 11.February.1942
Brest Harbor
Occupied France
21:14 hours

The massive, darkened warships silently and smoothly made their way from the bomb-damaged docks toward the open ocean. The formidable German battlecruisers DKM *Scharnhorst* and DKM *Gneisenau*, along with the heavy cruiser DKM *Prinz Eugen* were barely visible in the light of the waning moon that was low on and just above the eastern horizon. The six destroyers assigned as their escort for the mission had preceded the capital warships out of the occupied Atlantic port in their bold attempt to press the supposedly closed English Channel. The German Operation CERBERUS began.

By dawn the following morning, the German flotilla was past Cherbourg and halfway through the English Channel. Despite the precautions put in place, the British did not detect the Germans until they were abreast Dieppe at nearly 11 o'clock in the morning, when the Chain Home RADAR operators noticed unusual, increased aircraft circling over the French coastline of the Channel. The Royal Navy and Royal Air Force scrambled to execute their interdiction plan.

The bold and audacious naval mission that would become known to history as the Channel Dash would conclude the following evening.

———

Thursday, 12.February.1942
RAF Gravesend
Gravesend, Kent, England
United Kingdom
12:10 hours

No.71 Squadron landed quickly and smoothly through the overcast earlier this morning. Nothing had changed in their mission briefing other than Group gave up on the airfield restrictions at Martlesham and wanted a quicker response time, if needed. Their aircraft were lined up at Gravesend, and topped off with full fuel and ammunition. They were ready to go should the requirement bloom. As they waited at Readiness through the morning, Brian's thoughts drifted to his conversation with Charlotte. *Things seem to be humming along well on the farm. Ian is growing so fast, and I'm missing most of it. The sooner this war gets over, the sooner I can enjoy Charlotte and Ian, and who knows, maybe even make more babies. I don't want my son to be an only child like I was.*

The red telephone in front of Corporal Harris rang. Everything stopped, and every head turned to their operations clerk. "Scramble the squadron!" shouted Harris without the need to consult the squadron commander.

The pilots that did not have their flight equipment on grabbed what they needed. The doorjamb slowed them down exiting the Dispersal Hut, but they took off running to their aircraft.

Corporal Jacobs had the big Merlin engine in the nose of the XR-G Spitfire Mark V aircraft running smoothly at fast idle and stepped out of the cockpit as Brian reached the left, trailing edge, wing root. Henry stood just forward of the small access door, braced against the prop wash. He connected Brian's oxygen mask hose, microphone, and earphone cords, as Brian checked and tightened his parachute straps, and buckled his lap belt and shoulder harness together.

Brian quickly scanned his instrument panel. The engine oil pressure was in the normal range, and the temperatures were off the peg and rising smoothly. He was ready to go. Brian glanced at his two wingmen off his right-wing. They were not quite ready. He then looked to the XR-A Spitfire of Tug Meares, whose engine was just coming up to speed. In another 20 seconds, everyone was ready. Brian heard Tug call for takeoff, and the squadron was quickly cleared with the altimeter setting, and wind direction and speed. Tug's XR-A Spitfire moved forward. Brian signaled Jacobs at the right-wing leading edge to remove the wheel chocks, then signaled his rigger Leading Aircraftman Stephen Hawking ahead of his left-wing to do the same. Tug's two wingmen followed, and Brian advanced his throttle to initiate movement. Dusty and Frog followed. As they had briefed, they took off as sections and joined up en route.

"Sapper, Eagle Leader calling," Tug radioed Biggin Hill Control.

"Eagle Leader, Sapper, Splash launched from Monster. They are heading south-southwest at cherubs five. Heading one four zero for intercept and climb to angels five. Swift is airborne. Hammer will join you shortly."

"Roger, Sapper. We'll catch up to them in short order."

"Good luck, Eagle."

"Eagle, out."

Brian quickly scanned and confirmed the whole squadron was airborne, and in their briefed combat formation. Their pre-mission briefing called for the squadron to climb to 5,000 feet (angels five). Splash was the callsign for No.825 Naval Air Squadron, temporarily stationed at RAF Manston, which was southeast of them on the Channel coast. The Fleet Air Arm squadron was six, old, slow, Fairey Swordfish torpedo biplanes—the same planes that carried out the successful Taranto raid and contributed to the sinking of the *Bismarck*. They passed through a comparatively thin, low, broken cloud layer. *These clouds are not going to be helpful.* Fortunately, the sky above the low cloud layer was virtually clear if they ignored the high cirrus wisps.

"Eagle Leader, Swift Leader."

"Go ahead, Swift."

"Swift has Splash in sight. We are below the cloud deck."

I cannot imagine the Spitfires of No.72 Squadron trying to maintain position on those Swordfish torpedo planes that have a maximum speed of just 124 knots—not much more than the approach speed of the Spitfire Mark V. Worse, they are below an 800-foot cloud deck.

"Roger, Swift. We'll have the high post along with Hammer."

Tug leveled off, throttled back, and began slow, shallow, S-turns to add the clouds below to the continuous scan for enemy aircraft. Brian looked hard through the breaks in the clouds but only saw water with dispersed white caps. This is not going to be easy. The radio remained silent, which in turn meant no other aircraft had detected their targets or enemy aircraft, yet. They all knew from the mission briefing that the objective of the torpedo planes was to sink, stop or slow down the German capital warship making a dash through the Channel for the safety of their homeland. *Our mission is to keep the German fighters off those torpedo planes. If those ships are out there, this is going to get nasty very fast.*

"Got 'em," broadcast Sweet, "nine o'clock, low, through that closest hole."

"Splash, Swift, we have you . . . high off your right-wing."

"Eagle Leader, Hammer Leader."

"Hammer, Eagle, go ahead."

"Eagle, Hammer, tally-ho, your seven o'clock, level."

"Roger, Hammer, tally ho. Splash and Swift are below our left wing. We're going to shift to their left-wing. You can take the right-wing."

"Roger, Eagle. Wilco."

They watched No.32 Squadron—Mud Morrison's old squadron—overshoot their station due to the enormous speed differential. They recovered quickly and smoothly. Brian looked back down only to see the cloud layer.

"Eagle, Hammer, Sapper. Bandits left orbit, turning toward you. Looks like one group descending and the other group climbing."

"Roger Sapper," Tug responded. "Hammer, Eagle, you take the climbing group. We'll try to intercept the diving group."

"Roger Eagle."

The Spitfires of No.32 Squadron began their climb. Tug signaled for speed and descent. Brian pushed his throttle forward, and the Merlin eagerly complied.

"Tally ho," Tug broadcast. "Bandits, twelve o'clock, a fist above the horizon."

Brian picked up right away. He signaled for his wingmen to take up their combat spread and prepare for the fight. His master switch was latched in ARMED, gun camera in SYNC, and his gunsight was illuminated and set. Brian moved his right hand on the spade to place his thumb on the middle of the firing switch.

Tug maneuvered the squadron to intercept a couple of dozen Bf109 fighters diving for the clouds. *They're ignoring us. Man, oh man, those guys are really intent upon getting to the Swordfish.* The Spitfires were diving at their red line airspeed and gaining on the bevy of grey fighters.

Radio chatter picked up substantially as Hammer dealt with the upper cover fighters. Suddenly, six of the German fighters banked sharply to face the Eagle Spitfires.

"Eagle Green, take the challengers."

Brian responded by banking into the rapidly advancing German fighters. He did not need to instruct his wingmen on their part of the engagement swiftly approaching. Brian adjusted their high-speed closure to place his gunsight pipper just above the middle German fighter and depressed the bottom portion of his firing switch for a second. Tracers arced out and showed no signs of impacts, but they served their purpose in breaking the German formation without them firing back. The 109s and Spitfires passed in a flash. Brian pulled up hard, feeling the g-loading on his body. He pressed his throttle against the stop, already through the emergency gate. He strained to look over his shoulder. Frog and Dusty were well into their climbing turns as were the Germans. Brian shifted his right thumb to the top of the firing switch. He pulled the Spitfire's nose through as hard as he dared with his airspeed bleeding off rapidly. To his surprise, his direct adversary made a fatal mistake and rolled away toward Frog on Brian's left. That maneuver gave Brian the closure geometry enabling him to quickly adjust his pipper. The cannons erupted and shuddered the Spitfire. A half dozen impact flashes preceded the German's engine bursting into full flash just before the aircraft broke up into pieces. Brian did not watch his vanquished adversary. As his nose dropped below the horizon, Brian rolled right to pick up first Dusty, and then Frog. They both had targets. Frog had a trailer closing on him. Brian quickly rolled, pulled the nose down farther, shifted his thumb to the lower part of the firing switch, and squeezed off a stream of bullets in a very long shot. He saw no impacts, but the tracers broke the concentration of Frog's attacker.

Among all the radio chatter and scanning for German targets, Brian heard, "Splash has the targets. Spread for engagement. Making our run-in." Brian could not see what was happening below the cloud deck.

Brian looked toward his right shoulder and caught a flash in his rearview mirror. He rolled sharply through the inverted position and strained his neck to see a 109 closing on him. Brian pulled back hard on the spade. The Spitfire responded. He aggressively maneuvered to deny the German a shot on him. The cloud deck was not far away. Brian dove for the clouds with the German matching his maneuvers. He rolled hard right as large, blue tracer rounds passed under Brian's left-wing. *Damn, that was close.* The German had fired his 20mm cannons and nearly hit home. The cloud deck rushed sharply up to him. *I won't have much time to stop my dive below these clouds.* Brian had just enough time to level his wings and begin to pull his nose up. He penetrated the 300-500 foot cloud deck. Brian broke out under the clouds as he nearly arrested his descent rate. The water was surprisingly close. He banked sharply left as soon as he cleared the clouds—no assailant.

What Brian found himself in the middle of below the overcast had to be hell on earth. The three massive German warships with heavily boiling wakes were perhaps 5,000 yards off his right-wing. *Damn, they are big.* Red, yellow, and blue tracer rounds of various sizes crisscrossed the scene just ahead of him. One of the Swordfish bellied into the water. Another biplane launched its torpedo into the water only to explode in a brilliant flash. Then, the yellow tracers swung toward him from the trailing cruiser. Brian pulled back on his spade hard as he pushed the throttle to the emergency stop. He was back up through the cloud deck and climbing swiftly. His head spun quickly all around him looking for a lurking German fighter—nothing. Yellow tracers followed him up through the cloud deck. With no immediate threat, Brian began a shallow, left spiral climb. A quick scan of his instrument panel told him everything was as it should be, except they were close to their bingo fuel. The furball dogfight continued above and to the west of him. He did not want to enter the fight from below. Brian adjusted his climb to keep his distance and kept his spherical scan to detect attackers. Within minutes, he was above the fight and rolled to pick his next target.

"Eagle," broadcast Tug Meares, "bingo."

Brian rolled away from the fight, then scanned to see if he could help anyone with disengagement.

"Eagle, Hammer, we'll cover you."

"Roger Hammer. Thanks, mate."

The Germans did not give chase. Once they were clear of the fight with no Germans following them. Tug cruise climbed the squadron to 5,000 feet. Brian was relieved to see Dusty's XR-C Spitfire behind and below his right-wing, and Frog's XR-J Spitfire in a similar position off his left-wing. They both signaled they were in good shape. No.32 Squadron joined No.71 Squadron a couple of miles behind them. No.72 Squadron was five miles ahead of them. None of the No.825 Squadron lumbering Swordfish could be seen anywhere. *This is going to be a helluva debriefing.* Tug checked in with Biggin Hill Control and indicated they would land at Gravesend to refuel and rearm. Brian checked his fuel gauge, made a quick mental calculation, and agreed they had sufficient fuel to make Gravesend, but it would be close. Swift descended for Manston, and Hammer headed to Biggin Hill. There were no calls from Splash.

———

Friday, 13.February.1942
Cabinet War Rooms
New Public Offices
Whitehall, London, England
United Kingdom
17:15 hours

The prime minister entered the War Rooms conference room late, after tending to a request from the King. The Defense Committee joined the full War Cabinet for the closed meeting. All attendees were ULTRA cleared. "My apologies, gentlemen." He looked at Alexander and Sinclair directly. "Right, then, as if the threats to Singapore, Egypt and the Suez Canal were not bad enough, we turn to the first lord and air minister to pray report to the War Cabinet. You asked for a couple of days. Those days are past. What the bloody hell happened yesterday?"

First Lord of the Admiralty A.V. Alexander fidgeted in his chair, put his left fist to his mouth, and cleared his throat. "Yes, well, to the point, it was not a good day for His Majesty's Armed Forces."

"A bit of an understatement, as I understand things," interjected the prime minister, who seemed to be in a rather grumpy mood.

"Quite so, Prime Minister. We are still collecting a few last details, yet, what we do know to this moment, the German battlecruisers *Scharnhorst* and *Gneisenau* along with the heavy cruiser *Prinz Eugen* and six escort destroyers set sail from Brest before midnight Wednesday. The photoreconnaissance of just that afternoon showed the camouflage netting still in place. They made ready for sea in a matter of hours from dusk until they cast off."

"Bomber Command stood down that morning due to low overcast all along the Normandy coast," interjected Sir Archie. "The first indication we had that morning came from Chain Home. The operators noticed what appeared to be several squadrons of aircraft orbiting over the Normandy coast. Eleven Group dispatched a section of Spitfires to reconnoiter the detection. The fighters did not report until they landed since their orders were to maintain radio silence. As fate would have it, they had stood off from the unusually large fighter cover and spotted the German warships through breaks in the clouds. They considered dropping below the clouds to confirm, however, the anti-aircraft fire they encountered convinced them that discretion was the better part of valor."

"Bloody hell!" Churchill exclaimed and slammed his open hand on the table. "That one bloody order gave them another couple of hours to advance through the Channel—our Channel!" No one spoke, coughed, or even moved. Churchill scanned the room several times, as he tried to calm his anger. "Continue," the prime minister ordered.

Alexander cleared his throat and proceeded. "The sighting confirmation was communicated immediately, and Operation FULLER entered the execution phase. Shore batteries at South Foreland were the first to engage before they reached Calais. The Germans returned fire but did not maneuver. A squadron of Swordfish torpedo planes of the Fleet Air Arm out of Manston, escorted by a squadron of Spitfires, made their torpedo attack off Dunkirk. They flew undaunted into withering anti-aircraft fire from the German flotilla. The Spitfires had their hands full with several squadrons of German fighters. Half the torpedo planes did not make it within range to launch. The other half managed to launch their torpedoes. No hits were recorded. None of the Swordfish returned."

"None?" asked Churchill with a tone of incredulity.

"Lieutenant Commander Esmonde led what remained of his squadron—825 Squadron with six Swordfish aircraft, six pilots and 12 ratings—in their valiant attack on the Germans. Five of the 18 men were rescued from the water. All of the others perished, including Esmonde. It was a heroic but tragic action." Alexander paused and scanned the group to allow for questions. No one spoke. He continued, "Dover Command sortied five motor torpedo boats out of Dover as well as the 16th and 21st destroyer flotillas out of Harwick and Felixstowe. The Germans deployed all of their available E-boats to defend their capital ships and did so in an exceptional manner. The low overcast covering most to the Channel and the North Sea frustrated the efforts of Bomber and Coastal Commands to locate and engage the German warships. The *Scharnhorst* hit at least one mine during the transit, but there was no sign it slowed her down."

"In short," the prime minister said and paused to ensure everyone was listening, "the Germans made it through our Channel, despite the prior warnings they were going to press the Channel."

"I would not state it in such stark terms," Alexander responded. "We had a good joint plan. Everyone did their part. The weather was on their side this time. We deployed enormous resources to stop them."

"And, they made it anyway," Churchill said with solemnity.

"Yes," the First Lord answered.

This time, Foreign Minister Eden cleared his throat. "We just received this Boniface message before the meeting."

MOST SECRET - ULTRA

```
SECRET
DATE: 13 FEBRUARY 1942
```

```
TO: TYPE COMMANDER BATTLESHIPS
FROM: NAVAL COMMAND WEST
INFO: NAVY HEADQUARTERS COASTAL COMMAND
OPERATION CERBERUS
BREAK
IT IS MY DUTY TO INFORM YOU THAT OPERATION
CERBERUS HAS BEEN SUCCESSFULLY COMPLETED BREAK
WELL DONE TO OUR VALIANT FORCES BREAK BREAK
HAIL VICTORY BREAK HAIL HITLER
END
SECRET
DECIPHERED: 13 FEBRUARY 1942
```

MOST SECRET - ULTRA

The message made the rounds of the War Cabinet and Defense Committee. Eden continued, "Confirmation arrived from our field agents this afternoon, the Germans made port this morning."

Prime Minister Churchill pronounced, "The Nawzees won this one."

"It appears so . . . yes."

"No," Sir Archie jumped in. "Not yet!"

Churchill looked askance at the air minister. "Pray tell what you have in mind?"

"Per the contingency plans of Operation FULLER, and if the weather breaks enough, Bomber Command will execute substantial raids on Wilhelmshaven, Emden, and Brunsbüttel over the next few days to catch them before they can bolster their defenses."

"Good luck and good hunting," added the prime minister. "We do not need those warships on the High Seas. Is there anything more to contribute?"

"Not at present," the first lord responded. "We will inform the War Cabinet, as we collect more information as we learn more."

"Thank you. I eagerly anticipate better news. Now, unless anyone has something more to offer us, we shall adjourn. I am leaving for Chequers."

The War Cabinet and Defense Committee dispersed. Churchill left immediately by limousine to the prime minister's country estate and retreat.

Lieutenant Commander Eugene Kingsmill Esmonde, Royal Navy, had been awarded the Distinguished Service Order for leading his squadron off *Victorious* on one of the early torpedo attacks on the *Bismarck* the year prior. They were aboard *Ark Royal* when she was sunk and quickly launched to save the aircraft from going down with the ship. For his incredible courage in leading his squadron against the *Scharnhorst* flotilla, Commander Esmonde was posthumously awarded the Victoria Cross for conspicuous gallantry under fire, three weeks after the action.

———

Sunday, 15.February.1942
Chequers Court
Ellenborough,Buckinghamshire, England
United Kingdom
14:30 hours

"Colonel Menzies has arrived, Prime Minister," announced duty Private Secretary John Peck.

"Show him to the library, would you, John," Churchill commanded. "I will join him forthwith."

"Yes sir," Peck answered and departed to carry out his instruction.

The prime minister finished the last of his late lunch before heading to the classic country manor library that also served as his office and study.

"Good afternoon, 'C,'" Churchill said as he entered the library to see only the director-general of the Secret Intelligence Service dressed in a conservative, dark blue, business suit.

"It is not, I must say, Prime Minister. I am the bearer of tragic news."

Churchill's jovial expression vanished in an instant as he gestured to the facing plush chairs. "What have you?"

"It is my solemn duty to inform you that Singapore has fallen. General Percival surrendered the garrison a little over an hour ago."

"Dear God above," Winston responded with shock. "That is tragic news, indeed. This may be the worst disaster to His Majesty's Armed Forces in centuries of our glorious history, and this just on the heels of the successful German Channel Dash three days ago."

"As soon as the message came in, I conferred with Minister Margesson and First Lord Alexander before leaving London. They are preparing their assessments for your review."

"Thank you, Stewart."

Menzies nodded his head. "This late-breaking sad news was not the purpose of my request to visit with you privately. It happened to be incidental." Churchill's puzzled expression caused Menzies to smile and nod once. "We have field reports from several dispersed and reliable sources that something significant happened at a large estate on the shores of Wannsee on the outskirts of Berlin, on the 20th of last month," Menzies reported and paused. The prime minister remained expressionless and transfixed. "The evidence we have suggests the Nazi security apparatus, specifically Heydrich and an unknown number of party security leaders, met at the estate. We have seen references to that conference or meeting as the authority for transporting people of the occupied territories to what the Germans call concentration camps. This appears to be the execution of what we learned last year of what Göring called The Final Solution of the Jewish Question. Field agents have reported several trains with cattle cars packed with people—two in Poland and one from Holland. We do not know where these trains were actually headed since the switching instructions were not readily available."

"What can we do?"

"I'm afraid not much, Prime Minister. We have limited message space to query our field operatives to minimize German direction-finding location countermeasures. We have made several attempts with no results, as yet. These camps are remote, making it more difficult to investigate. Our analysts' belief most of the field agents instinctively know these are serious findings."

"Combined with the intelligence regarding the SS special action units operating behind the German army groups in Russia, Ukraine, and the Baltic States, this is rather ominous information."

"Yes, it most assuredly is."

"What exactly do you think it means?"

Menzies held Churchill's gaze as he considered his words. "To be brutally blunt and perhaps a bit crass, we think it means the Nazis, I cannot say the Germans, intend to exterminate the Jews, gypsies, homosexuals, political dissidents and other undesirables to the regime."

"Exterminate?"

"Yes."

"That is a rather harsh word in reference to human beings."

"Yes, it is, Prime Minister. That is the word that seems most descriptive to our cognizant analysts."

Churchill frowned deeply and wiped away a tear. "What has mankind come to with this tragedy?"

"Indeed."

"Do you have anything else for me on this chilly Sunday afternoon?"

"No sir."

"Very well then. Thank you for making the journey, Stewart. I trust you and your operations staff to carefully use your discretion to learn as much as you can about these camps, what they are doing there, and support structures that allow these operations, if for no other reason than to gather sufficient evidence for the prosecution of these beasts after the war. I have much to discuss with the Defense Committee. Perhaps we can find a way to lessen the severity of what these Nawzees are doing."

"We can only hope at this stage."

Churchill bade Menzies a safe journey back to London. The prime minister sat alone in the manor house library staring out the window at the usually elegant garden subdued by winter. John Peck recognized Churchill's pensive mood and stood guard outside the closed door to eliminate any potential intrusions.

—

Thursday, 19.February.1942
Oval Office
The White House
Washington, District of Columbia
United States of America
13:00 hours

One of the duty Secret Service agents wheeled President Roosevelt into the Oval Office and to his desk. Harry Hopkins waited for him at the left side of the desk.

Without looking at Hopkins, the president asked, "Is it ready?"

"Yes sir." The agent left the office and closed the door. "Before we get to the business at hand, Secretary Stimson asked me to inform you that the Japanese carried out a serious bombing raid on Port Darwin, Australia, this morning their time, last night our time. Henry indicated several reconnaissance patrols have detected no indications of invasion, although the Australians are understandably on edge. They are still assessing the damage and will brief you as soon as they have a more accurate picture of what happened and what it means."

"With the fall of Singapore, this attack takes on more ominous dimensions. I suppose it was expected, but I for one did not expect it so soon. I do not look forward to the briefing. Bad news is never pleasant." Roosevelt paused for a few moments' contemplation. "Please prepare a simple message of acknowledgment and condolences to the prime minister, the governor-general, and to the King and Prime Minister Churchill. There is not much we can do at the moment, but we should also offer to do whatever we can to assist them."

"Yes sir, right away," Hopkins responded. "I have nothing else on that matter." Roosevelt nodded. "The attorney general and secretary of war have reviewed the exclusion order without revision or comment."

"So, it is ready to sign?"

"Yes sir," Hopkins replied and placed the action folder on the desk, opened it, and slid the document in front of the president.

President of the United States Franklin Delano Roosevelt nodded his head in recognition, and then carefully read the document he was about to sign into effect.

The President
Executive Order

Executive Order No. 9066

Authorizing the Secretary of War to Prescribe
Military Areas

Now, therefore, by virtue of the authority
vested in me as President of the United States,
and Commander-in-Chief of the Army and Navy,
I hereby authorize and direct the Secretary
of War, and the Military Commanders whom he
may from time to time designate, whenever he
or any designated Commander deems such action
necessary or desirable, to prescribe military
areas in such places and of such extent as
he or the appropriate Military Commander may
determine, from which any or all persons may be
excluded, and with respect to which, the right
of any person to enter, remain in, or leave
shall be subject to whatever restrictions the
Secretary of War or the appropriate Military
Commander may impose in his discretion. The
Secretary of War is hereby authorized to
provide for residents of any such area who are
excluded therefrom, such transportation, food,
shelter, and other accommodations as may be
necessary, in the judgment of the Secretary of
War or the said Military Commander, and until
other arrangements are made, to accomplish
the purpose of this order. The designation
of military areas in any region or locality
shall supersede designations of prohibited
and restricted areas by the Attorney General
under the Proclamations of December 7 and 8,
1941, and shall supersede the responsibility
and authority of the Attorney General under
the said Proclamations in respect of such
prohibited and restricted areas.

I hereby further authorize and direct
the Secretary of War and the said Military
Commanders to take such other steps as he
or the appropriate Military Commander may
deem advisable to enforce compliance with

the restrictions applicable to each Military
area hereinabove authorized to be designated,
including the use of Federal troops and other
Federal Agencies, with authority to accept
assistance of state and local agencies.

I hereby further authorize and direct
all Executive Departments, independent
establishments and other Federal Agencies,
to assist the Secretary of War or the said
Military Commanders in carrying out this
Executive Order, including the furnishing of
medical aid, hospitalization, food, clothing,
transportation, use of land, shelter, and other
supplies, equipment, utilities, facilities, and
services.

This order shall not be construed as
modifying or limiting in any way the authority
heretofore granted under Executive Order No.
8972, dated December 12, 1941, nor shall
it be construed as limiting or modifying
the duty and responsibility of the Federal
Bureau of Investigation, with respect to the
investigation of alleged acts of sabotage or
the duty and responsibility of the Attorney
General and the Department of Justice under
the Proclamations of December 7 and 8, 1941,
prescribing regulations for the conduct and
control of alien enemies, except as such
duty and responsibility is superseded by the
designation of military areas hereunder.

Franklin D. Roosevelt
The White House,
February 19, 1942

Roosevelt closed his eyes and turned his face to the ceiling. Without changing his position, he said softly, "I know I must sign this order, but it gives me deep misgivings." Roosevelt raised his head and looked at Hopkins. "In normal, peaceful times, this order would be considered tyrannical—an abuse of presidential power. I seem to be the most reluctant participant."

Hopkins moved to the front of the desk to look directly at the president. "I think we can all appreciate your apprehension, Franklin. However, the security concerns, especially in the West Coast states, are very real and at grave levels. We have coordinated with the speaker and majority leader, and they both have agreed to follow up your executive order with legislation to codify the directive."

"Some solace."

"Congress is with you, Mister President," Harry said to reassure his friend and assuage his misgivings.

"Valiant attempt, Harry," Franklin responded and smiled. The president signed the executive order. "I know it is necessary, but I just hope I do not regret this one."

Hopkins blotted the signature and closed the folder. "I'll get this distributed forthwith."

Roosevelt nodded and turned his back to Hopkins to stare out the window at the whites and grays of winter in Washington. Harry departed and closed the door, undoubtedly informing Grace Tully to not disturb the president for a few minutes.

—

Wednesday, 25.February.1942
Oval Office
The White House
Washington, District of Columbia
United States of America
14:45 hours

When Coordinator of Information Bill Donovan entered the office, President Roosevelt looked up from the never-ending stream of paper crossing his desk. The president moved himself to his usual spot between the two long couches. "So, you have more information?"

"Yes sir. First and foremost, we have seen no signs of a Japanese invasion. To the best of our knowledge, the Japanese Combined Fleet remains in ports of the Home Islands, although Admiral Nagumo turned his carrier strike group south after supporting the siege and surrender of Singapore. They struck Darwin, Australia, last week with 150 carrier dive-bombers and fighters, killing 243 and inflicting sufficient damage to cause the government to reconsider the port as a supply depot. After the strike, the Japanese withdrew and could not be located."

"They are not done, are they?" asked Roosevelt with solemnity and sternness in his expression.

"No sir, I'm afraid not," Donovan responded and paused for the president to pursue his thought, which he did not. "You asked me to examine the events of the last couple of days on the West Coast. We have completed that assessment.

At 19:15 Pacific time Monday evening, a Japanese submarine surfaced a few miles off Goleta, California, just north of Santa Barbara and fired 27 shells from its 5.5-inch deck gun in an apparent effort to ignite oil storage and refining structures. If that was their objective, they failed. The damage done was minor and the repairs to the worst of it will be completed by the end of this week. As could be anticipated, news of the attack could not be suppressed as it spread by word of mouth in the region. The following evening, citizens were on edge and many telephoned police with aircraft sightings off or near the coastline. The situation quickly escalated with air raid warnings being issued in the Los Angeles area, and as the warnings persisted, several anti-aircraft units opened fire with explosive shells that detonated at preset altitudes, causing even more concern. Military commanders in the area eventually ordered a ceasefire and regained control. My folks visited the Los Angeles Times and other area newspapers in an effort to constrain coverage and reduce panic in the area. Some people have dubbed the incident the Battle of Los Angeles."

"We can hardly blame them for being jittery. Was anyone injured or anything damaged . . . other than the refinery at Goleta?"

"No sir, not that we are aware of here. As I said at the outset, we can find no signs the Japanese are even planning or preparing for an invasion. The shelling Monday evening was a message."

"Message received. Further, I intend to send a message directly back to their heart quite soon."

"Yes sir. We are assisting in the target intelligence analysis for the carrier strike on the Home Islands."

"Certainly, Bill, as it should be. The panic in Los Angeles is actually a more proximate concern. We have not discussed it, so I do not know if you are aware, but I signed an executive order last week that authorizes the military district commanders, especially on the west coast to relocate and confine enemy aliens or individuals of that descent, as much for reassurance of our citizens as for control of potential enemy agents."

"Yes, I am aware, Mister President. I am certain the attorney general has advised you that is very thin ice."

Roosevelt smiled in a rather mischievous manner like he occasionally did. "Yes, that he did, but these are the exigencies of war. Fortunately, for me, Congress is taking up legislation to codify the order."

"Yes sir."

"May I ask, do you have agents and sources inside Japan, on the Home Islands?"

"Mister President, you may ask whatever you wish to know," Donovan answered. "However, for the sake of us all, I would prefer not to divulge any details." Roosevelt waved his hand dismissively. "The succinct answer is yes, we do. We have sources in all the belligerent countries, as well as others. Our recruitment efforts continue in earnest."

"I would prefer not to know the details, and I trust you to make the assessment of accuracy and reliability."

"Thank you, sir. We shall endeavor to do our best to that end. I have a couple of other relevant news items, Mister President." Roosevelt nodded his consent. "The situation in the Philippines continues to deteriorate."

"Of that, I am quite aware. Henry Stimson and General Marshall briefed me this morning. We are trying to coax MacArthur off that island, but he is being quite stubborn, captain of the ship after all."

Henry Lewis Stimson was a prominent Republican politician and former secretary of state, whom President Roosevelt nominated, and the Senate confirmed in July 1940, to be secretary of war.

"The image of him being paraded through the streets of Tokyo is not comforting."

"My thoughts exactly. Our national pride is bigger than his ego."

Donovan laughed. "That may be a stretch, Mister President."

"Indeed," the president said, as he joined Donovan in laughter at the notion. "I may well have to give Douglas a direct order to avoid that possibility."

"May I ask, Mister President," Bill asked and received a nod from the president, "has the Navy briefed you on the Channel Dash debacle?"

"Yes, they have. Do you have anything else?"

"Only that the British have not given up stopping the German warships. The German operation, they called it CERBERUS, was successful beyond their expectations, although all the ships incurred some degree of damage, but they all completed the transit. Jumper Pike has localized the three large warships, and Bomber Command is in the final stages of preparing for an all-out raid Friday night, to at least put them out of action for a while."

"I wish them the best of luck."

"Mountbatten's Combined Operations command is on track to execute Operation BITING—the Bruneval Raid—Friday morning, after several days of unacceptable weather. The weather guessers apparently expect a break."

"Excellent. Winston and I discussed BITING several times. It is a modest but important step, if for no other reason than to demonstrate to Joe Stalin that we are serious about trying to relieve the pressure on his forces."

"The scope of BITING is far below his requirements and expectations."

"Yes, it is, but something is better than nothing."

"True. We will have several field operatives embedded as observers with the Commandos. I presume Mister Churchill informed you the highly classified primary objective is a radar unit the Germans have operating in that location." Donovan paused. The president nodded his head in affirmation. "The plan calls for specialists to switch the primary electronic units with prepared dummy units before they destroy them, a technique they used successfully to acquire a new Enigma coding box three years ago. If successful, they will extract the control units without the Germans suspecting and study them in detail to develop precise countermeasures."

"I did not discuss the details with Winston, but it sounds rather ingenious."

"The amphibious probe will hopefully mask the primary objective."

"Again, we wish them the best of luck."

"Yes sir. We will keep an eye on things." Donovan paused to check his wristwatch. "Now, I noticed I have already consumed more than my allotted time. I shall get out of your way."

"Thank you for the briefing, Bill. You continue to perform in an exemplary fashion, and I am most grateful."

"Thank you, Mister President."

Donovan stood. Roosevelt extended his right hand, and they shook hands. "Please ask Grace to find Harry if he is not already lurking outside."

"Yes sir, as you wish. Good day, Mister President," Donovan said and departed the Oval Office. Hopkins was indeed waiting just outside the door, next to Grace Tully's desk.

—

Friday, 27.February.1942
RAF Martlesham Heath
Woodbridge, Suffolk, England
United Kingdom
08:30 hours

The No.71 Squadron pilots had just arrived during morning twilight at their Dispersal Hut and checked in with Group as Available, when the telephone rang, and Corporal Harris shouted, "Scramble the squadron."

The pilots quickly grabbed their flight equipment and ran to their aircraft. It was extraordinarily rare these days for such an event to be launched without a mission briefing. Yet, it was not without precedent, especially for the more experienced pilots who survived the Battle of Britain during the summer of 1940.

As expected, they received the essence of their mission once they were airborne and heading south. They would cover the disengagement of No.74

Squadron that had been assigned to cover the extraction of a Commando force from the beach at Bruneval, Occupied France.

"Tiger, Eagle, inbound. We have you tally-ho."

"Eagle, Tiger, we appreciate . . . ," the leader of 74 Squadron stopped transmitting, presumably because of his situation. "Sorry, a bit crazy here. Two squadrons of bad guys."

"We've got you in sight along with the bogies."

"Cover the boats," he broadcast.

"Wilco. Break. Eagle Green, Eagle Leader, go low to cover the boats. We'll cover Tiger."

"Wilco," Brian responded. Brian descended to pass directly over the destroyer and two small ships making the best speed north. *They must be carrying the Commandos*, Brian thought. Brian had his throttle up to but not yet through the emergency gate. He quickly rechecked his weapons were armed and ready, then checked to make sure his engine was not overheating. *All is good.* "Eagle Green 2 and 3 take the E-boats closing. I'll take the fighters."

Brian's peripheral vision confirmed the divergence of his two wingmen to engage the two German torpedo boats heading directly at the small retreating flotilla. He focused on the three German Bf109 fighters also heading toward the flotilla at low level. They would reach firing range before Brian could get there. He placed his thumb on the top of his firing button, pitched the nose up slightly, and fired off a burst of cannons shells at the advancing German fighters. The first burst did not deter them. Brian repeated his long shot as he approached the British ships in front of him. *Thank God the ships saw me coming and stopped firing.* The second burst did the trick. All three German fighters pulled up and scattered. Brian pulled up with them and fired a lower-position, gun burst at the middle German as they passed. *No impacts.* Brian rolled left and pulled hard to bring the aircraft's nose around as quickly as possible, and pushed the throttle through the emergency gate. He regained sight of the three Germans who were making no attempt to reengage and appeared to be running for home. *Yep, they're leaving.* Brian turned his attention back to Frog and Dusty. His two wingmen continued to make gun passes at the now retreating E-boat. Then, he saw the white streak in the water heading toward the trailing destroyer. *Torpedo.* Brian rolled sharply to nearly inverted and pulled hard to bring the nose down quickly. He adjusted his alignment as the long dark cylinder producing the bubbling wake became visible. Brian thumbed the middle position on his firing switch. He mashed down the middle part of the switch, and all of his cannons and guns erupted. The spouts of impacts were slightly short and ahead of the speeding torpedo. He kept the combined guns firing as he adjusted the boiling, spouting impacts ahead of the torpedo. A massive geyser burst from the water. Brian rolled and pulled as hard as he could, but he was too close and penetrated the edge of the geyser, causing his engine to sputter. As quickly as he hit the massive waterspout, he was out. Brian rolled his wings level, gently pulled his nose up to give himself and his engine time, and retarded the throttle to give the Merlin the best chance to restart. As he reached for the canopy handle to prepare for ditching, the big Merlin engine re-fired and was soon humming nicely. *Damn, that was too fucking close. It would not have been pleasant to go into that cold water.*

"That was close," broadcast Dusty, as though he was reading Hunter's mind.

"Roger Eagle Green Two. Too close." Brian quickly scanned the sky to regain his situational awareness. Dusty and Frog were behind his right-wing about a half-mile and closing nicely.

"Eagle Green, Eagle Leader. That was quite a show. Glad you made it. Rejoin. The bad guys have bingo-ed. We'll remain overhead until our bingo."

"Roger Eagle Leader. Rejoining," Brian responded, but he had an interim step in mind. *The lessons of Dunkirk*! Brian began a gentle, right turn and stopped his climb to aid the join-up of his wingmen, which occurred halfway through his turn. With his wingmen in position, Brian began a gradual descent as he continued the turn to a spot through the middle of the Navy flotilla. He leveled off at 100 feet to give his wingmen sufficient maneuvering space. They knew what the leader intended and tightened up their formation position. Brian smoothly advanced his throttle to full power. As they approached the ships, they could see men in green uniforms on the decks waving and cheering as the three Spitfires roared through the center of the ship formation at just above deck level. Brian pulled up smoothly and reacquired the remainder of the squadron. Green Section smoothly took their assigned position in the squadron formation.

They orbited overhead the ships now on a beeline for the English coast. The squadron circled the flotilla for another 30 minutes until they reached the fuel level requiring them to return to base. Tug took them to higher altitude and throttled back to give them their best range power setting.

Their return to base was easy and uneventful. They landed sections in trail, taxied to their assigned parking spots, and shutdown.

Saturday, 28.February.1942
Cabinet War Rooms
New Public Offices
Whitehall, London, England
United Kingdom
16:45 hours

The complete War Cabinet and Defense Committee without the secretariat or military support staffs were assembled in the underground bunker conference room.

The newest member of the Defense Committee became Secretary of State for War just six days earlier in the wake of the Singapore debacle. Sir Percy James 'P.J.' Grigg, KCB, KCSI, PC, had been Permanent Under-Secretary of State for War, the most senior civil servant in the War Ministry since 1939. Sir James's appointment to the political position as War Minister produced substantial ripples in the political pond as the first major cabinet-level appointee who was not a member of Commons or Lords. Next to Sir James sat General Brooke.

The only guest, not a member of either the War Cabinet or Defense Committee, was Chief of Combined Operations Commodore Lord Louis Mountbatten.

"I asked for a closed meeting," began the prime minister, "to hear Lord Mountbatten's report on Operation BITING, the first Allied land operation on the Continent since Dunkirk, as it contains sensitive information of limited access as will become clear. Are there any objections?" Churchill scanned the room and saw no indications. "Hearing none, Lord Mountbatten, you have the floor."

"Thank you, Prime Minister," Mountbatten said as he stood, moved to the center of the wall facing the prime minister, and uncovered a detailed sketch of the Bruneval area along with several large-format aerial reconnaissance photographs. "After four days delay due to unacceptable weather in one area or another, we finally realized near perfect, albeit cold, weather for the operation. The plan was carefully constructed to present as a small-scale probe of the coastal defenses of German-occupied France. Beginning Thursday night, several para and Commando teams parachuted into drop zones here, here and here," Mountbatten said, pointing to the designated drop zones. "The transport aircraft encountered minimal anti-aircraft fire as they were inbound to the target area. The para-drops were fortunately and blessedly accurate with only a few minor injuries. The security teams moved swiftly to neutralize the local coast defense installations from behind, which proved to be quite effective. As a consequence, the exploitation team moved quickly and effectively to neutralize light security personnel, and secured the radar unit. As the team had planned, trained, and rehearsed, the specialist technicians removed the vital modular electronic units, and replaced them with similar boxes with wires and tubes. The specialists strove the get as close . . ."

"Please excuse the interruption," said Minister of Labor Ernest Bevin, "wouldn't the Germans be suspicious of British wire and vacuum tube construction, and markings?"

"Very good question, Minister. Yes, they would. However, the specialists were very careful to use German source material, where available to them, and to remove markings with burns and impact that would be common to explosive destruction. The plan called for specific large explosive charges being placed at or near the electronic components, so that it would appear to German investigators that we simply destroyed the unit."

". . . rather than stole their electronics," Bevin added. Many of the attendees laughed audibly.

Mountbatten smiled and calmly replied, "Correct, Minister."

"Do you believe your team was successful to that end?" asked Churchill.

"It is impossible to know for sure, until we determine the German reaction to the raid. We could not examine the bits since the destruction charges detonated during the withdrawal. The boxes were successfully delivered this morning to Watson-Watt's Radio Research Station for detailed examination. Of particular note, the various elements of the exploitation team were adroit and attentive enough to capture two of the principal operators in the proximate manor house that was their control center. The captives have been safely ensconced in specialty interrogation rooms at Trent Park with knowledgeable Air Ministry intelligence section personnel assisting MI9 with the interrogations."

"May I ask," said Lord Privy Seal Sir Stafford Cripps, "how many of the raid team know the primary purpose of the operation?"

"Very few," Mountbatten responded, "perhaps a half dozen . . . those assisting the technicians and planting the charges at the radar unit—a subset of the 'Jellicoe' assault team."

"Do you believe the primary mission is sufficiently masked?" Clement Attlee asked.

"Yes, I do. We were very careful in our planning. The primary mission was contained in a limited access supplement that appeared to be a detached leadership appendix. To most of the team, this raid was a probe, a test of the German coastal defense provisions as well as our airborne and amphibious procedures, along with the destruction of equipment and facilities in that specific area. We are still debriefing the various members of the assault teams, and the involved intelligence specialists have been discreetly instructed to query the men on what they believe the purpose of the raid was—no direct queries. We have done our best to minimize knowledge or even awareness of the primary purpose." Mountbatten paused to allow any other questions. None came. "The extraction of the assault teams in the morning proved to be a dicey, close-run affair. The naval and army forces worked well together, adapting to surprises that caused disturbances in the plan. We managed to get everyone off the beach and aboard the recovery ships in fine form. All told, we suffered two killed in action, six wounded, and six missing and presumed captured. None of the missing personnel were aware or knowledgeable of the primary mission supplement. The naval unit commander requested of me directly that I acknowledge the role of the air force in aiding the extraction and recovery of the assault teams. The Spitfires kept the German fighters occupied and at bay, and engaged two German E-boats that threatened the naval ships. In fact, the commander specifically noted the action of one Spitfire pilot who managed to destroy an E-boat torpedo launched and heading to one of the assigned destroyers—an incredible display of airmanship and gunnery."

"Bravo!" exclaimed the prime minister. "Bravo, I say. Well done to the whole team and to your Combined Operations group."

"Thank you, sir."

"I am certain you will properly recognize those noteworthy personnel."

"Yes sir, most assuredly."

"Are there any other questions for Commodore Lord Mountbatten?" asked the prime minister. Churchill scanned the room. There were probably many other questions, but none chose to voice them. "Very well, on behalf of the War Cabinet and the Defense Committee, thank you for your exemplary work, Lord Mountbatten."

"Thank you, sir."

"This concludes the BITING summary. If you would be so kind to excuse us, we have a few other items to discuss." Mountbatten knew precisely what was being asked. He stood, gathered his papers, saluted and departed the conference room, closing the door behind him. Churchill waited several seconds, and then scanned the room again, as if to check the credentials of each man remaining in the room. Satisfied, Churchill continued, "We have a few follow-up items. First, I will ask Lord Beaverbrook to meet privately and discreetly with his colleagues in the press to ensure they remain focused on the public aspects of this operation. As noted at the outset, this was our first land endeavor on the Continent since the Miracle of Dunkirk. This should be a welcome morale boost for our people. While it was modest in scale, I can and will inform Uncle Joe that we have begun taking action to help them. Beyond the public elements . . .," Churchill paused, changed his focus, and looked directly at Foreign Minister Robert Anthony Eden, MC, PC, Member of Parliament for Warwick and Leamington. "Anthony, please take the action to alert 'C' and Bletchley to watch for any German reaction, especially within ULTRA, to this raid and precisely the expected investigation involving the radar unit at Bruneval."

"Of course," Eden responded.

"The primary objective of the exploitation team," Air Minister Sir Archibald Sinclair interjected, "will be the development of countermeasures from what they learn. They will also have a number of secondary objectives regarding German technology and how that knowledge might benefit us."

"Quite so. Thank you, Archie. Further, I, for one, would like to know what we learn from the two captured operators regarding how they use their equipment. Let us all join our people in celebrating our first successful raid on the Continent." Applause and muffled cheers temporarily filled the normally subdued room.

The War Cabinet turned to other matters of supply and administration of government in wartime. It had been a good day and a welcome but a brief respite from the stream of defeats, setbacks, and bad news.

———

Chapter 6

Men, not having been able to cure death,
misery, and ignorance, have imagined
to make themselves happy
by not thinking of these things.
-- Blaise Pascal

Thursday, 5.March.1942
Air Ministry
Whitehall, London, England
United Kingdom
15:15 hours

Chief of the Air Staff Air Chief Marshal Sir Charles Portal returned to his office after his afternoon staff meeting. Air Commodore John Spencer had been waiting patiently for 15 minutes.

"Thank you for waiting, John."

"I could do no less, sir."

Sir Charles smiled and responded, "Indeed." He gestured to the circle of four plush chairs facing the center of a low round table. "Thank you for coming into Whitehall. Air Vice Marshal Leigh-Mallory is away on a specific task for the air minister, and this could not wait for his return."

Air Vice-Marshal Trafford Leigh-Mallory, CB, DSO, succeeded Air Vice-Marshal Keith Rodney Park, MC+Bar, DFC, as Air Officer Commanding-in-Chief, No.11 Group, after a protracted and raucous operational debate with his predecessor and the chief of Fighter Command. More than a few inside and outside the Air Force held Leigh-Mallory responsible for not only Park's transfer but also for the relief of Air Chief Marshal Sir Hugh Dowding—the father of Fighter Command.

"Yes sir. I am at your service."

"For clarity, and since we have not discussed such things, I must ask, are you aware of the Butt Report?"

"No sir."

"Well, it was close hold and you are in Fighter Command, after all." Sir Charles smiled, and John Spencer joined him. "Anyway, a year ago spring, the prime minister commissioned a study, encouraged by Professor Lindemann, that was conducted by David Bensusan-Butt."

Professor Lord Frederick Alexander Lindemann, FRS, first Baron Cherwell of Oxford, was a professor of physics at Oxford, and had been Churchill's science advisor and confidante since the 1920s. Bensusan-Butt had been recruited out of Cambridge by Lindemann, to serve in Churchill's newly created Statistical

Branch at the Admiralty. It was from that collaborative experience at Admiralty that led to Bensusan-Butt's selection to lead the bombing accuracy study.

Sir Charles continued, "The objective of the study was an assessment of flight crew reports of bombing accuracy. His report was released in August of last year. Let it suffice to say, the crew reported accuracy was not validated, in fact. As a consequence, the War Cabinet suspended our bombing campaign of German industrial targets for Bomber Command to reassess their procedures and to implement appropriate technology to improve the accuracy of night bombing. Three weeks ago, the War Cabinet approved, the Air Minister directed, and Bomber Command issued its area-bombing directive.

"With that background, we are reinstating CIRCUS operations. Your fighters will be escorting bomber formations into France and the Low Countries. Eleven Group can anticipate the full range of fighter operations into enemy territory."

The four principal fighter missions during this period of the war included: 1. RHUBARB – fighter or fighter-bomber sections, at times of low cloud and poor visibility, crossing the English Channel, and then dropping below cloud level to search for opportunity targets such as railway locomotives and rolling stock, aircraft on the ground, enemy troops, and vehicles on roads, 2. RODEO – fighter sweeps over enemy territory, 3. ROVER – armed reconnaissance flights with attacks on opportunity targets, and now, 4. CIRCUS – daytime bomber attacks with fighter escorts against short-range targets, to occupy enemy fighters and keep them in the area concerned.

"We are ready, sir."

"Excellent. As has been the case since the war began, Eleven Group will be the vanguard unit for the cross-Channel operations. Squadrons will be assigned from the other groups but will remain under your control. This will give you a head start on adjusting your operating procedures and informing your squadrons."

"It shall be done promptly."

"Of that, I am certain. Now, with my primary business done, have you managed to identify the pilot involved in that torpedo interdiction event during the German Channel Dash."

"Yes, we have. Flight Lieutenant Brian Drummond of Seventy-One Squadron."

"The Americans?"

"Yes sir."

"Lord Mountbatten and the destroyer's captain intend to nominate him for a Distinguished Flying Cross—his second, as I understand it."

"Correct sir."

"I will pass along the information to Combined Operations for their action . . . very quick thinking and commendable reaction that undoubtedly saved lives and one of the King's precious warships. Let's allow the award process to play out."

"Yes sir."

"It will be a genuine shame to lose American pilots like young Mister Drummond."

"Hopefully, Chief, they will just change uniforms and still be with us rather than transfer to the Pacific. Do we, or perhaps will we, have any say in the matter?"

"Well, John, I think the safe answer is not likely. However, detailed discussions have been suspended until the American Army Air Forces establish a command structure in England. It will be those commanders who will negotiate the final details. I think it safe to say that the transfer of the three American volunteer squadrons is inevitable, based on agreements reached at the ARCADIA Conference two months ago. What happens from that point is entirely an American affair."

"Thank you, sir, mum's the word."

"Thank you, John, for all you do. Great job! You should be due for promotion soon."

"What will be, will be," John Spencer responded.

"Indeed. Now, I'm afraid I'm late for my next appointment if you will excuse me."

Sir Charles led John Spencer out of his office.

———

Saturday, 7.March.1942
Headquarters, Secret Intelligence Service
No.54 Broadway
Westminster, London, England
United Kingdom
14:20 hours

The new head of Government Code and Cypher School (GC&CS, also known as Golf, Cheese and Chess Society) at Bletchley Park, was announced and entered the director-general's corner office.

Commander Edward Wilfrid Harry 'Jumbo' Travis CMG, CBE, replaced Commander Denniston as the head of Bletchley Park just last month. Travis had served in several GC&CS positions since 1925, which made for a seamless leadership transition.

"Good afternoon, 'C.'" Travis greeted his chief.

"And, to you, Jumbo. What have you?"

"I passed the routine . . . ."

"If there is ever routine messages with Boniface," Menzies interjected, referring the pseudo-code-name for the product of the Enigma deciphering process, and reported under the compartmented and classified code-name ULTRA.

Travis chuckled softly. "Quite so. We have had a string of productive days. I delivered the bulk of the decrypts to Carl and his lads," Jumbo said, referring to Carl Ambrose Acton, head of SIS Operations. "I pulled out two of our recent yield to discuss with you directly."

Menzies nodded. Travis extracted two sheets of paper from his manacled case and handed the first one to the director-general.

MOST SECRET - ULTRA

```
SECRET
DATE: 4 MARCH 1942
TO: OBW
FROM: DRG
TRANSPORT
BREAK
THIS MESSAGE CONFIRMS REQUESTED SWITCHING
INSTRUCTIONS FOR TRAIN 42025 ISSUED TO AND
ACKNOWLEDGED BY ALL JUNCTIONS TO DESTINATION
BREAK CRITICAL TO MAKE AMIENS YARD BETWEEN 0845
TO 0905 NO LATER THAN 0905 19420310 BREAK BREAK
HAIL VICTORY BREAK HAIL HITLER
END
SECRET
DECIPHERED: 5 MARCH 1942
```

MOST SECRET - ULTRA

Menzies looked at Travis. "So, if I read this correctly, German Rail is informing Command West that train," 'C' paused to glance at the message, "42025 must reach the switching yard at Amiens at a specific time on the 10th of March."

"Yes sir, that is how it reads."

"Do we know the cargo?"

"From other sources, we believe it will be carrying the ammunition and support equipment for the 61st Panzer Division. Elements of the division began moving east two weeks ago. This particular train must be considered high value to have its destination switching instructions so precisely defined. What is strange in this one is the Amiens constraint. If the train was that high value, it could just override any other conflicting traffic. Something of even higher value must be passing through Amiens right after this switching window."

"From what you've collected thus far, are there any other sources for this information?" 'C' asked.

Travis knew precisely why Menzies was asking the question. "No, not that I'm aware of on something like this. I think you have rail experts in the German Section. They might know if other sources might exist."

"Leave this one," Menzies said and held up the first message, "with me. I'm thinking of having one of our German Rail analysts sit down with the Air Intelligence Section without discussing sources to consider a hypothetical of this nature. I will also discuss this question at a broad level with the chief of the air staff to see if we can devise a reasonable plan and exploit the information without exposing our source."

"Very well, sir. The second message happened to be from the same lot as the last one out of German Rail," Travis said and handed the single sheet of paper to Menzies.

MOST SECRET - ULTRA

```
SECRET
DATE: 4 MARCH 1942
TO: CHIEF RSHA
FROM: DRG
TRANSPORT
BREAK
WANNSEE AUTHORITY FOR SWITCHING PRIORITY
ACCEPTED BREAK BREAK HAIL VICTORY BREAK HAIL
HITLER
END
SECRET
DECIPHERED: 5 MARCH 1942
```

MOST SECRET - ULTRA

Travis explained, "We picked this one up, and it is one of the few we have detected that refers to the Wannsee Conference we've discussed previously. It appears to our analysts that German Rail is confirming to Heydrich that he has apparently invoked priority for deportation and relocation trains among all the other rail traffic."

"Streamlining their Final Solution."

"So, it would appear when coupled with other information."

"The Germans, or perhaps I should not be so broad, the Nazis are quite intent upon genocide."

"We continue to collect information like this."

"The requirement for that task must remain until this outrageous conduct stops, and we can use the information to prosecute these bastards."

"Not this information," Travis said, pointing to the second message on the desk in front of 'C.'

Menzies smiled. "Well, point taken, not this message specifically. However, information like this can point the investigators and prosecutors to other files we will eventually capture. The Nazis will hang themselves."

The two intelligence leaders concluded their meeting. Travis headed back to Bletchley. Menzies picked up the telephone and talked to the secretary to the chief of the air staff for an appointment with Sir Charles later this afternoon, and then returned to the reports on his desk.

———

Monday, 9.March.1942
RAF Martlesham Heath
Woodbridge, Suffolk, England
United Kingdom
17:00 hours

The pilots of No.71 Squadron were seated, facing the blackboard between the squadron leader's office and the operations clerk's high desk. Corporal Harris was distinctively absent—a rare occurrence, probably intended. An RAF wing commander who was not introduced joined Tug Meares in front of the blackboard.

"OK lads, we are going to brief for a special mission that requires precise timing and is sufficiently sensitive to demand no discussion of this mission outside this briefing. We are restricted to base tonight, and once again, I urge you to not over-indulge your attraction to the beer and spirits offered at Mess. You will consider this briefing to be most secret. Is this requirement clearly understood?"

"Yes sir," came the chorus of pilots.

The wing commander provided precise information regarding a German high-value train that was expected to pass through Amiens, France. The Air Ministry wanted No.71 Squadron to attack the train at a bridge crossing the River Somme, 11 kilometers east of Amiens, and not quite to the village of Corbie. The primary target was the contents of that train. However, the secondary objective was the destruction of the Somme rail bridge using the explosive expected to be on that particular train.

How the hell do these guys get such precise information, Brian asked himself?

Several control points were established for timing. The first, designated Point One, was due south of Gravesend on the Channel coast near Eastbourne. Biggin Hill Control would clear the mission to proceed, and they would descend to 500 feet (cherubs five) for their crossing of the Channel. The second control point, designated Point Two, was 20 miles prior to penetrating the French coastline and would be their final abort point should something not line up for the planned mission. The wing commander's instructions emphatically stated they were not to cross Point Two without clearance, and beyond Point Two, there would be no further communications with Biggin Hill Control until they were returning inbound to the English coast.

They must have people watching that train and the switching yard at Amiens.

Tug continued the procedural portion of the briefing. Once cleared for the approach beyond Point Two, 'A' Flight would remain at 500 feet, and 'B' Flight would descend to wave-top, follow by treetop altitude over land, roughly a quarter-mile behind 'A' Flight. From Point Two, the split squadron would turn to a heading of 140° to the coastline, ideally halfway between Dieppe and Le Tréport. As they crossed the coast, they would turn to 115° for their next waypoint—a distinctive road junction at Piox-de-Picardie, and then turning to 090° for the base leg to Moreuil. From that point, the squadron would turn to 015° for the run into the target. Using the maximum range airspeed would give them a time-to-target of 46 minutes and give them plenty of speed margin to meet their waypoint crossing times. The route gave them roughly 45 minutes on target and allow for a maximum speed extraction.

Based on the experience since the end of The Blitz, the remaining German fighters in France were rarely allowed to challenge British fighters, but no detectible criterion for fighter-on-fighter engagement decisions could be determined. They had to expect to be challenged. The route minimized exposure to anti-aircraft fire; the worst exposure would be around Amiens. The mission planned called for 'A' Flight to serve as navigator and air cover for the low-level attack 'B' Flight. To keep all of the squadron fighters at roughly the same ammunition levels, the two flights would switch positions after 15 minutes on target, and bingo at 30 minutes. They needed to preserve some ammunition just in case they had to fight their way out of France.

The pilots discussed the operational aspects of the mission plan. The situation could easily turn bad at any point should German fighters show up, or they faced some unforeseen obstacles. As always, they would do the best they could to perform the RODEO mission as briefed, until that was no longer possible.

The wing commander stepped back. Tug Meares told them, "We will reconvene at 06:00 tomorrow morning . . . ."

"It's dark then," Salt interrupted.

Meares glanced over his shoulder to the senior officer, and then he smiled. "Yes, it is, Salt. Thank you for the observation. Is there a problem?"

"No sir. It is just we are daylight fighters, and rarely take off or land in the dark."

"This mission requires it," Tug said and stared at Salt as if to gesture whether there was anything else. "As I was saying, we will assemble here at 06:00 tomorrow morning. I will check with Group to ensure the mission is still on for execution. If so, we will launch . . . in the dark, Salt," laughter interrupted Tug, "and reposition to Gravesend. We will check with Group, again, to ensure the intelligence has not changed. Our mission timeline has us launching on the RODEO mission at 08:30. The mission plan calls for us to land at Gravesend to refuel and rearm unless we need to land short. From that point, several follow-on missions might bloom depending upon what occurs.

"Lastly, as I said at the outset, we are henceforth confined to base until this mission is complete. I am not to the threshold of closing the Mess bar to you, but I strongly urge each of you to restrain your usual enthusiastic consumption of distilled spirits until this mission is done. Any deviants will not be looked upon kindly. This is clearly a very important mission that has been entrusted to this squadron by the air ministry. We must stand worthy of that trust. Do I make myself clear?"

"Yes sir," came the unanimous chorus.

"Very well then, let's board the lorry outside. It is nearly time for the evening meal. Be good tonight, lads."

The pilots had long ago hung up their flight gear. The rumble of conflicting chatter filled the room as they filed out of the Dispersal Hut and climbed up into the covered bed of the truck. Meares and the wing commander did not join them and remained behind, presumably to acquire the wing commander's assessment of the mission briefing.

———

Tuesday, 10.March.1942
RAF Martlesham Heath
Woodbridge, Suffolk, England
United Kingdom
06:00 hours

They gathered before morning twilight. Tug Meares confirmed with No.11 Group that their mission, now designated RODEO 42-65, was still a go. They took off as the first slivers of morning twilight barely backlit the eastern horizon. It was rare for them to take flight in the dark, but it was not without precedent. The 20-minute repositioning flight was accomplished at maximum range power despite the broken clouds and pre-dawn hour. The Gravesend base operations crew had deployed a couple of dozen lights to define the landing area, although sufficient twilight made them unnecessary. They landed uneventfully, taxied to their designated parking spots at the far end of the flight line, and shut down.

To their surprise, the same unidentified wing commander who briefed them yesterday evening was waiting in the Dispersal Tent assigned for their use. The wing commander conferred with Tug Meares in private and seemed to be present as an observer, or perhaps to assist Tug if there were any last-minute adjustments.

The temporary crews topped off their fuel tanks and checked their aircraft thoroughly. The aircraft and pilots were ready. Nothing was added to the mission briefing. Even the weather en route and over the target area remained as forecast and better than the mission minimum threshold. They waited without words or other distractions.

—

Tuesday, 10.March.1942
RAF Gravesend
Gravesend, Kent, England
United Kingdom
08:30 hours

As the planned launch time neared, the pilots instinctively readied their flight kit for combat. Group called and gave the launch command. They took off just after dawn, and the whole squadron had their wheels in the wells on time.

"Sapper, Eagle Leader, with you climbing."

"Roger, Eagle Leader, climb to angels three, heading one eight zero. Cleared to Point One."

"Roger, Sapper, climbing to angels three, heading one eight zero, and cleared to Point One."

When they reached 3,000 feet, Tug leveled off and throttled back his engine to the maximum range power setting, and the others matched his flight condition. Brian checked his engine instruments—everything normal. He also ensured his armament switches were set for combat.

Five minutes prior to reaching Point One, which they could clearly see through the low scatter clouds, Biggin Hill Control radioed, "Eagle Leader, Sapper calling."

"Go ahead, Sapper."

"Roger, Eagle Leader, you are cleared to Point Two."

"Roger, Sapper, Eagle cleared to Point Two," Tug responded.

As they passed overhead the coastline a few miles to the east of Eastbourne, Meares initiated a gradual descend, maintaining their airspeed, and eventually leveled off at 500 feet. The Channel was surprisingly calm—swells but no whitecaps. Brian checked on his wingmen and received a thumb's up from each of them. He rechecked his instrument panel and switches—ready.

Ten minutes after crossing the English coastline, the radio crackled. "Eagle Leader, Sapper calling."

"Sapper, Eagle Leader, go ahead."

"Eagle Leader, Sapper, all is right with the world. You are cleared beyond Point Two. Good hunting."

"Roger, Sapper, cleared beyond Point Two."

So, this rodeo is going to happen, Brian thought and rechecked his armament switches were set for combat. *Here we go.* Brian held Green Section in their assigned position. He watched 'B' Flight descend to their planned altitude just above the water and slowly fell behind 'A' Flight. They could see the French coastal villages of Dieppe and Le Tréport. Tug adjusted their heading slightly to the left so that they would cross the coast between the two villages. They encountered no anti-aircraft fire and no German fighters could be seen, yet.

—

Tuesday, 10.March.1942
Headquarters, Special Operations Executive
No.64 Baker Street
Marylebone, London, England
United Kingdom
08:45 hours

A man dressed in a Norwegian army captain's uniform burst through the open office door of Director of Operations and Training Brigadier General Colin McVean Gubbins, DSO, MC. "Excuse me ever so much, General, this just arrived a few minutes ago in the clear." He handed the single sheet of plain paper to Gubbins.

MOST SECRET - CHEESE

10 MARCH 1942
SOE NOR IC1
CHEESE

HAVE STOLEN BOAT AND MAKING FOR SCOTLAND PLEASE
GIVE AIR PROTECTION CHEESE
END

MOST SECRET - CHEESE

"Why did he expose himself and steal a boat?" Gubbins asked.

"He did not brief us, so his actions were undoubtedly spur-of-the-moment and a reaction to circumstances. Our guess, by virtue of his recent work, is he is extracting himself and the engineer most familiar with the Norsk Hydro heavy water facility—a man by the name of Einar Skinnarland. He is probably being chased and anticipates the *Luftwaffe* will join in the effort to stop him," reported Captain Jorgensen.

Kaptein Liam Hansen Jorgensen succeeded the famous and original commander of NOR.I.C.1 *Kaptein* Martin Jensen Linge when the latter had been killed in action during Operation ARCHERY in Måløy on the Norwegian island of Vågsøy the previous December.

Agent Cheese was a former Norwegian army soldier who made his way to Great Britain after the fall of Norway to the Germans in July 1940. His name was Odd Kjell Starheim. He was also one of the founding members of the SOE's Norwegian Independent Company 1 (NOR.I.C.1)—the source of special operations teams trained to operate in occupied Norway. Starheim had been in and out of his homeland as an SOE agent several times already in the war. He had been working the means to penetrate Norsk Hydro Vemork hydroelectric plant just outside of Rjukan, Norway, to cripple or destroy the heavy water production capacity at the plant. Heavy water was an essential moderating fluid used in nuclear fission research. The Germans held control of the plant and, by consequence, sole use of the plant's unique product; thus, the Allied interest in the Norsk Hydro facility.

"How sure are you in this assessment?"

"We have no way to be sure, sir. However, based on our experience with Cheese, we believe his request is genuine and of the utmost urgency."

"I will call the air ministry directly. What location should we tell them? The North Sea is a big place."

"We anticipated the question. Based on what we know, we estimated his location an hour from now is most likely a 100 square mile area centered on 58° 17' 07" North – 1° 39' 05" East. He most likely departed out of Stavanger and is making for Aberdeen, Scotland."

Gubbins stared at Captain Jorgensen for several seconds. "That is not particularly informative. We do not get many passes at such shallow evidence. However, I recognize the importance, so in this instance, it is worth the risk."

Gubbins lifted his telephone handset off its cradle. "Chief of the air staff or the air minister, please." Brigadier Gubbins waited as the operators made the appropriate connections. "Yes sir. Good morning, sir. I'm afraid I have a bit of an urgent request." Gubbins relayed the essential information to Air Chief Marshal Portal and did not have to recount the importance of heavy water to nuclear research. The chief of the air staff asked several cogent questions to ensure he understood the request. "Yes sir. Thank you, sir. And, just to emphasize the need, speed is vital to protect this important asset. Yes sir. Thank you again, sir. Good day."

Gubbins looked back at Jorgensen. "OK. He is going to scramble the closest Spitfire squadron he has to Aberdeen."

"Thank you, sir. I just hope we are not too late."

"Likewise, Captain Jorgensen. If you can get word to Cheese, tell him help is on the way."

Jorgensen thanked Brigadier Gubbins for his support, saluted, and departed the office.

———

Tuesday, 10.March.1942
RAF Drem
Drem, Lothian, Scotland
United Kingdom
09:05 hours

No.609 Squadron had been temporarily assigned to the comparatively peaceful aerodrome east of Edinburgh and halfway into No.13 Group. They had been there for just over two weeks for their rest and restoration. The location had not escaped the awareness of Flight Lieutenant Kensington. He was one of the last pilots with No.609 Squadron, who had been stationed at RAF Drem two years earlier. He remembered those days with his close friend Flight Lieutenant Brian Drummond.

The telephone rang, and the operations clerk shouted, "Scramble the squadron."

The command caught most of the pilots by surprise and with some degree of incredulity. It had never happened since they had arrived at the distant airfield. Jonathan was one of the first pilots to reach the cockpit of his Spitfire. As was their practice in such situations, they would have to forego their pre-takeoff engine checks. Jonathan was ready to go first, as far as he could tell. Both of his wingmen signaled a thumb's up 20 seconds later.

Squadron Leader Jason Billings 'Stack' Long-Roberts led the twelve fighters of the full squadron into the air. "Harbor, Sorbo Leader, with you climbing through cherubs three, heading zero nine zero."

"Roger Sorbo Leader, Harbor, turn to zero five zero." Stack immediately adjusted the squadron's heading. "Climb to best altitude for surface search. Maintain maximum speed possible. Your objective is believed to be a modestly sized fishing trawler at 170 nautical miles and believed to be heading at best speed for Aberdeen."

"Roger, Harbor, we have the objective. What do we do when we find this objective?"

"Sorbo Leader, Harbor, provide air cover protection for the objective."

"Harbor, Sorbo Leader, wilco." Stack leveled the squadron at 1,000 feet altitude and kept his throttle at maximum power, which in turn gave the rest of the squadron emergency power to maintain station. Stack knew it would spread the squadron out a little, but those were the instructions from Turnhouse Control.

We're supposed to find a single fishing boat in the middle of the North Sea, Jonathan thought. *We used to launch out of Drem into the airspace above the North Sea, but we were always looking for Gerry aircraft. This is not going to be easy. There must be something very important on that fishing boat.* The clouds below them had gone from scattered to broken out over the North Sea. Stack increased their altitude to 2,000 feet.

After 45 minutes, Stack broadcast, "Sorbo, Sorbo Leader, we are approaching the rendezvous point. Throttle back to max endurance. Sorbo Green, take your section below the clouds. We need to initiate an expanding spiral search pattern until we find the objective."

Harness throttled back. "Roger, Sorbo Leader, Sorbo Green descending." Jonathan initiated a gradual descent.

"Mark, mark," Stack broadcast and started a shallow left turn.

Jonathan matched Stack's turn as they continued their descent. The clouds were broken and did not appear very thick. Jonathan chose not to seek the openings in the cloud cover but rather descended through the clouds. They broke out at 700 feet above the water.

"Sorbo Green, Sorbo Leader, you take the lead for the objective search. Sorbo will follow, keep track of you, and watch the sky."

"Roger Sorbo Leader," Harness responded. He used a hand signal to spread his wingmen.

Green Section droned on, expanding the spiral, as they looked for the fishing boat. They had seen nothing but the modest white caps of moderate seas below them. Jonathan tried to keep track of their position around the spot on his thigh map and the sun line when they got one. The maritime haze below the clouds made distant visibility more difficult, but they kept their search going.

Eighteen minutes after they began their search, Stack broadcast, "Tally ho. Bandits, three o'clock, level, ten miles. Break, Sorbo Green, heading zero eight five, about ten miles. Maximum speed. Bandits are pretty intent on that spot."

"Roger, Sorbo Leader, on the way, full power," Harness responded.

Jonathan advanced his throttle to full power, and the big Merlin engine responded in fine form. Harness checked his wingmen as they all increased speed below the clouds. Both of them were in a good position for engagement. *This haze is not helping.* A flaming grey fighter in a flat spin fell through the clouds and impacted the water. The chatter of an active aerial engagement came to them from above the clouds. Then, Jonathan saw two grey Bf109 fighters with red propeller domes that were turning from opposite directions behind the fishing boat that had clearly been hit. They were making another run on the trawler.

"Vicky, take the right bandit. I've got the left one," radioed Harness. No answer came, but Jonathan noticed his right wingman Pilot Officer Victor Hanson 'Vicky' Clegg veer to the right slightly. He pushed his throttle to the emergency stop and roared just feet above the trawler's yardarm. Jonathan thumbed the center position on his spade, firing switch. The German was approaching his line up line still in a hard-right bank. As the enemy fighter sharply rolled his wings level, Harness depressed the center position, and all of his cannons and guns erupted, jolting the Spitfire. The German exploded in a brilliant fireball. Jonathan rolled hard left to avoid the shrapnel, but felt the pings of small impacts on the bottom of his fighter. He had no time to worry about damage, as he pulled hard to bring the nose back around and stay below the clouds. Jonathan looked out the top of his canopy to see an almost mirror image. Vicky had caught the other German fighter still in his re-engagement turn. Jonathan adjusted his turn to pass just ahead of the trawler. He saw men waving and cheering, although he could not hear them over the roar of the Merlin.

"Sorbo Leader, Sorbo Green, splashed two bandits. The objective is damaged but still moving well."

"Roger, Sorbo Green. We splashed three. Some damage. Bandits disengaged."

Jonathan throttled back to maximum endurance power and signaled for the join up. Both wingmen complied. They took up a wide orbit below the clouds around the fishing trawler that was still on a beeline for Aberdeen. Jonathan checked his fuel and signaled the same for his wingmen. They were close and had perhaps another 30 minutes on station. He hand-signaled for them to take equal positions around the boat. Jonathan decided to make a low-speed pass from stern to bow, close off the starboard side of the boat to check on the people. A man in a blue knit cap, blue sweater, and an open heavy coat gave a series of hand signals—one wounded in the arm, another wounded in the leg, and finished with a thumb's up.

As Jonathan returned to his orbit position, he radioed the report. "Sorbo Leader, Sorbo Green, we are at maximum endurance in orbit around the objective with 25 minutes to bingo. The boat has two wounded but gave us a thumb's up."

"Roger, Sorbo Green."

Fifteen minutes later, they heard, "Sorbo Leader, Hornet Leader calling."

"Hornet Leader, Sorbo Leader, go ahead."

"Roger, Sorbo, we have you in sight, inbound to relieve you."

"Roger, Hornet."

Hornet was the callsign of No.54 Squadron—another Spitfire unit. They completed the transfer. Jonathan saw a section of 'KL' Spitfires appear below the clouds. They took similar positions. Jonathan held his shallow turn to enable a quick and easy join up, and then found a hole in the clouds. They quickly located the remainder of the squadron well above the clouds. They were all still flying, so the previously reported damage was not that serious. Once Green Section was in position, Stack turned the squadron for RAF Drem and held a maximum range power setting. Mission accomplished.

This will be an interesting debriefing. I wonder if we will find out who those men are?

———

Tuesday, 10.March.1942
Corbie, Somme, Hauts-de-France
Occupied France
09:25 hours

No.71 Squadron made their RODEO 42-65 ingress waypoints on time and without opposition. *So far, so good.* At Moreuil, they turned north. 'B' Flight went to full throttle and passed underneath 'A' Flight for the run-in to the target. As they neared the target, 'B' Flight was a half-mile ahead of 'A' Flight. The smoke and steam plume from the locomotive working to increase its speed made localization easy. Behind the locomotive and coal supply car was the first of three, quad 20 mm *Flakvierling* 38 anti-aircraft gun units secured to armored flatbed railcars. Ten flatbed cars followed with a Panzer III medium tank secured to each railcar. Roughly a dozen freight or passenger cars were between the middle and rear anti-aircraft gun railcars. The locomotive was nearly across the bridge over the River Somme.

'B' Flight spread for action. Whitey went after the locomotive to at least stop the train. Pete, Salt, and Sweet took the forward, middle and rear anti-aircraft, armored cars. Red tracer shells from those 20mm anti-aircraft guns initially rose toward 'A' Flight, until the gun crews realized their attackers were coming in just above the treetops.

Whitey was successful on his first pass. The massive, almost explosive, billowing steam erupted from the locomotive's boiler. The train's momentum carried the destroyed locomotive beyond the bridge over the River Somme. Between scans of the sky around them, as they orbited the train, Brian saw Whitey roll right into his re-engagement turn.

Buddy and Pete made quick work of their task. They disabled the forward and rear, anti-aircraft gun, flatbed railcars with multiple hits. A distinctive flash and blossom erupted, as the staged ammunition exploded on both anti-aircraft cars.

The German gun crew on the center unit fared better, training their quad gun emplacement and opening fire close enough to force Salt off his target before the Spitfire could open fire. The characteristic blue tracer elements from the German cannons followed Salt as he pulled hard through his sharp left turn. The German effort left that gun crew open. Sweet had effectively shifted from the forward anti-aircraft gun railcar to the middle unit and placed his cannon rounds all over the quad gun emplacement. The guns stopped firing, but there was no explosion of staged ammunition. The six Spitfires of 'B' Flight hit all three anti-aircraft gun railcars again to make sure they were out of action.

Brian continuously scanned the sky around their objective and wondered, *where are the German fighters?* The sky remained clear. German, large caliber, anti-aircraft guns positioned at Amiens 10 kilometers to the west fired several exploding shells in a somewhat desperate attempt to aid the beleaguered train but were ineffective and no factor as the Eagle Squadron pressed their attack.

'B' Flight made their third unopposed pass on the hapless train, and then pulled off into climbing turns to replace 'A' Flight. Tug led 'A' Flight as he rolled into a shallow dive and lined up on the length of the train from front to back. Brian was the fourth aircraft of 'A' Flight to roll into the attack on the train. He moved his thumb to the top of the firing switch and lined up on the first car aft of the middle gun car. The impacts from Jimmy and Hick were bright flashes on the freight and passenger cars. Brian fired but only expended a few rounds when the first freight car exploded in a massive expanding fireball with burning debris and shrapnel. Hunter pulled up as hard as he could and rolled hard left. Multiple impacts loudly struck the bottom of his aircraft and shuddered the fighter. He had avoided the delayed explosion of what had to be a freight car carrying ammunition. His Merlin began to sputter and cough in protest to engine damage.

Brian retarded his throttle to see if he could help the engine and used his momentum to gain altitude in case he had to bail out. "Eagle Leader, Eagle Green, I've been hit by shrapnel."

Brian passed through the 'B' Flight orbit. He still had oil pressure—no fluctuations, yet. Coolant temperature—normal. The engine was audibly running rough. The vibration and sound suggested one of the twelve cylinders was not firing. Brian looked to his wings—no holes on the topside. Both Dusty and Frog were now in close formation.

"Dusty, Frog, what damage do you see on my belly?"

"You've got skin damage, but no signs of leaking fuel or fluids," responded Dusty.

"Engine is running rough but still running. One cylinder seems to be dead."

"Eagle Green, Eagle Leader, bingo with your section. We'll finish off this train and catch up."

"Roger Eagle Leader, wilco."

Hunter rolled wings level at 3,000 feet on their initial egress heading of 312° to avoid population centers and known heavy defense positions. Frog and Dusty moved back into combat spread positions for better protection of their leader. The Merlin engine seemed to be stable but still running rough. *Damn, I've got a long way to coax this engine home.* Brian left his throttle at moderate power to give the damaged engine as much margin as he could and hold a reasonable airspeed to at least clear occupied France. Some advancing clouds gave some comfort. Several flak shells exploded not far from them, but not close enough for effect. Temperatures and pressures remained blessedly steady and normal. He was consuming fuel but not losing fuel. *If we can just avoid a fight, I might make it.*

Eagle Green Section crossed the coastline, visible through the broken clouds below them, when they heard Tug call bingo. The rest of the squadron had finished with the German train. Green Section was approximately mid-Channel when the nine other fighters of No.71 Squadron joined up with Hunter leading and still limping back to England.

"Eagle Green, Eagle Leader, can you make it back to Gravesend?"

"Eagle Leader, I just started getting metallic sounds, and oil pressure is dropping. I'm going to be lucky to make the coastline. I need to prepare for an emergency landing at Hawkinge."

"Roger, Eagle Green. Break, Sapper, Eagle Leader."

"Eagle Leader, Sapper, we heard. You are cleared to Hawkinge. Contact tower when ready."

"Roger, Sapper, wilco."

"Eagle Leader, Eagle Green, I'm going to remain at this altitude until overhead Hawkinge in case the motor quits."

The engine was sounding much worse by the time Brian reached the high perch overhead RAF Hawkinge. He was cleared for emergency descent and landing. Tug had decided to keep the squadron airborne and orbiting the aerodrome to observe and cover Hunter. Brian opened his canopy, closed his throttle to the idle position, and began a right spiral, gliding descent. Through a quarter of his turn, the engine gave out a terrible, grinding groan and stopped. He did not have time to get the undercarriage down without hydraulics. *Belly landing.* Brian closed the throttle and shut off his mixture lever to minimize any chance of fire. The remainder of the descent went smoothly without further trouble. As gently as he could, Brian slowed the Spitfire to just above flaps up stall speed and softly floated the fighter onto the grass. The aircraft slid to a rapid stop, slamming Brian into his harness straps. Fire trucks immediately surrounded him. Brian quickly unstrapped, disconnected, and then jumped out of the cockpit and off the wing. *I made it.* Clear of the aircraft, Brian turned and looked at his faithful and now floundered fighter. *Now, the maintenance folks will have to figure out what can be repaired or salvaged.*

———

Saturday, 21.March.1942
Shepherds Tavern
No.50 Hertford Street
Mayfair, London, England
United Kingdom
22:20 hours

The No.71 Squadron pilots took full advantage of the squadron's stand down from operations as much to celebrate Hunter's return from his ordeal in France.

They had enjoyed a hamburger with all the fixin's, crisp French fries, and a Coca-Cola at the Eagle Club, which was becoming progressively more crowded as more Americans arrived in London. They also decided *en masse* to forego the scheduled movie for the evening in favor of joining their brethren at their preferred Pub in London.

The raucous interior was surprisingly not as full as Brian had seen Shepherds on previous occasions, most notably on a weather day interrupting the Battle of Britain. The American volunteer fighter pilots blended into the sea of RAF blue broken by splashes of color from the ladies who joined them for an evening of libation, laughter, and rambunctiousness.

With a pint of beer in hand, Brian looked around the main bar room and immediately picked out his long-time comrade and best friend Jonathan 'Harness' Kensington with his back toward the door. Brian weaved his way through other pilots passing greetings and gibes to those he knew along the way. When he finally reached Jonathan's right shoulder. Jonathan glanced over his shoulder, did a double-take, and spun around to heartily embrace Brian as a long-lost brother. Jonathan introduced Brian to the handful of pilots he had been talking with when interrupted. Brian knew none of the pilots, and two of them were replacement pilots with Brian's old squadron—No.609 Squadron.

"Have you eaten?" Jonathan asked.

"Yes, but I'll go with you, so we can talk."

Jonathan nodded his head and excused himself. Brian followed the only brother he had ever had into the dining section of the Pub. Harness knew what he wanted and ordered a simple ham sandwich with Brussels sprouts. There were only three open tables—two with four chairs and one with six. Jonathan chose one of the four-place tables near the back window. Jonathan sat, and Brian took a chair across from him.

"First and foremost, how are Charlotte and Ian?" Jonathan asked.

"Doing well, thank you. That boy is growing like a bad weed on Momma's milk. How's Linda?"

"Well, between my flying and your countrymen descending upon our beloved emerald isle, I hardly see her. She really enjoys her Home Office job. Her current assignment is with something they call the location commission, working on finding and contracting for facilities for an enormous number of American soldiers and airmen."

"Lots of Americans have started showing up."

"I've not seen you since Pearl Harbor. Have they decided what to do with the eagle squadrons?"

"After the President declared war on Japan, Germany, and Italy, we petitioned Fighter Command for transfer to the Army Air Forces. Even Tug Meares worked his way up the chain of command to Douglas himself on our behalf. The Thursday after Pearl Harbor, a bunch of us met with Ambassador Winant at the Embassy. Everyone told us to be patient. It was going to happen, but until there is a command structure in place, we . . . ."

"Hey, there you two ingrates are," Mud Morrison interrupted Brian's explanation. He had an attractive, young woman with short, curly, brown hair in an odd pseudo-RAF blue uniform on his arm. "They told me you two were back here. Please allow me to introduce Third Officer Marilyn Powell." Brian noticed the odd pilot wings with 'ATA' on the shield and no crown, over the left breast pocket of her uniform tunic. "Marilyn, these two degenerates are Flight Lieutenant Jonathan 'Harness' Kensington and the infamous Flight Lieutenant Brian 'Hunter' Drummond."

"Nice to meet you, boys," Marilyn said in a pronounced Southern drawl. "Your reputation precedes you," she added looking directly into Brian's eyes.

"American? What kind of uniform is that?" Jonathan asked, looking Powell up and down.

"Air Transport Auxiliary. We arrived from the States three weeks ago and just completed our indoctrination training and got our wings," she answered and tapped her wings.

"Would you care to join us?" asked Jonathan.

"If we are not intruding," Mud said.

Jonathan and Brian both gestured to the table. Jonathan moved next to Brian so Mud and Miss Powell could sit next to each other. After all, they appeared to be more than recent acquaintances. They all sat.

"The only ATA pilots I've seen have been in flight suits and British," Brian added. "I've never seen the uniform before."

"We do occasionally clean up," Marilyn giggled.

"And, clean up nicely indeed, I must say," Jonathan said and smiled.

"Thank you."

"What brings you to this fight?" Jonathan continued his questioning.

"Easy now, lads. She's one of us now," Mud cautioned.

"To answer your question, General Arnold sent us over here to learn how the ATA works so that we can form a similar American unit."

"How many is us?" Brian asked.

"Twenty-five."

"And," Mud said, "before you ask the inevitable question, I met the lovely Marilyn two weeks ago. We developed an immediate affinity for one another."

"Oh, wow!" Brian exclaimed. "I just noticed the additional stripe, Mud." Morrison held up his right uniform sleeve with three medium stripes of a wing commander. "Congratulations, Mud."

"Thanks, mate. The air ministry thought it fit to promote me and take me out of the cockpit."

"Really?"

"Yes, indeed, they did. Made me the commanding officer of RAF Hamble, a small aerodrome south of Eastleigh on The Solent. That's how I met Marilyn. The ATA ladies use Hamble for their operations."

Mud stood. Harness and Hunter glanced over their shoulders to see what Mud saw. Another attractive but older woman in the same uniform with two broad sleeve stripes approached the table. "May I introduce First Officer 'Jackie' Cochran."

Cochran pulled up an empty chair with the back toward the table and sat at the end of the table between Marilyn and Brian. With the anticipated questions, Jackie explained that she was the senior pilot of the American contingent of accomplished American female pilots to prove themselves in a similar environment as Cochran had proposed to the Roosevelts and General Arnold.

Jacqueline 'Jackie' Cochran had been born Bessie Lee Pittman and, by the time of Pearl Harbor, was already a renowned aviator, certainly comparable to the missing aviator Amelia Earhart. As Europe went to war, Cochran proposed to First Lady Eleanor Roosevelt a women's auxiliary pilot corps to relieve men from routine ferry tasks, so that the men could be assigned to combat units. The First Lady pitched Cochran's proposal to her husband, who, in turn, introduced Jackie to Chief of the Army Air Forces General 'Hap' Arnold.

They laughed and drank as the quintet regaled each other with their accomplishments, although it was Marilyn who sung Jackie's praises, and Mud and Harness that touted Hunter's achievements.

After the third round, Jackie said, "Marilyn and I really must go. We have duty tomorrow, and we need to get back to Hamble tonight. If you will excuse us, gentlemen."

The men stood, and the ladies departed, but not until Marilyn kissed Jeremy Morrison passionately. They watched Jackie and Marilyn disappear out the front door. No sooner had that happened, another stunningly attractive woman stepped into their view and sauntered slowly toward them. Jeremy seemed to fidget as he stood waiting.

"Lord Morrison," she said, holding Jeremy's eyes.

"Lady Castlerosse," said Mud in reply.

The woman did not wait for an extension of the introductions. She slowly and demurely turned her eyes and head to Brian. "You must be the famous Brian Drummond."

"No ma'am," Brian responded. "I am just an RAF pilot who loves to fly."

"Please, Brian. My name is Doris." She extended her right hand to Brian. "May we sit," Doris said, looking at all three men.

"I'm afraid we must go," Mud said, backhanding Harness on the right shoulder.

"I'm Jonathan Kensington," Harness said. He shook hands with Doris and moved with Mud, leaving Brian alone with Doris.

Once things settle, Doris gestured for Brian to sit, and then sat next to Brian at the table. He did so. Doris took a sip of wine and looked to Brian. "Do you know who I am?"

"No ma'am."

"Brian, please, I am not an old woman matron. Please call me Doris." Brian nodded his head. "I first heard your name not quite two years ago. I have heard nothing but great things about you since that time. I am embarrassed to admit that I fled London and England in 1940, as the bombing started."

"Where?"

"New York."

"How did you get back?"

"Well, that is a rather direct query, is it not?"

"My apologies, ma . . . Doris."

She giggled and waved her hand dismissively. "I asked the prime minister for a favor."

"You know the prime minister?"

Doris smiled in a very mysterious manner. "Yes. I think it safe to say I do know Winston. Do you?"

"Yes, I do." Brian recounted his meetings with Prime Minister Churchill, both before and after his premiership.

"Well, then, we have more in common than I thought."

What on Earth is this all about? "How can I help you . . . Doris?"

The woman exuded seduction. She smiled and placed her hand on Brian's mid-thigh. When Brian did not react, Doris slid her hand up his thigh. Brian pushed his chair back slightly. Her smile turned into a broad, toothy grin that reminded Brian of the Cheshire Cat of fame. Her hand moved with him.

"Well, there is no denying your response, young Brian."

"I'm sorry, Doris. I'm married and not . . . not interested. We have a young son between us."

"Brian," she said, squeezing his reaction gently but firmly, "no need to be so provincial. Your body speaks for you."

Brian wanted to push back farther and stand, but his potential embarrassment kept him from moving. He needed to hide the now aching bulge. "What do you want with me?" he said more sternly and as a rhetorical question.

"I just want to get to know you better."

"Why me? I'm married," Brian repeated.

Doris smiled again. "I know, you declared that already. I have no interest in interfering in your marriage, Brian."

Hunter finally smiled. "Doris . . . truly . . . I am flattered that you are interested in me, but I'm afraid I cannot play." Brian thought for a moment. "You clearly know Jeremy, and he is single . . . well, although he seems to have a girlfriend at the moment."

"Wives and girlfriends have never stopped me," she said with a far more sinister grin. "Lord Morrison and I have a history, and those days are behind us." She stood. When Brian started to rise with her, Doris placed her hand on his left shoulder and held him down. "I think you should let that magnificent erection dissipate first." Doris leaned over and kissed Brian on the cheek. "Your bollocks are safe with me, Brian. I do believe you know how I feel. I will see you, again. I trust you will change your mind by our next meeting."

Brian opened his mouth to respond, but he only saw her rapidly retreating posterior. He sat dumbfounded for several minutes. *What on God's little green earth could she possibly want with me? I simply must find out more about her and what she is up to with this flirtation.* The image of Charlotte and Ian flashed into his consciousness in vivid color and vibrancy. *And, I must tell Charlotte about what just happened.*

—

Chapter 7

Success is the child of audacity.

-- Benjamin Disraeli

Saturday, 21.March.1942
Oval Office
The White House
Washington, District of Columbia
United States of America
17:15 hours

Secretary Stimson and General Marshall entered the Oval Office for their appointment with the president, after waiting 15 minutes for the commander-in-chief to finish other business.

"Thank you for waiting, gentlemen," President Roosevelt said as he wheeled himself to the couches and gestured for the two Army leaders to sit. Stimson sat on the president's right, while Marshall chose to sit opposite to the secretary of war. "And, thank you for joining me on this Saturday evening."

"As you know, Mister President, MacArthur safely landed in a B-17 Flying Fortress at Batchelor Field, south of Darwin, Australia, on the 17th, along with his family and senior staff."

"More than he was authorized to bring, I am compelled to add," interjected Marshall.

"Douglas has always seen himself as above the rules . . . quite an inflated ego and full of himself," Roosevelt commented matter-of-factly.

"We received confirmation of his acceptance this morning of his appointment as Supreme Commander, Southwest Pacific Area. He arrived in Melbourne this morning, Australia time, and immediately commandeered several luxury suites in the Menzies Hotel as his headquarters, for now. So far, the Australians have welcomed him with open arms."

"Well, we are blessed," Roosevelt said and smiled in a very mischievous manner. "I presume Admiral Nimitz is aware of MacArthur's acceptance."

"Yes sir, he is. While the strategy for our campaign against Japan is still evolving, MacArthur has made his opinions crystal clear. He apparently feels some embarrassment for being ordered off Corregidor and intends to argue forcefully to thrust northward from Australia to retake the Philippines. From there, his thinking is a little less firm, but he seems to favor the Formosa-China-Korea path to the Japanese Home Islands."

"What do you think, General?" Roosevelt asked, looking at Marshall.

"There is merit to General MacArthur's approach."

"Yes, but Admiral Nimitz is espousing a thrust directly at the heart of the enemy," observed Roosevelt.

"Yes sir. We have heard the arguments," Marshall responded. "We are not ready to propose the joint recommendation to you for our Pacific strategy."

"I look forward to hearing your joint," the president said with emphasis on the last word, "proposal. Thank you. Where are we on the special mission?" Roosevelt asked.

"Training of the aircrews is complete. Colonel Doolittle has proven the concept and plan. Each of the 16 handpicked flight crews has successfully performed five takeoffs at sea as required by the Navy. They will load the aircraft aboard the *Hornet* at Alameda next week and depart San Francisco Bay on the first of next month. If the Halsey task force does not encounter adverse weather that might slow them down, they expect to launch and carry out the attack on a half dozen industrial and military targets on Honshu on or about the 18th next month."

"Excellent. Please convey my best wishes to Colonel Doolittle and his team."

"We will do so, Mister President," Marshall answered.

"Now, I have a couple of relevant administrative items since I have you both here. First, I signed the congressional resolution affirming the policy direction contained in Executive Order 9066. This is not a moment or action I am particularly proud of. It is not a bright day for the republic. But I recognize that it is an action we must take given the realities we face, especially on the West Coast."

"Yes sir," responded Stimson. "The West Coast military district commanders have begun the relocation of residents with Japanese heritage in their areas of responsibility. The interior camps are being constructed and completed as the relocations are executed."

"This is a very distasteful enterprise," the president observed, "but it is a necessary one, I'm afraid."

"Agreed," responded Stimson.

"Also, I just signed Bill Donovan's promotion to brigadier general . . . effective on the 23rd."

Stimson nodded his head. Marshall wanted to say more. "Quite appropriate and timely, Mister President. Donovan's COI was instrumental in our target selection process for the special mission. His recruitment of personnel is progressing well ahead of any expectation, and he has an active and growing network in Northwest Africa in anticipation of the GYMNAST approval, preparation and execution if we get that far."

Roosevelt nodded his head. "When will the War Department be ready for me to review the plans?"

"The European plans are farther along with the adjustments we made at the ARCADIA Conference. The Pacific plans have proven to be a little more problematic as a consequence of the differences between the MacArthur and Nimitz proposals."

"And, Douglas's ego," mumbled Roosevelt.

This time Stimson smiled. "They are both strong leaders, Mister President."

The president chuckled audibly. "That is a rather delicate and diplomatic way to state the facts, Henry."

Stimson did not wait for further comments. "General Marshall and I have been through the planning several times so far. As a consequence of the realities we face, the European plans are close and should be ready for presentation to you a week from Wednesday. We have scheduled a couple of hours with you that afternoon."

"The first?"

"Yes sir. We are not close enough on the Pacific campaign to set aside time on your calendar, yet."

"Very well. Germany first, after all."

"Yes sir," Stimson responded succinctly without further discussion of the difficulties they were having with General MacArthur.

"Excellent. I eagerly await the review."

The three men concluded their business. The president asked them to stay for supper, but both of the War Department leaders had prior engagements planned. They excused themselves and moved on.

—

Sunday, 23.March.1942
RAF Martlesham Heath
Woodbridge, Suffolk, England
United Kingdom
17:35 hours

No.71 Squadron had been reported as Unavailable a half-hour ago, but they were not released. Tug had not provided an explanation. The grumbling had begun 10 minutes earlier. Squadron Leader Meares could hear some, if not all, of it through his open office door, and he ignored it for the time being. Brian chose his usual action at such times. He just saw no point in such grumbling.

A Royal Navy sub-lieutenant in a dress blue uniform and a gold-braided aiguillette on his left shoulder entered the Dispersal Hut and announced in a commanding voice, "Attention on deck." He stood aside from the open door.

Corporal Harris was the first to spring to attention. The pilots stood, although they did not show signs of a rigid position of attention, except Whitey. Brian nearly fell out of his leaned back chair but made it safely to his feet.

A Royal Navy commodore in full dress blue uniform entered the building just as Squadron Leader Meares emerged from his office and saluted the admiral, who returned the salute. The admiral stopped just inside to allow the building door to be closed by the lieutenant and gestured for the pilots to be seated.

Squadron Leader Meares said, "Gentlemen, it is my honor to introduce Chief of Combined Operations Commodore Lord Mountbatten." Tug moved a couple of steps to the side and remained standing.

"Thank you, Tug. It is an honor for me to be with you this evening. I requested this honor from Air Chief Marshal Sir Charles Portal, who graciously granted my request. My command is fairly new. We have been busy carrying out His Majesty's orders and taking the fight to the Germans. Our most recent campaign was known as Operation BITING—an airborne and amphibious probe of German coastal defenses at Bruneval, France.

"Tug informed me that you were not aware of the details of the ground and naval operations, but I am here to inform you that you," Mountbatten said, pointing and looking at each pilot, "that this squadron played a vital role in the success of the Bruneval Raid. On behalf of King George VI, Prime Minister Churchill, and Combined Operations, I offer each of you my heartfelt and sincerest gratitude for your skills and contributions to the operation's success. I wanted to convey these thoughts to you personally." Mountbatten, Meares and the sub-lieutenant applauded the squadron. The admiral glanced over his left shoulder to his aide-de-camp.

"Attention to orders," the sub-lieutenant commanded. The pilots rose, and this time stood at attention. "Flight Lieutenant Brian Arthur Drummond, CBE, MC, DFC, front and center."

Brian felt a jolt of shock, as he made his way around the chairs and his brethren. He stood at attention to the admiral's left and faced the other pilots. Brian was a couple of inches taller than Lord Mountbatten.

The sub-lieutenant read from a single page. "His Majesty King George VI takes pleasure in awarding Flight Lieutenant Drummond his second Distinguished Flying Cross.

"On the morning of the 27th of February 1942, Flight Lieutenant Drummond, as a section leader with No.71 Squadron, participated in Operation BITING, providing air cover during the extraction portion of the operation. While engaging enemy fighters attacking the naval support ships, Flight Lieutenant Drummond witnessed a torpedo launched by an enemy patrol boat running directly at the Royal Navy destroyer with its main deck crowded with commandoes being transported away from the beach. Skillfully and adroitly, Flight Lieutenant Drummond maneuvered his Spitfire fighter sharply, and used his cannons and guns to explode the torpedo before it could strike its target. His quick thinking and exceptional skill saved countless lives and His Majesty's destroyer. For his flying skill in direct support of Operation BITING, Flight Lieutenant Drummond is awarded the Distinguished Flying Cross."

Lord Mountbatten stepped in front of Brian and extended his right hand without taking his eyes off Brian's eyes. "Well done, Hunter," Mountbatten whispered.

"Thank you, sir," Brian said softly.

The admiral looked to the open award box held by his aide. He removed the DFC medal from its box and pinned it on Brian's uniform tunic below his wings and shook hands with Brian. "Where are your other ribbons, Lieutenant?"

"I don't usually wear them, sir, especially when I'm flying."

"You should," the admiral said and smiled.

"Yes sir."

Lord Mountbatten stepped back to face the squadron. "Thank you for waiting for me, gentlemen. I needed to do this one myself. As the first American volunteer fighter squadron in the Royal Air Force, we are very proud of your accomplishments in the defense of freedom. Now, I wish I could join you for a couple of celebratory pints at the Mess, but that shall have to wait for another day. Carry on," the admiral said and turned to shake hands with Tug. The pilots began to shuffle around, although none of them left. Meares saluted. Mountbatten returned the salute, and then he sidestepped to Brian. They shook hands again, and the admiral held Brian's hand. "I wanted to personally convey my awe of your accomplishments, Brian. We are blessed to have you with us. Also, if I may be so bold, cherish Charlotte and Ian in these troubled times." Mountbatten released Brian's right hand. Brian saluted and Mountbatten returned the salute, and then departed, followed by his aide-de-camp.

The other pilots slapped Brian on the back or punched him in the shoulder. Tug Meares shook Brian's hand and said, "Well deserved, Hunter."

"Thank you, sir."

"Now, gentlemen, you are released. Let us retire to the Mess and celebrate Hunter's second DFC."

They cheered and applauded as they made their way outside into the covered bed of the waiting transport truck. The squadron pilots sat for the evening meal, and then tossed a few pints in honor of Hunter, or so they claimed.

Brian had other things on his mind. When festivities dwindled, Brian quietly made his way to the bank of a half dozen telephone booths. The operators made the relevant connections, and eventually, he heard the familiar female voice.

"Bushey Heath two four seven one," Mary spoke with smooth sophistication.

"Mary, it's Brian."

"I'm afraid this is not one of the nights we are blessed with John's presence," she said with noticeable sarcasm.

"Actually, I wanted to talk to you."

"Oh my . . . a rarity these days. Are you calling for a date?"

The question surprised Brian, but it was not particularly unusual for Mary Spencer. "Not a bad idea, but no, that is not the purpose of my call."

"Well then, do tell."

"Do you know a woman by the name of Lady Doris Castlerosse?"

Mary laughed heartily as he rarely remembered. Brian waited quietly. "You are running in interesting circles, my lovely Brian." He did not respond and waited for her to continue. Mary calmed her jocularity and explained, "Lady Castlerosse is known in social circles by many names in London society, not least of which are Mistress of Mayfair, Sex Queen of Mayfair, and Notorious Lady 'C.' If I may be so bold, have you met her? Have you succumbed to her womanly wiles? And, if so, how did that happen?"

"Wow! Those are unusual titles."

"Not for her. Are you ignoring my indelicate queries?"

"No . . . no, I'm not ignoring your questions. I was just commenting. I had heard none of those titles. Yes, I have met her. I was enjoying a pint at Shepherd's Pub with Harness and Mud, when she approached our table and introduced herself. And, no, I have not been intimate with her, although she made it quite apparent that was her interest."

"How does she know you . . . a young American volunteer fighter pilot?"

"I do not know. I did not ask, and she did not say."

"Brian, my darling, you caught a glimpse of London high society, or some might say, the low side of high society. She is a renowned seductress, an equal opportunity lover who makes no distinction between men and women. She seduces them all."

"Have you met her?" Brian asked innocently.

"Yes, several times, although I have not climbed into bed with her."

"Wow!"

"Oh, it's not so shocking as it seems. She demonstrably enjoys sex and has a voracious appetite. So, the gossip goes, she is famous, some might say infamous, for what she calls Cleopatra's Grip, a use of her vaginal muscles to enhance male orgasm . . . and hers, so they say. I've tried the technique without the same success."

"Wow!" Brian exclaimed. *I had no fucking idea.*

"Oh, don't play so innocent, Brian. Since you are now running in a fairly narrow vein, another one to keep a careful eye on is Lady Edwina Mountbatten."

"What!" said Brian with pronounced incredulity. "Mountbatten? Any relation to Commodore Lord Mountbatten?"

Mary chuckled audibly. "Yes, my dear. Edwina is Dickey's wife, but that fact has not altered her ravenous enjoyment of sex with whoever will join her, again regardless of male or female."

"I just got an award from Lord Mountbatten a few hours ago."

"Congratulations. What was it this time?"

"My second DFC."

"I look forward to hearing the story, the next time we meet."

That sounds anticipatory.

"Have you informed Charlotte?"

"Not yet, but I will."

"The sooner, the better."

"I plan to tell her the next time I can see her, eye-to-eye. Not the best topic for the telephone."

"Wise. I do not know if Charlotte knows or is even aware of Lady Castlerosse, or Lady Mountbatten, and their reputations and accomplishments."

"Thank you, Mary. Now I know."

"All this seduction talk has made you all the more attractive, my dear Brian. Are you sure you would not entertain a rendezvous for old time's sake?"

Brian smiled to himself. "Thank you for your desire and invitation, but I must respectfully decline."

"Understandable but nonetheless regrettable," Mary said with unusual soft smoothness to her voice.

"Thank you for the information, Mary. Have a good night, and please convey my respects to the air commodore."

"I will do that the next time I see him. Good evening to you, Brian."

Mary disconnected first. Brian hung up the handset and sat quietly in the booth with his thoughts. Several minutes passed before he left the booth and went to his room for sleep. *This is more serious than I thought. Charlotte really deserves to know as soon as possible—no telling where this might go. Her approaching me was not some random occurrence. Memories of Anne Booth and her secret work flashed back into his consciousness, along with the close call his relationship with Anne had brought to his life and avocation.*

———

Wednesday, 25.March.1942
Camp X
Oshawa, Ontario
Dominion of Canada
10:55 hours

The two Bills—Little Bill Stephenson and Big Bill Donovan—had been discussing numerous aspects of mutual interest since breakfast this morning. Both of them had arrived at the training facility yesterday morning. The joint training camp had been in operation for not quite four months. Initial trainees were British SOE, American COI, and Canadian Commando personnel, although their joint plans called for expansion of trainees to include potential agents from other occupied countries in support of special operations missions behind enemy lines.

Chief Instructor Captain William Ewart 'Bill' Fairbairn entered the small conference room early. "Our guest of honor will be a few minutes late," he announced. "The tour of the facility is taking a little longer than expected."

The wiry, bespectacled, 57-year-old Fairbairn had a little-known reputation outside the small circle of the special operations community; however, within the world of commandoes and special operators, he was a respected and revered specialist in hand-to-hand combat, self-defense and especially the art of silent killing. Fairbairn was a former Royal Marine, who perfected his knowledge and techniques of close combat during his service as a patrolman with the Shanghai Municipal Police Department, at the time a British-controlled organization. During his tenure in Shanghai, he was attacked and stabbed multiple times by a Chinese separatist gang. As a consequence, he developed a combat knife known as the Fairbairn fighting knife that had become the preferred personal protection weapon for special operators along with the techniques to effectively utilize the knife. His reputation brought him the moniker "Dangerous Dan." Brigadier Gubbins had been instrumental in recalling Fairbairn, commissioning him in the British Army, and tasking Fairbairn with training SOE agents in his close combat techniques. After the formation of COI in the United States, Little Bill and Big Bill collaborated with Gubbins and MI6 to expand Fairbairn's charter that led to the creation of Camp X.

Bill Donovan had proposed the concept of a joint training camp before President Roosevelt chartered him as the Coordinator of Information. Bill Stephenson's British and Canadian contacts within the intelligence and commando communities enabled the two Bills to find the remote, rural, farmland on the north shore of Lake Ontario. They had mutually agreed the site gave them the privacy they needed as well as access to major transportation facilities.

The knock on the door announced the arrival of their guest. "Welcome to Camp X, Trevor," Donovan said, stood and extended his hand to Trevor Andersen.

"Thank you, sir," Trevor responded and shook Donovan's hand.

Donovan gestured to one of a dozen chairs around the rectangular conference table. "We will not impose on your purpose here, but Bill and I wanted to meet with you, once we had received confirmation of your training slot."

"Too many Bills," Andersen observed.

They all laughed. Donovan continued, "Yes, quite so, the luck of the draw, I'm afraid. To jump directly to the point, we," Donovan said and gestured to Stephenson, "thought it prudent to take advantage of your attendance in Captain Fairbairn's training program. We acknowledge and accept that your purpose here is to acquire close combat skills for your work. What we wanted to discuss with you is tapping your undercover techniques. We are aware of your work deep behind enemy lines on a variety of missions, not least of which was your experience during Operation FLIPPER."

Andersen grimaced and said, "That was a very close call. I was extraordinarily lucky. The main capture team was not so fortunate."

"Which is what brought you here," Stephenson added.

"Yes. Brigadier Gubbins believed it was far too close and that I needed to acquire some of Captain Fairbairn's unique skills."

"And, we would like our students to benefit from your experience. Admiral Pike and Brigadier Gubbins have been most forthcoming with your missions behind enemy lines. We jointly agreed that you can discuss general techniques for your activities without disclosing specific details, especially your operation in Poland during the spring of 1939."

Big Bill and Little Bill were broadly knowledgeable of Andersen's operation with his contacts in the Polish Secret Police that resulted in the capture of the most recent version of the German cipher device known as Enigma. While the details of that operation would be quite applicable to the mission of Camp X, the risk to ULTRA was simply too great. They could not discuss that particular mission, since Fairbairn and the students of Camp X, were not cleared for and on the access list for ULTRA.

"We would like you to provide an overview course," Donovan said.

"Brigadier Gubbins briefed me on your request before my departure, and my mentor Admiral Pike emphasized the importance. So, I am prepared to conduct such an overview."

"Excellent," responded Stephenson. "We have arranged for a specifically trained stenographer with most secret / top secret clearance from all three sponsoring governments to record your training course for follow-on use once you have departed."

"The brigadier made us aware of that feature as well."

"Very good," Wild Bill Donovan said. "We also must impose, by joint agreement, a restriction from discussing future missions open or in planning. However, as I'm sure you know, we are training individuals and teams that will operate deep into enemy-occupied territory. With Brigadier Gubbins' approval and the reason Captain Fairbairn is present for this meeting, we would like to discuss your White Rose effort."

"I am authorized to discuss aspects of that mission," Trevor responded. Diamond recounted his missions into Munich, Germany, to connect with and build a clandestine relationship with the White Rose Society, which was a loose coalition of mostly medical students at the University of Munich surrounding Professor of Psychology and Music Kurt Huber. White Rose grew from the rise of the Nazi Party in 1929 and had been focused solely on passive-aggressive actions like the distribution of leaflets and other intellectual material decrying the anti-democratic, brutally violent actions of the Nazis across all of Germany.

The men discussed how Allied special operations activities planned for France and Germany might be of assistance to Diamond's mission. Fairbairn would add a couple of specifically tailored courses for Andersen's benefit and especially for surviving an opposed egress effort. As lunchtime had arrived and the Camp X mess hall had rather limited hours of operation, they moved to the mess hall and confined further words to the unclassified level. At the conclusion of their lunch, Stephenson and Donovan excused themselves for an afternoon meeting in Ottawa with the Canadian government. Trevor 'Diamond' Andersen headed into the initial session of the self-defense close combat training courses.

—

Monday, 30.March.1942
Cabinet War Rooms
New Public Offices
Whitehall, London, England
United Kingdom
17:15 hours

Once more, Commodore Lord Mountbatten stood before the War Cabinet and the Defense Committee without the secretariat and staff in attendance; this time to report on the preliminary results of Operation CHARIOT—the St. Nazaire Raid. Combined Operations orchestrated the attack on the *Normandie* dock—the largest dry dock in the world when it was completed in 1932 and the only dry dock that could handle repairs on capital warships like the *Bismarck* sunk last year and her sister ship *Tirpitz*.

Prime Minister Churchill announced, "You have the floor, Lord Mountbatten."

"Thank you, Prime Minister. The flotilla sailed as scheduled on the afternoon of the 26th. Bomber Command began the planned bombardment of the port facility of St. Nazaire at 23:30 on the 27th to provide a distraction for the approach of the raiding party.

"The primary ship was the remotely controlled HMS *Campbelltown*, a modified Lend-Lease U.S. destroyer, the former USS *Buchanan*. The ship had been modified to appear like a German destroyer rather than a flush-deck, four-stack, Great War vintage, American destroyer, with a discreet, radiofrequency, helm steering motor and throttle installed. The bow of the destroyer had been packed with 10,000 pounds of Amatol high explosives fitted with a multi-path, time delay fusing mechanism, set to explode after the withdrawal of the Commando personnel. The *Campbelltown* struck home at the center of the seaward dock gates at 19 knots, at 01:34 on the 28th, and drove into the dock some 30 plus feet. I must say at this juncture, the approach of the whole assault force was aided by captured codebooks from the Vågsøy raid the previous December. The crew used proper codes to the Germans that caused them to hesitate for several minutes at a crucial time.

"No.2 Commando provided the core of the land assault force and was supplemented by specifically trained explosives teams from other Commando units. They had precisely defined objectives like the pumps and pump house for the *Normandie* dock, and they executed those plans with precision. The debriefings conducted so far suggest we were successful.

"The bow explosives were set to detonate at 04:30, after the disengagement and re-embarkation of the Commando raiding force. At first, we thought the detonator might have failed when dawn arrived, and the ship still had not exploded. For reasons we know not, the charge finally did detonate just before noon. Our preliminary assessment based on aerial photographs returned this morning indicates we achieved the primary objective of the operation. The engineers are performing a detailed analysis that should be completed within a month; thus, we shall have to wait for the final analysis to know the precise results."

Mountbatten paused to allow for questions. Surprisingly, there were no questions, as if they were listening with reverence to Lord Mountbatten's report.

The admiral continued, "While preliminary data suggest we were wholly successful in the execution of Operation CHARIOT, this was a very costly affair indeed. Of the 622 men of the Royal Navy and Commandos who took part in the raid, only 228 men returned to England. We know we have scores of dead, but the precise number of those killed in action has not yet been established—41 known as of this moment—and we believe the number is sure to grow. We have 353 presently listed as missing in action; some of that number will likely be added to the killed in action list, and others were captured. We presume they will be treated with respect as prisoners of war, and if so we will eventually achieve an accounting. We hope the majority of the missing is in the prisoner of war category, although we may eventually learn that some evaded capture and are in the process of escape.

"The heroism, courage, determination, resoluteness of purpose, and outright bravery are . . . ," Mountbatten choked back his emotions. Dickey placed his right fist in front of his mouth and cleared his throat. He wiped away a tear. "My apologies. I am humbled and awed by the selfless bravery of these men. We are gathering the requisite facts and rationale for appropriate awards and recognition. We are certain to have several Victoria Cross candidates and other awards of various degrees of courage in combat." Mountbatten bowed his head, as if in prayer. "That is the extent of my preliminary summary report to the War Cabinet."

Silence filled the room for several seconds. Prime Minister Churchill rose and applauded. The remainder of the War Cabinet and Defense Committee followed suit. Mountbatten smiled, nodded his head several times, and raised his right hand in a subtle royal wave.

The prime minister raised both hands above his shoulders and waited for quiet. As the room calmed, he gestured for everyone to sit. Churchill and Mountbatten remained standing. "On behalf of the War Cabinet," Churchill paused to look at each member of the War Cabinet and received a confirmatory nod for what the members knew was coming, "I offer our profound gratitude to Combined Operations command, and especially to the brave men who carried out this important action. We eagerly await your list of awards to acknowledge the bravery of these valiant men."

"Yes sir. It shall be done," Dickey replied.

"Before we move on to the more mundane of today's agenda, does anyone have any questions for Commodore Mountbatten?"

"No questions," Attlee said, "but I would like to add my voice in praise of the CHARIOT team for their accomplishments. Well done, Admiral."

"Thank you, sir."

"Thank you for your excellent report, Commodore Lord Mountbatten." Dickey stood, gathered his papers in his left hand, saluted palm forward, and departed the conference room.

The prime minister waited for the door to close before he turned the attention of the War Cabinet and Defense Committee to the necessary and routine business of His Majesty's Government.

The men who carried out the St. Nazaire Raid were awarded 89 decorations, including five Victoria Crosses, four Distinguished Service Orders, four Conspicuous Gallantry Medals, 11 Military Crosses, 24 Distinguished Service Medals and 15 Military Medals, among other combat valor awards.

—

Wednesday, 1.April.1942
1637 30ᵗʰ Street, Northwest
Georgetown, Washington, District of Columbia
United States of America
00:10 hours

Wild Bill Donovan emerged from his residence dressed in a medium grey business suit with a solid blue necktie and carrying his characteristic leather briefcase along with an overnight case.

"My apologies, James . . . urgent last-minute business," Donovan said to James Freeman, his long-term, loyal driver, as he handed the suitcase to James. "I have made us late."

"No worries, General. I'll get you to the station in time for your train."

Donovan had a first-class ticket on the 01:05 express train for New York City to meet with *Doktor* Heinrich Aloysius Maria Elisabeth Brüning—one of the last German chancellors before Hitler's ascension. He spent three years in England before coming to the United States in 1937. Brüning currently served as a visiting professor of philosophy at Harvard University. He was a social democrat by political leaning and had been with the Center Party when he became chancellor toward the end of the Weimar Republic. Friends of his warned Brüning of Hitler's bent for retribution that enabled him to flee Germany just 27 days before *Nacht der langen Messer*—Night of the Long Knives. He knew it had been a very close call in avoiding Hitler's vengeance. Brüning settled into his exile in Vermont and generously made himself available to Allied intelligence organizations. The purpose of the meeting was to learn as much as Doctor Brüning could provide about Adolf Hitler and the political situation in Nazi Germany.

The meeting last week with Trevor Andersen had reinforced the desired objective of cultivating anti-Hitler, anti-Nazi elements inside Germany to weaken the ability of the rogue country to sustain their war effort. Bill Donovan suspected there were veins of resistance to be nurtured, encouraged, and reinforced in the COI's clandestine operations charter from President Roosevelt.

The COI had just opened his briefcase to remove a relevant report for continued reading under the small lamp in the passenger compartment of his Cadillac limousine. Just five short blocks from his home, bright lights flashed into the driver-side rear window. The impact thrust Donovan across the back seat and into the site of the collision. Both knees struck various hard objects as he hit the damaged door. Flying glass cut him in several places but did no serious damage. The sharp pain in both knees was far more serious and seemed to have aggravated old injuries to both knees sustained during the Great War.

"Are you injured, Mister Donovan?" asked Freeman from the front seat with serious concerns.

"A little banged up, James, but nothing serious, I do believe. We'd better check on the other guy," the COI said and started to move toward the undamaged passenger-side door. Donovan winced and pulled up short when the pain in his knees made him hesitate with the thought that his injuries might be more serious than initially thought.

Fortunately, the driver's door was comparatively undamaged, allowing Freeman to get out. Donovan struggled against the pain in his knees and eventually made his way out of the car and around the back end. The car that hit them was a ten-year-old Chevrolet that had sustained far more damage than the Cadillac. The other driver had some cuts but appeared to be oblivious to what had just happened. Neither Freeman nor Donovan could find any serious injuries. The other driver babbled incoherently with obvious intoxication.

"What do you want to do, Mister Donovan?"

"The man is drunk, which is what probably saved him from serious injury. He is not going anywhere. The limousine appears to be functional. I'm afraid I must ask you to skirt the law and get me to Union Station as soon as you are able." Donovan took a small notepad from his inside jacket breast pocket and jotted down his name, the intersection of the collision, and the time of the accident. He added a telephone number at the bottom, then handed the note to Freeman. "As soon as you drop me off and get me on the train, please call the number on the note. It is the home telephone number for Mister Taylor from my law office." Jeremy Taylor was a capable, young attorney in the Washington office of Donovan, Leisure, Newton, Lumbard & Irvine. "Do not wait for dawn. Call him as soon as you are able. Tell him exactly what happened and allow him to contact the police to report the accident. Answer all of his questions as accurately as you can. He can call me for my statement if he or the police need it. Do you understand all of that?"

"Yes sir. I will tend to it as soon as we get you on the train."

Freeman supported his boss as he hobbled back to the right side, rear, passenger door. He checked the other driver one more time. Satisfied that the man was not in danger, at least from the accident, James drove the Cadillac to Union Station, parked the car at curbside, retrieved Donovan's suitcase, and helped his charge to the proper train and the seat in his assigned compartment. Donovan shook Freeman's hand, and thanked him for his service and help. He checked his wristwatch—ten minutes to spare. *A rather inauspicious start to this important journey!*

———

Wednesday, 1.April.1942
St. Regis Hotel, Suite 1906
2 East 55th Street
Manhattan, New York City, New York
United States of America
09:45 hours

The other invited attendees for the day's conference had been waiting for Donovan in the lobby of the hotel. Their guest of honor was not yet present that they could tell. The three men, all in business suits, stood when Donovan hobbled into the lobby.

Allen Welsh Dulles joined COI the previous October, having been recruited out of his New York law firm, personally by Donovan. Dulles managed the New York office of the COI.

Arthur Joseph Goldberg left his Chicago law firm and enlisted in the Army shortly after Pearl Harbor. At only 36 years of age, he had proven himself to be an accomplished labor lawyer, and Donovan had convinced him to transfer to COI and head up the intelligence organization's Labor Desk based in New York City.

Bill Stephenson had been invited but declined in favor of an urgent trip back to England. Little Bill nominated a German political expert from his Manhattan office to represent him. Donovan had met John Wheeler-Bennett several times during his many visits to Stephenson's British Security Coordination (BSC) office in Rockefeller Center and had been sufficiently impressed. Wheeler-Bennett articulated numerous times and in various forms the need to the Allies to nurture resistance factions within Germany. He was a welcome addition to the day's conference.

After the appropriate introductions and dismissing the concerns of his colleague for his injuries, Donovan and colleagues made it to the spacious suite that Bill retained for his use. Wild Bill quickly reinforced the purpose of the meeting and the need to glean as much as they could from Heinrich Brüning. They were still talking when the door knocks at precisely 10:00, shifted their attention.

Dulles answered the door, shook hands with Brüning, and invited him into the room.

"Welcome Doctor Brüning," Donovan said and winced as he stood. "Please excuse my sorry state. I am a bit sore from an unfortunate traffic accident early this morning."

"Oh my, General Donovan," Brüning said in English through his heavy German accent. "We can certainly postpone this discussion until you feel better."

"No, no, this is far too important and timely." Donovan gestured for everyone to sit and provided Brüning with a short description of each man's background and purpose in the meeting. "As we had discussed in setting up this conference, we would like to pick your brain to gain some insight into Adolf Hitler and the Nazi regime."

"I will gladly answer whatever questions you may have. I love my native Germany, and I am deeply saddened by what he has done to my country and our people."

"We are as well, Heinrich. May I use your given name?" Donovan asked.

"By all means, General."

"Please, Bill is sufficient. Let us keep this discussion as informal as possible. Let us start with your personal assessment of Hitler."

"As you know, Bill, I had firsthand, direct experience with . . . with . . . with the corporal. I must restrain my disdain for the man, as it will contaminate the purpose of this conversation. My opinion of the man has not changed since I first became aware of his political activities circa 1921, shortly after he became the leader of the National Socialist German Workers Party. I personally fought against his lenient sentence and treatment at Landsberg Prison after the beer hall *putsch* was crushed; wait, sorry for the German, the Nazi coup attempt in München. His book, *My Struggle* . . . have you read it?"

"Yes, I have," answered Donovan.

"As have I," added Bennett.

"I believe he was surprisingly frank and candid in his political thoughts, beliefs, and objectives. What we witness today is precisely as he described in his book. He told us what he was going to do and very few of us paid attention. I believe with little doubt that Hitler is convinced he was chosen by God to cleanse the world of undesirables and impose Aryan domination, as the natural state of God's intention, on all lesser peoples. As the chosen one, he alone will decide the fate of people. Many of us recognized him for what he was ten years before he became chancellor. We tried to sound the alarm. He is a demagogue . . . I think that is the word in English."

"Yes, that is the word," Donovan said. "Tell us about the 'many' you mentioned. Who were or are they? What did you do to try to stop Hitler's appeal to the lesser elements of German society? Where are they now?"

"First, General Donovan, I must object—strongly object—to your characterization of Hitler's appeal to the lesser elements of German society. There are good people among his believers, very intelligent, capable, accomplished citizens, among those who support him. They have been seduced by his Siren's Song." Donovan nodded his head and held up his hands, not wanting to argue the point. "There are Germans in all walks of life from common laborers to professional military and politicians who have rejected the Nazis strong-arm, brute force methods. The journalists who sounded the clarion call before Hitler's ascendency have gone underground or perished as the regime has used its police powers to eradicate any signs of opposition, and I must say, the Gestapo has been uniquely effective in suppressing any opposition they can detect. The voices of resistance can no longer be heard in public."

Bill Donovan wanted to inform Brüning the Allies knew of several assassination attempts and dissatisfaction within the professional military, but he did not want to disclose what Allied intelligence already knew. "Can any resistance be cultivated?" asked Donovan.

Brüning chuckled softly and smiled. "I would like to respond in the affirmative; however, I am a realist. There is dissatisfaction in the professional military; however, I do believe their sense of duty and patriotism would likely override any attempt to foment insurrection. Hitler has quite adroitly leveraged national pride for his purposes. Without a vigorous press, the people have no means of assessing the government's actions. When they do see glimpses, they discount their vision with the flick of the phrase, that cannot be so."

"Could like-minded Germans be mobilized to influence other Germans?" asked Bennett.

"That would be the best approach, but that is a very risky proposition. The fundamental fear of the Gestapo is palpable, and rightly so. It would only take one slight misstep by just one person in that string to collapse the whole thing. Reinhard Heydrich is a ruthless enforcer."

"Of that we know," Dulles added.

The four men continued their discussions through a private, self-service, working lunch and well into the afternoon. Bill Donovan kept the mounting pain in his knees to himself, except for the occasionally unavoidable wince with a shift in position or his effort to move to and from the dining table in the luxury hotel suite. Hitler remained the center of their talks. Dulles and Goldberg listened for the most part, although they were critical listeners as well as essential contributors to the evolving strategy of the COI in both the intelligence and clandestine operations arenas. Wheeler-Bennett added complementary information in numerous instances throughout the afternoon. As the productiveness of the day's conversations waned, Donovan graciously thanked Doctor Brüning for his frank answers and opinions, as the former German chancellor departed with an expressed willingness to contribute further as General Donovan saw fit. The four intelligence professionals remained in the suite. After the hotel's room service staff cleared their lunch dishes, they talked about the day's conversation.

"Well, what did you think?" asked Donovan.

"I think we have had enough talk today, General," said Dulles with determination. "You are clearly in pain, and it worsened all day. Your strength to soldier on is laudable, but you need to see a doctor."

Donovan waved his hand dismissively.

"No, General. You need to see a doctor, now. We can reconvene tomorrow, or within the next few days, and share our assessment of Doctor Brüning's insights."

"I agree with Allen," added Goldberg.

"Respectfully, General Donovan," Wheeler-Bennett contributed, "I expect to remain in Manhattan for the next few weeks at least, so I am at your service. Further, if we wait for a couple of days, Mister Stephenson should be back in New York and available to listen to our debriefing."

Donovan looked at each man, noted the concerned expressions, and finally nodded his head in consent. "My apologies, fellas. My knees are indeed getting worse. I will accede to your concerns and counsel to avail myself of medical treatment. I will inform each of you, and coordinate a proper meeting date and time for our debriefing. Thank you so very much for your time, concern and participation."

Dulles sprang to the telephone, immediately call the hotel's doctor, and then at Donovan's insistence, he called Donovan's personal physician for additional medical examinations and consultations.

Medical examination established that Donovan's automobile accident had indeed aggravated previous damage to both knees incurred during his combat service in France. The doctors unanimously agreed on the diagnosis and the treatment—bed rest followed by precise rehabilitation. The patient made numerous attempts to resist, but his lieutenants relentlessly worked to enforce the doctors' counsel. He would be predominantly immobile for a month to six weeks.

—

Wednesday, 1.April.1942
Cabinet Room
The White House
Washington, District of Columbia
United States of America
14:30 hours

The military leadership of the United States had gathered in the White House Cabinet Room to brief the president on the operations plans modified from the ARCADIA Conference agreements and guidance last January. The restricted attendees included the secretary of war, the secretary of the Navy, the Army chief of staff, and the chief of the Army Air Forces. Chief of Naval Operations Admiral Ernest Joseph 'Ernie' King, USN [USNA 1901], replaced Admiral Stark just two weeks prior. Stark had become another casualty in the aftermath of the Pearl Harbor debacle. Privately, both the president and secretary of the Navy had lost confidence in his ability to lead the naval war effort. The featured and sole speaker on the agenda for this particular meeting was Chief of the Army's Operational Plans Division Brigadier General Eisenhower. The Navy's Director of War Plans Captain Charles Maynard 'Savvy' Cooke Jr., USN [USNA 1910], had replaced Rear Admiral Turner the previous December and was present to support General Eisenhower.

One of the duty Secret Service agents wheeled President Roosevelt into the Cabinet Room. Everyone came to attention until the president gestured for them to be seated.

Once everyone was settled, Secretary of War Stimson began, "This is the requested presidential briefing on operational plans in the European Theater agreed to after the ARCADIA Conference, Mister President." Roosevelt nodded his head. "General Eisenhower, please proceed."

Dwight Eisenhower stood across the large conference table from the president and before a small-scale map of Europe, the Mediterranean Sea, and North Africa. He held a red-tipped, long wooden pointer with both hands in front of his service uniform. "Good afternoon, Mister President," Ike said to which Roosevelt nodded again. "We have modified a number of existing plans and added a new plan for Operation GYMNAST in accordance with the ARCADIA agreements. In a broad, general sense, GYMNAST is a joint invasion of Northwest Africa with specific objectives of occupying North Africa for future operations into Europe, coordination with the British 8th Army to eliminate Axis forces from that region, and third, to neutralize substantial Vichy French forces in their Northwest African colonies.

"I do believe we have convinced the secretaries and the joint chiefs that the sheer logistics obstacles have made Operation ROUNDUP, the invasion of occupied France, and the thrust into Germany and Berlin, impractical within the time window set at the ARCADIA Conference—this year, or the latest within two years. The ROUNDUP analysis scope included all known Channel and Atlantic landing beaches. The joint planning staff has agreed on the building of the necessary transport shipping and amphibious landing craft to facilitate an operation the size of ROUNDUP in conjunction with Pacific Theater requirements. The time required for preparation, planning, training, staging, and execution of a ROUNDUP size mission is roughly two years."

"Does your assessment include SLEDGEHAMMER?" asked the president.

"In a general sense, yes, Mister President. However, in a specific frame, SLEDGEHAMMER has more modest mission objectives, although the salient of interest for SLEDGEHAMMER is the intelligence estimates of the German order of battle the operation would face. Because of its more limited scope, SLEDGEHAMMER was confined to the Brest and Cherbourg peninsulas," Eisenhower said, pointing to each region on the map, "to restrict the lateral front the landing force would have to defend. It is that particular salient that remains a contentious topic between the combined planning staff. Both SLEDGEHAMMER and ROUNDUP would accomplish more for the strategic objective of aiding the Russians in their effort to stop and beat back the Germans on the Eastern Front. A further concern with SLEDGEHAMMER is taking and holding sufficient lodgment size to protect the necessary logistics support facilities for such an operation. The joint planning staff and, to a certain extent, the combined planning staff see the benefit of having a ready foothold on the Continent for the ultimate invasion to defeat Germany. As I indicated at the outset, the crux of concern remains the intelligence assessment. At the low end, the SLEDGEHAMMER force might face 10 divisions including up to two armor divisions. On the high side, they might have to deal with 50 divisions including 10 armor divisions. The latter would be an overwhelming force with Gallipoli implications."

"Or Passchendaele, as Prime Minister Churchill has noted," the president interjected.

"Yes sir," responded Eisenhower. "The potential remains a concern at the forefront of our thinking. We are deeply mindful of the risks as we evolve our planning."

"By your words," Roosevelt said, "I surmise you favor GYMNAST."

"Mister President, I am currently the head of the Army's planning staff. We do our level best to develop plans to achieve the direction and guidance given to us by the national leadership. We have no place to favor or disfavor any particular plan."

"My apologies, General Eisenhower," President Roosevelt said, pointing to Ike. "Your reply is very noble and diplomatic. Please allow me to rephrase my question. Tell me a little more about GYMNAST, and how will the logistics concerns you have noted earlier play into the operation?"

"There are several key facts that influence our thinking regarding a Northwest Africa operation. First and foremost, the Royal Navy dominates the Mediterranean, which constrains the ability of the Germans to reinforce the region. Second, thanks to the excellent intelligence work by MI6 and the COI, we see the Vichy French forces as more vulnerable to realignment."

"Realignment?" Roosevelt asked.

"Yes sir. We know that some of the general officers on duty with the territorial forces are quite sympathetic to the Allied cause and more precisely against the Germans. The intelligence community is unanimous in their assessment of French territorial forces in Morocco and Algeria," he pointed to each area, "and with good spadework, we might be able to negate any substantive resistance. The key will be consolidating gains enough to make any reinforcement impractical and excessively risky. There would be a monumental difference in resistance between French territorial forces and primary units of the German armed forces. Third, such an operation would serve the efforts of the British 8th Army in Western Egypt," pointing to the current location of British forces, "placing Axis forces in a difficult vice—the desert to the south, the sea to the north, and significant Allied forces on both flanks."

"I see. You paint a very clear picture," President Roosevelt commented.

"Just to be precise," interjected General Marshall, "we are not convinced that GYMNAST will satisfy Premier Stalin."

"The only thing that will placate Stalin is an all-out invasion this year. He still has not broken the German advance, especially in the south, although the advances on Moscow and Leningrad have been stalled, at least for now. I am quite keen on helping Stalin chew up the Germans and keep the Russians in this fight. The full-up invasion is very attractive to that end. However, Prime Minister Churchill offers a cogent and persuasive argument for the soft underbelly, as he puts it. I recognize the joint chiefs want to make quick work of this affair, which prompts me to ask you directly, do you think we can muster sufficient combat forces, transport, and landing craft to carry out a ROUNDUP mission this year, or even next?"

"Frankly, this year is impossible . . . even for us. Next year would be a sporty proposition."

"And then, when could GYMNAST be executed."

"We think it is feasible, later this year," answered General Marshall.

"Is the Navy in agreement here?"

"Yes sir," Secretary Knox responded promptly. "We have been integrally involved in this planning and General Eisenhower speaks for all of us. We can support GYMNAST. SLEDGEHAMMER is more demanding, and ROUNDUP is beyond our current capacity."

"Is there anything else to add to this discussion?" the president asked. No one spoke. "Very well, then. Prime Minister Churchill and I agree that we should focus our limited resources on a near-term achievable objective. As I see things, GYMNAST appears to be that effort. If there are no objections," Roosevelt said and looked at each man in the room, "let us focus on GYMNAST.

I shall ask and leave it to Prime Minister Churchill to use his formidable skills to assuage Stalin regarding the wisdom of a less ambitious operation than he wants. Are we in agreement?" Again, Roosevelt looked at each man and received a head nod or a thumb's up. "Very well, then. We are agreed. Thank you very much for your briefing, General Eisenhower."

"It was my honor, Mister President."

They adjourned and dispersed.

—

Thursday, 2.April.1942
Golden Gate Bridge
Between San Francisco and Marin Counties, California
United States of America
09:10 hours

The sight below the pedestrians and motorists crossing the bridge over the narrow opening into San Francisco Bay would be a singularly unique scene in their memory. Many who were on the bridge that morning—walking or driving—would remember what they saw and connect it with an important event in world affairs two weeks hence that they would not learn about for another month and a half.

Most citizens who happened to witness the passing would only remember that large Navy flattop warship with 16 comparatively large, green, twin-engine aircraft packed tightly on the stern of the ship. What observers on the bridge did not know and would not learn for another month, the aircraft were North American B-25B Mitchell medium bombers that had once belonged to the U.S. Army Air Forces 17th Bombardment Group and were specially configured for the mission they would execute in two weeks. Each aircraft had been lifted by dockside crane to the position in which it would remain until it was time to take to the air. Rumors had been intentionally spread when the bombers were being loaded onto the carrier that the purpose was merely to transport the bombers to Hawaii. A large numeral '8' on the bow of the flattop warship identified the vessel as the USS *Hornet* (CV-8)—the third and last of the U.S. Navy's Yorktown-class fleet aircraft carriers.

Once she was clear of the bridge, the churning and boiling wake indicated the large warship was increasing speed, heading due west. Unbeknownst to the observers on the bridge and contrary to the rumors, the *Hornet* and her one heavy cruiser plus four destroyers were now en route for a rendezvous with her sister ship, the USS *Enterprise*. Once joined up, the two first-line fleet aircraft carriers, three heavy cruisers, one light cruiser, and eight destroyers would become Task Force 16, under the command of Vice Admiral William Frederick 'Bull' Halsey Jr., USN [USNA 1904].

Task Force 16 had one mission—deliver the 16 Army medium bombers chained to the flight deck of the *Hornet* to their launch point and rendezvous with destiny. The unique USAAF squadron was under the command of renowned aviator, Lieutenant Colonel James Harold 'Jimmy' Doolittle, USAAF. Their mission had sprouted and bloomed from a 21.December.1941, meeting between President Roosevelt and Chief of Staff General George Marshall, and the president's desire to take the fight to the enemy as soon as possible, after the disaster at Pearl Harbor. The handpicked aircrews had assembled for the first time a month before their departure from San Francisco Bay, to rehearse the procedures they would use to accomplish their special mission. The aircrews knew they were training for a very special mission by virtue of taking an Army medium bomber off the flight deck of a Navy aircraft carrier. Their mission had been classified top secret from the inception, and Colonel Doolittle repeatedly cautioned them not to discuss what they were doing, or to speculate about what they might be training for with anyone. They were assured they would be properly informed when there was no risk of inadvertent disclosure.

The passing of the *Hornet* through the Golden Gate into the Pacific Ocean that morning began the next phase of their historic mission. They were ready.

———

Sunday, 12.April.1942
Standing Oak Farm
Winchester, Hampshire, England
United Kingdom
17:20 hours

"**W**elcome home, my hero," Charlotte shouted, as Brian walked into the barn near the end of the evening milking task. "Come over here. I want to show you this new milking machine contraption we've been using for a couple of weeks now."

Charlotte showed her husband the various items of equipment and demonstrated how they worked on the last of their cows to be milked. When the afternoon milking was done and the cows were turned out to pasture, the cleanup of the milking machine was left to the farm's helpers—the old men, Lionel Bridges and Horace Morgan, and the young one, 14-year-old, A-Level student Jacob Holden.

Once outside in the unusual moderate, early spring evening air, Charlotte literally jumped into Brian's welcoming arms and wrapped her legs around him. They kissed passionately, and then she nestled her head against his neck and shoulder. "I'm so glad to have you home," Charlotte whispered.

"With a welcome like this, I should desert."

Charlotte dismounted and grabbed her husband's hand. She led him to the house. "We need to feed the troops, so they can get today's product to market. How long do I have you this time?"

"I need to be back to Martlesham by noon Tuesday."

"So, you will be able to talk to Jacob's school class tomorrow?"

"That is the plan. Squadron Leader Meares was very supportive."

"Jacob is so excited. You are an immense figure in his life. He is so proud of you."

"I will try to be worthy of his pride."

"I'm sure you will."

As they entered the house, Brian smelled the delightful aroma of fresh bread and what had to be a rare beef stew—rich and earthy. "Evening, Edith," Charlotte shouted.

"Evening, Mum."

"Look who came home to us—our hero."

Edith Hanscom looked over her shoulder from her meal preparation effort. "Welcome home, Mister Drummond."

"Great to be home. Thank you, Miss Hanscom."

Charlotte looked at Brian. "She has been a godsend. In addition to helping me with Ian, she has stepped into the role of housekeeper and chief cook."

"Where is Ian?" As if on cue, their infant son cried out. Brian went to the boy's cries in the master bedroom. Charlotte followed. She watched as Brian checked Ian's diaper and approved of her husband's changing of their son. Ian fixated on Brian's face and eyes for quite a few seconds, as Brian carried him into the kitchen dining room. When his gaze finally broke, the infant voiced his unhappiness.

"It's feeding time," Charlotte announced. She sat at her usual corner chair and opened her shirt. Charlotte reached for Ian. Brian laid Ian into the crook of Charlotte's left arm, and he immediately found her breast and began to remove the milk he sought.

Edith had already set the table and began serving this evening's meal. The three farmhands entered just as supper was served. The process moved like a well-oiled machine. The men all greeted Brian as they took their places at the table. Once Edith was seated, Brian took his chair at the head of the table. Charlotte managed to eat with her free hand, stopping only to switch Ian to her right breast as they ate. The table conversation focused on Brian's talk at Jacob's school tomorrow. Everyone was interested. Edith, Lionel, and Horace regretted that they would not be able to attend.

With the evening meal complete, the men cleared the table. Horace and Lionel needed to get Jacob home, and then deposit the afternoon's yield of milk and cheese that had cured to the day. Brian washed the dishes, while Charlotte and Edith tended to Ian.

Once Brian finished his task, he caught Charlotte's eyes. "It looks like a decent evening. Can we talk out by the lake?"

A serious expression washed over Charlotte's face. "Should we take Ian, or is this serious?"

"Sure, we can take Ian, but we will need to bundle him up, probably a little chilly for him."

Charlotte completed dressing their son for the evening air and handed him to Brian. Holding Ian in his left arm, Brian reached for and held Charlotte's hand as they sauntered down the wide gravel path to the large bench under the oak tree near the shore of the farm's large pond.

"What is all this hero stuff?" Brian asked.

Charlotte chuckled. "Is that what you wanted to talk about?" Brian did not respond. "The *Hampshire Telegraph* had a front-page article about your latest flying award. They talked about you like you are a local hero. They could only say so much, something about quick thinking during the German Channel Dash. I imagine I will not like hearing about what really happened. They also mentioned our marriage. Numerous neighbors have called or stopped by, after the article to congratulate us and thank you for your service to the Kingdom."

"It was just luck, Charlotte. I happened to be in the right place at the right time."

"Knowing your modesty, I suspect there is much more to that story, but I am not going to ask, because I probably will not appreciate the truth."

They reached the bench. Brian gestured for Charlotte to sit. Ian was satisfied and quiet, apparently enjoying the new sights for him to absorb.

"How did you acquire the milking machine?"

Charlotte stared at Brian with incredulity. "It was the Brownfield's unit and part of the land that we acquired last October. They sold their cows before the transfer to us. So, I moved it over here a couple of weeks ago. We need to find a way to acquire more and a proper system. So, what is this serious topic you need to tell me about?"

"Directly to the point."

"You don't usually suggest the bench," she said, patting the wood beside her. "And, I do not know how much time we have with Ian."

"Two weeks ago, I was in London *with me mates*," he said with colloquial British emphasis, "to toss a few pints at Shepherd's Pub. I had a short chat with Jonathan and Jeremy that was interrupted by a woman who was rather forward. She surprised me . . . ."

"Who was this woman?" asked Charlotte, interrupting her husband.

"Mud greeted her as Lady Castlerosse. She said her given name was Doris."

Charlotte shook her head. "I don't know her, nor have I heard of her."

"Well, apparently she has quite a reputation. I was curious and I figured Mary might know; so, I called her. She told me she was Viscountess Doris Castlerosse, and Mary told me she was also known as the Mistress of Mayfair or Sex Queen of Mayfair."

"Why was she interested in you?"

"Precisely my question to her and to Mary. I gather from Mary's information that Lady Castlerosse wanted to add me to her trophy case."

"Did she?"

"Nope, but from her words, I suspect she is going to show up, again."

"Why are you telling me all this, Brian?"

"I thought you should know."

"Or, are you indirectly asking me for permission?"

"No, no, not at all. That thought did not enter my mind."

"Oh, come on, Brian. You are a virile, attractive, young man. She is undoubtedly an attractive woman. From what you've told me, she is doing all the work."

I need to change the direction of this conversation. "Mary also told me a rather interesting fact . . . well, I think it is a fact. Apparently, Lady Castlerosse is not the only such woman. She said Lady Edwina Mountbatten, wife of Lord Louis Mountbatten, is rather notorious as well."

Ian began to fidget and squeak.

"It is probably past his bedtime," Charlotte said. "We'd better get him inside and made ready for bed. But, before we go," she stopped and kissed Brian, at first with just a peck on the lips, but then she reached across with her hand to caress the back of his head and neck. Charlotte kissed her husband full on deeply. She pulled back just a few inches from his face. "Thank you for confiding in me, Brian. I truly appreciate your candor. I would like to talk more about this . . . perhaps tomorrow." Brian simply nodded his concurrence. "Now, let's get the baby to bed, and then I want you to make me a happy woman."

I know what that means. Brian stood, kissed Ian on the forehead, and wrapped his free arm around Charlotte's shoulders. They walked together back to the house in the dark. *I have no idea how she took all that, but at least I told her the truth. It is done.* Brian took a deep breath and exhaled slowly.

———

Monday, 13.April.1942
St Swithun's School
Alresford Road
Winchester, Hampshire, England
United Kingdom
14:20 hours

Charlotte's dark green 1936 Hillman Minx Magnificent Saloon automobile under her methodical, conservative, driving control carried them to Jacob's school ten minutes ahead of time. The vehicle was showing its years, however, between Charlotte's diligence and Horace Morgan's mechanical skills, the car was maintained in fine running form, along with her dark green, 1932 Bedford WSTB, stake side, flatbed, delivery truck the farm used for milk and cheese deliveries. The one insurmountable difficulty was fuel rationing that proved a constant challenge. Charlotte had to save two months' worth of petrol for the journey.

Jacob's instructions to Charlotte indicated they should check in with Headmaster Toby Michaels before speaking to his class at 2:30. Finding the headmaster's office took two separate queries from different students to reach the office. They were announced.

Charlotte made a striking companion in her conservative, medium blue dress with black stockings, to Brian in his freshly cleaned uniform with flight lieutenant sleeve stripes festooned with his medals and gold wings.

After mutual introductions, they sat in comfortable chairs across a low, small table. Michaels looked to Brian and said, "I hope you don't mind, sir, once Jacob told his mates that you were coming . . . word spread. It seems virtually the whole student body and staff wants to hear you . . . your story."

"I hadn't quite prepared for that, Mister Michaels."

"Will it be a problem?"

"I thought I would have a conversation with a dozen students or so. I have not prepared a presentation of any kind to a larger group—an assembly," Brian said and stood. Charlotte did not join him and reached out to grasp his hand, gently tugging him to sit back down. Brian looked into Charlotte's loving eyes as she glanced at the chair for him to sit. Brian did as his wife suggested.

"I appreciate your apprehension, Flight Lieutenant Drummond," Michaels said. "May I suggest you still have a conversation with the students, like . . . oh . . . like you, Jacob and a few of his mates are chatting around a campfire."

"Easier said than done, Mister Michaels." They sat there, staring at each other in silence.

"Mister Michaels," Charlotte offered, "my husband is an incredible fighter pilot, from what everyone tells me, but he is rather averse to crowds, prominence, and adoration." She paused, gathering her words. She looked into Brian's eyes for several seconds. "You can do this, Brian. Set aside your concerns, your worries . . . whatever it is that causes you to hesitate."

Brian stared into Charlotte's eyes. "I'm a bloody fighter pilot. I'm not a politician."

Michaels cleared his throat loudly, clearly uncomfortable with Brian's choice of words. "Well, then," he said, "there is no requirement for you to speak, Mister Drummond. I do believe Jacob thought you were excited to speak to him and his mates."

"I am. I always enjoy talking to Jacob."

"Well, then," Michaels continued, "just pretend you are talking only to him. He will be in the front row with your wife. Speak to them."

OK . . . OK . . . this is downright silly, now. I may not like doing this public speaking stuff, but I can do this. Let's do this and get it done, so we can go home. Brian stood. "Let's go. Jacob and his mates are waiting."

Headmaster Michaels smiled and stood. Charlotte smiled broadly with pride in her eyes as she stood and kissed Brian on the cheek. Michaels led them through numerous hallway turns, through double doors, and into a modest size, combination room that served as the school's gymnasium and assembly hall. Rows of folding chairs for 400 students and teachers were all full. The entire assembly stood, a clearly audible sound. A small dais with two steps and about 18 inches high had been installed along one long wall. Only a lectern stood on the platform and no chairs. Michaels gestured for Charlotte to join Jacob. Another open chair remained on the other side of Jacob from Charlotte. Michaels motioned for Brian to follow him on the stage and went directly to the lectern. Brian stood to the right and behind Headmaster Michaels. He held up his hands for everyone to sit and be quiet.

Michaels waited for silence. "Ladies and gentlemen, boys and girls, it is our privilege and honor to have Flight Lieutenant Brian Arthur Drummond of our Royal Air Force here to speak to us this afternoon. Flight Lieutenant Drummond is the third-highest scoring ace in the whole of Fighter Command, and he is an American volunteer from Wichita, Kansas, on the Great Plains of the United States of America. I'm sure you remember your geography lessons." The assembly laughed almost like a tension relief. "He joined the Royal Air Force in June of 1939 before the war began. Mister Drummond flew through the whole of the Battle of Britain a year and a half ago. He is currently assigned as a section leader with Number Seven One Squadron—the American Eagle Squadron. He is the holder of the Military Cross and two Distinguish Flying Crosses for heroism in aerial combat, and King George the Sixth awarded him the Commander of the British Empire medal. With Mister Drummond today is his wife Mrs. Charlotte Drummond, the owner of Standing Oak Farm and

Jacob's employer . . . when he is not in school." Again, the assembly laughed. "Please welcome, Flight Lieutenant Drummond." The assembly stood and applauded, and a few cheered loudly.

Brian replaced Headmaster Michaels at the lectern. He held up both hands, palms out. The gathering gradually quieted and sat.

"Thank you very much for the warm and generous welcome. Your classmate Jacob Holden asked me to speak to his mates. I didn't realize he has so many mates." The assembly laughed and some applauded. "I graduated from high school, the equivalent of your A-Levels, just after I turned 18 years of age, and could legally make such decisions. I left home and traveled by train to Windsor, Ontario, Canada, to join the Royal Air Force."

"Why?" one of the male students shouted.

The audience laughed. "Well, that is a very good question. The man who taught me to fly, Mister Malcolm Bainbridge, also helped me to appreciate the importance of service and the darkness of German nationalism. Mister Bainbridge joined and flew in combat with the Royal Flying Corps in the Great War. I just knew I had to serve in this war like Mister Bainbridge did in the last war."

"We read the newspaper," some anonymous person shouted, sparking enthusiastic cheers and applause.

I am not going to respond to that. Brian calmly and dispassionately waited for the audience to quiet.

"Bless you, sir," another anonymous person mumbled louder than he expected.

"Thank you. I truly appreciate your gratitude. I would be less than candid if I did not recognize and praise Reginald Mitchell. I have been privileged to fly his masterpiece—the Supermarine Spitfire, built just down the road in Woolston."

"What is that like?" asked another anonymous young man.

"With all due respect to my wife, Charlotte," *that sounded so strange. How did I ever deserve her?* "It is quite like heaven, I must say. It is better than your wildest imagination or dreams. It is arguably the finest flying machine ever built." Again, applause punctuated Brian's words. "I feel I am a part of England." Many of the young folks cheered. "I am still an American . . . ," Brian paused, ". . . volunteer. But . . . my history is now part of England's history." More applause interrupted this talk. "I'm a pretty ordinary bloke, just trying to do the best I can. I don't have much else to say, so do you have any more questions?"

"You don't sound like us," another anonymous young man observed and sparked a wave of laughter.

Brian chuckled a little. "No . . . no, I don't. I am an American volunteer pilot from Kansas."

A young boy in the middle of the left grouping raised his hand. Brian pointed to the boy. "What was it like to meet the King?" he asked.

"It was a distinct honor. He is a very kind and generous man." Total silence filled the room. "Much more so than we Americans remember King George the Third." Laughter and cheers mixed with clapping of hands and whistles. "Thank you. Please excuse a little colonial humor." Even more cheers and clapping filled the hall with warmth.

"How well does Jacob milk Mrs. Palm . . . er . . . Drummond's cows?" asked another boy without standing or raising his hand. Laughter and cheers filled the room.

Brian laughed hard, bent over, and held up his right hand. "Sorry . . . sorry," he said, while still doubled over with laughter, and before he stood and regained his stoic composure. "He milks Mrs. Drummond's cows very well, truth be told."

"Have we won the war?"

Brian's jovial expression vanished in an instant. "What makes you think that?" Brian said sternly. No answer or response came. "No, the war is long from being over. We are fighting every day. The Royal Air Force is fighting every day to defeat the Germans. And now, the Soviet Union Red Army and my countrymen are in the fight to beat the Germans." Brian paused to survey the audience. Everyone stared back at Brian with distant don't-care expressions. "My apologies for being so . . . so . . . forthright. We have not yet beaten the Germans . . . but, we will." The applause was delayed but grew with enthusiasm. Brian waited for another question and looked around the gathering.

"They are not bombing London anymore," another boy offered.

"No, they are not, thank goodness. The German invasion of Russia has demanded their nearly full attention," Brian responded.

"Are you afraid?" a girl asked.

"Afraid of what?"

"Afraid of the Germans, afraid of dying?" persisted the girl.

Brian stared at the girl for several long seconds, and then glanced at Charlotte, who saw his glance and smiled back at him. Connecting with the girl's anticipatory eyes, he answered, "Yes. I am afraid every time we fight the Germans in the air. They are good . . . very good . . . but they are not better than us." He paused to allow his words to sink in. No one spoke or reacted to his words. "When I fly on a mission, I focus and concentrate on the task at hand. My head is on a swivel, watching for those bloody bastards." Numerous audible gasps were heard. "Oh, sorry. Please excuse the profanity. I respect the

Germans. They are very skilled. We cannot let our guard down for an instant when we are up there," Brian said and pointed to the ceiling.

A boy roughly Jacob's age stood up in the middle of the left group. "If you are always looking for Germans, how do you fly the aeroplane?"

Brian laughed softly and put his right index finger to his lips. "Very good question! I suppose the only way to answer is, when you fly, the aircraft becomes part of your body, part of who you are, like a leg or arm. You do not think about how to move your hand when you are writing a letter, or eating your evening meal, or brushing your teeth in the morning. Your hand just does what you want it to do. That exact same process is how you fly a fighter airplane. You feel the machine—the sound, the vibration, everything. You don't think about what to do. You just make the aircraft do what you need it to do like it was your hand."

"Wow!" someone exclaimed.

"God bless you," a female teacher said loudly from the back row.

Brian nodded his head in recognition a few times. "Thank you for that, and may God bless all of us who cherish freedom."

Toby Michaels stood and walked to the podium that Brian readily turned over to the headmaster. He glanced over his shoulder to Brian, and then said, "Thank you very much, Flight Lieutenant Drummond." Michaels glanced over his shoulder again and nodded his head to Brian. General applause came from the assembly. A few students stood and continued to applaud. Other students joined until all the students and teachers were standing.

Mister Michaels dismissed the students to return to class. Brian and Toby stepped down from the dais. Jacob stepped forward to shake Brian's hand, and then Charlotte kissed his cheek. They said their good-byes. Headmaster Michaels gave Jacob permission to leave a little early, and go with Charlotte and Brian. By the time they reached Standing Oak Farm, it would be milking time. Horace and Lionel would most likely have begun the process.

—

Chapter 8

The wicked flee when no man pursueth:
But, the righteous are bold as a lion.

-- Proverbs 28:1

Wednesday, 15.April.1942
Office of the Chief of Staff
Munitions Building
Constitution Avenue & 20ᵗʰ Street, Northwest
Washington, District of Columbia
United States of America
14:00 hours

The gold leaf lettering on the frosted glass portion of the door was simple and direct.

Chief of Staff
General G.C. Marshall

Now Major General Eisenhower was not sure whether this requested meeting in the general's office was intended to be solo or with others. The subject of the meeting had been simply stated as plans. Ike brought his plans briefing binder, just in case anyone wanted details of their active plans.

The office staff filled the anteroom and was a beehive of activity. Aide-de-Camp to the Chief of Staff Lieutenant Colonel James Snyder announced Eisenhower's arrival and ushered him into Marshall's spacious office. Marshall gestured toward the four, comfortable, leather chairs facing each other across a low, round, coffee table, and then joined his chief of war plans, sitting directly across from Eisenhower.

Marshall jumped directly to the point of the meeting. "Well, Ike, the president asked me to personally convey his gratitude for your briefing a couple of weeks ago. As a consequence, you will leave for England in a couple of weeks with a set of specific tasks. One, you should bring the prime minister and the British chiefs of staff up to speed on the planning we have done so far. Two, you will need to dig deeper into British plans than we were able to do during the ARCADIA Conference. Three, make the rounds of the three-service headquarters to build your contact list. Four, and this one is personal and private, the president favors you to be the joint commander for GYMNAST as you planned it and briefed the president. He is concerned about British acceptance and support. You cannot even hint at this potential, but the point is, you need to sell yourself to the British. The president wants them to accept and fully support you to lead the combined joint operations staff for GYMNAST. Fifth, and this one is personal to me, I want the British to indirectly recognize that the leadership of the Army is quite concerned about Stalin's demand for a western front. The Soviets are a long way from having the upper hand against the Germans on the battlefield. We are eager to take the fight directly to the Germans, as much to assist the Red Army as to contribute to the early defeat of Germany. I want the British to feel, if not think, we are a little wild, and perhaps even reckless. However, we are fully committed to the president's strategic direction and Churchill's soft underbelly approach. It will be a fine line to walk, Ike. Are you OK so far?"

"Yes sir."

"The secretary and I both agree with the president's opinion that you have the requisite combined staff skills to make this partnership with the British work for both our purposes. Yet, the president is not willing to impose his will on Churchill or the British joint chief. You've got the necessary interpersonal traits to make this work. Now is the time for you to step up and prove it. You must convince Churchill. The ideal would be to make your appointment his idea. Hopefully, Brooke, Pound, and Portal will enthusiastically support the prime minister and you. The job is yours, but only if the British support your selection. This is not going to be easy, Ike. You've met all the players, but you need to connect with their lieutenants."

"I understand, sir. How much time do I have?"

"A couple of weeks, no more than a month. While you are there, I want you to conduct a subtle, as in it is not obvious or official, assessment of the ETO." As is common in military usage, the use of initials or acronyms became prevalent contractions; in this instance, ETO signified the European Theater of Operations.

"Yes sir. I can handle that."

"Events are moving fast, Ike. We need to get past this administrative and social stuff, so we can commit to the execution of GYMNAST. I know Mamie will not be happy with all this, but she is a trooper."

"That she is, sir. She will be fine. She knows what lays ahead."

"Excellent. You have a few days to get your affairs in order. You need to leave as soon as you are able. When you are ready, call Hap Arnold's office. He has aircraft heading to England virtually every day now. He will get you on the first available aircraft."

"It shall be done, sir."

"By the way, congratulations on your promotion. Well deserved, I must say."

"Thank you, sir." Eisenhower saluted and departed.

—

Saturday, 18.April.1942
USS Hornet
35° 18' North – 154° 54' East
08:20 hours

A Japanese picket patrol ship had spotted Task Force 16 at 07:38 that morning. The ship had been sunk by the USS *Nashville* main battery fire, but not before the picket sent a warning alert message to Japanese fleet headquarters. The element of surprise had been lost. They made the prompt and difficult decision to proceed with the mission. The bombers launched earlier than planned and meant the aircraft would be dreadfully thin on fuel even with their installed special extended range fuel tanks.

Colonel Doolittle completed the final pre-flight briefing along with the revised launch range and mission modifications. The aircrews all grabbed their flight gear and headed to the flight deck and their waiting aircraft. Jimmy watched the other crews mount up. He was the last of his crew to ascend the short ladder into the aircraft, closed and latched the access door, and made his way to the aircraft commander's seat on the left side of the cockpit.

The entire task force, including both aircraft carriers, had turned into the wind. The deck of the *Hornet* was pitching more than desired in heavy seas; however, they had to achieve a minimum wind speed over the flight deck. Their choices had dwindled to two after the morning engagement of the Japanese picket ship, and the second one was just not acceptable. After a quick consultation and recalculating their range options, Colonel Doolittle favored and recommended they take the risk and the only offensive action remaining. Admirals Halsey and Fletcher concurred.

Lieutenant Colonel Doolittle leaned over to his co-pilot, First Lieutenant Richard Eugene 'Dick' Cole, as they strapped into their cockpit seats. "Hey, Dick, they handed me this as I left the island," Doolittle said and passed the single piece of paper to his co-pilot.

```
TO COL DOOLITTLE AND HIS GALLANT COMMAND
GOOD LUCK AND GOD BLESS YOU
HALSEY
```

Cole returned the paper to Doolittle and nodded his head. "We're going to need all the luck we can find."

Doolittle placed the message in his leather jacket pocket. "Let's get the bird spun up. We need to get on the way as quickly as possible."

"Is this pitching deck going to affect our ability to get these big birds off this postage stamp?"

"We'll have to make sure it does not. We'll try to time our liftoff with a rising deck."

The crew reported the completion of the pre-takeoff checks. Both engines were running at fast idle. Temperatures and pressures had increased, and stabilized.

Colonel Doolittle said, "Here we go," as he pushed the throttles forward. It was all or nothing. There were no provisions for return to the carrier. At full power with the launch officers go gesture, Doolittle released the aircraft's brakes. The bomber lurched forward and accelerated across the pitching flight deck toward the bow. The aircraft bow began to sink as the aircraft left the flight deck, but it was flying. Doolittle gingerly coaxed the aircraft to accelerate, as Dick cleaned up the machine for cruise-climb. Once satisfied the bomber was flying comfortably, Jimmy began a shallow, climbing, left turn. As soon as he could, Doolittle looked over his left shoulder. He counted four other aircraft in the air and following his general path. Leveling at 1,500 feet altitude, Jimmy throttled back to hold the aircraft maximum endurance speed and watched each additional aircraft launch from the churning carrier. All 16 bombers were airborne. Jimmy kept a circling pattern around the *Hornet*.

When the 16th aircraft began his rendezvous turn to join up, Admiral Halsey ordered the task force to reverse course and head west, back to Pearl Harbor at the best practical speed give the sea state.

Doolittle switched to the intercom. "Harry, give me a heading to the Split."

Several seconds later, Navigator First Lieutenant Harry Potter replied, "Two five eight will do it, Skipper."

The Split was the point over the ocean about 200 miles from landfall in Homeland Japan, the squadron would separate into four attack groups and turn to separate headings: 10 aircraft to Tokyo, two bombers each to Yokohama and Nagoya, and one aircraft each to Kobe and Yokosuka.

The raiders hit their assigned targets and other targets of opportunity, and then set their respective courses across Honshu to China with one crew diverting to the Soviet Union due to inadequate fuel to make China. The premature launch farther out to sea than planned, due to the task force's detection by the Japanese picket patrol ship, altered their recovery plans. They did the best they could.

Of the 16 aircraft and 80 airmen who launched from the *Hornet*, none of the aircraft would be salvageable at the end of the mission; 69 of the men survived and evaded capture or execution at the hands of the Japanese forces;

most of those were repatriated or served with U.S. forces in China. Only three of their number were killed in action. The Japanese Army forces in China captured eight raiders and summarily executed three of those.

Four months after the raid, President Roosevelt awarded newly promoted Brigadier General Doolittle the Medal of Honor "for conspicuous leadership above the call of duty, involving personal valor and intrepidity at an extreme hazard to life while commanding the First Special Aviation Project in a bombing raid of Tokyo, Japan, on April 18th, 1942."

———

Saturday, 18.April.1942
Oval Office
The White House
Washington, District of Columbia
United States of America
09:30 hours

The president's informal war council—Secretary of State Hull, Secretary of War Stimson, and Secretary of the Navy Knox—arrived on time. As was often the case, Harry Hopkins sat in a straight back chair behind the president's left shoulder.

"Before we get started," Roosevelt began, "what is the status of the Special Mission?"

Stimson looked at Knox to answer. "Halsey's Task Force 16, including the embarked Special Mission aircraft, is under strict radio silence until the ships return to Hawaiian territorial waters. We will not know for several days. If they launched this morning Japan time in accordance with the plan, they have completed their bombing attacks and should be landing in China. It's approaching midnight in China. If they made the designated landing areas, we might get our first evidentiary radio transmissions tomorrow. We won't get Halsey's action report for another few days."

"So, we still pray they were successful and safe."

"Yes, Mister President. We will inform you and the council as soon as indications come in," Knox responded.

"Very well. Now, Cordell, what have you heard from Ambassador Leahy?"

"He has acknowledged our recall order effective on the 1st of May. He also confirmed the information we had from other sources that the Nazi-sympathizer Pierre Laval is now prime minister of Vichy, France. Our *charge d'affaire* Pinkney Tuck in Vichy is ready to assume responsibility for the embassy and consular affairs in the territory, as soon as the recall is effective. As we discussed, we issued a terse message to Marshal Petain to convey our displeasure with the Laval appointment and the implications to Allied relations. The British Foreign Office indicated they sent a similar message as well."

"Excellent. When will Bill Leahy arrive back here?"

"As you recall, Mister President, Ambassador Leahy's wife Louise is in the hospital for urgent surgery that cannot wait for their return to the States. I suspect she will not be able to travel for a few weeks. We intend to get them on a PanAm Clipper flying boat as soon as Louise can fly safely. My best guess from what Bill has shared with me is probably mid to late May."

"Please keep me posted on his status and return. I ask for your counsel on a move I would like to make." Roosevelt paused, just in case any of them might object. "When Bill returns, I would like to make Bill Leahy chief of staff to the commander-in-chief. What do you think?" None of the three cabinet secretaries jumped to answer. "Oh, come now, surely you have an opinion. I do believe each of you knows Bill. I envision this new position as a direct conduit for you inside the West Wing and especially the Oval Office."

Henry Stimson was the first to respond. "Yes, Mister President, we know Bill Leahy. He is an exceptional officer of high accomplishment, but he is retired from active duty and working in Cordell's State Department. At first blush, I am not too keen for yet another layer of bureaucracy between us, Mister President."

Roosevelt smiled with that particular devious grin. "I can certainly appreciate that concern, Henry. I do not want and will not look kindly upon any filter between us. We have gone to war with this council. I am quite pleased with your service and expect for us to be together until this thing is done. Frank, Cordell, what are your views?"

"Largely the same as Henry's view," Knox answered. "I feel we need to allow our chiefs to weigh in since such an appointment would likely affect them as well. I suspect Admiral King will look favorably upon such a position and appointment, as long as it does not interfere with or restrict access to you and your office."

"That is certainly not my intent."

"Would you recall him to active duty?" Frank asked.

"Yes . . . at his previous rank," the president responded. Knox nodded his head.

"Can we have a few days to consider this issue?" asked the secretary of state.

"Yes, of course. I want to meet with Bill as soon as he returns to Washington. You have that amount of time. I want to dispense with this as soon as possible."

The secretaries reluctantly accepted the task. They adjourned and departed.

———

Friday, 24.April.1942
Savoy Hotel
Strand, London, England
United Kingdom
13:30 hours

The luncheon, quasi-news conference had been set up by a loose coalition of American correspondents and journalists. The early afternoon engagement had been requested for many months, if not years, if Churchill had felt an urge to know the fact. They graciously allowed him to eat his meal in comparative peace. There was no apparent host or moderator, so the prime minister stood and took the podium next to his table.

"I do believe everyone has finished or nearly finished their lovely meal, and I have limited time to share with you today. I am grateful for your persistence and recognize your consistent request for such a news conference masked as a luncheon." Laughter punctuated Churchill's opening remarks. "I must apologize that it has taken me so long to avail myself of your gracious invitation. Rather than allow me to babble on, I stand ready to address your queries of The King's prime minister."

The first man stood. "Eric Sevareid—CBS News, how is the war going?"

Churchill smiled. "Skip the appetizer . . . straight for the dessert." Hearty laughter filled the modest size meeting room, and several clinked their water glasses. "War is never pleasant or orderly. As you well know, the Allied cause has suffered egregious losses the ultimate of which were the devastation of the American Pacific Fleet at Pearl Harbor and the loss of the Singapore garrison. We have had successes that I am not yet able to discuss in public, but those successes will become known. We will face many more losses ahead before we can see the banners of victory waving above our streets."

Several men stood. Churchill pointed to a distinguished young reporter in a better than average business suit. "Walter Cronkite—United Press. Mister Prime Minister, if I may, two related questions. One, are the Soviets going to stop the Germans, and two, how do you intend to satisfy Premier Stalin's demand for a second, western front?"

"That is a mouthful," Churchill responded with a light-hearted tone that invoked more chuckles. "Please allow me some latitude here, since I must be careful with my words. The Red Army stopped the Germans from taking Moscow last winter. Leningrad continues to hold and suffer against the German siege. We have worked hard and sacrificed to supplement the war supplies going to Russia. The Soviets are mobilizing and deploying their forces to take the offensive. While I cannot say they have stopped the German advances, the Soviets are in a noticeably stronger position than they were six months ago. We continue to support the Russians in their efforts to stop the Germans, which may come this year. Now, to your second question, I am certain you recognize that I would be foolish in the extreme if I disclosed our operational plans, as like it or not, press reports are read by our enemies as well. Let it suffice to say, we, and here I mean President Roosevelt and myself . . . we are keenly aware of the need for a second, western front, as you phrased it. We are gathering our forces and completing our plans. As I have assured Marshal Stalin, we fully intend to engage the enemy to relieve some of the weight of the German assault as soon as possible. Specifics beyond that shall remain outside your reach and justifiably so."

An older man jumped and did not wait for recognition, "Dan De Luce with the Associated Press. When are you going to take the fight to the Germans?"

"Well, that is a rather loaded question, verging upon an opinion. Nonetheless, I shall respect the query portion of your rhetorical question. Perhaps you have missed the fact that we have been fighting the Germans in the Atlantic Ocean since the war began nearly three years ago. Nary a day goes by that sailors pay a dreadful price in that running battle. The struggle with German aggression that persists in threatening our sustenance continues in grave, earnest manner every single day. The Royal Navy would not take kindly to the implication that they are not fighting the Germans. Further, as your colleagues have referred to them, The Few fought an epic aerial battle two years ago that halted the looming German invasion in its tracks. So, to characterize . . ."

"Excuse me, Prime Minister, I should have been more precise. When will France and the other occupied countries be liberated from German occupation?"

Churchill stared at the man as if he was deciding whether to answer the reporter. He chose a succinct response. "When it is time."

"Yes, but . . . ." De Luce stopped when the prime minister raised his left hand, palm out.

The prime minister gestured to another standing journalist. The others sat.

"Ernie Pyle with Scripps-Howard Newspapers. There seems to be a rapidly growing number of Americans in England. How have the British people adjusted to such an influx of patriots from your former colony?"

This time Churchill laughed deeply and placed his right index finger to his lips as he regained his composure. "Another interesting turn on the words. As you gentlemen are probably aware, my mother was an American citizen. I am half American, and I certainly feel a kindred spirit with you. To answer your question, I believe they are adjusting to the burdens quite nicely and will continue to do so. The British people know why American troops are showing up on our sacred islands. They welcome these arrivals because these men represent the path to victory. That said, I urge you," he said, looking directly at Pyle, "I urge each of you to talk to the people you meet. Ask them that question and allow them to answer. I believe you will find the veracity of my reply."

Churchill called upon a handsome young man.

"Charles Collingwood—CBS."

"My," interrupted the prime minister, "I see Bill Shirer in this gathering, fresh from his escape from Nawzee Germany. How many of you so-called Murrow's Boys are there here?"

Laughter again filled the room. Collingwood answered, "I do not know, sir. I have not counted, but more than a few."

"Quite so, apparently," Churchill said and waved his hand for him to continue.

"When will the war be over?" Collingwood asked and did not sit.

"You must have me confused with Nostradamus." More laughter. "I do not predict the future. I am incapable of forecasting what is to come. The only aspect of the future that I am certain of is our inevitable victory."

"Why?"

Churchill held a stern, near scowling expression. "The righteousness of good over evil," the prime minister answered, and then smiled modestly.

"But, how long will this go on—months, years, decades, how long?" Collingwood pressed.

"Young man, we are immersed in a desperate struggle against the consummate evil of our time. We did not ask for this fight. We did everything humanly possible, short of prostrating ourselves before the altar of military might to avoid this fight. But, that vile corporal was hell-bent upon world domination. We have no choice but to defeat fascism if freedom is to survive. So, my young reporter, it will take however long it will take to defeat the Nawzees to return the occupied lands to their citizens. Further, by this fight, we have inherited the additional burden of reforming German culture and society to avoid this tragedy again. We failed to care for the German people after the Great War. We must not falter or fail that task in the second conflagration of a generation." Silence occupied the space. Churchill stood resolute. John Martin, standing in the back, tapped his wristwatch. After a dozen seconds, the prime minister said, "Now, gentlemen, if you will excuse me, I have a war to fight. Thank you ever so much for your invitation to luncheon. We must do this again sometime." Churchill grabbed his bowler hat and departed the meeting room, as the gathering of skeptical journalists applauded.

—

Sunday, 10.May.1942
RAF Debden
Saffron Walden, Essex, England
United Kingdom
12:05 hours

The CIRCUS 42-52 mission had gone smoothly despite some ugly grey flak bursts among the bomber formation, and two, German fighter engagements. All of the bombers delivered their payloads and returned to England. It was the first mission for No.207 Squadron after transitioning to the Avro Lancaster, four-engine, heavy bombers. The mission's target had been the railway switching yards at Amiens. Brian had marveled at the view from their perch position 1,000 feet above the bombers with 'A' Flight on the left or east side of the bomber squadron, and 'B' Flight on the other side. From their altitude, he could see the railway bridge they had indirectly destroyed two months prior, although it was difficult to tell whether the river bridge had been restored to functional status. The bombs hit their intended target, and the railway-switching yard was soon obscured by the smoke and dust of the exploded bombs.

The fighter squadron landed singly in trail on runway 28. Brian appreciated the consistency of a hard-surface runway and tolerance to weather in dramatic contrast to the grass landing areas they were accustomed to using at the various airfields they had used since Brian began flying with the Royal Air Force three years ago.

The pilots taxied in trail to their respective parking spots. Brian shut down the Merlin engine with all normal indications.

As he usually did, Corporal Jacobs stood on the left-wing root forward of the open canopy and access door. "How did she do, Hunter?" asked Jacobs.

"Like the gorgeous lady she is . . . perfect. No squawks." Brian looked at Aircraftman Stanley George Easton from Blackburn, who served as the crew's armorer. "I've got some cannon shells remaining, Stan," Brian shouted to Easton. "I should be empty on bullets."

"We'll check the guns and load you back up with your standard load."

"Thanks, Stan."

Brian stood up and stepped out of the cockpit and jumped off the wing. He waited for Henry Jacobs to perform his post-flight checks and to jump down off the wing as well. Stan Easton came around the left-wing and joined them. Leading Aircraftman Stephen Hawking from Sheffield, the crew's rigger or mechanic came around the tail.

"Good mission, sir?" Hawking asked.

"Near perfect, I would say. We got the bombers in. They hit their target from what I could tell. And, more importantly, we got them out safely. No losses for them or us."

"No hits?" asked Hawking.

Brian knew he meant on the aircraft in case they had to make swift repairs. "I didn't notice any taps on the bad guys. She took no hits either."

"We'll give her a good look-see," said Jacobs, "and get her loaded back up in short order."

"Thanks, guys. Well done, as always."

"Thank you, sir," the three men said in unison.

Brian walked slowly toward the Dispersal Hut and looked over his shoulder several times to admire the curves of his Spitfire fighter airplane that he genuinely loved. He was the last of the pilots to enter the Dispersal Hut. The cacophony of excitement surprised Brian.

Salt Morton held up a folded copy of the *Daily Telegraph*. "We bombed Tokyo, Hunter," shouted Salt.

"Who's we?" asked Brian.

"The Army Air Forces," Salt shouted. "Sixteen B-25 Mitchell medium bombers took off the deck of the USS *Hornet* and dropped their bomb loads on five Japanese cities, including Tokyo."

"Hard to do much damage with so few bombers," Brian mumbled.

"Something's better than nothing," responded Salt.

"Yeah, don't try to wet blanket this news," contributed Sloppy Butterfield, looking directly at Brian.

"That is not my intention," replied Brian. "It is great news. After what they did at Pearl Harbor, it is a small token of what is to come for the Japanese." Brian gestured for the newspaper. Salt handed the paper to Hunter. Brian sat down in his usual corner chair and read the newspaper article. "Wow!" he exclaimed several times as he read the words. "Pretty damn bold. They apparently surprised the hell out of the Japanese, since the article says they encountered little to no opposition on the raid, certainly not like our bombers face on the Continent."

Several of the others continued to cheer, applause and shout expressions of bravado. It was the most enthusiastic celebratory expression among a group of pilots since he joined the RAF. Tug Meares had to remind the pilots they had their mission debriefings to complete.

Once they had completed their obligations, the Dispersal Hut activity returned to what they might call normal. Green Section gathered on either side of Hunter in the corner.

"Why do you think they did such a limited raid?" Dusty asked.

"Who knows, but my guess is, President Roosevelt wanted to make a statement to the Japanese and the world."

"He did that," commented Frog.

"Yeah," added Dusty. "Why not more?"

"What, more bombers, more raids, what do you want more of in this?"

"All of the above."

"Again, my guess is, they don't have the carriers and aircraft to risk. They also lost the element of surprise, now that the Doolittle Raiders have done it."

"True," said Dusty. "But, so is taking the fight to the enemy."

"Don't you feel the urge to join them?" Frog asked.

"The Doolittle Raiders had no fighter escort," responded Dusty.

"We have our hands full here with the Germans," Brian added. He leaned his chair back against the wall and closed his eyes. "Let's keep focused on the task at hand," he mumbled.

—

Tuesday, 12.May.1942
Cabinet Room
The White House
Washington, District of Columbia
United States of America
10:15 hours

"Before we turn to the agenda," President Roosevelt announced, "how are your new offices?" he asked, looking at Secretary Stimson and General Marshall.

"We just moved our offices across the river, and we are not yet settled in; however, the new building will be a dramatic improvement over the Munitions Building." The Pentagon was still under construction and would be so for another year, but the 3rd Floor, E Ring offices on the River and Mall Entrances were completed first. "The building should be completed by the middle of next year, and everyone moved over to the Pentagon shortly thereafter."

"The services are growing faster than we can build," added General Marshal, "so, I suspect we will need to retain the Munitions and Navy buildings on the Mall for our overflow."

"That should be acceptable to all."

"We thank you for your support in getting this new headquarters building approved," Stimson said.

"I am honored to be of service, and I am pleased that you like your new offices. Now, to our business."

"Excuse me, Mister President," Stimson said. Roosevelt nodded. "Please allow me to introduce our new deputy chief of staff for intelligence General Strong."

Major General George Veazey Strong, USA [USMA 1904], assumed his position as DCS G-2 just one week earlier. Previously, Strong had been Commanding General, VIII Corps, at Fort Sam Houston, San Antonio, Texas.

"Welcome to the party," the president said.

"Thank you, Mister President," Strong responded.

"I also asked for General Donovan to join us for this discussion. I have been informed that the Soviets initiated a broad counter-offensive against the Germans south of Kharkov this morning. We have been deeply concerned about the viability and sustainability of the Red Army for a host of reasons, not least of which are their capacity to absorb, protect and utilize Lend-Lease supplies we are diverting from England to Northwest Russia, and perhaps more importantly, the ability to occupy significantly large numbers of German combat units. The answers to those issues will seriously affect our assessment and approach to ROUNDUP, SLEDGEHAMMER, or even GYMNAST."

Everyone looked at General Strong sitting next to General Marshall. "You are well informed, Mister President. The Soviets took the offensive before the Germans could complete their preparations for their own spring offensive, after surviving the winter. We are watching the situation. So far, the Soviets appear to have caught the Germans with their pants down. This is the first major offensive initiated by the Red Army since the German invasion began last year. We hold an optimistic view that the Soviets may have turned the corner from the devastating losses of last year. The winter helped the Soviets regain their footing."

"I sure hope so," Roosevelt commented. "However, this is just the beginning."

"Quite so, Mister President," added General Marshall. "General Timoshenko did a masterful job during the winter to stop and push back the Germans south of Kharkov. He is a very capable officer." Marshall looked to his left at General Strong. "Give us a general summary of the orders of battle for both sides at Kharkov."

"By the numbers, the Soviets have deployed a significantly greater force for this offensive. They exceed the Germans in virtually every category—nearly three-quarters of a million men for this offensive alone."

"The numbers are staggering, to say the least—the number of armed men fighting over a vast terrain."

"Yes sir. The numbers are huge."

"While we are encouraged by the Soviets committing such a large force and taking the offensive before the Germans," Marshall said, "it will likely be several weeks before we can measure the results."

"General Donovan, your assessment, please," Roosevelt requested.

Bill Donovan leaned forward, placing his elbows on his knees. "The COI agrees with the G-2's summary. We are also encouraged. However, I strongly urge caution. Timoshenko is facing the German 6th Army under the command of General Paulus, who is somewhat of an unknown to us from a combat command perspective. The Germans maintain considerably sharp teeth. This is not going to be an easy fight."

"If I understand everything, you are collectively suggesting we hold the *status quo* until we obtain a clearer view of the Soviet offensive."

"I do believe that accurately states things, Mister President," Secretary Stimson said.

Roosevelt nodded his head in consent rather than concurrence. "I must gauge the balance between Stalin's pressure for us to deploy a comparable force to create a western front and our judicial use of scarce resources while we build-up our capacity."

"I do believe we all appreciate the relevance of that issue. To that end, we have dispatched General Eisenhower to England to solidify a consensus on our European strategy."

"I look forward to hearing his assessment. Is he aware of this latest information of the Kharkov offensive?" asked the president.

"I doubt it, Mister President," answered General Marshall. "I will ensure that he is as soon as possible."

"Very well. I am eager to make a demonstrative action to help Stalin without unnecessarily exposing us to greater losses. I am quite mindful of the fall of Corregidor and the surrender of General Wainwright, along with the remainder of our forces in the Philippines. The Navy tallies the Battle of Coral Sea as a victory, since they stopped the Japanese southward probe toward Australia, again; but it was very costly, losing the *Lexington* and other warships."

"We have had some setbacks, Mister President," Donovan interjected. "But, judging from the reaction we have seen inside Japan, the Doolittle Raid was wildly successful."

"And, also very costly. None of the aircraft were salvageable, and we are still working to recover our surviving aircrews."

"True, Mister President; however, the Doolittle squadron accomplished your objective of taking the fight to the Japanese, and that fact is reflected in the Japanese Home Island reaction," Donovan added.

"There is that. I do not want to be overly cautious. War requires sacrifice, but we must be prudent with the sacrifice we ask of our citizens. We walk a very fine line, while we mobilize our industrial capacity. Nonetheless, I believe I have made my point. Thank you for bringing me up to date. Please keep me posted."

Stimson understood the implicit meaning. The meeting was over. The others joined the secretary of war, and they departed the Oval Office.

———

Thursday, 14.May.1942
Station HYPO
Administration Building, Naval Station Pearl Harbor
Russell Avenue and Port Royal Street
Pearl City, Honolulu County, Oahu, Hawaiian Islands
Territory of the United States of America
10:00 hours

The small group of Pacific Fleet intelligence leaders gathered in the concrete and steel-reinforced, secure basement facility of the headquarters building—the home of the radio intercept and deciphering station. The austere furnishings of the small conference room reflected the functional configuration of the facility.

Officer-in-Charge Station HYPO Lieutenant Commander Joseph John 'Joe' Rochefort, USN, requested and set up the meeting with his immediate supervisor Commander Edwin Thomas 'Ed' Layton, USN [USNA 1924], who had been the combat intelligence officer for the U.S. Pacific Fleet for nearly a year and a half. With the two senior intelligence officers was Senior Chief Petty Officer Bradley Robertson, head of the Japan desk for Station HYPO.

"Take it away, Chief," Rochefort stated after the door was closed, and the three men were seated.

Robertson had a small stack of papers in from of him but did not refer to the pages. "We have been collecting a growing amount of traffic under MAGIC," the American code word for decryptions of the Japanese Purple naval coded messages, "that refer to a pending action they call Operation MI and a primary target they call AF. The decoded messages suggest whatever this operation is, it is big; perhaps, not quite to the scale of last December, but on that order of magnitude."

"We received a couple of recent separate messages through ONI," Office of Naval Intelligence (N-2) in Washington, DC, "that report increased activity at several main ports and anchorages on Honshu."

"We are convinced, especially from similarities to the activity of November and December, that something big is approaching the execution phase."

"Yeah, but where? What is their objective, or perhaps objectives, like December?" Layton asked.

"We have looked for those clues," answered Rochefort. "We have found none so far."

"Then, it could be anywhere."

"Exactly."

"The Japanese have solidified their occupation of the Philippines, Malaya, Indochina, with pressure on Burma, and continue to expand their holdings in China," Layton observed like he was thinking aloud. "They have carried out several bombing raids on Australia, which must be considered a prime target. The Dutch East Indies has only limited occupation, so the consolidation of those islands has to be another target. Last December, they failed to take Midway but did subdue Wake Island. The fact that Midway remains in our hands may be a little too close for their comfort. If they have designs on finishing off Oahu, they would need Midway. And, as we are reminded constantly, the West Coast is seen as a target, at least in the minds of the DC folks."

"Perhaps we can plant a few seeds to at least eliminate a few potential targets," suggested Rochefort.

"How so?"

"Well, we need a simple unclassified statement regarding one of the potential targets that the Japanese would surely hear, and hopefully think it was routine administrative traffic."

"Such as?"

"What if we send a coded message to Midway instructing them to send a routine communication in the clear, like their water supplies are running low—something innocuous and not particularly important. They might see it as a small but relevant item of intelligence. Such a transmission poses no risk to the Midway defenses, but might provide an association regarding the objective of MI."

"What about the other potential targets? We do not have much time since they are rapidly approaching the execution phase for whatever it is they are planning."

"The other locations are not isolated like Midway. Anything that would be significant militarily would not be transmitted in the clear. Further, their choice of MI as their mission designation within their secure communications may simply be shorthand for Midway Island. The best I can say is, let's try this one. It costs us nothing, and if they take the bait, we will know as well as we can probably ever know that it is Midway. On the side of caution, they might well ignore the information."

Layton considered the risks and benefits as he stared at that spot on the wall map of the Pacific Ocean. "OK. Let's do it. We might get lucky."

Rochefort looked at Chief Robertson. "Can you handle it, Chief?"

"Sure. Just to make sure of what you want, we are going to send a message in operational code to Midway command instructing them to send an uncoded, clear text, simple communication to headquarters Pacific Fleet that they are running short of water and request resupply."

Layton nodded. Rochefort answered, "You got it."

"Very well. I'll get it on the wire within the hour."

"Now we pray," Commander Layton said as he stood to leave.

———

Wednesday, 20.May.1942
Office of the Commander-in-Chief
Administration Building, Naval Station Pearl Harbor
Russell Avenue and Port Royal Street
Pearl City, Honolulu County, Oahu, Hawaiian Islands
Territory of the United States of America
15:20 hours

"**W**hat is so urgent, Ed," protested the commander-in-chief.

Admiral Chester William Nimitz, USN [USNA 1905], had been selected by President Roosevelt 10 days after the Pearl Harbor attack to replace Admiral Stark as commander-in-chief U.S. Pacific Fleet and promoted him over his peers to full admiral effective on the 31st of December. He never held the rank of vice admiral. Six weeks earlier, the American joint chiefs of staff (JCS) divided the Pacific Ocean into Southwest Pacific Area under General MacArthur and covering the Dutch East Indies, South China Sea and the Philippines, and the remainder of the Pacific was designated Pacific Ocean Areas, and Nimitz was given command of all Allied forces in his area of responsibility.

Commander Ed Layton, along with Lieutenant Commander Joe Rochefort, entered and closed the door to the admiral's third-floor, corner office overlooking the primary American naval station in the Pacific Ocean area. The smoke was gone, but the damage from the Japanese attack was still being cleared and remained quite visible from the admiral's windows.

"We just decoded this message just a few minutes ago," Layton said, as he handed the red-striped border folder to Nimitz.

The admiral took the proffered folder and removed the single page of red-striped border paper.

———

TOP SECRET - MAGIC

```
TOP SECRET
DATE 19420521 0719 HOME
FROM SUPREME COMMANDER TOKYO
TO COMBINED FLEET OPERATION MI
AF SHORT ON WATER SUPPLIES
TOP SECRET
```

DECIPHERED: HYPO 210235Z MAY 42

TOP SECRET - MAGIC

Nimitz looked up and across his busy desk at his intelligence chief, as if to say what the hell is this drivel.

"Sorry sir. You're missing a few steps in between," Layton said.

Nimitz placed the message back in its folder, closed the cover, and leaned back in his plush leather chair.

"As you know, we have been struggling with identifying the objective for the pending Japanese Operation MI and their primary objective known as AF. A week ago, Commander Rochefort and I agreed to a simple seed bait message that might give us a clue. That routine unclassified administrative message was sent from Midway Island stating they were short of water."

"I did not know Midway was short of water."

"They are not, sir. We asked Midway command to send the message knowing the Japanese would pick it up."

The light went on, and Nimitz smiled broadly. "So, this message," he said, tapping the closed folder, "indicates that their Operation MI AF objective is a large-scale attack on Midway Island."

"Yes sir. Precisely!"

"I'll be damned. Ingenious. And, you and Joe dreamed up this little trick?"

"Joe did, sir. It was entirely his idea. We didn't bother you or the staff with our action, because it was such a long shot. We got extraordinarily lucky."

"Better lucky than good, as the aviators like to say. If I recall the prior discussions of our intelligence, you believe the attack date is on or about the 4th of June, and you believe this message," again, tapping the closed folder, "establishes the location of that attack is Midway Island."

"Yes sir, exactly."

"If my memory serves me, you last determined their order of battle for Operation MI to include four of their fleet carriers and two battleships."

"Your memory is accurate, sir."

"We've only got three functional carriers in the whole of the Pacific."

"Yes sir, but we know where they will be and when. They do not. We have seen nothing in MAGIC to even remotely suggest they might be suspicious of compromise."

"So, this is going to be an all-in gamble. And, my boldest carrier admiral is ill."

"Ill?"

"Yeah. Halsey is due back to Pearl on the 26th, and he has a bad case of shingles. He will be hospitalized as soon as we can get him there, and he will likely be incapacitated for four to six weeks, so the doctors tell me."

"Oh, dear. It is outside our wheelhouse, admiral, but who can replace him?"

"Halsey is one of a kind. I will not assign a replacement until I can talk to him on the 26th, but I will probably have Ray Spruance assume command of Halsey's Task Force 16, with Jack Fletcher in command of Task Force 17 aboard *Yorktown*."

"They are both very capable leaders," Layton observed.

"Yes, they are, but we are betting the ranch on this one, and we have very little margin for error. Keep a very close eye on this, fellas. I will need you to prepare a non-MAGIC intelligence briefing for Spruance and Fletcher, to give them the best we have. They will need all the help we can give them since they will have the whole of our available carrier strike capacity and going against a significantly larger enemy force."

"Yes sir. We understand the situation. We will be ready when you need us, and we shall remain at utmost vigilance."

"Thank you, both. Please convey my sincerest, genuine gratitude to your teams. Bravo Zulu. Well done."

The two intelligence officers thanked their commander-in-chief and departed the office.

———

Chapter 9

A desperate disease requires a dangerous remedy.

-- Guy Fawkes

Wednesday, 27.May.1942
Cabinet War Rooms
New Public Offices
Whitehall, London, England
United Kingdom
16:30 hours

The combined War Cabinet and Defense Committee, along with the secretariat and military support staff, gathered in the underground conference room to hear the initial report of the results of Operation ANTHROPOID. By invitation, the minister of economic warfare, and the SOE director of operations and training, as the operative supervisors for the mission, were the featured guests.

Roundell Cecil Palmer, 3rd Earl of Selborne, succeeded Hugh Dalton as minister of economic warfare in the ministerial adjustments made in the aftermath of the Singapore catastrophe in February. Brigadier Gubbins sat to the left with Lord Selborne at a green felt topped table across the mouth of the U-shaped conference room table.

War Cabinet Secretary Sir Edward Bridges opened the meeting. "This session is convened to hear the initial preliminary report of the Special Operations Executive regarding recent activities. Lord Selborne, you have the floor."

"Before we hear Lord Selborne's report," interjected Prime Minister Churchill, "I would like to note this is Lord Selborne's inaugural War Cabinet briefing for on-going operations, since assuming his duties as minister of economic warfare. I would also like to welcome Brigadier Gubbins again." Both men nodded their acknowledgment. "That said, as Sir Edward stated, Lord Selborne, you have the floor."

"Thank you, Prime Minister. In the form of background for a common basis, I remind the ministers that Operation ANTHROPOID was created last fall by SOE in the weeks after Reinhard Heydrich assumed his additional duties as deputy protector of Bohemia and Moravia. While Heydrich was titled as the deputy to Konstantin Baron von Neurath, there was no doubt whatsoever that Heydrich was chartered by Himmler, and quite likely Hitler himself, to be the *in situ* authority in Czechoslovakia. The assignment of Heydrich to this role was a clear statement of dissatisfaction with the perceived softness of Neurath with respect to the implementation of Nazi territorial policies. Local intelligence sources quickly established Heydrich's arrogance and his apparent sense of invulnerability in his daily routine in and around Prague. With the cooperation and contribution of the Czech government-in-exile here, we began formal planning and training of Czech-exile, SOE agents at Camp X in Canada. Upon the presentation of the intelligence and plan, the joint decision by the prime minister and the president of the United States in December initiated deployment of the assault team. They inserted by parachute from a Halifax bomber that was embedded in a bombing raid formation. The objective of the mission was the assassination of Heydrich, as the most visible persona of Nazi oppression in Czechoslovakia.

"With that background, Operation ANTHROPOID was executed this morning at 10:30, as Heydrich's convertible Mercedes touring car passed the same tight bend in the roadway he traveled every morning, with the top down, weather permitting. Our agents made their escape and are believed to be making their way to one of the planned extraction points. Multiple independent sources indicated that Heydrich was injured in a car accident this morning and taken to a hospital. We believe his injuries are actually wounds sustained during the assault. There has been no mention of the attack. Police action began immediately as expected, and we suspect the search for our agents will grow rapidly in scope and intensity. We have no contact with our agents, as yet, but we remain hopeful to be able to debrief them on the details of the attack. We are also working through independent operatives to establish the details of Heydrich's injuries and, more importantly, his prognosis."

"So, we do not yet know if the operation was successful?" asked Churchill.

"No sir. That process may take several days or weeks to determine."

"Regardless of the outcome, we should anticipate reprisals by the Nawzees," the prime minister added.

Selborne looked to Gubbins to respond. "Yes sir. Regrettably, there is not much we can do to avoid that consequence. Based on past performance in such circumstances, we should anticipate a grossly disproportionate response to this action. If Heydrich eventually dies, we must expect the reprisals to be brutal."

"Our hearts go out to the Czech people who shall suffer this abuse," commented Attlee.

"I will ask the obvious question," said Churchill, "is there anything we can do to mitigate the abuse that is sure to come?"

"Win the war," responded Gubbins in almost a mumble.

Lord Selborne quickly jumped in. "We have considered that very question as we were finalizing our planning. We could not forewarn the populace for obvious security reasons. We also consulted the Czech government-in-exile in London. Their official position in simplistic terms is, we must weather the storm."

"Not very reassuring to Czech citizens who will bear the brunt of the Nazis wrath," Ernie Bevin said.

"No, no, it is not," Selborne responded. "If we ultimately achieve Heydrich's death, perhaps history will record this action as a worthy endeavor."

"We can only pray," said Churchill, "for the Czechs who stand in harm's way, and for our agents. Pray tell me the measures we are taking to recover these gallant men."

"The plan established several escape routes that were rehearsed multiple times during their preparation. It will likely be several days before they can reach one of the planned signal points that would give us our first indication of their status and progress. The three primary routes are north across Germany to the sea, west across Southern Germany to Vichy France, and south across Austria to the Adriatic. Their egress will likely take a month or more, since penetration so deep into Nazi-occupied Europe is not possible with our current resources."

"That sounds rather dicey at best," Eden commented.

"Yes, it does, but that is the best we could do to achieve the result."

"Let us not forget, gentlemen," said Churchill, "this was Lord Selborne's initial preliminary report. I am certain the earl will return as our knowledge of ANTHROPOID clarifies and solidifies. Does anyone have any additional questions for Lord Selborne or Brigadier Gubbins?" The prime minister scanned the room. "Thank you for your report," he said, looking directly at Selborne and Gubbins. "You are welcome to remain, if you wish, or depart if you have more pressing business. The next topic is our discussions with the Soviet foreign minister."

Selborne and Gubbins whispered, and then Lord Selborne said, "We would like to listen if that is acceptable."

"By all means," Churchill responded, and then the prime minister glanced at Sir Edward.

"The next item on the agenda is Foreign Minister Eden's report on negotiations with Soviet Foreign Minister Molotov and Ambassador Maisky," Sir Edward announced and looked to his left at Eden.

Minister of Foreign Affairs Vyacheslav Mikhailovich Molotov succeeded Maxim Maximovich Litvinov in May 1939. Litvinov was now the Soviet ambassador to the United States.

Ivan Mikhailovich Maisky had been the Soviet Union's ambassador to the Court of St. James since 1932.

Anthony Eden began, "We concluded our discussion with the ambassador and foreign minister yesterday. As a consequence, we signed the negotiated Twenty-Year Mutual Assistance Agreement between our countries that provides for defense support."

"Is that anything like the agreement they had with the Germans in August 1939?" facetiously asked Oliver Lyttelton.

Minister of State for Production Oliver Lyttelton, DSO, MC, PC, had been elevated to the War Cabinet in the February ministerial shuffle, succeeding Lord Beaverbrook. He was a member of Parliament for Aldershot, a member of the Conservative Party in good standing, and had held the ministerial position as president of the Board of Trade, since his initial election to Parliament in the by-election of November 1940, to replace Roundell Palmer when he was elevated to the peerage.

"The two agreements are not the same thing," Eden responded. "The Germans sought to nullify the potential interference of the Soviets for the invasion of Poland, and to that end, sought to placate the Russians by ceding Polish territory east of the River Bug to them as an enticement for their agreement and cooperation. Our agreement simply formalizes the support we have been providing since the invasion last year. We are only recognizing what we have been doing for almost a year now. Further, this agreement was long overdue, especially since the United States extended Lend-Lease support to the Soviet Union in September of last year, three months after the invasion." No one spoke.

The prime minister said, "After Anthony concluded the formal negotiations with Molotov, I had the opportunity for a private chat with the foreign minister. As expected, Molotov made an impassioned plea for our western front to help them with the Germans. By the way, those are my words, not his. He was very careful to make not even an implication that the Soviets need our help with anything, including the Germans. Their pride gets in the way. Nonetheless, I chose not to share any details of our operational planning and preparations. I did try to assure him that cooperation with his country is a primary concern in our efforts. We recognize and acknowledge the need. To put a fine point on it, I told him that the last thing the Red Army needs is for us to fail on the western front objective. They need a successful western front. I felt compelled to remind him we are not facing a land campaign. We must transport massive, sufficient forces and supplies across bodies of water. These will be amphibious campaigns, and the logistics demands are far greater. We have landing craft to build. He listened and, I believe, he understood the challenges for us.

"Beyond the extant agreement and the still perilous position of the Soviet Union, I wanted to feel him out how Premier Stalin and the Soviet Union saw the post-war world? He was somewhat and understandably surprised by my query. Perhaps that surprise aided him in giving me a candid view. I shall summarize my perception of his words in one simple word—beware. While he said nothing directly, I believe they expect the territory they take back from the Germans to be the spoils of war. We discussed elections, but elections have little meaning for a state that regulates the outcome. I mentioned the notion of Allied supervision, and he dismissed it as an unnecessary complication.

"While I laud Foreign Minister Eden's exceptional effort to attain the understanding we now have in this mutual assistance agreement, I want to inform the War Cabinet and Defense Committee of this word of caution. A factor in our calculus for victory must now include linking up with the Red Army as far east as humanly possible. It is my private opinion that the Soviets intend to impose their governance system and values on the peoples they liberate. Post-war Eastern Europe is going to be a problem in many ways. To be blunt, I am afraid the Nawzees have uncaged the beast."

"Surely you jest," Ernie Bevin protested.

"I wish I was. I am only offering this august council my perception of what lays ahead."

"And, Winston, we must pay attention, whether we appreciate the message or the messenger," Clement Attlee pronounced. "You made similar observations in the 1930s, and we did not listen."

Bevin flashed a scowl at the leader of his party but did not speak.

"Are you now suggesting you are in favor of ROUNDUP?" Lyttelton asked.

"The question is not whether we favor ROUNDUP. The objective of ROUNDUP or something like it is inevitable, so yes, ROUNDUP must happen. The issue is when. Attempting to press ROUNDUP this year is verging upon suicidal. Crossing the Channel by the summer weather window next year seems beyond reach at this moment, but we must reserve judgment. The key to such an operation will be the rapidity of buildup for sufficient forces and the accumulation of appropriate amphibious landing support craft. The Americans have been pressing rather hard for ROUNDUP this year. I cannot see the path to that objective. BOLERO will give us a good metric of when sufficient forces can be gathered up."

Silence blanketed the room for a handful of seconds, and then Deputy Prime Minister and Dominions Secretary Clement Attlee spoke. "What do you want us to take away from this conversation?"

Churchill smiled and glanced at Attlee, sitting to his right. "Only to be cautious, wary, and methodical in our dealings with the Soviets. The fact remains; we need the Russians in this fight. We need them to grind down the Nawzees. We have no choice but to support the Soviets, but I fear the Russians will become the enemy once the Germans are vanquished. I do not wish it to be so, but that is my impression at the moment."

"You can't be serious, Winston," exclaimed Ernie Bevin.

Churchill did not look at Bevin. "No more so than I was ten years ago when I sounded the clarion call regarding Hitler's ascension to power in Germany. I am not asking for or recommending any action—only awareness. The burden for the present rests upon the foreign minister and me. Any of you may well be our successors—better informed than ignorant." Prime Minister Churchill paused. No one chose to extend the discussion. Winston looked at Sir Edward and nodded.

"That completes our agenda for this meeting," announced the cabinet secretary. "We are adjourned."

The Blond Beast, also known as the Butcher of Prague, died seven days later from sepsis—infection from the wounds he received in the attack. Mission accomplished.

The SS tracked down the two Czech-national, SOE agents—Jozef Gabčík and Jan Kubiš—hold up in the Church of St. Cyril and St. Methodius on Resslova Street in Prague. They died in a four-hour gun battle on the 18th of June.

The SS reprisals over the weeks following the assassination were brutal beyond imagination. The bishop and priests of St. Cyril Church were arrested, interrogated, tortured, and executed. The villages of Lidice and Ležáky were obliterated—every single dwelling and building razed to the ground. The Gestapo, SD, and SS arrested, and interrogated roughly 13,000 Czech citizens, with an estimated 5,000 men, women, and children executed or sent to the extermination camps for liquidation. Some women were raped and relegated to pressed brothel service. Children with the "correct" anatomical features were sent to "Germanization" programs. The Czech people paid a terrible price for the assassination, but the operation also served notice—the Allies were coming.

—

Friday, 5.June.1942
Oval Office
The White House
Washington, District of Columbia
United States of America
14:30 hours

Secretary of the Navy Frank Knox preceded Chief of Naval Operations Admiral Ernie King into the president's official office. Newly installed Chief of Staff to the Commander-in-Chief Admiral Bill Leahy stood beside the president's desk dressed again in his summer khaki working uniform. President Roosevelt wheeled himself to his usual spot. Knox and King took the couch to the president's right, while Leahy stood opposite them. They waited until the president was in position, and then they sat.

"I hear you have news from the Pacific. I eagerly await your report," Roosevelt said after their cordialities were exchanged.

"While we are a long way from declaring victory," began Knox, "the initial reports are quite encouraging. It is dawn the next day at the longitude of Midway. The Japanese naval assault force appears to be withdrawing, which would fulfill our primary objective—the defense of Midway Atoll. The results of the naval battle north of the island are a little sketchy at the moment. On the debit side of the ledger, the *Yorktown* was hit hard, multiple times during the battle. She is in serious trouble, but as of a few hours ago, she is still afloat. Other ships are damaged, but none as badly as *Yorktown*. We have also lost an as yet uncounted number of aircraft and pilots from the garrison on Midway as well as the combined task force. Admiral Spruance is still collecting the details, and that process will likely take days and weeks. On the positive side, we sank two Japanese fleet carriers yesterday, and the other two are essentially dead in the water, but still afloat so far."

"Is the battle over?" asked the president.

Admiral King answered, "Beyond the damage control activities, Admiral Spruance will use today to finish off any remaining enemy ships he can find. Submarines on both sides remain a threat. Our forces are aggressively searching for the remainder of the strike force and trying to find the assault force."

"So, it is not over."

"No, Mister President, we cannot declare the battle to be concluded, just yet," King responded.

"Also," added Knox, "we now know their companion Operation AL is an invasion of the Aleutian Islands. They hit Attu and Kiska Islands at the western end of the Aleutian chain. As a historic note, this is the first foreign invasion of U.S. territory since the War of 1812."

"What are we doing about that?"

"At the moment, there is not much we can do," Secretary Knox responded. Dealing with the Japanese invasion will have to come as we build up our forces. We are simply too thin and vulnerable at present."

"Is there a threat to the remainder of Alaska?"

"We do not believe so," Knox answered. "The AL force is too light for expanded operations, and no reinforcements have been detected."

"Turning back to MI, is it possible the Japanese will regroup and make another attempt?"

"Not likely, Mister President," Admiral King said. "There is always the potential; however, the loss of half and potentially all of their carriers would leave his task force extraordinarily vulnerable, especially since they now know we have three fleet carriers in the vicinity. Our guess is they are withdrawing at best available speed to preserve their remaining forces."

"I would like to engage the press to the fullest. The Doolittle Raid announcement a couple of weeks ago was a big boost for our people. We need to take advantage of this success in the constant challenge to build and sustain the morale of our people. With Doolittle, we had to wait until the raiders were safely recovered. We do not have the same problem here."

"Quite understandable, Mister President," said Knox. "However, we need to be careful not to celebrate too soon."

"Yes, yes, quite so. How about this, let's release the preliminary results in part with the proviso that we are still assessing the results, and expect to know more in the coming days and weeks."

Knox looked at King and then Leahy. Both admirals nodded their consent. "That should be acceptable. I would only caution against overzealous disclosure."

"I think we can live with that," Roosevelt said, and then looked at Leahy. "Bill, would you kindly coordinate with Bill Donovan's War Information Service to get the word out. This appears to be our first victory against any of our enemies. We need the people to know."

"Yes sir. I will see to it," Leahy responded.

"I will send a personal note to Admirals Nimitz, Spruance and Fletcher for their accomplishment. I trust there will be appropriate awards for those involved in this victory."

"From the sounds of it," said King, "there will be a list of awards from this action. Heroic is a word that is not unreasonable—to use a double negative appropriately."

"Thank you very much, gentlemen." The three men stood. Knox and King bade their *adieu*. Roosevelt gestured for Leahy to remain seated and waited for the door to close. "What did you think of all that, Bill?"

"I think we shall soon realize that the Battle of Midway was a far greater victory than we currently appreciate."

"That was my impression, as well. I must confess I felt a boyish glee, which I tried desperately to contain, that we finally bloodied their damnable nose. The Doolittle Raid was important, but it did very little toward winning the war. I suspect historians will look back on this naval battle as the inflection point at which the Imperial Japanese Navy was never the same or as formidable."

"I am not sure I can go that far, Mister President, but you may well be correct."

President Roosevelt nodded his head and wheeled himself back to his desk. The meeting was done, and the rest of the day's agenda awaited.

Once the tally could be completed, the magnitude of the U.S. victory came into clear focus. The limited combined forces of the U.S. military stopped the assault on Midway Atoll. All four of the deployed Japanese fleet carriers had been sunk, along with the loss of 250 naval aircraft and their experienced combat flight and maintenance crews. More than 3,000 Japanese naval personnel perished, and 37 were captured. The United States lost the *Yorktown* three days after the battle and the destroyer *Hammann*, along with 150 aircraft and 300 naval and land-based personnel killed-in-action and many more wounded. With the clarity of hindsight, the Battle of Midway was a decisive American victory in the Pacific Ocean Areas and proved to be the turning point in the war against Imperial Japan. Long, hard fights lay ahead before victory was achieved, but the process of reducing Japanese held territories had begun.

—

Monday, 8.June.1942
Pentagon Building
Arlington, Virginia
United States of America
08:30 hours

"**W**elcome back, Ike," General Marshal greeted Major General Eisenhower and gestured to the comfortable chairs in his new spacious office. "I trust your journey was without difficulty."

"A B-17 heavy bomber is certainly not the most luxurious mode of transportation, but it is effective. Both going and coming home were textbook transits with a few turbulent spots, but nothing dramatic."

"Excellent," the chief of staff said with noticeable eagerness to jump into the agenda. "So, tell me first your impressions of the ETO."

"To be blunt, I was not impressed with the organization, the staff efficiency, or the productivity of the ETO staff. They are definitely not ready to go to war."

"I am sorry to hear that . . . but that is my assessment as well." Marshal stared at Eisenhower. Neither man spoke. "Please give me your assessment of your coordination activities with our cousins."

"My impression is we are in general agreement. They are keenly aware of our collective need for the western front and the direct assault on the western flank of the Germans. BOLERO has begun in earnest. The British Home

Office has an excellent plan to quarter our troops. They are now and should remain ahead of our forward deployment schedule. So, for now, BOLERO gives us a good metric for our capacity. We are in broad agreement with the objectives and the broad plan agreed to. There is still considerable detail to be resolved, although we collectively agreed that we can get everything finalized by the September approval deadline with a late October, early November execution date. The British joint chiefs are agreed."

For the first time, Eisenhower noticed the stapled dozen pages on the table between them. Even upside down, the title was easily readable—"Directive for the Commanding General, European Theater of Operations."

Marshall glanced down at the same report, then tapped it with two fingers. "I've read your draft several times, Ike—excellent piece of work that shows me your grasp of the situation and the mission."

"Thank you, sir."

"I would say it is perfect, but that leaves little room for improvement. The secretary and the president have approved the directive and the OPD draft plan for GYMNAST. The president and prime minister have agreed as well. This is going to be your show, Ike. We all believe you are best suited to lead a joint, combined, assault force. That said, we have several gates to get through. First, you will depart for England and assume command of the ETO on or about the 24th of this month. Second, you will need to make good progress on fleshing out the GYMNAST plan with an eye to British officers to fill key staff positions. You should already have a good idea of whom you want."

"I do."

"Good. You can expect to present the plan to the combined joint chiefs in London by mid-August, with approval by the president and prime minister within a week or two after that. From that point, we, and here I mean all of the combined joint chiefs, expect you will be confirmed as the supreme commander of Allied Forces with the mission of executing Operation GYMNAST. Are you good with all that?"

"Yes sir. What of General Chaney?" asked Eisenhower.

"He will be transferred back to the States and given a training command. He is no longer your concern. On that note, whom do you want as your deputy?"

Without hesitation, Eisenhower answered, "Mark Clark."

Newly promoted Major General Mark Wayne Clark, USA [USMA 1917], had been friends with Dwight Eisenhower since their days at West Point. He was an accomplished and decorated infantry officer who served in combat during the Great War. Clark was currently the deputy chief of staff of Army Ground Forces and the youngest major general in the entire U.S. Army.

Eisenhower continued, "I would like him to serve as CG II Corps for the nucleus of the BOLERO forces. And, if it is not too much to ask, I would like to have 'Beetle' Smith as my chief of staff. He has unique staff skills to make all this joint operation approach work."

Brigadier General Walter Bedell 'Beetle' Smith, USA, had enlisted in the Indiana National Guard and commissioned from Officer Candidate School. He served on the Western Front during the Great War and was currently secretary to the Joint Chiefs of Staff.

Marshall smiled. "You don't want much, do you, Ike?" Eisenhower smiled in response. "We will make it happen. Beetle has done an exceptional job as our staff secretary in these turbulent times. I am sure you recognize the difficulty of making a combined military force work. There should be no doubt that GYMNAST will be your test, Ike. Make it work and you will be in the vanguard for the leadership of the much larger ROUNDUP class invasion of the Continent. If you are not aware, you should know that General Brooke has his eye on the larger prize, and to be candid, so do I. The invasion of France will be the premier combat command of our time. You will have competition, but this opportunity will be yours to lose."

"Yes sir. Understood."

"One last important observation here . . . Churchill takes a far more direct, hands-on, approach to political leadership than does President Roosevelt. The president will respond to performance. Churchill will take more cultivation to ensure his support. He will want to feel assured in his relationship with you, and as such, it will take more of your time to ensure he is on your side. There should be no doubt this will be a very demanding, difficult, and frustrating assignment, Ike, but you must know and believe the president, the secretary and I have faith in your ability to navigate the rocks and shoals."

"Thank you for that, sir. I hold no illusions. I will do my best to make this work."

"We know you will, Ike. Now, you have two weeks to finalize things with the staff here, organize your movement to London, and get Mark and Beetle on step with you. Please take some time for Mamie and your family. This is going to be a long, hard slog—mind your family."

"Yes sir. I will. We will get this done."

They concluded their meeting. Dwight Eisenhower was on his way and set on a course of prominence in history.

—

Friday, 12.June.1942
RAF Debden
Saffron Walden, Essex, England
United Kingdom
15:45 hours

The overcast had been with the pilots of No.71 Squadron since yesterday morning. The Meteorology Office forecast remained bleak for the next week. Many of the aerodromes were grass fields that the rain usually made unusable; this was one of those times. The hard-surface runways at Debden kept the squadron at Available status from dawn to dusk—nearly 17 hours, a week before the summer solstice.

Recognizing the unusual burden placed on the pilots, Tug Meares split the squadron with the two flights taking 10-hour shifts with a four-hour overlap at mid-day when they might face the greatest demand. Surprisingly, few complaints or protests could be heard among the pilots. They all seemed to understand the peculiar situation. Although Tug stayed at the Dispersal Hut from dawn to dusk, 'A' Flight had the afternoon shift on this Friday.

All three telephones on Corporal Harris's high desk had the same ring tone, so any call for any reason piqued the attention of the pilots. Each of the three telephones was identical except for color: red for operational, blue for administrative, and black for on-base. The distinctive ringing bells turned all heads to Harris.

"Group on blue, Skipper," Harris shouted.

A minute later, Tug appeared at his office door. "Group intends to launch a section to watch over a freighter departing the Thames Estuary. Hunter, you're up. Green Section has been moved to Readiness. Once the controller receives confirmation the ship is clearing the estuary and the anti-aircraft umbrella, he will launch you. The Met Office indicates broken low clouds off the coast, so you will have to decide whether your mission is better served above or below the clouds."

"Roger, Skipper," Brian replied. He checked to make sure he had all his flight equipment on his body or in hand. Dusty and Frog followed their leader. They sat in their usual chairs. Brian leaned his chair back against the wall.

"Before you go," said Frog, "this seems odd, sending us out to cover one ship."

Brian looked at his left wingman. "You know the answer, Frog."

"Just seems strange."

"Perhaps so, but with this weather, I imagine most of our fighter squadrons are grounded. This mission is up. We got the assignment, full stop." Brian closed his eyes. Frog Forcier respected the hint.

The squadron had flown nearly double their usual number of sorties just since yesterday, and the Meteorology Office forecast predicted a continuation of the extra workload.

The telephone ring abruptly brought Brian to instant upright alertness. With all heads turned to the squadron operations clerk, Corporal Harris raised the red phone handset to his right ear, then placed it back in the cradle two seconds later. "Launch Green Section."

The three Green Section pilots headed to their aircraft. Since it was a comparatively routine sortie, they walked rather than ran, and the ground crews had not started the engines.

"Nothing serious?" asked his crew chief.

"Nope."

"Babysit a worried ship?"

"So we are told," Hunter answered.

When Brian completed strapping in and connecting to his trusty steed, he looked to his left and received a thumb's up from both wingmen. He signaled for engine start. The whine of the starter, followed by the firing of the first couple of cylinders, produced a billow of smoke and unburnt fuel before the big Merlin quickly rose to fast idle. Brian noted his oil pressure rising normally. As he switched on his generator and electronic equipment, he uncaged his attitude gyro and aligned his heading indicator. Engine oil and coolant temperatures were rising nicely. A light drizzle began to fall. Brian closed his canopy. The tower cleared them to taxi to runway 28 for takeoff with a light and slight crosswind.

They took off in trail. Once airborne and cleaned up, Brian made a slow turn to the left and picked up a heading of 135° for their rendezvous with their assigned charge. Hunter throttled back to stay below the low cloud ceiling. Dusty and Frog joined up off the wings of the XR-G Spitfire. Hunter signaled they would climb through the clouds, and his wingmen tightened up their formation position. The Meteorology Office had indicated the tops of the low overcast were at 4,000 feet, with broken and scattered layers above the overcast. The clouds were going to make the mission a little sportier.

Their cloud penetration was comparatively easy with moderate turbulence along with patches of heavier rain. They broke out above the overcast and validated the Meteorology Office data. Again, as forecast, the overcast began to break up a little over the mouth of the Thames Estuary and the North Sea. His wingmen spread out for better searching. When Hunter calculated they were over the rendezvous coordinates, Brian throttled back to maximum endurance and set up a shallow bank, wide orbit, as they scanned the spots of the sea they saw below the clouds. After two turns, they found nothing.

"Green Three, Green Leader, get below the clouds and find our charge."

"Wilco," responded Frog and rolled left into a dive through one of the holes in the clouds. The XR-J Spitfire disappeared under the clouds. The search took nearly ten minutes. "Tally ho, Green Leader. Objective positively identified."

"Roger, Green Three. Too many clouds. We're coming down to you. What is the ceiling and your altitude?"

"Ceiling at cherubs seven. I'm at cherubs three. Patches of drizzle. No serious weather."

"Roger, Green Three. Green Leader descending."

Dusty tucked in behind and below Hunter's right-wing. Brian turned to head east to ensure they were clear and penetrated the clouds. Both aircraft broke out underneath the overcast at just above 700 feet. He leveled off at 500 feet, spread Dusty for better search, and began to look for the ship and Frog. The process took just 20 seconds. They could not quite see Frog, but a single ship was northwest of them at about 8-10 miles in the obscuration of the light rain. Brian turned toward the ship and waited until he saw a single Spitfire fighter in a wide orbit around the ship. "Tally ho, Frog. Approaching from the southeast. About five miles and closing."

"Tally ho," Frog broadcast.

Hunter's hand signaled Dusty to take up an equidistant orbital spacing around the ship. They split and meshed with Frog in a one-mile radius orbit at 300 feet altitude around the larger than usual freighter, making good speed to the north. Like Frog, they throttled back to maximum endurance to extend their time protecting the ship.

Brian scanned the sky up through the occasional hole in the clouds above them. The mission was boring and dragged on for over an hour; however, on the plus side, they were flying. At the reduced power levels, Brian's engine temperatures and pressures remained comfortably in the normal range, even at low altitude.

Several times during their mission, Hunter popped up through a hole in the clouds to communicate with Debden Control. He informed Control that the clouds had required them to go low for the mission. The simple instruction was to let them know when they needed to return to base. They would mark the position of the ship with Hunter's Pipsqueak—the rudimentary transponder utilized to identify RAF fighters for the Chain Home radar operators. There was no other way to describe the mission, circling the ship was boring, even with the potential threat of enemy fighters converging upon them.

Brian's fuel gauge approached the threshold for their return to base. He chose to not broadcast a query for Dusty's and Frog's fuel level, but rather he flew to each wingman and hand signaled for their fuel level. Both of them had slightly less fuel than he did. It was bingo time. Brian signaled for Frog to join up, which he did smartly. Hunter crossed the circle, and Dusty did not need a signal to take his position off Hunter's right-wing. Brian saw another hole in the overcast layer ahead of the ship and decided that was a good enough reason for a stern-to-bow, high speed, low pass . . . for morale purposes, of course.

Once his section wingmen were in position, he signaled for increasing throttle. He slowly advanced his throttle and increased speed, allowing a margin for his wingmen to adjust. Brian extended astern of the ship to allow their speed to build, made a wide, low-g turn to keep their speed, and aligned for their pass down the starboard side of the ship at bridge height. As they approached the ship's stern, Brian noticed the name in big letters across the square stern— *Liverpool Lady. I'll be damned. That's the same ship that brought me to England in '39.* They roared past the ship, and noticed several crewmembers on deck and waving. Brian pulled back on his control spade, trading airspeed for altitude, as they zoomed up through the break in the clouds. Once above the cloud layer, Brian rolled the section to his calculated initial heading, leveled off just above the cloud tops, and throttled back slowly to the maximum range setting.

"Garter, Eagle Green Three calling."

"Eagle Green Three, Garter, go ahead."

"Roger, Garter. We are bingo."

"Roger, Eagle Green Three. We have your Pipsqueak. Eagle Blue is inbound to your position. You are cleared to Catpaw."

Hunter set the best initial heading for RAF Debden based on their estimated position. He would likely have to refine the heading once they observed the coastline. Ten minutes later, they passed three Spitfires in their typical 'V' formation, heading in the opposite direction, a couple of thousand feet higher and two miles off the left side. *That's Tug, Jimmy, and Hick taking station.* Neither section broadcast to the other.

Brian gradually increased altitude to give himself a better shot at the geographic location. The clouds had filled in and were solid once again. He requested a vector for Debden. Garter provided the proper heading from the radar return, indicated the cloud layer ceiling at 900 feet, and cleared them to penetrate. Brian began their descent. Dusty and Frog tightened up. Just after they entered the clouds, the rain started to mist and then spatter their canopies. They broke out at 900 feet, although the light rain made visibility only a couple of miles. Brian throttled back some more to maintain sufficient maneuvering margin, and yet give them a little more time for navigation. The rain continued to spatter on the windscreen and streak back, distorting his field of view. He identified the village of Sudbury to the east-northeast of Debden at 18 miles. Brian adjusted their heading for what he thought was a good initial approach point, signaled for Dusty and Frog to configure for landing, and then take up a trail position. They would land in sequence on runway 28. The tower did not have them in sight on their initial call. They received the proper current altimeter setting, and the winds were light and nearly down the runway. When Brian estimated their position at five miles, he began a gradual descent, rechecked his landing gear was down and locked, and his flaps set for landing. At two miles, he saw the runway and adjusted for a good lineup. The tower reported him in sight and cleared them to land. The XR-G Spitfire touched down smoothly. Brian had plenty of runway, so he kept his tail up as long as he could to minimize his deceleration and give his two wingmen the most room he could.

As Brian taxied off the runway onto the taxiway, he looked back to see Dusty and Frog behind him with good separation and spacing between them. He kept his canopy closed to minimize the water intrusion to the cockpit. Only the three crew chiefs were on the ramp in full raingear to assist in shutting down the aircraft.

When Brian came to a full stop in his designated parking spot, Henry Jacobs blocked the wheels with chocks. As usual in rainy conditions, Henry did not get up on the wing and waited at the trailing edge of the left-wing tip, clear of the propwash. As the propeller stopped, he moved to the wing root. Brian completed his shutdown, unstrapped and disconnected. He quickly slid the canopy back, hopped out without opening the access door, and then closed the canopy behind him.

"No squawks, Henry," Brian shouted as he jumped off the trailing edge of the wing. "No shots . . . just fuel."

"Very well, sir."

Brian ran to the Dispersal Hut. It was odd to enter with no pilots and only Corporal Harris inside. Dusty and Frog were right behind him.

After they shut the door to keep the rain out, Corporal Harris said, "Welcome back, gentlemen."

"Skipper replaced us," Hunter said.

"Yes sir. Intel blokes just phoned to say they would come here for the debriefing."

"Excellent."

"Save us from getting wetter," added Frog.

"I have reported Green Section as Available in 30 Minutes, until your aircraft are reported ready."

"Thank you, Jimmy."

Green Section completed their routine, mission, intelligence debriefing in short order as there was not much to report. Blue Section would take the mission until nearly dusk, so Brian decided to lean back in his chair and take a nap.

———

Friday, 12.June.1942
Office of the Secretary of War
The Pentagon
Washington, District of Columbia
United States of America
14:30 hours

Bill Stephenson arrived last and just prior to his appointment. Also, in Henry Stimson's office at Bill's request were the Army chief of staff and the chief of military intelligence (G-2). Bill had also requested Wild Bill Donovan's attendance, but the COI was en route to England. Ned Buxton attended, as Donovan's deputy, representing the COI and soon to be announced the Office of Strategic Services (OSS).

"How is the new office in what will be a most impressive building, Mister Secretary?" asked Bill.

"An upgrade from the old office," Henry answered. "Welcome to what will eventually be the Pentagon building when it is finished . . . sometime next year, the experts tell me."

"Thank you, sir."

"You requested this meeting, Bill, so what brings you here?" Stimson asked.

"His Majesty's Government has tasked me to request and carry out this rather distasteful but necessary briefing, as delicately as possible with minimum essential involvement."

"That sounds rather ominous, Bill," Stimson noted. "I suggest you get directly to the point."

"Yes sir. Last fall, we became suspicious of the Germans seeming anticipation of every move we made in the desert of Cyrenaica. Time after time, Rommel was repeatedly and extraordinarily lucky, it seemed, too lucky to be coincidental. We opened a highly restricted investigation by a dedicated team of MI6 and MI5 officers into a possible mole with access to operational plans of General Wavell's Middle East Command. The team narrowed the potential sources down to a rather small number by February. The last several months of effort refined out suspicions, and we received confirmation last week. Rommel has had our detailed operational plans for months now."

"And, the winner is," General Marshall said with considerable sarcasm.

"We narrowed it down over the course of several months of vigorous investigation to your military attaché in Cairo," Bill said with quiet solemnity.

"That's pretty specific," Marshall said with an air of irritation in his voice.

"Who is he?" asked Stimson. "Who might that be?"

Marshall looked at Lee to respond. The G-2 cleared his throat. "Colonel Fellers, sir."

"That is our information," Stephenson added. "Colonel Bonner Frank Fellers."

"That's correct. Fellers was class of 1916 at West Point . . . Coastal Artillery Corps," added Lee.

"One and the same . . . that is our information as well. I must hasten to add, we do not believe he was or is an agent for the Germans. We believe he has been using a code the Germans have broken and passing operational information he was privy to in the normal conduct of his assignment. He was an unwitting player."

The room remained quiet for several minutes.

"You are sure?" asked Stimson.

Stephenson held Stimson's eyes and eventually nodded his head in the affirmative. "I am authorized to share physical evidence. Once we were certain, we carefully planned a false seed. Confirmation came . . . ," Stephenson looked around the room to confirm for himself that all of the attendees were MAGIC and ULTRA cleared for access, " . . . confirmation came from ULTRA a week ago last Thursday. So, yes, Mister Secretary, we are certain, absolutely certain."

"Then, he must be removed immediately," General Marshall pronounced.

Stephenson held up his hand to stop. "We are convinced Colonel Fellers is innocent. He does not deserve to be punished. Yes, he must be reassigned and hopefully in a positive transfer, so that we can mask the necessary code change. But, far more importantly, we are asking for the diplomatic code to be suspended without prejudice, to avoid alerting the Germans. We might consider using the compromised code for the dissemination of disinformation. Nonetheless, we must carry out these changes in a natural and normal manner to avoid German suspicions."

"Suspicions of what?" Stimson asked.

Stephenson smiled. "Suspicions that we are reading their mail," Bill spoke with firmness.

"Ah, yes, that would not be good," Stimson said. "Well then, perhaps to disconnect the two actions, Ned, can we depend upon you to coordinate with State to quietly terminate the use of the appropriate diplomatic code, and replace it with a more secure code, and make it look routine?" Buxton nodded his agreement. "General Marshall, I know we can depend upon you to find an appropriate advancement assignment for Fellers. We also need to replace him . . . with an appropriate senior officer, who is privately and carefully made aware of the cause of Fellers removal as a cautionary tale for his vigilance and care."

"That should work in fine fashion," Stephenson offered. "We have taken great care on our side to avoid any compromise of the U.S. military attaché in Cairo, or even our intimate relationship. We must plug the leak, but far more importantly, we must preserve our intelligence sources and our cooperation, so the fewer people who know of this action the better."

"Agreed," Stimson acknowledged.

"Excellent," Stephenson said. "His Majesty's Government sincerely appreciates your understanding and support in this matter. Now, if you have no further questions for me, I must be off. I depart this evening for England. Wild Bill got a head start on me, but I need to be in London."

"Yes, I am sure you do," Stimson said. "Wild Bill is briefing the prime minister and the government on the creation of the Office of Strategic Services. We expect the President to sign the order tomorrow."

"Thank you for seeing me on such short notice. I shall beg your forgiveness for running along so quickly. Thank goodness for the majestic flying boats. The journey across the Atlantic is far easier than by ship."

The men shook hands and departed.

———

Saturday, 13.June.1942
Shangri-La
Naval Support Facility Thurmont
Catoctin Mountains
Thurmont, Frederick County, Maryland
United States of America
16:15 hours

The mountain retreat had been completed in 1938 as a Works Progress Administration project for federal agents and their families. President Roosevelt commandeered the mountain lodge and its surroundings, as a presidential retreat in early 1942, and renamed the site for the fictional paradise in James Hilton's 1933 novel *Lost Horizon*.

"Welcome to Shangri-La, Edgar," Roosevelt said as FBI Director J. Edgar Hoover entered.

"Thank you, Mister President. The mountain air is delightful with its hint of pine, and the lodge is quite nice, I must say. This is my first time up here."

"Mine as well. Attorney General Biddle indicated you had an urgent matter to discuss."

"Yes sir. In the earlier hours of this morning, an unarmed Coast Guard patrolman came across a man wearing a German Navy sailor's uniform in the dunes at Amagansett, Long Island. The man accosted the Coast Guardsman, threatened him and tried to bribe him with $260 in valid U.S. currency. The Coast Guardsman feigned cooperation and immediately returned to his station. After a quick debriefing, an armed patrol returned to the site and located a substantial cache of explosives, primers, fuses, incendiary devices, grenades and several handguns. The Coast Guard immediately notified the New York field office. We have begun a massive search for the man based on the description from the Coast Guardsman."

"Was he alone?"

"Yes, at the encounter with the Coast Guardsman. The preliminary interrogation of the sailor by our field agents suggests the man is likely an ex-patriot American with a good New York accent. We believe he is not alone and is likely part of a larger team that landed from a submarine. The discovered cache is simply too big for one man. The Navy was immediately notified and an aircraft search for the submarine has begun over the waters off Long Island. Based on the detailed description provided by the Coast Guardsman, we expect to find the man before he can leave New York City, and if he is an ex-pat, we hope to turn him quickly."

"Anything else?"

"No sir. That is the extent of what we know, so far; but, our investigation is only hours old."

"Understood, Edgar. Please keep me posted on your progress."

"Will do, Mister President."

"Since I have you here, I will avail myself of your opinion. This morning I signed the executive order disbanding the COI and creating the Office of Strategic Services under General Donovan. I understand from Attorney General Biddle that you contributed to the draft and reviewed the final order. Is that correct?"

"Yes sir, that is correct."

Roosevelt handed Hoover a single piece of paper. "Here is your copy of the order."

Hoover quickly re-read the document.

```
                MILITARY ORDER
BY virtue of the authority vested in me as
President of the United States and as Commander
in Chief of the Army and Navy of the United
States, it is ordered as follows:
    1. The office of Coordinator of Information
established by Order of July 11, 1941,
```

exclusive of the foreign information activities
transferred to the Office of War Information
by Executive Order of June 13, 1942, shall
hereafter be known as the Office of Strategic
Services, and is hereby transferred to the
jurisdiction of the United States Joint Chiefs
of Staff.

2. The Office of Strategic Services shall
perform the following duties:

(a) Collect and analyze such strategic
information as may be required by the United
States Joint Chiefs of Staff.

(b) Plan and operate such special services
as may be directed by the United States Joint
Chiefs of Staff.

3. At the head of the Office of Strategic
Services shall be a Director of Strategic
Services who shall be appointed by the
President and who shall perform his duties
under the direction and supervision of the
United States Joint Chiefs of Staff.

4. William J. Donovan is hereby appointed
as Director of Strategic Services.

5. The Order of July 11, 1941, is hereby
revoked.

FRANKLIN D. ROOSEVELT
Commander-in-Chief
WHITE HOUSE,
June 13, 1942

"So, you are in agreement with and in support of the new OSS organization?"

"Yes sir, although not without reservations, as I expressed to the attorney general."

"General Biddle has informed me of your concerns. I trust you will make us aware of any evolving apprehension you may find as the OSS grows. I wanted to stress to you personally, Edgar, that we will watch carefully for germination of your concerns, but we need this strategic intelligence apparatus. I trust you will give General Donovan and the OSS your fullest support, and cooperation."

"Yes sir, Mister President," Hoover responded without enthusiasm.

President Roosevelt nodded his head, smiled, and then thanked Hoover for making the journey into the Maryland mountains.

Federal Bureau of Investigation Director J. Edgar Hoover departed Shangri-La and returned to Washington.

The German agent discovered on the beach in New York was George John Dasch. He was an illegal immigrant American with an odd history in the United States before the war and a German intelligence agent. After landing on the Long Island beach, he got cold feet and called the FBI New York field office from a payphone in Manhattan's Upper West Side, two days after his landing. The FBI arrested him and promptly turned him. Dasch convinced one of his fellow saboteurs, Ernst Peter Burger, to cooperate, as well. Between the two captured German agents, the FBI rounded up the Operation PASTORIUS agents that included Dasch, Burger and two others in New York, and a similar team of four men who landed on a beach just south of Jacksonville, Florida. The mission of the two teams was the sabotage of infrastructure targets like hydroelectric facilities, oil storage sites, bridges, railroad switching and repair yards, and river locks in several states. All eight had been captured within two weeks of landing. A military tribunal in Washington tried the saboteurs on espionage charges. All eight were convicted. Six were promptly executed. Dasch and Burger were spared, imprisoned, and deported to the American Sector of Occupied Germany after the war. Hitler rebuked the head of German military intelligence Admiral Canaris for the failed mission, and the Germans never attempted another sabotage mission inside the United States.

—

Tuesday, 16.June.1942
Cabinet War Rooms
New Public Offices
Whitehall, London, England
United Kingdom
15:00 hours

Sir Edward Bridges brought the meeting of the War Cabinet and Defense Committee to order, and then immediately turned to the prime minister to introduce their guests and the first order of business on the agenda.

"Thank you, Sir Edward," Churchill began. "We have with us this afternoon Office of Strategic Services Director Brigadier Bill Donovan along with our head of the Passport Control Office in New York City Bill Stephenson. I also invited Lord Selborne and Brigadier Gubbins, since the SOE is an essential part of Brigadier Donovan's charter for this visit, as well as Admiral Lord Mountbatten. Without further ado," he said and looked directly at Donovan, "Bill, you have the floor."

Donovan stood. "Thank you, Prime Minister, ministers and the joint chiefs of staff, for this opportunity to brief you regarding recent changes in the

U.S. government. President Roosevelt asked me to personally convey his best wishes to His Majesty's Government on behalf of the United States.

"As you know, since last year, I have had the honor of serving the president as Coordinator of Information. Three days ago, President Roosevelt signed an executive order disbanding the COI and creating the Office of Strategic Services, or OSS, and appointed me as the head of the new agency. The intelligence and special operations elements of the COI have been transferred, intact, to the OSS. The propaganda and information warfare functions established under the COI have been transferred to the newly created Office of War Information. For the most part, what was established under the COI is now the OSS. Further, while the COI reported to the president on a temporary basis, the OSS is under the operational control of the joint chiefs of staff to ensure proper coordination with and support of combat operations of the military services. The director of strategic services will continue, as the COI did, to report to the president on matters of strategic intelligence.

"I am grateful to see Lord Selborne, Brigadier Gubbins, and Lord Mountbatten in attendance, and I must express my gratitude for their contributions and cooperation during this transition. We have more work to accomplish over the next few days to ensure our separate and joint clandestine operations are synchronized, and to minimize and hopefully eliminate any conflict or overlap in our efforts. I am heartened by our achievements, so far, and eagerly anticipate our combined successes in support of the battlefield soon to come.

"That is my summary of this change. I will close my introductory remarks by saying that President Roosevelt asked me to reassure His Majesty's Government of his commitment to the purposes of the new Office of Strategic Services. Are there any questions I can answer?"

"Thank you, Director Donovan," Churchill said. "I am satisfied since I had the benefit of our private chat over the weekend. I invite the War Cabinet and the Defense Committee to ask what you wish to know."

"We wish you the best of luck," Clement Attlee stated. "We look forward to the accomplishments of our combined efforts."

"Thank you, Mister Attlee. I should add that while my focus on this trip is upon special operations," Donovan nodding to his British colleagues, "I must emphasize our continuing good communications with Brigadier Menzies and MI6 regarding intelligence matters. We have a long, arduous journey ahead, and I shall do my part to ensure we achieve victory together."

No one else chose to speak. Churchill thanked Donovan for his briefing, then excused the Defense Committee and their guests to allow the War Cabinet to continue on a private matter.

———

Chapter 10

Defeat in war is not the greatest of evils,
but when that defeat is inflicted by an unworthy enemy,
then the evil is doubled

-- Aeschines

Wednesday, 17.June.1942
54° 55' North – 5° 1' West
Loch Ryan Estuary
Stranraer, Dumfries and Galloway, Scotland
United Kingdom
23:15 hours

Prime Minister Churchill stepped from the motor launch onto a moored platform tied to the left sponson of the British Overseas Airways Corporation Boeing Model 314 flying boat with Berwick lettering on the nose—the same aircraft he had flown back to England after the ARCADIA conference. As he stepped through the port hatch, Winston was pleased to see the smiling face of Captain John Kelly-Rogers—the same pilot who flew the Berwick last January.

"Welcome aboard, Mister Churchill," the aircraft commander greeted his prominent passenger.

"Thank you, Captain."

"We are prepared for takeoff as soon as your party and baggage are aboard. We have a few patches of rough weather that we will try to avoid, and we expect to arrive on the Potomac River tomorrow in late afternoon."

"Excellent."

"Before I head up to the flight deck, I would like to personally thank you for limiting the size of your party. We have loaded full fuel and provisions to make this journey as quickly as possible." Churchill nodded his acknowledgment. "As on our previous flight, you are most welcome to join us on the flight deck and take your hand with the controls."

"Thank you, Captain. Once we are airborne, I shall avail myself of your finest cognac and retire for some sleep. Perhaps I shall enjoy your invitation after dawn tomorrow."

The prime minister chose a small entourage for this quick trip to the United States and the ARGONAUT Conference with President Roosevelt. Boarding the plane were Generals Brooke and Ismay, Churchill's personal physician Doctor Sir Charles McMoran Wilson, and Churchill's faithful bodyguard Detective-Inspector Walter Henry Thompson. John Martin had volunteered to be the prime minister's duty private secretary for this trip. The men with him were precautionary—just in case. By mutual agreement with

Franklin Roosevelt, the single purpose of this visit was a personal, private discussion between the two leaders on the atomic development program.

"Very well, sir. Now, if you will excuse me, we will get the engines started and be on our way."

"By all means. Thank you."

Kelly-Rogers went to the galley and ascended the spiral ladderway to the flight deck. The chief steward showed the prime minister to his compartment and quickly provided a healthy snifter of Hine cognac—his favorite.

Everyone was on board. The entry hatch was secured. The first of the four engines started smoothly, followed by the other engines. Within minutes, they were skimming across the dark water and bounced into the air.

—

Friday, 19.June.1942
Springwood Estate
4097 Albany Post Road
Hyde Park, Dutchess County, New York
United States of America
17:10 hours

Winston Churchill tightly gripped the passenger door handle of the president's unique, 1936, Navy blue, Ford Phaeton convertible automobile outfitted with hand controls for handicap operation. The prime minister tried desperately to contain his apprehension with Franklin Roosevelt's almost cavalier speeding along the narrow country roads from the railway station to the president's country estate.

The prime minister had been pushed back on his heels from the very first "hop in" from the president in the driver's seat of the bright blue car—the only automobile to pick him up at the railway station. He never really recovered from the shock.

The president rambled on about the beautiful late spring day, the wind of their passage, the quality of the country road, and even the eagles, hawks, and vultures soaring intermittently over their heads. Winston listened and barely heard a word with his attention focused on the roadway ahead of them, or at least what he could see of it. The president was in an ebullient jovial mood as he feverishly worked the hand controls at breakneck speed and babbled on about the delightful spring weather, exquisite earthy scents on the land that flashed past them, and the pleasures of life in general. Winston could not speak or take his eyes off the road, and the president seemed to be unaware of his passenger's apprehension.

Churchill finally found relief when Roosevelt slowed the car and turned off the paved road onto a comparatively wide gravel road. Blessedly, Franklin did not accelerate as he began a guide's narrative of the Springwood Estate, its sights, and its history.

The first order of business after showing Churchill to his room was lunch with Eleanor and Anna, their oldest child and only daughter. All four of Anna's younger brothers were in uniform in service to the nation. The conversation remained light and personal, dominated by the women, which Churchill thoroughly enjoyed. The one question he managed to inject to their table conversation dealt with the acquisition of Franklin's unique automobile. It was a sensitive topic, as Eleanor made it quite clear she was not supportive of her husband's use of that car. The Ford vehicle had been delivered to Franklin in April 1936 and remained a serious irritant between wife and husband.

All too soon, Franklin and Winston excused themselves, and retired to the president's personal and private study. Settled with a brandy and cigar for Winston and a cigarette in his signature holder for the president, Franklin began, "Please tell me candidly how you feel about the joint planning underway so far."

Churchill took a good swallow of his brandy. "To be as succinct as I can, which is not my nature, I will respond in two words—exceptionally well. There is much work to be completed before we have an executable plan, but planning is progressing well. At this point, I must compliment you, Franklin. I have been most impressed with General Eisenhower. He has quickly built the connections with our joint chiefs of staff and their planning departments. He works well with other forceful characters and has a palpable knack for connecting with colleagues, even those he disagrees with, in one topic or another. I have tested him, Franklin, and I must proclaim, he has a keen appreciation for a wide range of vital topics in military affairs."

"Well, I had not expected that, but thank you very much for your candid views. So, if I interpret your words properly, I do surmise you are in favor of General Eisenhower for joint command of GYMNAST."

"Yes," responded Churchill. "That was not my opinion before I had the opportunity for several in-depth discussions with General Eisenhower, but that is my opinion today."

"I think that can be arranged. I shall discuss the matter with Secretary Stimson and General Marshall."

"Now, if I may," Churchill said and paused. Roosevelt nodded. "The purpose of my hasty visit is rather singular and focused." Again, the prime minister paused, and the president remained stoic and attentive. "Our nuclear scientists are rapidly becoming more apprehensive."

"About what, pray tell?"

"We have discussed the development of an atomic weapon to counter the suspected lead of the Germans in their efforts to produce such an extraordinary weapon. Our scientists expected rapid acceleration of our joint development efforts once the United States declared war, and to be blunt, we have not seen such advancement. I share the apprehension of our scientists in that the thought of the Nawzee villain gaining access to such a device before us might well be decisive and fatal for all of us. I am here to encourage a more energetic joint approach to our atomic development."

"Thank you for bringing this matter to my attention, Winston. To be candid, I trusted that we were proceeding under Doctor Bush within the defense research domain."

"Please," interjected Churchill, "do not infer criticism of Doctor Bush. Our scientists have nothing but praise for his leadership and technical understanding. Again, to be candid, it appears the development effort is being treated as a feasibility research project. If you will permit me," Churchill said but did not wait for consent, "this effort should be the highest priority for both our governments. We have made all of our knowledge available to your physicists and engineers. We are no longer discussing feasibility. I believe we are jointly convinced such an extraordinary explosive is indeed feasible. The matter before us now is design, manufacture and testing. Deployment is a political question for another day. The science is clear, Franklin. Well, perhaps overstated a bit, allow me to clarify. The science is as clear as we can make it. We need industrial commitment, now, at the most urgent and aggressive level."

"That is an impassioned plea, Winston. Let me assure you, I am in full agreement with your articulation of the requisite urgency. I will confess my neglect in keeping up with Van Bush. I shall promptly take up the matter with Doctor Bush and Henry Stimson to reorder our priorities. We will stimulate the urgency for this important program. We will get ahead of this effort, and we will do it together."

"Thank you, Franklin. Then, I have accomplished the purpose of my visit."

"Excellent. What do you say we take a tour of the grounds?"

"In your Ford automobile?"

Roosevelt laughed heartily. "No. I shall not subject you to that excitement again. I shall have my driver take us in a more appropriate convertible limousine."

Churchill chuckled. "I would be honored."

The two national leaders took the rest of the afternoon to travel the various roads, trails, and paths around the sprawling, 800-acre, country estate. They continued their discussions on less sensitive matters as they enjoyed the late spring day.

———

Saturday, 20.June.1942
RAF Debden
Saffron Walden, Essex, England
United Kingdom
13:25 hours

The CIRCUS mission had gone well—a comparatively rare daylight-bombing raid on the railyard southwest of Arras, France. The 10 Short Stirling, four-engine, heavy bombers of No.7 Squadron they had rendezvoused with over the English Channel were still ahead of and below the 12 Spitfire Mark V 'B' fighters. No.71 Squadron engaged two German fighter squadron intercepts and kept the enemy at bay. The bombers dealt with flak near the target, but none of the bombers appeared to have taken any serious damage. The fighters stayed above the bombers. Brian remembered watching the bombers press their target and endure the flak bursts around them. The entire formation turned a few miles from Arras to pass down the long axis of the rail yard. As the formation turned north for their egress, Brian glanced down several times within his scan for enemy fighters. He eventually saw the bombs explode all along the railway tracks and the spread of tracks in the railway switching yard at Arras.

As the formation passed over the White Cliffs of Dover and No.71 Squadron was released, Tug gathered up the squadron to make a high-speed pass, diving from above, from behind to ahead of the bombers, as if to salute the bombers. The fighters rolled right toward the east for their return to base, and left the bombers for their return to RAF Oakington, north of Debden.

Tug had lined up the squadron in trail. They would land in sequence.

Brian would be fourth to land. He pulled his canopy back, opening the cockpit. Brian switched off his oxygen supply and detached his oxygen mask. The swirling airstream with the scent of earth felt refreshing. Brian rechecked his landing gear were down and locked, and the confirmation pins extended out of the upper surface of both wings. The flaps were set for landing. Brian stepped through the landing acronym Malcolm had taught him all those years ago—GUMPS. Gas – fuel level, sufficient for approach and go-around, if necessary; Undercarriage – landing gear down and locked, witness pins up; Mixture – rich; Prop – high; and, Speed – approach speed maintained and stable.

As he crossed the threshold of runway 28, Brian closed his throttle. The big Merlin engine coughed and sputtered in protest of being at idle. As the aircraft settled, Brian flared the aircraft gradually to make a precise three-point landing on the centerline of the runway. He kept his ground rollout speed up to allow space for those who followed him.

Brian swung his tail into his parking spot, switched off his electrical equipment, and pulled the mixture lever to CUTOFF. The engine and propeller clicked to a stop.

Corporal Jacobs stood at his usual position with the access door open. Hunter removed his gloves, headgear, goggles and oxygen mask before he stood to exit the cockpit. "Squawks, Mister Drummond?" asked Jacobs.

"Nope. She was perfect. Petrol and ammo only, I should think. Give her a good look-see, Henry. I don't think I took any hits, but better safe than sorry."

"Will do, Mister Drummond. We will have her ready to go in 20 minutes."

Brian smiled and chuckled as he stepped off the wing to the ground. He turned and looked directly into Corporal Jacobs' eyes. "I would bet good money you and the crew will beat that time."

"Thank you, sir."

Brian walked to the Intelligence Office and waited for his turn to debrief the mission. The process took a little longer than usual since the debriefing corporal asked him for his observations of the bombing raid. When he completed his post-mission duty, Brian made his way to the Dispersal Hut and was the last to enter. He hung up his flight equipment on his peg and sat in his usual chair.

Dusty leaned toward Hunter and whispered, "Skipper's been in his office since before we got back."

"I wonder what could be so important," added Frog, also in a whisper.

"I'm sure Tug will tell us if he feels we need to know," Brian responded.

Salt and Sloppy started a game of checkers. Several others were reading newspapers or magazines. Brian yawned, leaned his chair back, and closed his eyes. He did not know how long he had dozed off, but the checkers game was complete when Tug's attention statement brought Brian back to erect alertness.

"First," Tug began, "Group indicated the preliminary assessment of today's mission has been very good, and Air Commodore Spencer commended our squadron for successfully protecting the bomber formation and enabling at least the temporary closing of a vital east-west railway junction." No one reacted, as if they all knew they had been successful.

"Second, Commodore Spencer and I spent some time discussing a planned deployment of our squadron to Russia."

"Whoa!" exclaimed several pilots. Others added various profanities. Squadron Leader Meares held up both hands for quiet.

"The Royal Air Force has stationed a fighter wing, Hurricanes to date, in Northern Russia, since the fall of last year. The Air Ministry has rotated squadrons every three to six months since then. It is our turn, and the government wants to upgrade the fighter support."

"When?" "Where?" "Doing what?" There were repeated questions among others in a confusing barrage of concern and curiosity. Again, Meares raised both hands.

"Look, gentlemen, I just received the Air Ministry's alert notice. Ferry Command will pick up our aircraft in early July. The aircraft will be flown to a port facility, disassembled in part, loaded aboard a freighter, and delivered to Murmansk, or possibly Archangel, where they will be reassembled, checked, and staged for our arrival. The plan calls for us to replace a Hurricane squadron at an airbase southwest of Murmansk. They have flown defense missions to protect the port facilities, but they have also flown offensive operations against German positions around Leningrad. We are slated to transit by ship shortly after our aircraft are moved. That is the most I am allowed to share with you at this stage. We do not want to be confined to base for the next month, so the details will have to wait."

"What do we do with this?" asked Salt.

"This is no different from deployment to North Africa, India, or any other site our skills are needed."

"It's colder," Hick interjected. Everyone laughed. Even Tug smiled.

"Indeed, Hick, it is colder where we are going, but that does not alter our impending orders. We will be given more information as the deployment date approaches. Until then, the best I can say is, tend to your affairs with this deployment in mind. That is all I can share with you. Are there any other questions or statements you blokes wish to make?" No one spoke or moved. "Very well." Tug turned to Corporal Harris, who knew what the commander wanted to know without asking.

"Maintenance has reported the aircraft are all serviced and ready, sir," Harris reported.

"Very well. Please report us as Available."

Harris did as he was instructed. Meares returned to his office. The Dispersal Hut was warming in the afternoon sun more than Brian was comfortable with, so he went outside, found a lawn chair, and sat in the shade. With his eyes closed and drifting toward slumber, Brian heard others join him, although he was not curious about who might be enjoying the day with him.

———

Sunday, 21.June.1942
Residence
The White House
Washington, District of Columbia
United States of America
09:25 hours

The journey back to Washington on the overnight train had been devoid of difficulties or delays, perhaps because the special train had been designated as a presidential train. Winston and Franklin talked about family and friends during the first few hours of the trip. Franklin retired to his compartment before Winston. They both slept well with the undulation of the train clickity-clacking down the rails. The president and prime minister enjoyed a delightful breakfast prior to their arrival at Union Station Washington.

Harry Hopkins stood patiently on the platform as the train had come to a stop and indicated where the presidential limousine was located out of a less traveled side entrance. The president's black, 1939, Lincoln K-Series limousine, popularly known as the Sunshine Special, had been waiting with its powerful V-12 engine purring smoothly at idle and the retractable roof pulled back. The Secret Service agents had assisted the handicapped president, as they had done so many times. Hopkins sped ahead in a Ford staff car. Churchill joined in and followed the lead of President Roosevelt in waving to the appreciative citizens on the morning streets en route to the White House.

At the president's direction, the Secret Service agents wheeled the commander-in-chief to the elevator. The device was just large enough for the president's wheelchair and two agents. Churchill waited for the elevator to return and lift him to the residence floor.

As Churchill entered the Yellow Oval Room, the residence living room, he found Hopkins standing next to the president. Roosevelt extended his right hand and a small piece of notepaper toward Winston. He took the note and read it. Roosevelt read another paper.

Tobruk has fallen.

"Oh, dear God, this is dreadful news." Churchill thought of and considered raising the matter of the Fellers compromise Little Bill Stephenson had dutifully raised with the secretary of war a week ago. The discussion between Stephenson, Stimson, and Marshall had gone exceptionally well. Winston shook his head, rejecting his inclination. "I do not have my usual staff with me on this brief visit. I will need to contact Lord Halifax to see what the Embassy can tell me."

"By all means. We have unfortunately bad news as well," Roosevelt said and handed the second paper to Churchill.

```
June 21, 1942
     Early this morning, a Japanese submarine
fired 17 shells on Fort Stevens, Oregon, at the
mouth of the Columbia River. Coastal artillery
garrison commander ordered his guns not to
return fire out of concern that doing so might
give away their position. No one was injured.
Minimal, insignificant damage was done.  Local
anti-submarine forces are in pursuit of the
enemy submarine.
```

As soon as Winston looked up and before he could speak, Roosevelt said, "We experienced a similar attack on an oil refinery and storage facility near Santa Barbara, California, four months ago."

"I did not know. The note says minimal damage."

"Yes, also similar to the earlier attack."

"Hardly an invasion, and certainly not comparable to your bold Doolittle Raid."

"True, but an annoying disturbance to public morale that we must contain."

"One of many burdens we share, Mister President."

Roosevelt gestured for Churchill to sit on one of the couches. The prime minister did not move, initially. "I should visit the Embassy to get caught up with events, Mister President."

"Yes, yes, of course. However, if I may impose . . . ," Roosevelt said. Churchill nodded and went to the closest couch. Hopkins retrieved the two messages and departed, closing the double doors behind him. "My question may be applicable to your queries at the Embassy. We have not yet discussed Operation RUTTER. What is the status?"

"Pardon my oversight, Franklin. Dickey Mountbatten has an approved plan. The necessary tides and conditions have established the execution window from the 4th through the 8th of next month, roughly two weeks away. He has planned several rehearsals for the first of the month. I must say, Lord Mountbatten has been most impressed with your Army Rangers and OSS agents assigned to the assault team. I will get an update at the Embassy and share with you any additional information. Further, I shall endeavor to keep you informed of progress as well as results."

"This is a larger amphibious operation than Operation BITING—the Bruneval raid."

"Yes, it is much larger and more complex. The core of the RUTTER operation at Dieppe, France, is the 2nd Canadian Infantry Division, with supporting regiments and battalions, including armor vehicles. This will be our first direct assault on German coastal defenses. We expect to learn a great deal about the difficulties that should help us shape ROUNDUP and our final drive for victory."

"I imagine you discussed RUTTER with Molotov during his visit with you last month. What was his reaction, if I may ask?"

"Franklin, please, I would like to think we are personal friends above being the first ministers of our respective governments. I want nothing hidden or beyond reach from you." Roosevelt nodded his head. "Molotov's response was positive and encouraging. However, since his visit, Anthony Eden received a rather terse message from Molotov, undoubtedly conveying Uncle Joe's dissatisfaction with anything short of a full-on invasion. I was quite patient and diligent in my explanation of the logistics threshold that must be attained before ROUNDUP or something like it could be safely and efficiently conducted. I informed him, and I believe he understood, that the issue for us is not just landing a force on the continent, but also installing the logistics facilities to bring on the necessary follow-on forces of all types to drive into Germany, link up with the Red Army, and achieve ultimate victory."

"As you know, Winston, I remain quite apprehensive about sufficiently supporting the Soviets to keep them in this fight."

"Yes, as I am, and I share your apprehension."

"Indeed."

"We are going to face persistent and aggressive pressure from Uncle Joe until ROUNDUP is successful, and we are firmly on the Continent, on our way to Berlin. Until that time, I'm afraid we must endure his relentless demands and unreasonable stance."

Roosevelt stared at the floor for several seconds, then looked back at Churchill. "The Red Army's offensive south of Kharkov appears to have failed."

"I would say it a little more strongly, Franklin. Marshal Timoshenko closed the offensive when the Germans completed their encirclement of his army. Several hundred thousand prisoners of war were caught in the German encirclement. The Second Battle of Kharkov has become one more tragedy the Russians must endure before they turn this around. The Soviet situation, while encouraging in spots, remains tenuous at best. They have not turned the corner yet."

President Roosevelt frowned and nodded his head. "I have already kept you too long, Winston. Thank you for taking the time with me. Now, you should be off. Harry should be in the hallway. He will see to your transport. Will you be back for lunch?"

"I have no idea what awaits me at the embassy. Let us leave it at this; I shall lunch with Lord Halifax and his staff. I will return later this afternoon.

If you are agreeable, I would enjoy a private supper with you, so we can catch up on our situation."

The two men agreed. Prime Minister Churchill departed. President Roosevelt refreshed himself and headed down to the Oval Office on a delightful spring Sunday.

—

Wednesday, 24.June.1942
Headquarters, European Theater of Operations, United States Army
20 Grosvenor Square
Mayfair, London
United Kingdom
08:30 hours

The spacious corner office overlooking Grosvenor Square Park befitted the commander of the U.S. Army in Europe, well actually just the United Kingdom at the moment, but they all had ambitious expectations. Major General Dwight Eisenhower surveyed his new office.

"Rather fancy accommodations for a military commander," pronounced Major General Mark Clark.

"Yeah, you got that right," responded Eisenhower. "I am not accustomed to such opulence."

"Might as well get used to it, Ike. We're going to be here for a while."

"I suppose."

"Do you want me here for your meeting with Sir Alan."

"Yes, Mark, that is why I invited you."

"Just wanted to be sure, Ike. What is the purpose?"

"Primarily . . . officially social."

Clark chuckled. "I can do that. When does Beetle arrive?"

"There are more than a few assumptions in that question. I made my request to General Marshall, and I hope we get him here in a few weeks, maybe a month."

"He will help a . . . ."

After a knock on the door, Eisenhower's new aide-de-camp Captain Julius 'Juli' Calhoun, USA, from Macon, Georgia, stepped halfway into the office and announced, "Chief of the Imperial General Staff General Sir Alan Brooke has arrived, sir."

"Please show him in, Juli."

General Brooke entered the office and immediately extended his hand to Eisenhower, "Welcome back to England, Ike, and congratulations on your new command."

"Thank you, Sir Alan. May I introduce my deputy and the Commanding General of II Corps, General Mark Clark. Mark, this is General Sir Alan Brooke."

The three generals shook hands, and then Eisenhower gestured to the facing couches. Eisenhower and Clark sat at opposite ends of the same couch, and Sir Alan sat across from Eisenhower.

General Brooke began, "I wanted to be the first to officially welcome you back. I am so pleased that our governments have selected you as Commander-in-Chief, Allied Forces. I look forward to working with you for the success of GYMNAST and subsequent operations." Brooke looked to Clark. "I presume II Corps is the initial skeletal command for the accumulation of BOLERO forces."

"Yes sir," answered Clark. "The build-up of our forces should progress rapidly."

"We received your joint staff requests, and we should have a definitive response for you early next week. I trust you will allow us to offer recommendations."

"Of course. We must make this joint staff and task force work . . . for both our sakes."

"We also continue to refine our forces allocation. The sooner we can establish and agree on a mutual, operations plan, the better. GYMNAST and October are not that far away."

"Quite true, Sir Alan. We are going to flesh out the staff as quickly as possible. We have a skeleton. We will flesh out the plan as quickly as we can. We should have it ready for the combined joint chiefs review by late next month or early August."

"Excellent," Brooke acknowledged. "I know it is a bit soon, but how are you settled for quarters?"

"Not yet, but I have a good lead on a delightful cottage in the Combe Hill district."

"Nice area. If I may be of any assistance, please do let me know. I would be honored to help. I understand you also have a knowledgeable driver to help you navigate the streets of London."

"Yes, I do—Kay Summersby of the Mechanised Transport Corps. She has proven herself to be a very capable driver."

Kathleen Helen 'Kay' Summersby, née MacCarthy-Morrogh, joined the Mechanised Transport Corps in 1939, as the war began. Serendipitously, Summersby had been assigned as Eisenhower's personal driver since his coordination visit in May.

"Excellent. As long as you are happy with your support, then all is right with the world."

"Thank you, Sir Alan."

"You are most welcome, Ike. So, on behalf of Sir Dudley and Sir Charles, we welcome you to the fight. We eagerly await your plan for our endorsement and the approval of the president and prime minister."

"Thank you again, Sir Alan. We shall not disappoint."

General Brooke stood. He extended his right hand to Clark. "It is a pleasure to meet you, General Clark. I look forward to working with you."

"Likewise, sir."

Brooke shook Eisenhower's hand, then departed.

Once the door closed, Eisenhower gestured for Clark to sit. "What did you think, Mark?" Ike asked.

"Seems like a straight-up guy."

"Yes, he is—quite the gentleman, actually, although he can turn prickly in an instant."

"We certainly did not see that trait this morning."

"No, we did not; but I only caution that we will. He is an accomplished combat commander. He knows the business. He is also a strict taskmaster. He will not make it easy, but he will make it better when we get to the approval stage."

"Then, we will both learn from him."

Eisenhower smiled. "Of that, I am certain."

"Now, if you will excuse me, Ike, I've got a meeting with my command that I must attend."

Eisenhower nodded his head. They stood, shook hands, and then Clark departed.

———

Friday, 26.June.1942
RAF Gravesend
Gravesend, Kent, England
United Kingdom
16:10 hours

The repositioning transit had been uneventful and routine for the entire No.71 Squadron. The grass landing area exhibited clear signs of repaired damage from attempts to use the grass during the protracted rain period earlier in the month. The landing rollout was a bit bumpy as a result, but the aircraft handled the bumps smoothly.

They parked their fighters in the designated spots. Temporary crewmembers tended to their aircraft. Brian had no problems with his aircraft. He just needed fuel.

The pilots gathered in a tent that had been erected as their dispersal hut away from home. The wooden plank floor gave their footsteps pronounced clunky sounds. Wooden, folding chairs had been evenly distributed through the simple but clean interior.

Squadron Leader Meares immediately went to the telephone and lifted the blue handset. He reported the squadron as Available in 30 Minutes while the refueling and turnaround of the aircraft remained underway. The telephone conversation lasted several minutes, punctuated with a handful of yes-sirs. When he finally completed the telephone conversation and replaced the handset to its cradle, Tug stood before the pilots.

"We knew we were being deployed to support a cross-Channel operation of some sort. I am informed that we will be providing fighter cover for Operation RUTTER—a Combined Operations amphibious raid on the French coast. We will participate in at least one rehearsal tomorrow and perhaps others depending upon accomplishments and problems. The time window for the operation is the 4th to the 8th of July. We will not be briefed on the actual target and plan so we can avoid being sequestered."

"What does that mean?" whispered Frog.

"Restricted to base," Brian promptly whispered back.

"So, Group expects us to be here until the operation is complete. Our ground crews are expected here later this evening. We are released for this afternoon; however, we are not free to leave. We are being billeted at Cobham Hall, the estate of the 9th Earl of Darnley. As such, the duty rests upon me to instruct you on proper decorum while we are guests of Lord Darnley.

"First and foremost, we were invited to reside and mess at Lord Darnley's residence. He and his family live there, so you will conduct yourselves as guests. This is not your house or your property. Second, Lord Darnley is a fellow Air Force officer, having attained the rank of major in the Royal Flying Corps during service in France during the Great War. He is one of us by his service, but you must not forget he is not one of us by his station.

"How high is an earl?" asked Sloppy.

Several pilots chuckled softly.

Tug visibly displayed his annoyance but answered, "Above a viscount and below a marquess, duke, and prince." Sloppy nodded and asked, "Why isn't an earl a count, or the countess an earless?" No one seemed to think that was a funny question.

Squadron Leader Meares smiled. "Let's get all these silly questions out of the way here, so we can avoid any awkwardness or unpleasantness at Cobham Hall. To be direct, I do not know, but years ago, I was told that an unspecified prior king thought count was a little too close to cunt," laughter erupted and interrupted Tug. He waited for quiet. "As a consequence, the king mandated the title change. England is the only country that uses earl, while the rest of the continent uses count. I do not know if any of that is true, other than the observation; however, that is what I was told." Numerous profane comments were overlapped as they absorbed the bawdy information.

Meares again held up his hands for quiet. "To continue, third, as guests, we will strictly abide by the rules of the household as established by the earl and represented by his service staff. I will not tolerate any colonial rambunctiousness, am I clear?"

"What does that mean?" asked Hick.

"It means no debate, no argument nor any deviation. Do you understand?" asked Meares with mounting irritation.

He is clearly nervous about our conduct, a bunch of Americans who do not recognize social station or noble titles. I had better reinforce Tug's words with my guys at a minimum.

"Yes sir," Hick responded.

Meares stared at Hickerson, then looked each pilot in the eyes. He nodded his head in no particular acknowledgment. "Because of his station, he will be referred to as lord, his lordship, or the earl of Darnley. I do not know him, and no one has given me guidance, so the best I can say is, take your lead from the earl and countess. Are there any questions?" No one spoke. "Very well, then. Your silence is consent to and agreement with my instructions. Now, the lorry for our transport is waiting outside. Oh, yes, one last thing, we are strictly forbidden from discussing any current or future operations, even amongst ourselves outside of this tent."

"Yes sir," they all responded in unison.

Meares gestured toward the open tent flap. The pilot's understood the signal. They silently hung their flight gear and boarded the truck. As soon as all of them were seated, the truck began the 10-minute journey to Cobham Hall.

———

Friday, 26.June.1942
Cobham Hall
Brewers Road
Gravesend, Kent, England
United Kingdom
17:15 hours

The twelve pilots jumped down off the covered bed of the Air Force truck. Tug and Whitey appeared to take in their surroundings as just buildings. The Americans could only stare with their mouths agape at the sprawling, complex structure.

They could not see the whole brick and stone building. The wings they could see were two and three stories high with a couple of four-story turrets at the ends of two wings. Dozens of chimneys spiked above the peaked roof.

Squadron Leader Meares and Flight Lieutenant Whittington stood next to a rather tall man in a dark business suit, and an elegant, conservatively dressed, attractive woman roughly the height of Tug Meares and a good foot shorter than the tall man.

Pete Peterson was the first to break the spell, began tapping the others on the shoulder, and gestured to the waiting welcoming committee. They gathered in front of Meares.

"Gentlemen, I am honored to introduce Lord and Lady Darnley." He turned to Lord Darnley. "On behalf of 71 Squadron, thank you for inviting us to your residence. We are grateful for your generosity."

Meares introduced each squadron pilot to the earl and countess, and each of them shook hands like a receiving line.

"Welcome to Cobham Hall. It is our honor and pleasure to make our home available to you for however long your staging for the pending mission lasts. Countess Darnley and I want your stay with us to be as comfortable as possible. Please let any member of our household staff know what you need. Our household butler, Mister Armitage," Lord Darnley said and gestured to a stately, middle-aged, handsome man dressed in formal attire with a wide, black, bowtie, "will take you on a tour of the facilities you will need and has your room assignments. After your tour, a member of the staff will show you to your rooms. The evening meal will be at half six as is your routine, and the countess and I would be honored to join you. As requested by your squadron commander, morning meal will be at half five; however, please forgive us, we will not join you at that hour."

Everyone laughed, including the earl and countess.

"Are there any other questions I may be able to answer before we get you settled into your temporary quarters?" asked Lord Darnley.

"What is your given name?" Hick asked.

The earl smiled. "An appropriate question from an American. My given name is Esmé Ivo Bligh."

Hick smiled and said, "Wow! Any relation to Captain Bligh?" Several of the Americans laughed.

Lord Darnley chuckled in good humor. "A common question, if I must say. The familial name is the same, however, to the best of our ancestral knowledge, no, there is no relation. Our familial name is rather unique, so I suspect there may be a distant connection, but my family has not identified that link."

"How old is Cobham Hall?" Salt Morton asked.

"The answer is rather complex, I must confess. The original manor house dated back to the 12th century. Segments of the current buildings date back to 1587. I inherited the estate upon the death of my father when I became the 9th Earl in 1927. You are a curious lot. Are there any other questions?" No one spoke up. "Very well, then. Mister Armitage and the staff will get you settled. The countess and I will see you for supper."

The tour took roughly 30 minutes. One of the chambermaids showed Brian to his assigned room—the Green Room. The room was indeed very green with a light seafoam green above the polished wood of the chair rail molding and a green fern print wallpaper below the railing. The furnishings and linens were shades of green or the browns of wood.

"Incredible," Brian said aloud when he was finally alone. "This is going to be interesting."

No.71 Squadron remained at Gravesend and Cobham for a week. The rehearsals had gone well. They knew their part. However, when the weather turned bad the day before the tide conditions window opened with the forecast remaining unsatisfactory through the tide window, and worse, as the assault flotilla gathered in The Solent Estuary, the Germans carried out a rare bombing raid of the assembled ships, as if to say, we know what you are planning. Operation RUTTER was canceled, and the squadron returned to Debden.

Additional intelligence in the following weeks transformed the Dieppe Raid into Operation JUBILEE that tentatively scheduled for execution in the August tide window. During the intervening weeks, the operational plan was revised, and the assault force strengthened.

—

Chapter 11

[B]ut those who hope in the Lord
will renew their strength.
They will soar on wings like eagles;
they will run and not grow weary,
they will walk and not be faint.

-- Isaiah 40:31

Wednesday, 1.July.1942
Quaglino's Brasserie
16 Bury Street
St. James's, London, England
United Kingdom
20:35 hours

Clementine and Winston Churchill arrived a few minutes late. Vice Admiral Lord Louis 'Dickey' Mountbatten, resplendent in his dress uniform, and his elegant wife Lady Edwina Mountbatten dressed in a delicate purple lace dress with matching hat, sat at a corner table in the small but elegant restaurant that had been spared by The Blitz. The *maître d'hôtel* recognized the prime minister before he and Clementine entered the restaurant, introduced himself immediately, and gestured to the corner table.

"Thank you," Churchill said. "We can find our way."

Patrons in the nearly full restaurant stood, applauded loudly, and cheered. Several people patted the prime minister on the shoulder as he passed them. Churchill tipped his bowler and thanked everyone for their gestures of support.

The Churchills and Mountbattens greeted each other as the friends they were. Clementine took the seat across the table from the admiral. The four of them sat.

"Welcome to Quaglino's," Louis opened. "So, this is your first visit?"

"Yes. I had heard a few distant comments about the restaurant, but never enough to cross my curiosity threshold."

"Well, at least you are here now. Edwina and I have always enjoyed this place."

"Quite so," Edwina added with a luminous smile.

The waiter arrived with four, single-page menus attached at the corners to padded, black leather boards. He took the drink orders for Clementine and Winston—house Chablis for the ladies and Johnny Walker Red neat for the gentleman.

"How have you been, Edwina?" asked Clementine.

"Better, now that the Germans have moved on."

"We should all say that."

"Wait, now," Winston interjected, "Clemmie commanded me to not talk war, and here you ladies have violated your own rule."

"Winnie, you know better."

"Yes, dear. I most certainly do. And, more importantly, I intend to abide by your wishes." Winston looked at Louis. "Thank you for the invitation, Dickey. We finally . . . ," Winston stopped when he noticed Louis' attention diverted behind him.

"Ernst," Louis said, "excellent to see you again."

"Lord Louis, Lady Edwina, thank you for your patronage. Welcome Prime Minister and Mrs. Churchill."

"Clementine, Winston," Dickey said, "may I present Ernst Quaglino, younger brother of Giovanni 'Johnny' Quaglino, owners of this esteemed and exquisite establishment."

Greetings and salutations passed among them.

"My apologies to all of you," Ernst said. "My brother is away on urgent business. He will truly regret missing this opportunity. I must also apologize for our rather limited menu of late. War rationing has been devastating on our master chef's creativity. However, I assure you, he has done exceptionally well within the constraints of the day."

"I am certain Chef Roberto has rendered his finest," Louis said.

"Thank you, Lord Louis. It is an honor to have you with us, Prime Minister. I trust you will be sufficiently impressed and return to us frequently."

"Thank you, Ernst. Please convey our respects to your brother."

"I will most certainly do so," Ernst Quaglino said. "Our chief waiter, James, will take your orders. Now, if you will excuse me, I have a restaurant to run. Enjoy your meals, ladies and gentlemen."

They bid their *adieux*. All four of them ordered the chef's featured entrée—*Rotini dal Mare con Merluzzo*—with a fine Pinot Grigio to complement the seafood pasta with Cod filet.

As they waited for their meals, Edwina said, "Thank you for joining us, Winston." She looked from Winston to Clementine. "And, Clementine. It has been far too long since I've seen you both." Edwina looked back to Winston. "Since you promoted Dickey and gave him that new job, I've barely seen him either."

"My respectful apologies. There is a . . ."

"We have," Clementine demonstrably interjected, looking to Edwina, "not seen Brook House, since you renovated. How do you like the changes?"

"Nicely done, Clemmie," Edwina gushed.

Clementine smiled. "I was trying to save my husband from the trap."

Edwina smiled back in knowing form and nodded her head slightly. "Yes, indeed, and again, well done. To answer your query, we are quite satisfied . . . and more importantly, the building came through The Blitz virtually unscathed . . . well, except for repeated broken windows and some façade damage when a bomb fell too close. The damage was comparatively easy to repair."

The waiter and his assistant arrived with the meals. With appropriate *panache*, the waiters uncovered their dishes simultaneously. They tasted their food, and all nodded and cooed their appreciation.

"Do I understand correctly," Clementine began, "you subdivided the building?"

"Yes, we did, several years ago," Edwina answered. "Brook House was far too much for us. We installed a dedicated elevator and separated the top two floors, which is still more than we need, but comfortable, nonetheless. The lower floors were converted into separate apartments that we sublet. Harry Selfridge himself rented one of the flats."

"Another transported American," Winston said.

"Yes, indeed, quite so," Edwina added, "and very accomplished, I must say."

"Isn't this meal delicious," Louis said, taking his turn at changing the subject.

Winston chuckled softly, "Yes, Dickey, despite the constrictions of wartime food rationing, Chef Roberto managed to create quite the sumptuous dish with the ingredients he had."

Everyone laughed.

"Most enjoyable," Clementine added.

"Well," Edwina said, "please forgive me for being so bold, but it is rare these days to be sitting next to the prime minister during a time of war," she paused. All eyes were on her, anticipating the remainder of her statement. "When is this damnable war going to be over?"

All eyes then turned to Winston. "I'm afraid, Lady Edwina, that day is not close at hand." Churchill stopped to gauge the reaction. No one budged and reacted in any form. Winston chose to continue. "Just today, Rommel has restarted his assault on El Alamein in Egypt, and the Germans have taken Sebastopol and Crimea in the Soviet Union. The Russians are hanging by a thread, but they are still engaged. Our current supply convoy PQ17 to the Soviets is in a dreadful struggle in the Arctic. We will suffer more setbacks before victory is in sight."

Edwina grinned at Winston. "That was a little drearier news than I anticipated."

"My apologies, Lady Edwina, but these are the times in which we live. Yet, on the positive side of the ledger, American forces are arriving every day and building up for the ultimate crusade."

"When?" Edwina asked.

Winston smiled. "I think you recognize I cannot say anything about such a sensitive event." The table remained silent and inanimate, while the white noise of indistinguishable conversations of the restaurant's patrons occupied their audible space. "I can assure you that plans are afoot to press our efforts to take the fight to the enemy." Dickey winked at Winston. The two men knew that Allied armed forces had been within days of executing Operation RUTTER, but inclement weather produced excessive surf at the landing beaches, precluded the necessary air support, and made cross-Channel naval operations problematic. Also, just this morning, unspoken beyond Dickey's wink, the War Cabinet, on the recommendation of the Chief of Combined Operations Command, postponed Operation RUTTER and transformed it into the more ambitious Operation JUBILEE, now planned for early August. "I am confident our inevitable victory is assured. It is only a matter of when and at what cost."

Edwina looked at her husband, who, in turn, nodded his head in agreement with the prime minister. She glanced at Clementine, then back to Winston. "Well, I did ask, didn't I?"

"Do not despair, my dear. He did that to me all the time," Clementine said, "until I stopped asking."

That concluded the serious conversation, and the group reverted to more benign topics like the ever-changing weather in England and the earthy, simple pleasures of the English countryside.

"You really must come spend the weekend with us at Chequers," Winston said.

"Ah yes, the prime minister's country estate," Dickey observed.

"One and the same. We did use Ditchley Park during The Blitz, in deference to the worries and apprehensions of the War Cabinet and Security Service. But now, it is mostly Chequers for the weekends and holidays."

"What about your beloved Chartwell?" asked Edwina. "Have you sold the property? Do you still have it?"

"Yes," answered Clementine. "We had to shutter the place when Winnie became PM. We will probably leave it in that limbo state until victory and the end of the war is closer."

"It would be an honor for us, Winston," Dickey said. "Then, you both must spend a weekend with us at Broadlands." Like Brook House in London, Edwina had inherited the palatial estate known as Broadlands near Romsey in

Hampshire, nestled sweetly on the east bank of the River Test. She had inherited enormous wealth and real property holdings from her maternal grandfather and her father.

They enjoyed an exquisite bread pudding with sweet embellishments before they savored their after-dinner cognac. Laughter and joviality bonded the two couples. The Churchills were both quite aware of the social gossip, rumors, and stories surrounding Edwina and Dickey, but neither of them was coarse enough to even hint at the topic. They rarely discussed those hints and clues even in the privacy of just the two of them. Winston was pleased with Dickey's performance as Chief of Combined Operations Command. That is what counted in the grander scheme of things. Lord Louis was the first to break the event. They paid their compliments and respects to Ernst, and Johnny *in absentia*, as well as Chef Roberto. They said goodnight to each other in the familiar fashion. Detective-Inspector Thompson and Sergeant Carrick waited with the prime minister's limousine at curbside. They rode in silence and would not discuss the evening until they were safely ensconced in their wartime residence at No.10 Annexe.

———

Friday, 3.July.1942
Headquarters, Special Operations Executive
No.64 Baker Street
Marylebone, London, England
United Kingdom
10:15 hours

"**W**elcome back," Brigadier Gubbins greeted Trevor Andersen, as the field agent entered the small conference room.

"Thank you, sir."

"How was your training event?"

"Exceptional, I must say. Captain Fairbairn is a unique character, an excellent instructor, and knowledgeable beyond description."

"Excellent. Trevor, a lot has happened since you inserted last. Please allow me to introduce Lord Selborne, 3rd Earl of Selborne, who replaced Minister Dalton late last February, while you were in the field."

The two men shook hands, and Selborne gestured for them to sit.

"What happened, if I may ask?"

"Surely," responded Selborne. "When Singapore fell . . ."

"Singapore is lost?" Trevor asked with incredulity.

"Yes, I'm afraid so. The garrison surrendered to the Japanese on the 15th of February. Also, the German battlecruisers *Scharnhorst* and *Gneisenau*, along with a small flotilla, successfully ran through the Channel to Germany on the

12ᵗʰ of that month. As a consequence of these setbacks and others, the prime minister felt it necessary to shuffle the War Cabinet and make a number of other ministerial changes."

"What happened to Minister Dalton?"

"He moved to be president of the Board of Trade, and I was chosen to replace him. There were other changes; probably most notable to our line of work, Sir Percy Grigg replaced David Margesson as minister of war."

Trevor smiled and shook his head. "I had heard the *Scharnhorst* mentioned in conversation in late winter, but I never did ascertain what that was all about. I had my mind on other matters."

"Which brings us to the extant conversation. How did it go in Germany?" Selborne asked.

"In one word . . . better . . . at least compared to my attempt last October, which is why I extended my time in country. I made a connection with Hans Scholl, who seems to be one of the leaders of what they call the White Rose—a resistance group based primarily at the University of Münich. Hans, along with Alexander Schmorell, are the drivers. They are both medical students, who were pressed into service in the medical corps in support of operations on the Eastern Front. They had just returned from their rotation when I returned to Münich and were quite disillusioned. I took a bold step of reciprocity with Hans and confided in him my purpose. That risk paid off. I was introduced to Hans' sister Sophie, who has also become very active in the group, and Professor Kurt Huber, who is the intellectual philosopher of the group."

"What does he teach?" asked Selborne.

"Psychology and Music."

"Interesting combination," commented Selborne. "Why is this group worth the risk we are asking you to take?"

Trevor smiled. "First, I did not initiate this mission."

"He is correct," interjected Gubbins and spoken directly to Lord Selborne. "Minister Dalton and I asked him to enter Germany last fall. We heard rumors from various reliable sources in Germany that something was afoot at the university. Agent Diamond found threads of resistance, but nothing substantive. After discussing the potential and risks, we mutually agreed to take another bite of the apple."

Lord Selborne nodded his head and looked back to Trevor. "Pardon my interruption, and thank you," he said, nodding and looking at both men, "for my education. Let's get back to your report."

"The group is small and rather loose, but they are also realists. They know what they are up against, with the Gestapo and SD squashing even hints of dissent. Yet, they distributed several of what they call Leaflets of the

White Rose—*Flugblätter der Weißen Rose*, in High German. The messages have been those of passive resistance, as well as the futility and folly of the eastern campaign."

"Are they open to more aggressive action?" asked Gubbins.

"That is hard to say, General. They have the political fervor for such action, but I do not sense that level of aggression, but that could change. They lack that focus, and to the best of my knowledge, none of them have military experience or training for offensive efforts."

"Perhaps, we can supplement their motivation," Gubbins added.

Trevor stared at Gubbins as he considered the general's statement. "These are medical students who have been exposed to the brutality of war. They are far more interested in passive measures at this juncture. They seek peace, not engaging in the violence of war. Their ideological inclination might change, if the German fortunes on the eastern front turn negative. There are not enough of them to take any substantive offensive action. They want peace, not war, as I said."

"So, what is your recommendation?" asked Lord Selborne.

"If this student group was located anywhere else other than München, or Bavaria, I would say we should keep a distant eye on them. The risk of maintaining contact is substantial. However, this student group is smack dab in the middle of Hitler's political base. As such, the political impact of their efforts—passive or aggressive—could be substantially amplified. Thus, I recommend we maintain contact, feed them information on Soviet advances that would not appear in the Nazi-controlled press, and watch for the opportunities to mobilize their political dissatisfaction to more direct efforts. Their mood might well change. Yet, I do urge caution. We cannot compromise them with information they would not have access to except from us. The vast majority of German casualties are on the eastern front, and they would likely witness those losses directly; thus, less exposure for them."

"You are the person they trust, Trevor," said Selborne. "The risk is yours. We will abide by your recommendation. What do you propose?"

"Full-time immersion is probably too much. I'd suggest another visit to assess their evolution. We can adjust from that point."

Lord Selborne looked at Brigadier Gubbins, who nodded his head in agreement. "Very well, then. That is the plan. When do you think it is the appropriate time to return?"

"I would say, late summer or early fall. A number of the students will likely have to endure at least one more rotation in support of medical services on the eastern front during that period. If nothing has gone off the rails by then, I should be able to gauge the progress of dissatisfaction and the potential for aiding their resistance."

"So it shall be. Let us prepare for that next step. Now, you justly deserve a rest and refreshment period. Take a couple of weeks of rest. If you need more time, just let either of us know. Upon your return, we will consider your next assignments."

"Thank you, sir."

The meeting concluded, and Trevor departed.

———

Friday, 10.July.1942
The Fighting Cocks Public House
London Road
Wendens Ambo, Saffron Walden, Essex
United Kingdom
19:30 hours

Squadron Leader Meares had contracted with the local public house for the dedicated use of their food and bar services for the squadron's farewell dinner. No.71 Squadron was now formally scheduled to take three-plus days for rest and recuperation. They would gather back at Debden on Tuesday for transport to Liverpool and the ship that would take them to Arkhangelsk.

Brian had met Charlotte at the rail station. They enjoyed a simple and quiet lunch before they walked to the hotel and checked into a small but well-maintained room. The Drummonds took full advantage of the few hours of slow time and paucity of any distractions to renew their union with zeal and vigor. They laughed, giggled, and played like two teenage lovers. By mutual agreement, the Drummonds dressed for dinner and arrived at the pub over an hour early to enjoy a pint together, which they did.

Squadron Leader Meares and his wife Edith were the next to arrive. The other pilots began to trickle in, each of them with a gorgeous woman of various descriptions, except Pete Peterson, who was the only other married pilot. Pete's wife remained in Utah. The pilots had assembled with their lady friends. Introductions and cordialities were exchanged, and beers filled all around. Tug Meares allowed each pilot to invite guests, and Brian used his allowance fully. The farewell dinner was a good excuse to gather friends.

The reason for the dinner was quite serious and solemn. Yet, as was so often the case, the pilot found laughter and joking about a wide range of contemporary subjects. Their laughter was contagious. With the expanding frivolity, an observer might think they had just won the war. Even the staid and distant Peterson laughed and enjoyed himself.

Wing Commander Lord Jeremy Morrison arrived in typically flamboyant fashion with his American lady-friend ATA Third Officer Marilyn Powell. It was Marilyn who garnered the attention of the other pilots. Half of them had not seen or talked to a female pilot, set aside a female pilot who was flying the same combat aircraft they were flying. Charlotte had questions that would have to wait.

Linda and Flight Lieutenant Jonathan Kensington came along with his sister Rosemary, who had just graduated from Oxford University with her undergraduate degree and was preparing for her medical doctorate education. The Drummonds had not seen Linda or Rosemary since the Kensington's wedding a year ago.

Mary and Air Commodore John Spencer were the last to arrive and just in time. As the senior officer, Tug Meares engaged John Spencer. To Brian's surprise, Charlotte went directly to greet Mary Spencer. The two women clearly engaged in friendly, mutual discussion. He was curious about Charlotte's motive and what they were talking about. Jonathan leaned toward his best friend and whispered, "They seem to be quite chummy." Brian nodded his head but did not answer.

With all members and guests present, Tug Meares clinked his glass so loudly Brian thought it might break. "Ladies and gentlemen, kindly make your way to the dining room for our supper," he commanded.

The cacophony of conversation continued as the assembly moved to the tables. Nametags had been distributed for seating. The Spencers and the Morrison couple sat at the head table with the Meareses. The Kensingtons and Pete Petersen joined the Drummonds. Rosemary did a great job of making Pete feel part of the group.

The meal was promptly and efficiently served, and well prepared. They enjoyed a surprisingly delightful fillet of smoked haddock, slow poached in milk on a bed of mustard mash with a baked potato and seasonal vegetables that included steamed broccoli, cauliflower, sliced carrots, and a light cheese sauce. The dinner table conversation remained purely social about the early summer weather, the trials of shopping in a wartime economy, and the incessant challenges of making do without males present. The men generally remained observers of the conversation. Everyone appreciated the meal choice and the exquisite bread pudding made exceptional by the light vanilla cream sauce with sugar-rationing of wartime England. As supper concluded, the ladies excused themselves to attend the powder room. Other ladies took the cue.

Pete was the first to turn the conversation. "Did I see correctly," he asked, looking at Jonathan, "that you became an ace late last month?"

"Yes . . . number five."

"Congratulations," Pete and Hunter said simultaneously.

"Thanks, mates."

"A 109 on a RODEO mission over Northern France," Harness added. "He was too focused on his attack on one of my wingmen."

"Serves him right," said Pete.

Brian nodded his head in agreement.

The women began to return. Tug Meares waited for the ladies of the head table to return before he clinked his glass again. He waited for quiet. "Thank you for joining us this evening. As a squadron, we thought it appropriate to gather our loved ones and friends before we deploy. Unfortunately, we are not able to share with you our destination due to operational security, but it is outside of the United Kingdom in defense of the realm, which is our excuse for this gathering. So, on behalf of the pilots and crews of 71 Squadron, thank you so very much, again, for joining us. Now, it is my distinct honor to introduce our distinguished guest, Chief of Operations for 11 Group, Air Commodore John Spencer, Companion of the Most Distinguished Order of Saint Michael and Saint George, and holder of the Distinguish Flying Cross . . . Air Commodore Spencer." The assembly applauded.

John Spencer stood and shook hands with Tug Meares. "Thank you very much for the warm welcome, Squadron Leader Meares. I had not expected or planned to make any remarks, but I certainly respect the occasion. Just 27 years ago, I deployed to France. A mere two years ago, many of the pilots in this room stood as part of the very thin line of defense against what all indications told us was an inevitable invasion of our beloved emerald isles. Our prime minister has coined the term for those pilots who served during those tenuous months—The Few. Please join me in applauding the accomplishments of The Few." Applause and cheers filled the room. Even the wait staff applauded. Charlotte patted her husband and his best friend on the back, then kissed them both on the cheek. Rosemary stood and kissed on the cheek her brother, Brian, and even Pete, who did not join the RAF until after the battle had been won. "We all owe you a debt of gratitude that can never be repaid. Now, with all that, I must also add that what distinguished this group of The Few, with the exception of Tug Meares and Whitey Whittington, these members of The Few are American volunteers. And, this squadron," John said and waved his arm across the room, "is the first of now three American volunteer squadrons to join us in the fight against the fascists. Yet, to me, and I think it safe to say on behalf of all of us in uniform, we owe our most profound appreciation to those who stand by us and support us as we do our duty." Cheers and applause again broke out.

Brian leaned toward Charlotte, gently touched her far cheek, and kissed her. He withdrew just a little, looked into her loving eyes, and whispered to her, "Thank you for loving me."

Charlotte smiled at her husband and kissed him back. She whispered back to him. "I am blessed to have you in my life."

John Spencer continued, "With all the love in this venerable establishment, we should probably retire to the privacy of our rooms." Many in the room laughed heartily. "I have taken too much of your precious evening already. Please allow me to close by thanking Squadron Leader Meares for arranging this celebration. Well done." Everyone applauded, and Tug nodded his acknowledgment. "Thank you for inviting Mary and me to your celebration," John said and nodded to Brian. "I wish you all a good night and a successful deployment."

"That concludes our planned farewell dinner. The bar will remain open as long as the proprietor will have us."

The mixture of cheers, chairs moving across the wooden floor, and people shuffling with their movements marked the transition of the evening. Several of the pilots and guests departed—most remained in the bar with laughter and conversation. Charlotte, Linda, and Rosemary wandered off for some unknown purpose. Brian watched the service staff clear the tables and return the dining area to its customary configuration. He felt a tap on his left shoulder and turned to see Mary Spencer standing comparatively close. She was beaming with radiance.

"So, my dear Brian, did you inform Charlotte of your encounter with Lady Castlerosse?"

"Yes, of course . . . after I talked to you."

"What did she think, or should I ask her?"

"Mary, I told her I talked to you about the incident. I also told her what you told me about the Sex Queen of Mayfair. So, if you want to know what Charlotte thinks, you should ask her. There is nothing to hide."

"Has Doris contacted you since we talked?"

"No."

"Will you tell me if she does?"

"If you wish?"

"I would like that. I am curious," Mary said. They heard Brian's name called from behind Mary. She turned and brushed his groin with the back of her hand, then said softly to Brian with a smile, "Don't forget."

Brian did not recoil. *Don't forget what? Did she do that on purpose?* Brian started to ask, but Mud Morrison joined them.

"Lady Spencer, great to see you again."

"Lord Morrison, always a pleasure, and who is your lady friend?"

"Mary Spencer, may I introduce Marilyn Powell. Marilyn, this is Mary Spencer, wife of our guest of honor Air Commodore Spencer." The two women shook hands delicately. Mud did not wait for the conversation to develop. He looked at Brian and said, "How is our ace of aces?"

"Still alive," Brian answered succinctly and devoid of enthusiasm. "Great to see you, again, Marilyn. I'm surprised you have endured this obnoxious bastard." Everyone laughed, including Mud.

"It is a challenge," Marilyn responded, "but I give as much as I get." Again, laughter.

What the hell does that mean? Why do all these women talk in codes?

"So," Mud said to change the subject, "how many are you up to now? It's 21 by my count."

"Close enough."

Mud turned to look into Marilyn's waiting eyes. "He's the third-highest scoring ace in the whole of the RAF, so far, and I trained him."

"Congratulations, Mister Drummond," Marilyn said. "That's quite remarkable."

"Not really . . . just lucky."

"He lies," interjected Mud. "He is a natural killer and uses a Spitfire like his own hand. So, what happened after I left you with Lady Castlerosse?"

Mary laughed heartily. "I already asked him."

"Who is Lady Castlerosse?" asked Marilyn.

"They often call her Notorious Lady 'C' for just reason."

"Or, in the more vernacular," added Mary, "she also has more profane monikers like the Mistress of Mayfair and Sex Queen of Mayfair." Just then, Charlotte returned and smiled at Mary. "My apologies, Charlotte. We were just enjoying a bit of fun at your husband's expense."

"He is an easy target," Charlotte responded. Brian smiled but did not respond. "He's been a good boy . . . so far . . . but, my goodness, who knows what the future holds for our young knight."

Mud Morrison renewed the drinks for everyone. As the evening progressed, John Spencer joined Mary, and Jonathan, Linda, and Rosemary returned as well. The conversation topics remained far lighter and less focused on Brian. Laughter continuously punctuated their chitchat. As the population of the bar thinned, the little group disbanded as well. The pilots of No.71 Squadron were technically already on leave. The entire small group had rooms at the same hotel. They agreed to meet for breakfast before they went their separate ways. Brian and Charlotte walked to their hotel in the cool evening air, as they discussed the evening's conversations.

—

Saturday, 11.July.1942
Standing Oak Farm
Winchester, Hampshire, England
United Kingdom
14:20 hours

The breakfast with the group had been pleasant and peaceful. The whole group walked to the railway station. The Kensingtons had been the first to depart on the northbound train 20 minutes before the others. The Spencers, Drummonds, and Jeremy and Marilyn had taken the southbound train to Liverpool Station in Northeast London, where they split.

The journey home for the Drummonds took the rest of the morning and into the early afternoon. They arrived at Standing Oak Farm on a sunny and warm afternoon. Brian immediately occupied himself with Ian, who was now 13 months old and all too content to play with his father, while Charlotte tended to her catch-up on the farm's business.

When the relentless time of day arrived, the Drummonds and their hired hands took care of the farm's afternoon milking and tending the cows. With the afternoon chores dispatched, the extended members of the Standing Oak Farm staff were fed, while young Ian managed the milking of his mother. The staff was paid and sent along their way.

As the house settled, and Ian was off to slumber, Brian looked at Charlotte and said, "Let's take a walk."

Charlotte displayed puzzlement in her eyes, nodded her head, and responded, "It is a good evening for a walk."

Instead of heading toward the property's entry portal as they usually did, Brian took Charlotte's hand and turned left toward the oak tree and their bench beside the lake.

"Well, this must be serious," Charlotte said.

Brian did not answer and only gently pulled her closer, put his arm around her shoulder, and kissed her forehead. He equally gently guided her to sit on the bench and joined her.

"Are you going to confess to succumbing to Lady Castlerosse's seduction?"

Brian laughed. "Nope, not even close. I am going to trust you with information I am obligated not to tell you or anyone."

Somewhat frustrated, Charlotte said, "How long are you going to keep me in suspense. Get on with it!"

"The reason for the farewell dinner and our extended leave is we are being deployed to Northern Russia next week."

"Oh, Brian, I'm so sorry. That cannot feel good . . . the Eastern Front."

"I am far more worried about you, my dear. We'll handle the bloody Gerries. Our rotation should be completed before winter sets in, even up there, but I don't see the combat risk to be any different from what we deal with today. My concern is the distance and difficulty of communications, especially for this deployment." Brian turned on the bench to look directly into Charlotte's anticipatory eyes. "My God, woman, I do love your gorgeous eyes."

"Oh, Brian, stop. You are trying to say something important. Get on with it."

"As I hope you recall, I changed my last will and testament a year and a half ago, when I was last in Kansas. I just recently took the step of formally producing a legal power of attorney for the period of this deployment, giving you full authority over any and all of my holdings. I received confirmation from Mister Braddock, my lawyer in Kansas, from Mister Atherton, my general manager, and Bobby Joe Sales, the manager of my aviation company. They now understand. This is partly to inform you of what I have done, but more to the point, I wanted to talk about our business situation here."

Charlotte shook her head with clear confusion displayed in her expression. "What on earth are you talking about?"

"I think it is time that we hire a general manager here."

"What?"

"Your property holdings . . ."

"Our!"

"OK, our property holdings are growing. They are taking more and more of your time in direct management. In many ways, I do not see our circumstances here as particularly different from our holdings in Kansas, and perhaps soon the United States. You need to take a more supervisory role, Charlotte, with a broader vision for what to do with our property. I would offer Trevor Atherton, but he is an American, not British."

"Where do you think we are going to find such a qualified man? This country has been at war for nearly three years now. Horace and Lionel are just too old; they should be retired by now. And, Jacob is far too young and will soon be of conscription age. Worse, most eligible males are already in uniform and military service, many of them outside the country."

"Who said it had to be a man?"

Charlotte smiled. "I applaud your sense of equality and humanity, but realism must govern our actions."

"We never know unless we try."

"Good point. It does not cost us anything to ask."

"I think it is time and worth the effort to see what we can turn up, what you can turn up, since I will be deployed and largely unavailable."

"Agreed. I'll begin the process next week to see what we can find."

"Now, to our Kansas holdings. I have been receiving monthly reports from Atherton, Sales, and Braddock. In issuing my power of attorney to you, I asked them to send the reports to you until further notice. I ask you to read the reports carefully and reply to each report, if for no other reason than to confirm receipt. But, if you see or feel something needs to be said as direction or guidance, please do so."

"Brian, you have shared with me on a broad scope of your inheritance, but I have no idea how to deal with day-to-day operations."

Brian smiled. "That was the point of my earlier suggestion. They are being paid handsomely for the operations of our holdings. Don't worry about daily decisions. Take a higher, more expansive view. You understand business. You have kept this farm in the black, even during the challenges of wartime rationing and restrictions. You can do the same for our Kansas holdings."

"What have you done to that end?"

"I have brought my files of correspondence—past reports and my replies—for you to review to get a feel for what I have done. We've got several days before I must report back to Debden, so we can discuss anything you wish to know."

"Very well, my darling. You have been so generous with me."

"Generous, woman!" Brian protested. "The hell you say. You saved my life. There is no greater generosity than that."

"I did what had to be done."

"As I have done."

"Enough. The sun is below the western horizon, and it is starting to get chilly."

"Very well, then. We can go warm ourselves by the fire, and then we can play some tickle n' wiggle."

"You are incorrigible, Brian Drummond, but I love you for it. Let's check to make sure everything is OK with Edith, and she is settled for the night, and then we can tend to our passion."

"You have a deal, my dear."

The two lovers made quick work of the prelude and jumped into their purpose with vigor.

———

Tuesday, 14.July.1942
RAF Debden
Saffron Walden, Essex, England
United Kingdom
13:05 hours

Squadron Leader Meares kept poking his head out of his office every few minutes. Sloppy Butterfield had not returned to his duty station by the appointed hour of noon. The Right-Wing of Yellow Section was not the first to be late, and he would undoubtedly not be the last. Tug appeared to be more animated and concerned than he was on previous late arrivals.

"Corporal Harris, kindly report the squadron present."

Can't be Available. We have no aircraft.

"Right away, sir."

Odd. He is not reporting Sloppy missing. He's taking a helluva risk in reporting the squadron present for duty while missing one of his pilots. I guess that is sufficient reason to be nervous.

Just then, Sloppy entered the hut.

"You are over an hour late, Pilot Officer Butterfield."

"I'm sorry, sir. My train was delayed a couple of hours after hitting a horse-drawn cart, we were told."

Meares ignored the excuse. "Gather up, lads. Have a seat, Sloppy." Tug waited for the sounds of shuffling to cease. "Our orders have changed," he announced. No one reacted. "The ship carrying our aircraft was sunk yesterday by a U-boat torpedo." That information produced a rumbling among the pilots. "The ship with our aircraft was part of convoy PQ17. Out of 34 ships that sailed from their assembly port in Iceland, only nine made it to Arkhangelsk, four days ago."

"Damn!" exclaimed several pilots.

"I was informed that the convoy had been ordered to disperse on the 4th after reports the *Scharnhorst* was maneuvering to engage the convoy."

"That's the battleship we missed in the Channel five months ago," observed Salt Morton.

"That's the one," responded Whitey. "An opportunity lost."

"Our aircraft were loaded on the Dutch merchant SS *Paulus Potter* that was struggling with a propulsion problem when they were hit and sunk yesterday morning. There were no survivors."

"What do we do now?" asked Hick Hickerson.

Tug smiled. "First, we are not deploying to Russia."

Cheers, applause, and grateful words filled the Dispersal Hut.

"I am informed by Group that our replacement aircraft will be delivered tomorrow. According to Group, they will all be Mark Five 'B's—most new, a few reassigned. Once our aircraft are checked out, painted with our designator, and released by Maintenance for flight, we will take the air for check flights. Group expects us to be back to Available status by Friday."

"Does that mean we are released?" Buddy Courtland asked.

Meares chuckled. "You are an anxious lot, aren't you? Yes, even though we just got off four days of leave, we have no horses. I expect all of you back in this building no later than eight o'clock tomorrow morning, including you, Sloppy." They all laughed.

"Yes sir. I'm not going anywhere. Thank you for not reporting me missing, Skipper."

"You are welcome. No one should make a habit of being late," Tug said, pointing to each of the pilots. "Enjoy your afternoon and evening. You are dismissed."

Brian sat in his chair, while the other pilots stood and shuffled out of the Dispersal Hut. *I need to call Charlotte with the news. I'll leave the power of attorney in effect to give her some experience with my stuff.*

"Are you coming, Hunter?" asked Dusty.

Brian smiled, stood, and said, "Sure."

———

Wednesday, 15. July. 1942
Office of Strategic Services Station London
No. 70 Grosvenor Street
Mayfair, London, England
United Kingdom
15:15 hours

OSS Deputy Director Ned Buxton had arrived yesterday, representing Director Donovan, who was on an extended trip to India and Australia. Wild Bill wanted the OSS ready in advance of the combined joint chiefs of staff review of the Operation GYMNAST plan over the next week. The pending operation was going to be the first major test of the OSS, and the organization's contribution to a successful, conventional, military combat operation.

Chief of Station Tangiers Bill Eddy had arrived yesterday, as well, having been called to London for this meeting. Eddy had been in place for seven months and was responsible for all OSS operations in Northwest Africa.

Chief of Station London William 'Bill' Phillips hosted the meeting in their new headquarters for European operations. Phillips was a career diplomat with the U.S. State Department, serving in a wide variety of positions, including undersecretary of state in the Harding and early Roosevelt administrations. He had resigned from the State Department, the previous October. Bill Donovan snatched him up to be chief of station London.

"Director Donovan is quite concerned about the impending GYMNAST review and our part in support of the operation. He is tending to the other side of the globe and entrusted this task to me," Buxton said. "So, Bill, why don't you bring us up to date on your preparations."

"Yes sir. As we discussed and agreed last December, before I took my present post, Bob Murphy and I have worked to: first, establish the alignment of French officers in Morocco and Algeria, and second, to determine which of those officers were amenable to our objectives in North Africa. At a broad summary level, the French Army and Air Force appear to be supportive of Allied operations in North Africa to rid them of German influence. The Navy, however, is still smarting from and resentful of the British Operation CATAPULT—the preemptive strike at Mers-el-Kébir, two years ago. Major General Charles Mast, commander of the French XIX Corps in Algeria, appears to be the most closely aligned. From everything we have learned so far, Mast should be the focus of our efforts. We turn him, and we bring along the other army generals, and quite likely air force generals as well."

"Those are positive results, so far," said Buxton. "However, this state is likely to be too soft for General Eisenhower and his generals. What can we do to solidify French alignment, or at a minimum neutralize the Vichy French territorial forces?"

"The French have low and mid-level flag officers in Northwest Africa. None of them wants to get crosswise with their senior colleagues. The one thing that unites them all is the Germans. However, they are loyal to the French Republic first and foremost, and that is the Vichy government, for better or worse," Eddy reported. "I say this because there are two political realities in this question. One, none of them wants to be hanging out there alone. Two, they want their senior generals to sanction or support any assistance to the Allies. Without such a demonstration, they all articulate their obligation to comply with their orders, which means the defense of French territory."

"General de Gaulle?"

"Absolutely not," Eddy responded emphatically. "Many of the Vichy generals see de Gaulle as a traitor, who deserted his nation at their ultimate time of trial. If I had to point to one flag officer that could be pivotal with the entire Vichy French military, I would say Admiral Darlan. He is the *de facto* leader of the joint chiefs and holds considerable sway among his colleagues.

"Another candidate might be General Henri Honoré Giraud. We have information from several diverse sources that Giraud has escaped from the senior officer's POW camp Four-B at Königstein, Saxony, last April—a rather daunting mountain fortress near Dresden. The SOE aided his disguise, movement, and support. Giraud rejected broader assistance from the British. We know he made it safely to Switzerland. The SOE lost contact with him when he sought support from his friends. We believe from the SOE that he may be *en route* to Marseilles or Toulon area of Vichy France. General Mast told me directly that Giraud is held in far higher regard than de Gaulle. He stood his ground and did not run."

"We might be able to help on that end," offered Phillips. "We have assets in Switzerland and Vichy France."

"Whatever we do," responded Eddy, "we must coordinate with the SOE and MI6, to work together to the same end. I would not advocate for any action that might interfere with Giraud's safety and progress. Brigadier Gubbins believes, presumably from his field agents, that Giraud is hell-bent on convincing Pétain that the German defeat is inevitable, and Vichy France should resist German activities, if not openly fight against the Germans. If Gubbins is correct, Giraud has taken a potentially more pro-Allied position than Admiral Darlan."

"OK, Bill," interjected Buxton, "what is your recommendation based on your groundwork?"

"First, we cannot put all our eggs in one basket. Second, I have sketched several potential paths to achieve our objective. Third, neither the OSS nor SOE can do this alone. We must work together. That said, we must convince General Eisenhower that we have a viable plan to neutralize or flip the Vichy French territorial forces during the Northwest Africa operation. If our efforts are not accepted as an essential part of the operations plan, then we should have a secret supplement with Eisenhower's sanction."

"The plan?" Buxton asked with some annoyance.

"My recommendation is that we should pursue each of the fulcrum points I have summarized. Each will require a different approach, so we must specify. Giraud is not likely to be successful in convincing the Vichy government in joining the Allies or even resisting in their own ways. Our objective should be to protect Giraud, as best we can. We need to quietly consult with Darlan through whoever is best positioned to get close enough to Darlan in private. Admiral Pike should be of considerable assistance to that purpose. We should do what has to be done to get Giraud out of France and to stand in person with the territorial forces in Africa. Bob Murphy and I will continue to work on General Mast and the others we know are sympathetic to see how we can strengthen their support of our efforts. Ned, Bob and I both agree; the French in Northwest Africa are ripe for turning. We may encounter some resistance. The landing forces must be prepared to deal with that resistance in measured fashion to avoid alienating the generals as the British did at Mers-el-Kébir."

"Churchill argued he had no choice," observed Buxton. "The risk of the Germans gaining control of the French warships at the moment of their greatest vulnerability was simply too great, and the French naval commander did not accept the ultimatum. What about de Gaulle?"

"Based on what I have heard from every one of the officers I have talked with directly, I would exclude and prohibit de Gaulle from this effort."

"That presents a political problem, which I am sure you recognize."

"Yes, it does, but that is my recommendation. The French officers in Morocco and Algeria have no faith in de Gaulle—none, zero."

Buxton stared at Eddy in contemplation for several seconds. "Very well. We will take that approach." Buxton shifted his gaze to Bill Phillips. "Who is invited and will attend your dinner party tonight?"

"Eisenhower and Clark were invited but declined due to other commitments," responded Phillips. "Those who were invited and accepted are Patton, Doolittle, and Strong."

Buxton smiled. "That should work, a good mix—armor/infantry, air, and intelligence." He looked at Eddy. "It will be showtime for you tonight, Bill. You'll have a good cross-section of senior officers to try out your proposal. One word of caution, though . . . do not oversell your recommendations. Patton will likely lead an armor corps for the invasion. Doolittle may well be the aviation commander. And, you know George Strong, as the new Army G-2, has an ax to grind with us. He has not hidden his disdain for General Donovan, the OSS, and our mission. I say this as a word to the wise, not as a constraint. Our focus in this matter should be on the supreme commander."

"Understood, sir."

"Play it straight up the middle," Buxton added. "Just know what you're up against. Now, unless you have something more to add . . . ."

"Just details, sir."

"Very well. I will excuse myself to tend to the message traffic. I doubt I will get word back from General Donovan before dinner, but we shall see. We are not going to wait for the director's approval."

Buxton departed and apparently knew the way to the secure message center.

Eddy looked at Phillips. "Nice headquarters building, Bill."

"Yes, we were very lucky, and I'm sure we had a little help from our friends. We have this building as our storefront, and we also have the building next door, number 72. Bill was quite demonstrative when we started this process. He wanted room to expand. He sees London Station as the center of European operations before and after the war."

"After the war?"

"Yes, Wild Bill Donovan is quite the visionary. He has seen the OSS as a national intelligence and special operations agency. He also believes that once the Germans and Japanese are beaten, the nation will have to deal with the Soviet Union and likely the Communist Chinese."

"Surely, you jest."

Phillip's expression remained neutral and steely-eyed. "Not in the slightest. Wild Bill is definitely taking the long view of international affairs."

"That is a lot to think about."

"Bill, there will be time to consider the long term. Right now, we need you to focus on the command structure for this effort."

"Got it. To that end, I will excuse myself as well to get ready for tonight and the next few days."

The two chiefs of their respective OSS stations shook hands, and Eddy departed. Bill Eddy walked to Claridge's on Brook Street to rehearse his proposal again.

—

Wednesday, 15.July.1942
RAF Debden
Saffron Walden, Essex, England
United Kingdom
16:10 hours

Brian Drummond sat outside with his two wingmen in the shade of the Dispersal Hut. The summer afternoon sky was clear and the air warm. They waited for the last four of the replacement fighters to arrive, along with perhaps one or two station spares. Eight other aircraft arrived just after lunchtime and were all in the maintenance hangers going through the required acceptance checks and having the unique designators for each aircraft added.

Hunter saw the five Spitfires five miles out in right echelon formation. They were not descending. The flight of five approached the airfield at full throttle and high speed. The melodious roar of the five Merlins grew in volume as the aircraft closed the distance. At the threshold of runway 28, the lead aircraft banked hard left. The other aircraft followed at three-second intervals. The five aircraft landed in sequence and taxied to the squadron flight line. All five aircraft were smooth and freshly painted with the standard camouflage paint scheme, with only the empennage roundel and tail fin flash markings. All five aircraft appeared to be brand-spanking-new Spitfire Mark VBs.

The Green Section pilots watched the new aircraft shutdown. Brian was focused on the fifth aircraft for some reason.

"Hey, isn't that the female pilot from the farewell dinner last week?" observed Dusty.

Brian looked at Dusty, and then looked to where his right wingman was looking. The light brown wavy shoulder-length hair and her porcelain face identified ATA Third Officer Marilyn Powell. As Brian recognized Jeremy's girlfriend, he stood and walked toward her. A few seconds later, Marilyn recognized Brian and turned toward him.

Marilyn reached out and hugged Brian. "Great to see you, again, Hunter."

"Likewise, Marilyn."

"We brought in your replacement aircraft—brand new, straight from the factory."

"Thanks. We were cavalry without horses."

"What happened?"

"The ship carrying our aircraft was sunk by the Germans before they reached Archangel."

"So, you fellas were headed to Russia?"

"Yes, that was the plan, until our aircraft were lost."

Just then, ATA First Officer Jackie Cochran joined them, and she did not wait for salutations. "So, you jokers lost a whole squadron's worth of Spitfires."

Brian laughed. "Great to see you, again, Miss Cochran. Yes, we did, and thank you, ladies, for delivering these new ones. We should be back in business tomorrow."

Dusty and Frog joined Hunter. Introductions were completed. Dusty kept gushing over Jackie Cochran and her pre-war, aviation speed exploits.

"Mister Drummond," a female British voice came from behind Brian, "we meet again."

Brian turned to see a familiar face, short blond hair, and captivating, brilliant, blue eyes.

"You don't remember me. I'm hurt."

"Oh, I remember you . . . but I'm struggling to remember your name."

"Jennifer Brentwood," she said and extended her right hand. "I delivered a new Mark Two to you nearly a year ago, to replace your tired old Hurri."

"Ah, yes, great to see you again. Allow me to introduce you to my two wingmen—Dusty Langford and Frog Forcier." They all shook hands.

Brian noticed the two female pilots from the fourth and fifth aircraft walking toward them. The ground crews had already begun towing the new Spitfires to the hanger for their acceptance checks. He also noticed a twin-engined Avro Anson taxiing toward the squadron area.

"Our ride is here," said Cochran. "I'm afraid we must excuse ourselves, fellas. We have one more set of deliveries to make before dusk. Great to see you, again, Hunter. Nice to meet you guys. We must go." Cochran swung her right hand over her head, then pointed toward the Anson. The transport aircraft stopped, the pilot kept the engines at idle, and the empennage hatch opened. The last two turned, joined the first three, and the five female pilots climbed into the Anson transport. Cochran was last and waved as she boarded the aircraft. The extendable steps were pulled in, and the hatch closed. Within minutes, the Anson took to the air and disappeared.

When the sound and sight of the Anson were gone, the Green Section pilots remained standing by the flight line.

"I had no idea Jackie Cochran was here or that you know her," Dusty said without moving.

"Yeah, I met her and Marilyn for the first time at Shepherd's last March."

"You do get around," observed Frog.

That was the same evening I met Lady Castlerosse. If they only knew . . .
"Just lucky."

"Better lucky than good, right boss?" said Frog.

Brian smiled.

"What is Cochran doing here . . . besides ferrying aircraft?" Dusty asked.

"She brought a couple of dozen female pilots over here to learn how the ferry business works. According to Jackie, General Arnold wants to create a similar female ferry command in the United States, to free up male pilots for combat assignments, just as the Air Transport Auxiliary does for the Royal Air Force. Cochran and her lady pilots will be the core of the American version of the ATA."

"Wow! That is history in the making," observed Dusty.

"I suppose so. I'm going to go check on our aircraft."

"We'll go with you."

The three Green Section pilots walked to the hangars. The beehive of activity was reassuring. These men knew their jobs well. The first of the aircraft to arrive began to roll out of the acceptance process. *We will be ready for tomorrow.*

———

Wednesday, 15. July. 1942
No. 54 Berkeley Square House
Berkeley Square
Mayfair, London, England
United Kingdom
18:05 hours

Bill Phillips welcomed his guests. Ned Buxton and Bill Eddy had arrived 20 minutes earlier. The three men greeted the generals. The three intelligence officers mutually agreed to dress in business suits, even though they all held military rank in the OSS.

Since January, Major General George Smith Patton, Jr., USA [USMA 1909], had been Commanding General, I Armored Corps, at the Desert Training Center he had created in California. Eisenhower personally asked him to temporarily join his staff in planning the North Africa campaign. Patton was widely considered the best and most aggressive armor general in the Army. He was not wearing his trademark pistols.

Brigadier General James Harold Doolittle, USA, had been an accomplished and celebrated aviator before the Pearl Harbor attack. The Tokyo Raid that bears his name to this day and the Medal of Honor President Roosevelt awarded to the intrepid aviator cemented his place in aviation history. Doolittle had only recently joined the 8th Air Force, like Patton, to help plan the aviation supplement for the upcoming North Africa campaign, as well as the strategic bombing campaign for which the Army was quickly building its heavy bombing force in England.

Brigadier General George Veazey Strong, USA [USMA 1904], had just become Assistant Chief of Staff, G-2, the chief of the Army's Military Intelligence Division, a month ago. He had served previously as the head of the War Plans Division at Army Headquarters, and the Chief of the Army Mission to the United Kingdom.

Drinks of preference were served. They assembled in the spacious living room with large windows overlooking the trees of Berkeley Square Park.

"Nice accommodations, Bill," Doolittle observed.

"Yes, it is," added Strong. "To be direct, accommodations like this," he paused and swung his arm around the room, "are far more lavish than an Army lieutenant colonel equivalent can afford."

"This place is a lot more than I need, but it also serves as part dormitory, part hideaway, for transient OSS members," Phillips responded.

"Well, I must say, it could pass for a fancy whorehouse," Patton chuckled. "You're not planning a lucrative side business, are you, Bill?"

Phillips chuckled uneasily. "Absolutely not. Strictly the nation's business."

"Oh, come now, no need to be prudish around us. We're all Army here, right."

"I'm a Marine, General."

"Yeah, sure, Army with gills and webbed extremities," Patton quipped. Everyone laughed.

"Since you brought it up, why aren't you officers in uniform?" asked Strong.

Phillips changed the subject. "Dinner will be served in a few minutes. Would anyone like to freshen their drink?"

Patton chuckled. Everyone did. "So, to pick up the lance, why are you here? I mean, the deputy director, the London station chief, I understand their presence, but why is a Marine intelligence officer, working for the OSS, showing up at a dinner given by the Chief of Station?"

"Well, sir, since you asked, I am the U.S. naval attaché to Morocco by day and the OSS Chief of Station Tangiers by night." Patton gestured for Eddy to continue. Eddy smiled. "We have an appointment with General Eisenhower tomorrow afternoon to discuss our—the OSS—support of Operation GYMNAST."

"I didn't know the OSS had armored divisions?" quipped Patton.

Eddy smiled again. "No, sir, we do not, General. We have a proposal to diminish or negate the resistance of the territorial forces."

"Well, now, colonel, that piece of news captured my attention."

"Since January of this year, Bob Murphy and I . . ."

"Excuse me, Bob Murphy?" Patton asked.

"President Roosevelt's appointed special representative to French North Africa, essentially the ambassador without the title." Patton nodded his head. "Anyway, since January, Bob and I have been working the flag officers of the French Territorial Army, to carefully ascertain their leanings. We masked our intelligence purpose in the form of political outreach." Patton impatiently gestured to get on with it. "To put our efforts in simple summary form, we believe we can take action to neutralize the army, potentially the air force, and we have a long shot with the Navy."

"What about turning them to support us against the Germans . . . and the Italians?" Patton queried.

Bill Eddy repeated his proposal and recommendation.

"That is outrageous!" protested Strong.

"Easy now, George," interjected Doolittle. "He has laid out a potential to at least neutralize the opposing force."

"They are suggesting we expose our operational plans to the enemy."

"Bill is suggesting they might be able to thwart the French in North Africa," said Doolittle.

"Exactly, sir," Eddy said. "We need the support of the supreme commander and specialized military assets to exec . . . ."

"Like what?" interjected Patton.

"A submarine, for example," answered Eddy.

"Submarine? We don't have submarines," said Patton.

"The Royal Navy does."

"Ahhh . . . the supreme commander has that access."

"Exactly, sir. Fewer people involved. The benefit at issue is the reduction of casualties to gain control of Northwest Africa and close on the Germans from the west. The cost is the potential failure of the invasion and higher casualties. As leaders of your prospective elements of the projected landing force, you should be aware of our proposal. General Eisenhower might well ask you for your assessment and/or support."

"I might add," inserted Phillips, "Generals Eisenhower and Clark were invited but could not attend."

"Yeah," Patton responded. "Ike and Mark are in Scotland. We understand."

"I'm against it," Strong declared.

"Against what?" asked Buxton.

"Against this whole cockamamie nonsense. This is not what we do."

George Patton sharply looked directly at George Strong. "And, perhaps, that is the root of the matter."

Strong huffed but did not answer.

Buxton jumped in, "We wanted to make you aware of our initiative since the supreme commander and his deputy could not be present. I believe each of you will have opportunities to contribute to and review the plan."

The chief steward appeared and announced dinner.

"Before we sit down to the evening meal," said Patton, "you are not going into a sit-down with Ike without having a good assessment of the likelihood of success. Y'all clearly believe you have a better than a 50-50 shot at success. Why?"

Buxton smiled and looked at Eddy. Bill caught the cue. "I speak fluent Arabic, including numerous dialects, including Moroccan, as well as Metropolitan French. I believe I have gained the confidence of General Mast, Major General Emmanuel Charles Mast, Commander Algiers Division. I also believe we have several paths to convince the French generals to help us rather than resist us."

Buxton raised his hand and said, "We believe General Eisenhower is amenable to OSS special operation support of GYMNAST."

"Well then, George," Patton said to Strong, "I suggest we hear what the supreme commander thinks, and then we can deal with the details when we see the plan.

Strong nearly sneered at Patton. "Very well, general."

Phillips gestured toward the dining room. The officers went to their assigned positions at the dining table. The discussion over supper and afterward dealt with other topics away from the war, like the rationing in England compared to the still abundant supply in the United States. They all believed the U.S. was headed toward similar rationing provisions to protect resources for the war effort. The conversation was cordial, respectful, and occasionally even humorous.

As the party broke up, the three OSS men remained behind.

"I thought the evening went well," Bill Phillips observed.

"Yes, it did. I agree. I do believe you carried the day. Now, we'd better get you back to your hotel for your beauty rest. We have a date with General Eisenhower at eight tomorrow morning. That will be truth or consequences time for us."

"Thank you, sir. Thank you, Bill, for the delightful meal and evening. Well done," Buxton commented. "I think we did some good spade work."

Buxton and Eddy excused themselves. An OSS unmarked automobile waited outside. The driver took them back to Claridge's.

—

Saturday, 18. July. 1942
Headquarters, European Theater of Operations, United States Army
20 Grosvenor Square
Mayfair, London
United Kingdom
14:30 hours

The rather exclusive club, otherwise known as the combined joint chiefs of staff, had reviewed the three major plans. They even managed to have yet one more spirited debate of ROUNDUP versus GYMNAST with the same conclusion they had arrived at in their prior discussions. Prime Minister Churchill attended and conveyed the King's regrets for not being able to attend. Harry Hopkins was attending as President Roosevelt's observer and representative.

The group assembled around the rectangular conference table with Churchill and Hopkins sitting side-by-side at the far end opposite the small podium and the large wall map of North Africa, the Mediterranean, and Southern Europe. The senior officers chose to sit by service rather than by country. Generals Brooke and Marshall on one side, and Air Chief Marshal Portal, General Arnold, and Admirals Pound and King on the other side.

General Eisenhower stood at the podium and tapped a small stone on the wood. "Welcome, Prime Minister and Mister Hopkins." Both men nodded. "We cleared the last of the concerns presented by the chiefs in our review yesterday evening. In summary, we have collectively agreed to a three-pronged assault plan." Eisenhower retrieved a long, red-tipped, wooden pointer from the corner where it was leaning. "The Western Task Force will land at three beaches in Morocco—Safi, Fedala, near Casablanca, and Mehdiya," the general said and pointed to each site. "The Center Task Force will land at three sites bracketing Oran, Algeria," he said, again pointing to the three designated sites, "and, the Eastern Task Force will bracket Algiers."

"Excuse me, General," interjected Churchill. "This plan seems to violate one of Sun Tsu's essential principles of warfare—the massing of forces."

"In evaluating the various conflicting aspects of this operation, we needed to balance our exposure to any French, territorial, or indigenous opposition. Each task force will have substantial force. While our distribution of forces may change as our intelligence estimates evolve, we have provisionally assigned the British 78th Infantry Division and the American 34th Infantry Division, along with numbers One and Six Commandos, to the Eastern Task Force. The American 1st Infantry Division and U.S. 1st Armored Division, augmented by elements of the American 509th Parachute Infantry Regiment, are assigned to the Center Task Force. The Western Task Force includes the American 3rd and 9th Infantry Divisions with the U.S. 2nd Armored Division. British and American naval and air assets are allocated to each task force. The assault force will deploy from the United States and the United Kingdom"

"That's a lot of moving parts," Churchill observed.

"Yes sir, it is. We collectively agree that this is a manageable plan. We have responded to intelligence estimates of the French forces we will face at each landing site. Neutralizing the French forces to minimize casualties on both sides is our primary objective to ensure our foothold for subsequent operations with the 8th Army in Egypt to close the jaws on the enemy forces we face. Our secondary objective is to convince the French to join us. To that end, I must acknowledge and laud the impressive groundwork of the SOE and OSS in Northwest Africa. We have also agreed to a secret, compartmented, supplemental plan to accomplish those objectives *vis-à-vis* the French Territorial Army. If the heads of state approve this plan, we will commit the necessary assets to support the supplemental plan. The preparations of our operational plan, and especially the supplemental plan, raised an important political issue."

"Pray tell us how we may be of assistance?" Churchill asked.

Eisenhower looked at General Marshall, who subtly nodded his head to proceed. "We believe General de Gaulle must be excluded from knowledge or support of this operation."

"Why?"

"The work accomplished so far is unanimous. The French generals view de Gaulle as a traitor, who ran rather than stand by his country. The assessment of the intelligence specialists to date tells us the local generals will not respond positively to any involvement by de Gaulle."

"That is quite the conundrum. Pardon me, General Eisenhower, in this matter, I need to hear from the chiefs."

General Brooke jumped in directly. "General de Gaulle was not popular or well respected by his colleagues before the war. His flight as France fell cemented their disdain. As the supplemental plan outlines, we intend to make a valiant attempt to capitalize on General Giraud's escape from captivity. His colleagues, and especially those serving in North Africa, hold him in very high regard. Giraud needs to be approached carefully and precisely by our American brethren. To the best of our knowledge, he does not look favorably upon us."

"Mers-el-Kébir?"

"They are still smarting," interjected Admiral Pound.

"They were given more than ample opportunity to accommodate our serious concerns."

"Yes sir, they were," Sir Dudley answered, "but that does not alter the devastating and I must say humiliating losses they suffered at our hands that day."

"A regrettable consequence for which we must atone, but vitally necessary. We had no choice. The French commander gave us no choice. So, I assume you are all unanimous in this recommendation?" Churchill looked at each of the chiefs, both British and American, and received a confirmatory acknowledgment. The prime minister smiled. "My goodness, this is a rare moment to have so many general officers in agreement on anything." Many laughed and chuckled. "President Roosevelt has already expressed his concerns about General de Gaulle's legitimacy as the titular head of the Free French Forces. Nonetheless, I shall take the matter up with President Roosevelt forthwith. I cannot say I disagree. However, you are asking us to walk a very thin and wavy line here."

"I do believe we recognize the difficulty," Marshall said. "We shall have to assuage de Gaulle's vaunted ego. We collectively," he said, gesturing to the senior officers at the table, "are in complete agreement with the field reports. Our best likelihood of success is to follow their recommendations as outlined in the supplement."

"Thank you for that, General."

"If I may add, Prime Minister," the first sea lord said. Churchill looked at Sir Dudley and nodded. "With Admiral Pike's assistance and Brigadier Menzies's support, I sent a personal message of introduction with one of Admiral Pike's senior agents with whom François Darlan was familiar."

Amiral de la Flotte Jean Louis Xavier François Darlan had been Commander-in-Chief of "*La Royale*," *Marine Nationale* since 1939, just after war was declared. He took on the additional responsibility of the prime minister of Vichy, France, reporting only to his friend and comrade Philippe Pétain, until the Germans insisted Pierre Laval replace him in April

1942. Darlan held considerable sway within the remainder of the French government, even as a minister without portfolio.

"He responded favorably but guardedly. Like many in the French Navy and armed forces in general, he is distrustful after the insult of Mers-el-Kébir. However, that said, Jumper and I both believe his response to our outreach indicates he is not happy with the direction Laval is headed and may be amenable to throwing his weight with us. Jumper suggested an addendum to the secret supplement that is simple and rather ingenious, I must say. Darlan's son is a Navy lieutenant serving in Algiers. The young man may serve our purposes to get Darlan to Algiers as the invasion is to begin and may well provide decisive influence in turning the territorial forces to our cause."

"Excellent," Churchill responded. "My compliments to you and Jumper, Sir Dudley. I'm certain there is much work to be done before the plan is ready to execute, but a good start. May I ask a routine question?" Churchill paused, but no one responded. "Do you have the necessary shipping and landing craft assigned? And, do you have sufficient follow-on logistics support to sustain and augment such a large and dispersed assault force?"

"The direct answer," Eisenhower began, "is those elements are a work in progress. We do not have sufficient dedicated assets either for the initial lift or sustaining support. Some of the required shipping is still under construction in the United States. We have tentatively agreed to a temporary diversion of some live assets from the Atlantic supply force. We have coordinated with the ministers of Shipping and Supply to absorb the near-term shortfall during the invasion. Admiral King has offered direct coordination with the construction organizations during the preparation phase to ensure the pending shipping we need will be ready and accepted into service in time to move Western Task Force units and necessary supplies in time." Admiral King nodded his head in agreement. "There is no question this operation will be more on the fragile side than we would like, but we collectively agree these risks are required to meet the 'this year' timeline objective."

"Are you arguing for a delay, General Eisenhower?"

General Marshall raised his hand and stepped in. "We have spent inordinate time discussing the risks in this plan," the chief of staff said, looking around the table. "I do not presume to speak for the whole of the combined joint chiefs; however, I think it safe to say the planning staff and command leadership have successfully addressed our concerns. We support this plan, Mister Prime Minister."

Churchill looked at each officer and received a sign of affirmation. "No one said war is not without risk. We need this important operation to be successful, not just for ourselves, but perhaps more importantly, to assist our Soviet colleagues who remain deeply engaged in a mortal struggle." Churchill looked to his left. "Mister Hopkins, do you have anything you wish to ask or say on behalf of the president?"

"No," Harry answered softly. "You have said it all quite well, Mister Prime Minister."

"Very well, then, I am in agreement with and in support of this plan. I will transmit my thoughts to The King and President Roosevelt as soon as I return to the War Rooms. Thank you, gentlemen. Please convey my appreciation to your planning staff, General Eisenhower. We have come a very long way since the ARCADIA Conference seven months ago. Well done, I must declare."

The meeting adjourned, and they disbanded.

———

Friday, 24.July.1942
Headquarters, European Theater of Operations, United States Army
20 Grosvenor Square
Mayfair, London
United Kingdom
16:15 hours

Mark Clark entered Eisenhower's office. "Your message said you had news."

Ike extended his right hand with a single sheet of red candy-stripe-bordered paper. "This just arrived."

Clark took the message and read it.

———

TOP SECRET

```
NO
WAR TOP NR 11347
TS 241422Z JUL 42
FM SECWAR COSARMY
TO CG ETOUSA
T O P   S E C R E T
OPERATION TORCH
BT
GYMNAST RENAMED TORCH BREAK PMUK AND POTUS
APPROVED PLAN OF 18 JULY 1942 BREAK YOU ARE
HEREBY APPOINTED SUPREME COMMANDER ALLIED
FORCES BREAK EXECUTE OPERATION TORCH ON OR
```

```
ABOUT 31 OCTOBER 1942 BREAK GOOD LUCK GODSPEED
END
BT
COPY TO WPD WAR DEPT
NNNN
```

TOP SECRET

"I'll be damned, Ike. We are a go for execution, and they changed the name."

Eisenhower smiled. "They called our bluff. It is on us now."

"Have faith, Ike. We have a sound plan. Have you considered your commanders?"

"Yes. First and foremost, I know you want a combat command, Mark, but selfishly I need you as my deputy for a host of reasons."

This time Clark smiled. "I am grateful for your confidence in me. Yet, I would be speaking a falsehood if I denied my desire for a combat command, and our honor to the Long Gray Line cannot be broken.

"Thank you, Mark. You will get your time. It may not be of much solace, but you will gain far more insight into combat command as my deputy than you would leading a division. You are destined to command, Mark. Just be patient."

"Easily said, not so easily done. So, if you don't mind me asking, what are your thoughts on your field commanders?"

"I still have considerable barter work to accomplish. So far, I think the Eastern Task Force will be British. I would love to have Alexander, but that is not possible. The leading contenders are Anderson and Montgomery—both very capable armor generals. I want George Patton for the Western Task Force, but his assignment seems to be a little more problematic with the British. I'm still up in the air with the Center Task Force."

"Good choices all. If there is anything I can do to assist you, I am ready, willing, and able to help."

"I know, Mark. Thank you for your understanding. To be blunt and candid, Operation TORCH will be a test for both of us. We must not fail."

"We won't, Ike. We won't."

After a good pause, Clark excused himself and departed.

Saturday, 25.July.1942
Chequers Court
Ellenborough,Buckinghamshire, England
United Kingdom
16:25 hours

The last scheduled event for the combined joint chiefs of staff had begun—a weekend retreat at the prime minister's country estate. All of the chiefs arrived together before lunch. The prime minister had just reappeared after his afternoon nap and found General Eisenhower.

"Walk with me, if you would, General," Churchill said.

"Certainly."

Churchill gestured for them to exit the manor house and into the immaculately manicured garden. "First, I wanted a personal, private word to convey my genuine admiration and appreciation for the extraordinary work you have done to bring the joint staff together. The integration has been impressive."

"Thank you, sir."

"As we both know, the plan is only the plan until the first bullet is fired, then we must adapt to evolving circumstances. We have a solid and sound plan in large part as a consequence of your personal efforts to meld both groups into one cohesive staff." The prime minister reached into his inside jacket pocket and extracted a single folded sheet of paper. He handed it to Eisenhower. "I received this message after my nap."

Eisenhower took the paper, unfolded it, and read the message.

MOST SECRET

```
WH
TS 251317Z JUL 42
FM POTUS
TO PMUK
T O P   S E C R E T
OPERATION TORCH
BT
TORCH APPROVED PER 18 JULY 1942 PLAN STOP
RECOMMENDATION FOR SUPREME COMMANDER ACCEPTED
STOP EISENHOWER SO INFORMED END
BT
NNNN
```

MOST SECRET

Ike refolded the message and handed it back to Churchill, and they continued to saunter through the exquisite garden.

"Congratulations, Ike. This is your show now. We look forward to great things from you and your team."

"Thank you, sir."

"We did not discuss commanders at the review conference a week ago. I know you have given that question considerable thought. If it is not premature, what are your thoughts?"

"You know how I feel about Alexander."

"Yes, I do . . . and you know how I feel. It is looking like I am facing changes in Egypt, sooner rather than later, and Sir Harold Alexander features in those changes."

Ike nodded his agreement. "Short of Alexander, I favor Ken Anderson to command the Eastern Task Force."

"I do believe Sir Alan supports that choice."

"Yes, he does. I am also considering George Patton for the Western Task Force."

"He is rather mercurial it seems to me, but from everything I have read, seen and heard about Patton, he is a very capable armor officer. North Africa is armor terrain. I have not met the man as yet. However, I do look forward to the opportunity, regardless of your choice."

"I do not need to sing his praises. His performance will speak for him. I have not decided, I must say. He was here for a few weeks to help us with the battle plan. I will probably need to have him back here before I decide. I would be happy to arrange a meeting for you with him, as soon as you are ready."

"That would be helpful. I hope you view me as a resource, Ike. I will eagerly assist you, as you may wish. We need you to be successful in your new assignment. To that end, I would like to suggest we establish standing personal meetings. I have a standing luncheon date with The King on Mondays. May I propose we set a Tuesday luncheon date for just the two of us, and Friday evening supper for a standing social interaction with us and a few others from time to time."

"Thank you very much for the generous offer of your time. I am honored to accept your invitation, as I am able. I am sure you recognize there will be days I am in the field in the months ahead."

"As will I, Ike. We shall do our best. We can also hold to our standing meetings in the field when we are both co-located."

"Agreed."

"Now, I am mindful of the time, and we have a bevy of generals in the house conspiring for God knows what purpose." They both laughed. "Shall we return to our guests?"

Eisenhower nodded. They turned and headed back to the famous manor house. All of the members of the combined joint chiefs of staff offered their collective and individual congratulations to Eisenhower, and their commitment to helping him be successful with the first major Western Allied effort in the European Theater.

—

Chapter 12

The truth is often a terrible weapon of aggression.
It is possible to lie, and even to murder, for the truth.

-- Alfred Adler

Thursday, 6.August.1942
RAF Debden
Saffron Walden, Essex, England
United Kingdom
16:05 hours

Yellow Section returned after a long patrol over a rare English Channel convoy—east to west. The squadron had been at Available all day except for a quick lunch, and Yellow Section had been and was quite likely the only section to fly on this particular day. Brian and the remainder of the squadron pilots continued to wait, as they had been doing all day. The intelligence debriefing for Yellow Section had gone comparatively fast.

"That was boring as hell," announced Sloppy Butterfield, as the three pilots entered the Dispersal Hut and hung up their flight gear.

"We didn't have any fun on the mission, but we did pick up a good rumor," Sweet Sweeney offered.

"Do tell," shouted Hick.

"We had to stop at Biggin Hill for fuel on the way back. I ran into one of the 133 guys I know. He said some senior RAF officer, a group captain, told them the Air Ministry was in the final stages of negotiating our transfer to the Army."

"All three squadrons?" asked Dusty.

"Yeah, all three of the American volunteer squadrons, and that includes us."

"When?" Salt asked.

"He didn't say, well, at least he didn't get an indication from the officer. He guesses in a month or two."

"And, your friend thinks it's really and finally going to happen?" Salt pressed.

"Based on what I heard, yes, I think so." Sweet looked to Pete and Sloppy. "You guys heard what Jerry said, what do you think?"

"That's what I heard, too," Sloppy answered.

"Me, as well," added Pete, "but, more importantly, the 133 guys had their first encounter with the Focke-Wulf 190s. They were quite impressed . . . to the point."

"I guess we are going to see more of the 190s," Whitey said, "although the intelligence blokes claim most of the German production is going east. Some are apparently coming our way."

"My guess, as well," responded Pete. "The 133 guys were pretty emphatic about the 190 being more capable than the 109s."

"We've seen a couple of photos and the three-view from the Air Ministry," added Whitey. "We've also studied the intelligence estimates. We're ready for the 190 when we eventually face them." Several seconds of silence suggested the pilots were absorbing Whitey's observation.

"Makes me wonder what the Army knows?" Dusty thought aloud.

"I probably won't find out," Whitey quipped. Everyone laughed.

"Good point, though," Pete said.

"So, based on what we were told last December," interjected Hick, "the Army has the required command structure in place . . . including intelligence?"

"From everything I have heard so far," Pete answered, "I think the answer is yes. The 8th Air Force has established its headquarters in London. Included in that command is the 8th Fighter Command under Brigadier General Hunter—an accomplished fighter pilot I hear—not an ace like our Hunter, but still accomplished."

"Then, what are they waiting for?" Hick asked.

Pete laughed hard. "Hick, my dear fellow, we are just stick-and-throttle jockeys. What the hell do we know, or can we know. I suspect they are working out the details."

"What details! Just wave the wand . . . puff . . . we're in the Army now," declared Hick.

Laughter filled the Dispersal Hut.

"Listening to you blokes," Whitey interjected, "I'd think you folks don't like it here . . . with us Brits."

More laughter punctuated Whitey's comment.

"That ain't so, Whitey," Hick protested. "We love you guys."

The laughter was beginning to water eyes; they were laughing so hard. Tug Meares joined them, smiling as he leaned against the doorjamb to his office. Even Corporal Harris was laughing.

As the laughter subsided, Pete added, "We will know when they want us to know, my brothers. Until then, we have seats in the premier fighter of our times and a place at the table defending freedom."

Several of the pilots clapped. Quiet returned when Tug moved to the briefing map. "I think Whitey and I understand and appreciate your desire to serve with your countrymen. Let it suffice to say, Pete is close enough. I am not at liberty to disclose any pending action, but I am allowed to tell you, the transfer is being finalized as we speak. I cannot tell you when. To be candid, I am really not sure the leadership has set the date, as yet; but, I do believe the transfer is close. So, as we were informed last December, we must remain focused on our assignments. It will happen when it is time. Let us not be distracted from our mission."

—

Friday, 7.August.1942
Guadalcanal
Solomon Archipelago
British Solomon Islands Protectorate

One month earlier, amphibious forces of Imperial Japan landed on the island and immediately began construction of airfields that would directly threaten Northeast Australia.

At 06:00, on this day, the heavy cruiser USS *Quincy* opened fire with her 8-inch, main battery guns on coastal defense targets on the island, known by the code-name 'Cactus.' Allied Operation WATCHTOWER had been conceived with one primary objective—stop the relentless expansion by Japanese armed forces, and take back the island and the archipelago. The combined strike force was under the overall command of Vice Admiral Frank Jack Fletcher, USN [USNA 1906]; he had commanded Task Force 17 aboard *Yorktown* during the Battle of Midway. Commander, Task Force 62 Rear Admiral Richmond Kelly Turner, USN [USNA 1908], led the amphibious forces, after serving as the Chief of the Plans Division prior to the Pearl Harbor attack. The First Marine Division, under the command of Major General Alexander Archer Vandegrift, USMC, landed and established a beachhead. The Battle of Guadalcanal began. Landing force air support came from none other than Brigadier General Roy Stanley Geiger, USMC, Commanding General, First Marine Air Wing, and the core of what would become known as the Cactus Air Force. The island-hopping, offensive operations in the Pacific Ocean region would take back the territory acquired by Japanese imperialism.

Ground, air, and naval engagements associated with the pitched battle for the island would last seven months with repeated very thin margins for error on land, sea, and in the air. Eleven Medals of Honor would be awarded to Marines, Army, and Navy personnel during the course of the battle. Legends sprang from the epic engagements.

—

Saturday, 8.August.1942
Air Ministry
Whitehall, London, England
United Kingdom
10:00 hours

Air Chief Marshal Portal had departed London a week ago to support Prime Minister Churchill on his special mission to Moscow and his meeting with Premier Stalin. Chief of the Imperial General Staff General Brooke was also with the group. The First Sea Lord remained behind.

By mutual agreement, the scheduled meeting was going ahead as planned. Air Chief Marshal Sir Wilfrid Rhodes Freeman, KCB, DSO, MC, Vice-Chief of the Air Staff, took the meeting and hosted Major General Carl Spaatz, Commanding General of the U.S. 8th Air Force. They had only one item on the agenda, although that one item had several sub-elements.

"Top of the morning to you, Sir Wilfrid," said Spaatz.

"And, the rest of the day to you, Carl. So, the day has finally arrived?"

Spaatz chuckled. "From the sound of your words, I would think you want to retain your American volunteer fighter squadrons."

"Of course, we do. They are valuable elements of our air defense system. Yet, we also recognize reality and the agreements of six months ago."

"That is quite a switch from the conversation between Sir William Douglas and Hap Arnold a year and a half ago."

Freeman smiled. "Indeed! They have matured and risen to worthy status, but that is not why you are here."

"No, true, it is not. Yes, the day is here. We are ready to accept the transfer of the three squadrons."

"Very well. As we agreed last month, all of the aircraft, support equipment, and American personnel for all three squadrons will be transferred to your command. We will retain the British pilots that are currently in leadership positions, so you will need to replace them with your leaders. The exception for the short term will be the British ground crews and assigned maintenance personnel. The Americans in the training process have already been transferred."

"Yes, they have."

"As I understand your acceptance, you intend to base all three squadrons at Debden."

"Correct. Upon transfer, they will become the 334th, 335th, and 336th Fighter Squadrons, and collectively they will become the 4th Fighter Wing. The commanders have already received their orders and are en route. We are in the process of scheduling interviews with each of the pilots to determine their suitability for service in the Army Air Forces. We began the interviews earlier this week. We estimate the whole process will take four to five weeks, with potentially another week for follow-ups, if required."

"What do you expect to do with those who may be rejected?"

"If they are suitable for other specialties, they will be given the opportunity to transfer. If they are not suitable for any assignment, our plan is to transport them back to the United States as soon as transportation can be arranged. I suppose you can or should have the choice of retaining those who cannot transfer."

"They have all been serving honorably," Freeman answered with a slight air of protestation.

"I'm sure they have. However, the secretary of war has directed the individual assessments as part of the commissioning process to ensure uniformity with the regulations."

"Understandable. I will discuss this aspect of the transfer endeavor with Sir Charles upon his return. On the face of it, I suppose we could allow an individual to request continued service with the RAF. However, unless we notify your headquarters to the contrary, we will stand with your assessment being the final word. They are your citizens, after all."

"That is acceptable to us," Spaatz affirmed. "We are prepared to make the final determination and take the necessary consequent actions with each American citizen currently serving in the RAF. One other matter, you have 121 Squadron at Southend, 133 Squadron at Biggin Hill, and 71 Squadron is already at Debden."

"Correct."

"If it is not too much to ask, we would like all three squadrons at Debden prior to the transfer. It will enable us to have one simple ceremony at Debden and start off clean."

"Excellent. We will gladly accomplish that task. That makes maintenance support easier. We will transfer our other squadrons from Debden before the transfer date, and the base will become yours to operate from that date. We will transfer the remainder of our support personnel as they are replaced by yours."

"That is the plan, sir. We expect to complete that process within a month of the transfer date, which brings us to the transfer date. We propose the end of September—the 29th to be specific."

"Based on the various moving parts, it would appear the appropriate date to move 121 and 133 Squadrons to Debden would be a couple of days prior to the transfer date." Sir Wilfrid checked his desk calendar and sat back down. "The 29th is a Tuesday. I would suggest we shoot for the end of the prior week, to have the relocation of both squadrons completed by Saturday, the 26th."

"That should work just fine. I will confer with General Hunter, who has been selected to command the 4th Fighter Wing, to give him a voice. I do not anticipate any problems with any of this. We, of course, have other administrative support actions to complete as well, commissioning documents, physicals, uniforms, indoctrination, and such, but that is on us. We will plan for those actions to be completed by the transfer date. Now, for planning purposes, let's tentatively set 11:00 hours on the 29th for the transfer ceremony."

"Agreed."

"Outstanding! It's been a pleasure doing business with you, Sir Wilfrid. Either General Hunter or I will coordinate any adjustments, over the ensuing six weeks, to what we have agreed to this morning."

The two men stood, shook hands, and the deal was done. Now, all that remained was to execute the plan as they had finalized and set in motion.

—

Monday, 10.August.1942
Headquarters, European Theater of Operations, United States Army
20 Grosvenor Square
Mayfair, London
United Kingdom
13:30 hours

Major General George Patton entered now Lieutenant General Eisenhower's corner office, after being announced by the commander's aide-de-camp.

"Welcome back to London, George."

"Thanks, Ike. When the commander of the ETO calls, I come running."

Eisenhower grinned and gestured for his guest to sit on the plush chairs facing each other across the low coffee table. "Just a couple of news items that you may not have heard during your transit," Eisenhower paused without finishing his sentence. Patton nodded his head. "Prime Minister Churchill departed a week ago for Moscow and a meeting with Stalin. He intends to brief Stalin on TORCH and assuage his apprehension regarding the western front."

"How is our favorite commie dictator?"

Eisenhower shook his head in disapproval but did not answer. "En route, he stopped in Egypt, and executed major changes in the British command leadership." Patton's interest piqued, but he did not speak. "Early this morning, the prime minister relieved General Auchinleck. His fate is not yet known. He recalled General Alexander from Burma and installed him as Commander-in-Chief Middle East Command."

General Sir Harold Rupert Leofric George Alexander, GCB, GCMG, CSI, DSO, MC, had been educated at and commissioned from the Royal Military College, Sandhurst, and served with distinction on the Western Front during the Great War. Most recently, Alexander had been Commander-in-Chief, Allied Forces Burma, since March 1942.

"Bloody hell, as the Brits like to say," Patton responded.

"Is that a good or bad exclamation, George?"

"Good, I would say. Auchinleck was always too cautious, too tentative. Nothing about combat, and especially large-scale armored warfare, is precise, pretty, or dignified. The Auk is certainly not a worthy adversary for Rommel. The German has proven himself an able armor general officer—bold, aggressive, and accomplished. Alexander has an excellent reputation, although I have not seen that much of him in the field. What about the 8th Army?"

"Nice that you asked, George. After Richie was relieved of command in June, Auchinleck assumed acting command. Churchill largely holds Auchinleck responsible for the failure of the desert offensive last month. The prime minister chose General Gott . . . ."

"'Strafer' Gott?"

"Lieutenant General William Gott."

"That's him. He earned his moniker. Aggressive leader. He understands armored warfare. Good choice, it seems to me."

"Well, Sir Alan and Sir Harold were not too keen on his selection—too impetuous and mercurial for their liking—but, Churchill felt those qualities were precisely what was needed."

"I agree with the prime minister, if that matters to anyone."

"The point is moot. Gott was killed three days after assuming command."

"Damn it all to hell. What the hell happened?"

"He had just completed his field survey and was returning to Cairo in a Bristol Bombay transport when they were jumped by German fighters. Only three of 18 aboard the transport survived the crash."

"Didn't they have fighter escort?"

"I have not wanted to intrude in their processes at this critical time, as it is currently outside my domain, so I do not know, but my guess is apparently not."

"Damn!"

"Churchill, on the recommendation of Sir Alan, selected General Montgomery for command of the 8th Army."

"A very capable officer, but a bit of a peacock, if you ask me."

"Is that the pot calling the kettle black?"

Patton smiled broadly and replied, "*Touché*, Ike, *touché*. I suppose I am seen by others as a bit colorful."

"An understatement, George."

Patton smiled, again, then his expression turned stone cold. "You didn't bring me back here to convey the latest news, as interesting as it is."

"No, I did not. You have seen our approved Op Plan for TORCH." Patton nodded his head. "I have not yet submitted my command request to the combined joint chiefs, and you and I have not discussed the command positions," Eisenhower paused, expecting a retort from Patton. None came. "I would like you to lead the Western Group."

Patton remained expressionless and silent. Eisenhower gestured, well? "I belong in command of the Eastern Task Force, closest to Rommel." This time, Eisenhower remained expressionless and silent. "Or, at least the Central Task Force. Casablanca is quite a distance from the real action. I don't want to be fighting the French. I am destined to be fighting the Germans, to face and beat Rommel at his own game. I have trained all my life for this moment, this opportunity. Who are you looking at for the Eastern and Central Groups?"

"We are not discussing those assignments, George."

Patton shook his head in disapproval. "I will take what I can get, Ike, and be grateful for your confidence, but if I may ask, why? You know I am the best armor general you've got. That's why you brought me here to help with the plan last month."

"George, I am going to be uncharacteristically blunt and direct with you. There are more than a few people in important positions who do not appreciate your arrogance."

"Arrogance!" protested Patton. "Hell, Ike, it's not arrogance. I've got balls. I do not sit around considering options. I act! I deliver and you know it."

"Which is also why I want you to command. I want to get you in the fight, to show them what you are capable of doing, George."

"So, there are those who don't want me in this operation?"

"Correct."

"I'll be damned. I'm no diplomat general. I am a fucking hard fighting general . . . sorry, Ike . . . ," Patton paused to regain control of his emotions. "I need to stop and listen." Eisenhower did not react. "I'm sure you have your reasons, and I respect the extraordinary job you are doing in such a broad, disparate command." Patton stared at Eisenhower, as if clues were bound to arrive in the commander's eyes and expression, and then shook his head when none came. "Do I have any choices?"

"Yes. You can accept my offer or wait for another command opportunity."

"It's really that bad?"

"Yes."

Patton thought about the reality of the moment, as he understood it. "Very well, then. I accept your offer."

"Hold on just a minute, George. I do not have that authority, as yet. I must gain the approval and sanction of the combined joint chiefs—that's both British and American chiefs. I have not submitted my request, yet. I wanted to talk to you first, to lay out the current resistance against you, and to try to impart a degree of sensitivity regarding the situation. If the chiefs approve my request, I think you should view your situation as a probationary assignment. Those above us who are not appreciative of your aggressive war-fighting spirit are and will be looking for evidence that they were correct in resisting your assignment. I need you to control your natural inclinations and prove them wrong. I must know you understand and are prepared to accomplish that private objective in this assignment."

"I certainly and emphatically understand, and I am ready, willing and able to accept this . . . this . . . this probationary assignment, as you call it."

"Very well, then. That will be my request and recommendation. I expect this process will take several weeks. Assuming you are approved for command, you should receive orders to include the transfer of your current command, along with time to find quarters here. The ETO G-4 will assist to that end. When do you head back?"

"Would it be helpful for me to meet with the British chiefs while I am here?"

"Under normal circumstances, yes, but these are not normal times. I am in a somewhat tentative or probationary status as well—a product of this combined staff construction. I would suggest you lay low, keep your mouth shut, and await the decision of the combined joint chiefs."

"That is against my nature, but I will abide by your counsel, Ike. Marshall will give me a fair shake, and Arnold, if I read him correctly. Thank you for your confidence and the opportunity to serve. I know I am the man for this assignment. I expect to depart tomorrow and await your orders."

"The orders will come from the War Department."

"Yes, yes, of course. Again, thank you for the opportunity." Patton came to a sharp, standing attention, clicked his heels and saluted smartly. The two generals said good-bye, and Patton departed.

———

Wednesday, 12.August.1942
Residence, General Secretary of the
Central Committee of the All-Union Communist Party
Kremlin
Moscow
Union of Soviet Socialist Republics
20:15 hours

Winston Churchill walked confidently behind a Russian foreign ministry representative and a burly serious-looking man with a very tight suit, close-cropped hair. The latter was most likely a member of Stalin's personal security detail or one of the security services. Behind the prime minister in his medium blue suit, white shirt and dark blue necktie were Detective-Inspector Thompson and Major Arthur Herbert Birse, the last minute, stand-in interpreter from the British Military Mission to Russia in Moscow. The scheduled Embassy interpreter had taken ill just that morning. Churchill had arrived that afternoon by aircraft, and at the chairman's personal invitation, their first meeting would be this unofficial private dinner with the general secretary in advance of the BRACELET Conference.

The series of voluminous hallways were all decorated with ornate, gilded scrollwork, elaborate historical frescos, and other historical artifacts. The journey through the labyrinth of hallways proved much longer than Churchill had anticipated. Eventually, they arrived at two, tall, wide double doors and two armed guards in fancy, 18th Century, ceremonial uniforms that seemed so out of place in these times of mortal struggle. As Churchill approached, the guards opened the doors and presented their rifles in salute to the prime minister. Winston returned the salute.

The formidable, gruff figure of Marshal Josef Stalin stood alone on the far side of the large anteroom. Just the parts he could see suggested the general secretary's apartment was expansive and ornately furnished. The scene offered no signs of war, privation or austerity. As Winston entered the residence, Stalin sauntered forward to meet his guest, and Churchill's small escort stopped short, except for Major Birse, who remained a pace behind and to the right of Winston. A small, rather mousey appearing man appeared and joined Stalin in the same position as Birse maintained with Churchill.

The two, wartime leaders shook hands and smiled at each other.

Through his interpreter, Stalin said, "Welcome to Moscow, Mister Prime Minister."

"Thank you for your generous welcome and invitation to join you for dinner, Marshal Stalin."

Stalin gestured for them to enter what was probably the living room or perhaps the reception room. Two drinks had already been poured on the center table. He had handed the amber one to his guest, and he lifted the clear one, presumably vodka. "Red Label, no?" Stalin said.

Churchill smiled. "Your intelligence is quite good."

"This one was easy. Your reputation precedes you," Stalin said and laughed rather coarsely.

The two men offered toasts to their respective countries, to each other, and to their heroic military forces. They talked about the history of the Kremlin and the colorful onion-domes of St. Basil's Cathedral. Stalin was clearly quite proud of Russian history, and specifically the Kremlin offerings.

"Thank you for agreeing to this conference," Churchill said.

"I was surprised but grateful for your request. Direct talks in these troubled times are exceptionally important. Our gallant armed forces have pushed back the Germans from their closest point of approach last December, but they are still less than 200 kilometers from here, thus my surprise at your meeting request."

"Much better than 25 kilometers."

Stalin laughed. "Indeed! Yet, we are a long way from Berlin."

"We will get there together."

Stalin nodded his head and gestured to the dining room. They sat across the end of the long, 24-place, dining table from each other, with their interpreters seated next to them—only the four of them at the end of the table. The appetizer course was lobster dimples with a dollop of Azov sturgeon caviar.

Winston found a moment, leaned over and whispered to Birse, "Who is Stalin's interpreter?"

Major Birse turned his head to place his mouth next to Churchill's left ear and answered softly, "Vladimir Nikolaiovich Pavlov, the principal English interpreter at the Foreign Ministry."

Churchill nodded his head. "He's good."

"Yes, he is, sir . . . very good."

Both men sat back up straight as their main course of a rich beef stroganoff was placed before them. They found delight in the traditional Russian dish exceptionally well prepared. For dessert, a cheesecake-like wedge tasted sweet and delicious, but it was not cheesecake.

"What is this delightfully exquisite dessert?" Churchill asked.

Stalin smiled and laughed modestly. "*Ptichie Moloko.*"

Churchill recognized that Stalin understood English. Pavlov nodded his head and said in perfect English. "It is called Birds' Milk Cake. I will add, it is traditional fare in Russia."

"I really must ask Mrs. Landemare to learn this one."

Stalin nodded his head, apparently pleased with the dinner's success. He said in Russian and Pavlov translated, "Let us retire to the study for cognac and cigars."

The four men went to another large room on the far side of the living room from the dining room. Shelves of books lined the walls in very English fashion. Stewards served a large snifter of French cognac to each of the leaders. The interpreters did not partake. One of the stewards held out a humidor to each leader.

Churchill withdrew one, examined it, smelled the length of it, pronounced, "*Cohiba Robustos* . . . very nice choice . . . rather expensive, as I recall."

"Nothing but the best for our guests."

"Thank you, Your Excellency."

The two leaders prepared and lit up their cigars. After several puffs, Stalin's smile and jovial expressions vanished in an instant. His eyes took on an icy coldness. "When are you going to help us beat the Germans?"

The question shocked Churchill. With uncharacteristic uncertainty, Winston stammered and stuttered. "My gracious, Marshal Stalin, the British people sacrificed an entire convoy of vital supplies that were diverted mid-Atlantic last summer to support your efforts. We have sent other convoys of supplies that we need in England."

"Yes, yes, we are grateful for what you sent, but it is never enough. What we really need is many of these German divisions drawn away from the Motherland. We need a second front immediately."

Churchill smiled and nodded his head. "That is one of many reasons I requested this meeting." Churchill paused. Stalin listened to the Russian translation with the unchanging cold expression and his eyes riveted on Churchill, without blinking once. "President Roosevelt and I reviewed the plan for Operation TORCH."

"Which is?"

"The invasion of Northwest Africa."

"That will not help us. We need fewer Germans in front of us."

"We understand. We have undertaken many operations. The United Kingdom is stretched to the limit. The build-up of United States forces in England is well underway. President Roosevelt and the American people have agreed to a Germany first strategy and their industrial mobilization is growing rapidly. We are limited by the number of landing craft and amphibious ships we have to conduct landing operations."

"Yes, yes," Stalin said with visible irritation, as he waved his cigar. "We need you to attack, not talk, or plan, or build. We need you to attack."

"We had to postpone a division size amphibious landing in Northern France last month, due to inclement weather in the Channel and the area of operation. That operation will be executed next week."

"Not big enough. The Germans will barely twitch. Just not big enough. What is this TORCH you mentioned?"

Churchill again nodded his head. "The plan we approved a couple of weeks ago will land 10 armor and infantry divisions at three sites in Morocco and Algeria, with more to follow. We have worked hard to engage Vichy French forces in the region. We fully expect to neutralize, and then mobilize those forces to join us.

We will capitalize on the coming successes of the British 8th Army in Cyrenaica and Tripolitania, to link-up, encircle and destroy the German and Italian forces in North Africa."

Stalin stared at Churchill without moving and devoid of expression. Several minutes passed as he considered the prime minister's information. "Africa is not Europe. Most of the German Army and Air Force are in Russia. I do not think this TORCH operation is going to help us."

"We think it will. Our strategy is to negate Axis forces in North Africa, threaten the soft underbelly of Europe, take Italy out of the war, and force the Germans to divert forces to the Aegean, Adriatic, and Southern France to counter our forces. We have already seen Hitler drawing forces off the Eastern Front to reinforce the *Afrikakorps*. We will draw off more forces to defend against our inevitable invasion."

"You must attack France. France is the only country that will get the attention of Germany. France is the only nation on Germany's border, on their frontier. You must attack France," Stalin repeated.

This time it was Churchill's time to think. "Marshal Stalin, I understand and appreciate your position. I can assure you I will convey your words to President Roosevelt. Ultimately, we will be constrained by the limits of our shipping. The last thing we need, or you need, is our forces to be insufficient to defeat the Germans at our landing site that results in a stalemate of attrition. We cannot and will not allow another Passchendaele."

"So, are you intending to bleed Russia?"

"Not at all. Just as you do not have unlimited forces, neither do we. The Americans are fighting the Pacific war virtually by themselves. We are doing our part in India, Australia, and New Zealand, but the rest of the Pacific is up to the Americans. And yet, President Roosevelt and the American joint chiefs of staff are committed to the Germany first strategy. I can assure you, both the president and I are doing our utmost to defeat the Germans as quickly as possible."

Stalin chose to change the subject, talking about Russian life in and around Moscow before the war. The second front appeal would be pressed many more times as the Red Army struggled to gain the upper hand against the Germans. However, for the rest of this opening evening, they laughed and enjoyed tales of Russian folklore and happier times.

—

Thursday, 13.August.1942
Pentagon Building
Arlington, Virginia
United States of America
14:15 hours

The meeting had been scheduled for several weeks. Only Secretary Stimson knew the direction for the action they would take this afternoon came directly from President Roosevelt and his personal meeting with Prime Minister Churchill a month ago.

The knock at the door preceded his secretary's appearance. "Mister Secretary, General Reybold is here. General Marshall indicated he had an urgent matter to tend to and will be here shortly."

"Thank you, Cynthia. Please show him in while we wait for the chief of staff. When General Marshall arrives, please ask him to come right in."

"Yes sir."

Major General Eugene Reybold, USA, CE, had been Chief of Engineers, U.S. Army Corps of Engineers, since October of last year—the commander of the Corps of Engineers.

"Welcome, General." Stimson extended his hand. "Great to see you again."

"Thank you, Mister Secretary."

"General Marshall has been delayed slightly. Would you care for some coffee?" Stimson asked as he gestured to the facing couches across a large rectangular coffee table. The silver service tray had just been refreshed.

"No, thank you, sir," Reybold replied as he sat.

Stimson sat across from the general. "How are the recruitment and expansion efforts going?"

"Surprisingly well, I must say. I continue to be impressed and inspired by the highly qualified and certified engineers who are volunteering to serve. We are well ahead of plan."

"Excellent. We have a long way to go in this affair. The Corps of Engineers will . . . ," Stimson paused, as the door opened and General Marshall entered, paid his respects and apologies, and sat next to Secretary Stimson. "The Corps of Engineers is going to play a greater than normal role in this war."

"We will be ready," Reybold said.

"We know you will. Now, to the business at hand," said Stimson.

"Yes, sir. As you requested, I have drafted an order creating the special office for the development project and reporting directly to you." Reybold removed a single sheet of paper and handed it to Secretary Stimson.

WAR DEPARTMENT
Corps of Engineers
Office of the Chief of Engineers

General Order 33

1. Effective immediately, the office of
the Manhattan Engineer District (MED) shall
be established in appropriate office space in
Manhattan, New York City, New York.
2. Funding for the office and the
operations of the MED has been allocated by the
Secretary of War.
3. Appropriate security provisions shall be
provided and maintained to handle, discuss, and
act upon compartmented TOP SECRET material.
4. Personnel assigned to MED shall be
prepared for major, multi-site, multi-state,
general-purpose construction with appropriate
supervision in direct support of the scientific
and civil engineering personnel team known
as the Laboratory Development of Substitute
Materials (DSM), for the purpose as defined
by the DSM team. This task shall include the
acquisition of properties through reasonable
purchase or eminent domain that will require
prompt response.
5. Colonel James C. Marshall, CE, is
hereby appointed Chief MED, and shall report
directly to the Secretary of War for the
duration of this assignment.
By order of,

Eugene Reybold
Major General CE
Chief of Engineers
Date: August 13, 1942

Stimson passed the draft order to General Marshall. After reading the document, the chief of staff nodded his head to the secretary. "This says what we need it to say. Before we ask you to sign it and distribute it to the appropriate parties, please tell us a little about Colonel Marshall," Stimson requested with a curious expression.

The chief of staff smiled. "No relation . . . that I know of."

Stimson nodded and smiled, and then he looked back at General Reybold.

"Colonel 'Jimmy' Marshall is a West Pointer, Class of 1918. Most recently, he has been the district engineer in Syracuse, responsible for several major ammunition and explosive plant construction projects. He is an exceptional engineer, an accomplished manager, and a credit to the service. From your general description requirements, Colonel Marshall is one of the best we have."

"Does he understand the special nature of this assignment?" asked General Marshall.

"Yes sir, I believe he does. I interviewed him myself and gave him as much information as you gave me."

"My apologies for the cryptic nature of this assignment. We have shared as much as we are able to offer at this stage. This will be a controlled-access project, tightly controlled, as a consequence, I'm afraid the chief of MED must report to me directly—no one else."

"He understands that peculiarity, as do I," said Reybold. "I can also report, Mister Secretary, that we have secured dedicated, temporary, office space in Manhattan. We have contracted for the entire 18th Floor of a modest building at 270 Broadway. It is not as large as we need for growth, but it will suffice for the next six months or so."

"Very good," Stimson pronounced. He looked to his right. "And, your judgment, General Marshall?"

"General Reybold has satisfied all of our launch requirements. I say let's get on with it and get this show on the road."

"I agree," Stimson said and looked directly at General Reybold. "You are authorized to sign Order 33."

"Yes, sir." Reybold removed a fountain pen from the inside pocket of his uniform tunic. He signed the order, blew on the ink to dry it, and handed the document to Secretary Stimson.

They traded words of encouragement for the Corps of Engineers' supervision of the construction of their new headquarters. The three leaders separated. Marshall returned to his office—a leg away clockwise on the 5th Floor, E Ring. Reybold rode in his waiting staff car back across the river to the Munitions Building

———

Monday, 17.August.1942
RAF Polebrook
Oundle, Northamptonshire, England
United Kingdom
13:00 hours

The 12, comparatively new, Boeing B-17E Flying Fortress heavy bombers of the 340th Bombardment Squadron, 97th Bombardment Group, lined up in trail on the taxiway with all four engines on each of the bombers turning at idle speed. The aircraft were painted in green livery with an empty triangle on the vertical stabilizer that identified them as the 97th Bombardment Group.

"We got the green flare, Skipper," announced Corporal Jenkins from his tail gunner station, as the only member of the crew with a clear direct view of the control tower.

"Here we go fellas," said Major Paul Warfield Tibbets Jr., USAAF, from the left seat of the lead bomber. As the squadron commander, Tibbets initiated the first combat bombing mission of the 8th Air Force in Europe. Their target was the railroad marshaling yard at Rouen, France, to reduce the east-west railroad traffic of the German occupation forces.

Tibbets taxied on the runway centerline and smoothly pushed all four throttle levers forward. The aircraft accelerated nicely. The airspeed indicator needle bounced a few times and began to rise. Tibbets checked the gauges of all four engines. Everything was normal. The tail rose, and the big aircraft continued to accelerate. The bomber lifted off the runway smoothly. Tibbets commanded, "Gear up." When the landing gear indicated they were up and locked, Tibbets commanded, "Flaps up." He initiated an overhead orbit at 3,000 feet altitude to await the join-up of the rest of the squadron. Within a few minutes, all 12 bombers were airborne and in formation.

Tibbets banked slightly and rolled out on a heading of 162 degrees magnetic and continued their climb to their planned bombing altitude of 23,000 feet. They had another 50 minutes to their mid-Channel rendezvous point with their fighter escort for the mission.

———

Monday, 17.August.1942
50° 25' North – 0° 10' East
Over the English Channel
16:10 hours

The bomber squadron No.71 Squadron was assigned to protect on this CIRCUS mission to attack the rail yard at Rouen, France, was easy enough to locate. The bomber formation was ahead of and above the squadron. They were also slower, and the Spitfires were gaining on the bombers quickly. Within minutes, they were in position and throttled back to maintain their escort station. 'A' Flight was a thousand feet above and to the left of the bomber formation. 'B' Flight had the same position on the right side of the formation. *Damn, those machines are big. Look at all those 50-cal machine guns. No wonder they call those things Flying Fortresses.*

Tug Meares must have given Hick a hand signal command. The Blue Section Left Wing climbed smoothly, trying to detect the altitude their condensation trails would become visible.

"Mark," broadcast Tug.

"Angels 25, cherubs three," Hick responded.

They all now knew that above 25,300 feet, their condensation trails would be visible all around them and from the ground, marking their position.

The weather remained near perfect over Northern France. A few, fair-weather cumulus clouds dotted the landscape below them.

Brian noted a half dozen ragged, dark grey flak bursts ahead of the bombers that caused no apparent harm or deviation by the bombers, as they crossed the French coastline. *Fifteen minutes to their Initial Point for their bombing run.* Brian kept his eyes and head in constant motion, searching for the enemy fighters that had to be out there. His diligence did not take long to yield results.

"Tally ho. Bandits nine o'clock level," Brian radioed.

"Apple Flight engage," commanded Tug, and rolled smoothly toward the approaching Germans. The Germans split—six went high, six went low. "Hunter, you take the low ones. We've got the high group."

The six German Bf109s were maneuvering to attack the bombers from below, but then they angled away and ahead of the bombers. Brian kept Green Section between the low German group and the bombers, and then quickly searched above and behind him. The fighter engagement above the bombers kept the enemy fighters away from the bombers. *Looks like 'B' Flight has joined the fight. What are those guys doing*, Brian asked himself as the other six German fighters remained below and ahead of the bombers? Red tracer rounds burst out from several bombers toward the Germans but without effect. Brian tried to keep an eye on what was happening above them and hold a position between the low group and the bombers, and clear of the bombers, just in case the gunners decided to take more long shots.

Flak bursts began to explode ahead of the bombers. In an instant, the Germans disengaged to the east. Brian looked over his shoulder to see the bomb bay doors were open on the bombers. He banked away from the bomber formation, pushed his throttle to full power, and checked on both wingmen. They had not anticipated the change but were adjusting smoothly. Brian led Green Section to rejoin Blue Section and re-form 'A' Flight. The city of Rouen and the large multi-track rail yard clearly lay ahead of the bombers. The bomber formation tightened up in a diamond of four inverted 'V' sections. The bomb load from the lead bomber fell in quick succession, followed promptly by the same release from the remainder of the squadron. Flak shells continued to burst around and among the bombers.

Tug and Whitey adjusted their positions as the bombers turned to the withdrawal heading. When he found a moment, Brian stole a quick glance at Rouen. The bombs were no longer visible and seemed to take a very long time to reach their target. In his next glance down, the rail yard had disappeared in a massive cloud of smoke, dust, and debris, as the orange flashes of the last bombs marked their detonation on the railroad tracks leading into the Rouen railway-switching yard.

Flak shells continued to burst around and among the bombers. Black smoke trailed from several bombers. The engine fires appeared to be quickly extinguished. Propellers were feathered to a stopped position. Two of the B-17s fell out of formation—one with one engine feathered, and the other with two engines feathered.

"Eagle Yellow, this is Eagle Leader. Stay with the stragglers."

"Wilco, Eagle Leader."

Pete maneuvered Yellow Section to a protective position with the two lame bombers.

The flak bursts stopped at the same time Tug broadcast, "Tally ho! Bandits ten o'clock high."

Brian spotted the enemy fighters before Tug finished his alert message. *Looks like we're going to have to fight our way out.*

"Whitey, stick with the bombers. We'll try to keep the bandits away."

"Roger, Tug."

Meares turned 'A' Flight and climbed to face the German fighter squadron. They spread to match the Germans. Gun bursts erupted from both sides as they passed. Brian pulled hard into a climbing left turn, strained his neck looking out the top of the canopy, picked up his adversary, who had continued straight toward the bombers. *Whitey will have to pick them up.* Three of the Germans pressed the attack on the bomber formation, but Brian could not watch with more immediate threats. Frog was in a tight ball with a white nose Bf109 fighter. Brian adjusted his nose to engage Frog's adversary. The German must have detected Brian rolling to intercept and dove into Brian, making his solution more difficult. Frog rolled sharply back to the right and pulled his nose through hard to pick up the German if he tried to turn back on Frog. The German continued his dive away from the fight. Brian quickly scanned for another target. The green and brown Spitfires appeared to have the upper hand on the grey and black 109s, at the moment. Brian rolled into the closest engagement to help Hick with his adversary but did not push the trigger button before Hick smoked his opponent, who arced in an odd wingover with a thick black smoke tail into a lazy spiral toward the ground. Brian quickly checked on the bombers; they were still lumbering on toward home. The glint of a canopy alerted Hunter—a 109 turning toward him. He did not have the time to counter. He rolled sharply and pulled the nose hard to dive underneath the potential attacker. The German fired a burst while still in his roll-in turn. The tracers passed above Brian. When they passed virtually canopy-to-canopy, Brian rolled hard in the opposite direction and climbed for a perch. Hunter searched all of the sky he could see—no 109s could be seen. The Spitfires were closing on what had to be Tug's Spitfire. Brian pulled his throttle back and maneuvered to regain his position in 'A' Flight.

"Eagle Yellow, Eagle Leader, how are you doing back there?"

"Eagle Leader, Eagle Yellow, good so far. Quite a show y'all put on for us."

"Eagle Flight, Eagle Leader, let's keep a keen eye out, lads. We are not clear yet."

The French coastline was in sight. A few flak bursts pocked the air around the bombers, but they pressed on. From their altitude, they could see Le Havre and Dieppe. Their current track split the difference between the two occupied port cities to minimize their exposure to anti-aircraft fire.

"Bandits, seven o'clock, two fingers above the horizon."

Brian looked instantly over his left shoulder. *That sounded like Sweet.* He could not see anything other than empty sky. Hunter widened his scan.

"Eagle Leader, Eagle Yellow. Bandits closing. Looks like a squadron, maybe more. We could use some help."

"Roger, Eagle Yellow, break, Eagle Green, peel off and assist Eagle Yellow."

"Wilco," Brian responded and rolled his section into a 180° turn and advanced his throttle smoothly to full power.

"Sapper, Eagle Leader calling." Meares radioed Biggin Hill Control—the assigned mission controller.

"Eagle Leader, Sapper. We heard the call. Boost scrambled." The codeword meant two, fighter squadrons had been launched to support them.

Brian spotted the two lame bombers, holding their heading. It took another few seconds to locate the three, much smaller Spitfires of Yellow Section. Pete had turned to face the Germans. Brian adjusted their heading to the expected engagement point. *We're not going to get there in time.* They saw the Germans. *Sure looks like two squadrons of bad guys.* They watched the furball bloom as Yellow Section engaged the superior German force. Six Germans maintained their heading straight for the two bombers. *Nope, not gonna happen.* Hunter adjusted their heading for an intercept point between the Germans and the two damaged bombers. As they closed with their intercept point, a half dozen tracer streams burst out from the bombers. The Germans took evasive action to avoid the intersecting machine gun fire from the bombers, but they were not deterred. *I sure hope those gunners see us coming. We don't need any friendly fire.* The tracers did indeed stop as Green Section passed overhead of the bombers. The Germans maneuvered to counter the three rapidly closing Spitfires. A couple of enemy fighters tried long-shot bursts from their guns before they had to face the diving Spitfires.

Brian fired a short burst of machine-gun fire at the two center Bf109s with green nose spinners. The Germans tried the same, all to no effect. An additional furball ensued. Brian took some shots, but their focus was defensive maneuvering to occupy the Germans and keep them off the bombers. Green tracers passed his XR-G Spitfire several times.

"Eagle Leader, Hornet Leader. Hornet and Tiger, have you in sight. We've got 'em."

"Eagle Flight, Eagle Leader. Disengage and rejoin."

Brian took a quick glance over his right shoulder and saw the 12 Spitfires closing fast. The Germans did as well. They turned to engage the newcomers, enabling Green and Yellow Sections to disengage. The two, No.71 Squadron sections took up their positions on either side of the two straggler bombers over the English Channel. They stayed with the two bombers until they were over England. They could see waves and salutes from the bomber crews. At the designated point, the Spitfires departed and returned to Debden. Mission accomplished.

—

Chapter 13

Our pleasance here is all vain glory,
This false world is but transitory.
-- William Dunbar

Tuesday, 18.August.1942
RAF Gravesend
Gravesend, Kent, England
United Kingdom
19:30 hours

No.71 Squadron landed without incident or problem. They were directed to the same parking spots and dispersal tent they used nearly two months ago, for the canceled Operation RUTTER. When the last of the pilots entered and sat in the folding chairs, Tug signaled for Sloppy to switch on the electric lights even though it was not yet sunset.

"As we briefed in late June, we have been staged closer to the Channel for a pending amphibious operation. We are one of ten fighter squadrons so deployed. It might be of interest that the other two American volunteer fighter squadrons—121 and 133—are included. We are assigned as fighter cover for the assault force. Out part in this operation is not complicated. We do what we've always done—keep the enemy fighters and bombers at bay. We have no assigned targets. The mission briefing indicates we should be prepared to conduct ground support strafing if required. What is different with Operation JUBILEE, as it is now known, is our assigned period.

"We will have a breakfast meal at 03:00 hours tomorrow morning."

"That's still night," interjected Sloppy.

"Yes, Pilot Officer Butterfield, it will still be night. We will arrive here at 03:30 and get any last-minute adjustments from Group. I expect we will launch the squadron at 04:20 hours. I will carry out the mission briefing in the morning before we launch, but it should be pretty straight forward." Tug paused. No one reacted. "I gave you this information because we need to make it an early night, get as much sleep as you can. The batmen will awake us at 02:30 hours. All of this information, so far, remains sensitive and classified, so no discussion once we leave the tent. I see the lorry is outside for our transport. As we did last June, we are guests at Cobham Hall, but there will be no social time. Evening meal is being held for us. We will get fed, tend to our personal affairs, and get to bed as soon as possible. It is going to be a very long day tomorrow. Any questions?"

Several of their number shook their heads. A couple of them stood in anticipation. No one said a word.

"Very well, then. Let's hang up our kit and board the lorry. Dinner awaits."

The shuffling of compliance marked their response. Tug was the last man out. He switched off the lights and closed the simple, wooden slab door. The ride to Cobham Hall was quiet. This time there was no welcoming committee. The pilots went directly to the dining room, ate their meal without words, and retired to their assigned rooms.

—

Wednesday, 19.August.1942
RAF Gravesend
Gravesend, Kent, England
United Kingdom
03:50 hours

There had been no grumbling during the early morning activities up to and including their arrival at the dispersal tent. Tug was the first to enter and switched on the lights. He had gone immediately to the telephone. Half the pilots, including Brian, took the few moments of calm to don their SidCot suits for protection against the high altitude cold, their flotation vests, and their shoulder holsters and pistols. They held their gloves and leather helmets with goggles and oxygen masks attached. Those who were not already sitting took their seats when Tug Meares appeared.

"The mission today is fighter cover for Operation JUBILEE—the amphibious landing of a Canadian division along with British Commandos and American Rangers at Dieppe, France. The task force is currently approaching the beach. They've got a night fighter squadron overhead during the approach. We will launch at 04:20, to relieve 604 Squadron—Nighthawk. Our initial position will be at Angels 18 for the landing at dawn. H-Hour is dawn—04:50 hours. The airspace below Angels 12, three miles either side of Dieppe, two miles prior to and five miles inland from the landing beaches has been assigned to naval gunfire in support of the landing force, and thus an exclusion zone for aircraft."

"What if the Germans strafe the beaches?" asked Hick.

"In the exclusion zone, anti-aircraft actions are the responsibility of the naval task force. The risk is too great."

"What about outside the exclusion zone?" Sloppy asked.

"That's open airspace," responded Tug. "They stationed a fighter squadron overhead because they are presumably more concerned about bombers striking the landing force than marauding fighters." He paused for any other questions. None came. "Our mission will be to keep enemy aircraft of any type away from the landing beaches. We may encounter anti-aircraft fire, so we'll need to stay on our toes. This could be simple, surely will not be boring, and could be a rather hairy mission. To minimize our exposure, we'll maintain a five-mile, racetrack orbit over and along the beach, and disperse the sections 90° apart. Depending upon what we may face, we may rejoin to respond as a squadron, a flight, or a section. We have no way to anticipate what we may face. Any questions?"

"What about the ground attack you mentioned last evening?" Salt asked.

"Ground attack is not on our assigned mission list. The Hurricanes, Blenheims, and heavy bombers will handle that part of the mission."

"I thought you said we should be prepared for ground strafing."

"Yes, Salt, that is what I said. We have no assigned ground attack mission elements. Group suggested that if we have ammunition and fuel remaining, the flagship HMS *Calpe*, callsign Maple Leaf, might direct us to aid ground operations. We will need to remain agile." Several of the pilots nodded their heads. "Any other questions?" No one spoke. "Very well," Tug said. He checked his wristwatch. "We've got seven minutes to our planned launch time. Let's get suited up. I'm going to call Group one last time. We'll spin up in five minutes."

Meares went to his makeshift office. Brian gestured with his head for Green Section to head to their aircraft. Morning twilight had just begun to lighten the eastern horizon as the pilots checked their aircraft with flashlights. Brian was strapped in and ready to start, when he watched Tug jog to his XR-A Spitfire.
04:20 hours

The eastern horizon continued to lighten, but the sun was still not up when Tug began his takeoff roll. The rest of the squadron followed their leader. They headed south, climbing to 18,000 feet. As they passed 9,000 feet, the sun appeared on the eastern horizon.

At mid-Channel, Tug made the contact call. "Nighthawk Leader, Eagle Leader calling."

"Eagle Leader, Nighthawk. Welcome to the party."

That sounds like 'Cat's Eyes' Cunningham. He must be the commander of No.604 Squadron, now.

"Roger Nighthawk. We are ten minutes out."

"Not much action yet. We dealt with a flight of Me110 night fighters an hour ago; nothing since then."

Hunter spotted the eight, twin-engine, Bristol Beaufighters. Tug made the call before Brian did.

"Nighthawk, we have you in sight. We have assumed the watch."

"Roger, Eagle. Nighthawk, we are bingo."

They watched the night fighters depart north. Without broadcasting, Tug throttled back to maximum endurance and banked away to set up their patrol orbit. Brian led Green Section to their assigned position three miles behind Blue Section. After scanning the sky, Brian glanced at the scene playing out below them. The destroyers firing their guns at the shore. Landing craft at the shoreline discharging their troops. The second and third wave landing craft lined up abreast and heading toward the shore. Dust and smoke obscured much of the port city.

Brian carefully scanned the sky around them as they trundled around their orbit pattern—still no business for them. Tracer streams could be seen crisscrossing the battle zone. Even from their altitude, the battle below them appeared desperate, but it was the first amphibious or land battle they had been in a position to observe. *Damn, I'm glad I'm not down there.*

"Tally ho!" broadcast Pete. "Bandits, south-southwest, three fingers below the horizon. Looks like six Junkers 88s, no fighter escort."

"Roger, got 'em. Eagle Red, you're closest. Take Beer Flight to intercept."

"Wilco," Whitey acknowledged.

Red Section rolled to intercept the German bombers. Yellow Section rolled to join as 'B' Flight. *Where are the fighters? They are not going to fare well with no fighters.* Whitey and his six Spitfires closed rapidly. *Wow!* All six German medium bombers dropped their bomb loads over open countryside and sharply reversed course. *They're running.* 'B' Flight gave chase for more than a minute, then broke off their intercept. They smoothly climbed and returned to their station in the orbit pattern.

Where are the damn fighters? The frustration of what surely had to be out there, but remained unseen or undetected, began to mount on Brian, and undoubtedly, the others were feeling it as well. The smoke and dust in the air above Dieppe increased, probably indicating the pitched battle that played out below them. And, *we are essentially observers of this whole affair.*
06:45 hours

"Eagle Leader, Freema Leader calling."
No.64 Squadron Spitfires.
"Freema, Eagle, go ahead."
"Eagle, we have you in sight."
"Not much action up here. All of it on the beach."
"Roger, Eagle, you stand relieved." The 'SH' Spitfires of No.64 Squadron replaced the No.71 Squadron fighters.
"It's all yours. Break. Eagle, join up. We are bingo."
Tug turned his section north.

Hunter maneuvered his section to join up with Blue Section. *We never got to fire a shot—not even any strafing of surface targets.* The squadron landed at Gravesend. They refueled and were quickly raised to Standby status that kept them strapped into their cockpit seats, ready to go in an instant.

Operation JUBILEE—the division-sized amphibious raid on German defenses at Dieppe, France—proved to be a very costly action. The Canadian 2nd Infantry Division and its attached Commando units suffered an 88% casualty rate—killed, wounded, and captured. Everyone suffered losses—heavy losses. Many people outside the operation called it a calamity or a disaster. What only a few knew . . . No.30 Commando had a very specific, classified, embedded mission within the overall operation—the capture of a new four-rotor Enigma encryption device and associated codebooks, along with any other intelligence they could collect from the local *Kriegsmarine* headquarters at Dieppe. All agreed that the lessons learned from the Dieppe Raid would help planners for the eventual invasion of German-occupied France.

While No.71 Squadron did not see serious combat during Operation JUBILEE, the Royal Air Force and fledgling U.S. 8th Air Force in England experienced the most intense, large scale, aerial combat since the Battle of Britain. Such was the nature of combat operations.

Three Victoria Crosses were awarded to members of the Dieppe assault force—Captain Patrick Anthony Porteous, Royal Regiment of Artillery, attached to No.4 Commando; Captain John Weir Foote, Canadian Chaplain Services, Royal Hamilton Light Infantry; and, Lieutenant Colonel Charles Cecil Ingersoll Merritt of the South Saskatchewan Regiment.

———

Sunday, 23.August.1942
Telegraph Cottage
Warren Road
Coombe Hill, Kingston upon Thames, London
United Kingdom
21:15 hours

General Eisenhower hosted the dinner and social occasion for the U.S. Joint Chiefs of Staff. They scheduled to depart for the return to Washington in the morning. This was also the first occasion the chiefs had been introduced to Kay Summersby.

Corporal Kay Summersby assigned as Eisenhower's driver during his first exploratory visit to London the previous May and had been specifically requested when he was posted to London. Now, she was also serving as his girl Friday at the commander's residence.

"Well done, Ike," pronounced Ernie King. "We would never know there is wartime rationing in London. That was a delicious and sumptuous meal."

"Quite so," added Hap Arnold.

"Yes, indeed," said George Marshall. "Well done all the way around. We have an approved and worthy plan, and you have your requested commanders."

The combined joint chiefs of staff had just unanimously agreed to Eisenhower's three, requested, landing force commanders for Operation TORCH. George Patton would have the Western Task Force. Major General Lloyd Ralston Fredendall, USA [USMA 1905], would serve as Commander-in-Chief Central Task Force, and Major General Kenneth Arthur Noel Anderson, CB, MC, had been selected to command the Eastern Task Force.

"Thank you for that," Eisenhower said. "We have our first commanders' conference on Tuesday. It will be the first time all of the amphibious and landing force commanders will have met each other. Now, we get down to the process of preparing for battle."

"We'll go to work on getting you more forces as soon as we get home," King said.

"Any additional units would be greatly appreciated," responded Eisenhower.

Marshall chuckled. "There is no general worth his salt who would not appreciate more troops." Marshall looked directly at Eisenhower. "You have done a masterful job of explaining the limitations. Even if the British or we could stand up several more divisions in time, we do not have the landing craft to move them ashore. I think you have a plan that satisfies the direction and guidance of the prime minister and the president."

"Then, we must focus on reducing the threat we face," responded Eisenhower.

"And, you have a good plan for that," Marshall added.

"Yes, we do, but there are far more dependent loose ends on that aspect."

Again, Marshall chuckled. "If there is anyone who can bring this puzzle together at the appointed hour, we have faith it is you, Ike."

"Hear, hear," added King.

"Agreed," Arnold contributed.

Hap Arnold refreshed his drink, and only George Marshall availed himself of Hap's offer to serve.

"The Germans successfully crossed the River Don this morning," said Arnold. "The Russians have still not figured out how to stop the German juggernaut, and the bad guys are one more natural obstacle closer to the Caspian oil fields."

"So far," commented Ernie King with solemnity.

"They are fighting better than last year," Arnold added.

"Thank goodness for small favors," Eisenhower said.

"Yes, indeed, as we must consider the big elephant 'what if' in this discussion," Marshall said. "We'd better win this thing as quickly as possible, just in case the Russians bail on us. Our calculus changes dramatically if the Russians are subdued."

"We will do our part," Ike said. "We'll cross that bridge if we get there, but it is not on the horizon yet."

"After the JUBILEE disaster," King began, "the prospect of SLEDGEHAMMER, or something like it, would become immensely more difficult with the weight of the German armed forces in France rather than Russia."

"JUBILEE demonstrated what can happen with insufficient forces," Ike said calmly.

"Point taken," King affirmed.

"JUBILEE faced German forces in reinforced defenses with insufficient ground forces to overwhelm the resistance. Their armored vehicles bogged down on the beach. The raid was never planned to hold the ground."

"Horrific casualties for a raid," observed King.

"Yes, exactly! We cannot allow that to happen again," Ike pronounced.

"Nothing is certain in combat," added Marshall. "We have a good plan. The key will be neutralizing the French to secure the beachhead."

"Agreed," responded Eisenhower. "We have a lot more work to accomplish toward that objective."

"We have faith, Ike," proclaimed George Marshall. "With that, I'm afraid I must be the party-pooper here. We've got an early morning call for our return to Washington. As much as I think we would all appreciate the enjoyment of your hospitality, Ike, we need to get back to the hotel."

"As you wish, sir."

The three senior flag officers paid their compliments to the staff and their host, then departed after an enjoyable exclamation point to this latest visit to the European Theater.

———

Monday, 24.August.1942
RAF Debden
Saffron Walden, Essex, England
United Kingdom
14:10 hours

"Hunter, Dusty and Frog, a word please," Tug called with a commanding voice from the doorway to his office. Meares was sitting at his desk when the Green Section pilots entered. He gestured for them to close the door and sit. "It appears the day you lads have been waiting for has finally arrived. The three of you are scheduled to be interviewed and examined by the American Army, to determine your suitability for service with the Army Air Forces."

"What does that mean, Skipper?" Forcier asked.

"I am not privy to the process, Frog, but I surmised they are trying to fulfill the same requirements for each of you, as for all of the other American Air Forces pilots."

Dusty looked puzzled, but it was Frog that pressed the interrogatives. "What if we are not accepted? Or worse, we are rejected?"

"I do not know the answers from Army Air Forces personnel. However, Air Marshal Leigh-Mallory has instructed me to inform each of you that you have a place with us regardless of the decision. I think the appropriate Army personnel will inform you of the options available to each of you after the physical examination and interviews are completed."

"So, you are telling us not to worry?" Frog said.

"I suppose, in a form, yes, that is what I am telling you. Each of you has a seat in the premier fighter aeroplane of our time. If, for whatever reason, you do not transfer with the squadron, I am authorized to tell you that you will transfer to another RAF fighter squadron, if you wish. You are all volunteers. That right still remains."

"Where and when do we report?" Brian asked.

Meares referred to a piece of paper on his desk in front of him. "I am informed that you should report to Brigadier General Hunter . . . ."

Both Dusty and Frog chuckled. "Any relation, Hunter?" asked Dusty.

"His family name, not mine," Brian coldly answered.

Meares ignored the interruption. "As I was saying, you are to report to General Hunter at the U.S. Army headquarters of the European Theater of Operations, 20 Grosvenor Square in the Mayfair District of London at 13:00 hours tomorrow. That's quite near the U.S. Embassy. I would suggest you arrive early. Perhaps, the three of you should have lunch in London to ensure you are not delayed for this important event."

"So, we will be released from duty?" Dusty asked.

"No. You will be on duty. Your duty, in this instance, will be to attend the interview and examination as described."

"In uniform?" Forcier pressed.

"Yes, in uniform, Frog. Each of you remains an officer in good standing in the Royal Air Force. I know this is perhaps a bit daunting, but it is the specified process. Further, I am suggesting that you try to relax. Be proud of your service with us. The American Army will decide what is best for them, and over that, you have no control. Let the chips fall where they may. As I said previously, each of you has a seat with us if you wish to avail yourselves of this offer, for whatever reason you wish."

Brian had heard enough. "Thank you for the information, Skipper. Is there anything else we need to know?"

"One last point . . . once we are released this afternoon, the three of you will be released for tomorrow, so you can depart for London when you wish. I will expect all three of you to report back here Wednesday morning, as usual. You will need to check with your mates tomorrow evening for the exact reporting time. Understood?"

"Yes sir," they responded in unison. They stood and returned to the common room.

—

Tuesday, 25.August.1942
Headquarters, European Theater of Operations, United States Army
20 Grosvenor Square
Mayfair, London
United Kingdom
13:00 hours

The plainly lettered sign, in addition to the address plaque, told the Eagle pilots they had arrived at the correct building. None of them had seen or even been aware of the new command in London.

"Looks like this is the place, fellas," Brian said. "Our fate lies beyond those doors," he said, pointing to the guarded main entrance.

The three pilots completed the required security checks with the desk sergeant. They were, in fact, scheduled to meet with the pilot evaluation board. Since they were technically foreign military officers, an Army corporal was summoned and assigned to escort the three RAF officers to the designated second-floor office. The interior of the ornate building was a veritable beehive of activity with officers and enlisted men walking at various paces.

"I don't think I've seen so many bloody generals and colonels," Frog whispered louder than usual to overcome the din of movement around them.

Brian chose not to respond, but he actually agreed.

"You're sounding very British, Frog," added Dusty. Frog punched Dusty in the shoulder.

The corporal stopped at an unmarked, heavy-looking door, knocked twice and opened the door, gesturing for the three pilots to enter. The room was filled with five simple desks and assorted administrative furniture and equipment—file cabinets, typewriters, wire file baskets, desk blotters, pen & pencil holders, and other accouterments of an administrative office. Two corporals, a sergeant, a staff sergeant, and a captain sat at the distributed desks. The captain rose and came to them. The escort corporal introduced the officers.

"Gentlemen," the Army captain in pink & green service uniform with General Staff branch lapel insignia stood before the three men attired in Royal Air Force uniforms with pilot wings, "thank you for arriving on time. I am

Captain Strange, and I'm the staff coordinator for the potential transfer pilot evaluation board. Pilot Officer Langford, you will go first before the board. Flight Lieutenant Drummond, you will be last. While Langford is before the board, the flight surgeons one floor down will evaluate Drummond and Forcier. Pilot Officer Forcier will be next before the board. Do you have any questions?"

"What are they going to ask us?" Dusty inquired.

"I am not privy to that information, but I think it safe to say, they are focused on your adaptability to the Army. To be blunt, most of you Eagle Squadron pilots were not trained in the Army ways."

That sounds rather condescending, Brian thought.

"Who are the members of the evaluation board?" Frog asked.

"The chairman is Brigadier General Hunter, Commanding General, Eighth Fighter Command. The other members of the board are Colonel Anderson, Commanding Officer, Fourth Fighter Wing; and, Colonel Zemke, Commanding Officer, Fifty-Sixth Fighter Wing."

"What are they going to ask us?" repeated Dusty.

"That is their business, not mine nor yours," the captain answered rather abruptly. "To my understanding, the board is charged with determining your suitability for Army service . . . since you did not receive Army training, as I mentioned earlier." He paused to look at each of the Eagle pilots. "Now, if there are no other questions," he said with discernible impatience. Strange looked to all three pilots. None of them responded. "Pilot Officer Langford, the board is ready for you in the conference room. Drummond and Forcier, you can head to the flight surgeon."

Dusty nodded his head to Hunter and Frog, opened the conference room door, stepped inside, and closed the door behind him. They heard Dusty report to the board.

Brian and Joshua easily found the flight surgeon's office. The nurse-receptionist instructed Brian to sit in the waiting room while the doctor examined Joshua, since he was next up with the board. Brian was soon alone in the small anteroom with only the last few issues of *Stars & Stripes* newspaper on the end table of a half dozen, wooden, straight back chairs. He had not seen the newspaper before, so it was somewhat fascinating about the success of the naval Battle of Midway last June. *Nice to see a success finally.* In the most recent issue of the newspaper on the table, a page three article caught Brian's attention—"Army Air Forces Board to Interview RAF Eagle Squadron Pilots." The article did not tell him any more than he already knew, except one important element. The chairman of the Board was the Commanding General, VIII Fighter Command, Brigadier General Frank O'Driscoll Hunter, USAAF, with the Commanding Officer, 4th Fighter Group, Colonel Edward

W. 'Ed' Anderson, USAAF, and Colonel Hubert A. 'Hub' Zemke, USAAF – Commanding Officer, 56th Fighter Group. According to the article, all three senior officers were experienced, fighter pilots. Their mission was to evaluate the suitability for transfer of the American volunteer pilots serving with all three American volunteer squadrons serving in the Royal Air Force. *And here we are!*

After an unrealized amount of time, Frog appeared, gave Brian and thumbs up, and left the room. The nurse appeared and called Brian's rank and family name. She measured and wrote down Brian's age, weight, blood pressure, heart rate, and temperature. His visual acuity was checked with both short and far charts. When the nurse finished all of the basic, common tests, she took him to an examination room, asked Brian to undress, don a flimsy hospital gown, and wait for the flight surgeon. The doctor reviewed Brian's medical history that he had obviously received from the Royal Air Force and completed the medical portion of the examination. The doctor pronounced Brian medically fit for service in the Army Air Forces, although Brian thought he showed inordinate curiosity about the scars of his prior wounds and the circumstances of their infliction.

Dusty was waiting in the medical office lobby when Brian came out. "How'd it go?" Dusty asked.

"All clear," answered Brian. "More importantly, how was your interview?"

"Pretty straight forward, it seems to me—standard stuff—like they wanted me to confirm what they already knew."

"Did the board members introduce themselves or tell you their assignments?"

"No . . . just a one-star and two colonels. At least they spoke American English."

Brian looked at the issue of *Stars & Stripes* that had an article about the interview board. He found it and passed it to Dusty. "Here, read this . . . page three, as I recall."

"What's it about?"

"The interview board. Seems the brigadier is the commanding general of 8th Fighter Command, and the two colonels are the commanding officers of two of the fighter groups—4th and 56th—that are forming up. My guess is, we will be in one or the other fighter groups."

"OK. I'll read it."

"I'd better get going," Brian said. "I'm up next, after Frog, so I'd better be waiting for the call."

"Good luck."

"Thanks, mate."

Brian made his way back to the conference room. One of the corporals asked him to sit. He did not have to wait long, perhaps ten minutes. Frog came out with a broad smile on his face. Brian's left wingman made a zip-his-lips, then gave a thumbs up with another smile. Another corporal from inside the conference room appeared.

"Flight Lieutenant Drummond."

Brian stood and followed the corporal back into the conference room. The corporal gestured to a single chair in front of a long rectangular table. Three Army Air Forces officers sat on the other side of the table—a brigadier general in the middle and a colonel on either side of him. The corporal took a seat at the end of the table. He was apparently the board recorder.

The brigadier did not introduce the board and jumped right into it. "You are Brian Arthur Drummond?"

"Yes sir."

"You have quite the story." Brian tried to remain stoic and expressionless. "How did you get into the Royal Air Force?"

"I took the train from Wichita to Detroit, crossed the border over the Ambassador Bridge, and joined the Royal Air Force in Windsor, Ontario, Canada."

"How did you know how to do that? Did you have help?"

"Yes sir . . . the man who taught me to fly and his squadron mate in the Great War."

"Who were those men?"

"Malcolm Bainbridge and John Spencer."

"John Spencer, as in Air Commodore John Spencer?"

"Yes sir. Operations Officer, Eleven Group."

The general glanced to the colonel on his right. The colonel asked, "Did you attend or graduate college?"

That's an odd question. I'm a fucking fighter pilot, not a professor or an engineer. "No sir."

The colonel shook his head as if that was an unsatisfactory answer. "Are you aware that a college degree is a prerequisite to being a pilot in the Army Air Forces?"

"No sir. I thought being a good pilot was."

None of the three officers smiled and simply stared at Brian. The general spoke next. "I would suggest you curtail the snide remarks, Mister Drummond. There is no guarantee you will be accepted for transfer. You must meet all the requirements for Army service. We are charged with making that determination with respect to you Americans, who chose to violate the law and fly for the French and now the British"

Again, the board members paused in silence and stared at Brian. *Maybe they are antagonizing me to see how I will react. I'm not going to give them the satisfaction.*

The other colonel took his turn. "What will you do if you are not accepted for transfer?"

"Does that question mean I'm not going to be transferred with my squadron mates?"

"We will ask the questions, Drummond. You will provide your answers. Understood?"

"Yes sir."

Again, the three senior officers stared at Brian. It took several minutes to realize he has been asked a question and not provided his answer. "I have not considered that possibility. I am an American. I am a decent fighter pilot. I thought you would need pilots."

"Do not presume, Drummond. You do not technically meet the requirements to be a pilot in the Army."

"Are you kidding?" Brian asked.

"Does it look like we are kidding?" the colonel said, rather than asked.

"No sir." The board members again waited for his answer. "I suppose I will remain in the RAF. They seem to appreciate my skills without a college degree."

"You are apparently quite impressed with yourself," the general observed.

"No sir . . . with all due respect, sir. I'm just a pilot who truly loves flying and using my skills in the defense of freedom."

"Quite righteous and noble," the general said.

"This is not going well, General, certainly not as well as I expected. I don't know why. May I speak freely?" Brian requested. The general nodded his head in consent. "I'm not sure what I've done to offend you, all of you. I don't know why you don't like me, or why you think a college degree would make me a better fighter pilot, but that is your choice entirely. If you don't want me, I think the British will. You know what I have done. If you don't want my skills, I will not understand, but I will accept your decision."

"That was quite the speech, Mister Drummond. We are keenly aware of your accomplishments." The general actually grinned. "You are a decorated, four-time ace. You have more combat hours than any active American pilot I am aware of, and we are just getting spun up for this war." He paused. Brian did not react in the slightest. The general looked to each colonel, who nodded his head in turn. "Let me explain what is going to happen. We must make a recommendation to the War Department. We are required to submit a waiver request for your lack of a college degree. If our recommendation is accepted and the waiver approved, you will be transferred to the Army with the other members of your squadron."

"Thank you, sir."

"Do you have any questions for us?"

"When will I find out?"

"They tell me two to three weeks. If there is nothing else, you are dismissed."

Brian stood, saluted in proper British fashion, did a proper about-face, and departed the conference room. Dusty and Frog were waiting for him in the outer office. Brian checked with the captain to ensure they were complete with the interview process, and then they departed the HQETO building. Frog and Dusty tried to talk several times as they walked to the Bond Street Underground Station, but Brian held up his hand to stop them each time. It was not until they were several stations out on the Central Line to Debden that Brian finally recounted his experience with the evaluation board. Neither Frog nor Dusty could believe what Brian told them. Once their shock subsided, they rode in silence with their section leader in contemplation.

———

Saturday, 5.September.1942
Telegraph Cottage
Warren Road
Coombe Hill, Kingston upon Thames, London
United Kingdom
20:45 hours

"Thank you for your gracious invitation to feed us, General," Bob Murphy said, as they left the dining room and walked down the short hallway to Eisenhower's study. Only Colonel Eddy and Chief of Station Phillips joined them before the doors were closed.

"You indicated you had vital information," Ike said.

"Yes sir. At General Donovan's insistence," Bob Murphy began, "I briefed President Roosevelt on the intelligence situation in Northwest Africa. The briefing went well, and the president instructed me to proceed directly here and give you the same briefing. I arrived this morning. Colonel Eddy arrived earlier this afternoon from Casablanca. I requested that Colonel Eddy and Chief of Station Phillips join us to ensure all four of us hear exactly the same things—our facts and your questions."

"Very well."

"Colonel Eddy and I have made progress with General Mast. What has changed since our last discussion of the topic is Mast's emphasis on engaging General Giraud in the process. General Donovan has directed OSS assets in

Vichy, France, to locate and track General Giraud. We are not there yet, but the reports from the field suggest we have essential leads. Once he is located, it is our intention to approach him in private to arrange his extraction from France to Algeria. General Mast believes that Giraud's presence and hopefully his cooperation will ensure the neutralization of Vichy French resistance to our landings . . . well, at least the Army and probably the Air Force. The Navy situation remains more problematic. Neither Mast nor the OSS has identified a senior like-minded naval officer comparable to the general.

"What about Admiral Darlan?" asked Eisenhower.

"Neither MI6, Admiral Pike nor ourselves have approached Admiral Darlan regarding our notional plan to move him to Algiers. I think we all feel that the timing of the approach is crucial. We don't want to surprise him, but we don't want to give him too much time to think. While we are convinced he is more closely aligned with our purposes, we do not believe he is as far along as Giraud. Our plan for the Darlan channel is to carefully contact the admiral's son for his cooperation. Whether his son chooses to participate or not, we suggest approaching the admiral a few days before the TORCH landings begin, at the same time he receives a message that his son is hospitalized with a serious case of influenza. Darlan experienced the 1918 influenza pandemic. We intend to inform him the message is a cover for him to fly to Algiers to lead his troops, save lives, and hopefully join our cause."

"That sounds reasonable, but that does not sound appreciably different from what we already have from State and the OSS."

"That's fair, sir. I asked Colonel Eddy to attend so you could hear his news directly. I had to represent him in my briefing for the president." Murphy nodded to Eddy.

"Since our briefing last July, I have made direct contact with two regimental commanders in Morocco, without exposing our purpose. We are in the process of contacting others in Algeria. General Mast has been most helpful to that end. They have colored our view of the territorial army. They are a force to be respected. However, the dissatisfaction with the conduct of Pétain and especially Laval after the armistice is palpable. They are torn between loyalty to the country and their disgust with Laval. The other common element we are finding among the officer corps is distrust of the British. The Navy is still quite bitter about the CATAPULT action. Admiral Pike believes Admiral Darlan understands why Prime Minister Churchill took the decision he did, initiating CATAPULT, but he is a realist in walking the line between the general bitterness of the fleet and the recognition of the British interdiction. It is against this background that Bob emphasized the keystone position of General Giraud. While Admiral Pike and Admiral Pound have committed to supporting us, the extraction of Giraud must have an American face, to avoid raising pride barriers with Giraud and other flag officers."

"OK, OK," Ike said with noticeable frustration in his voice. "What are you proposing?"

Murphy again nodded to Eddy. "In addition to the Giraud-Darlan-Mast channels, we are proposing a direct gesture from you."

Eisenhower sat back into his chair sharply, as if he had been struck. "Me?"

"Yes sir. The ideal would be for you to meet directly with the French generals, and others we might be able to gather up in the interim, but we recognize that is not likely."

"Quite so," responded Eisenhower, "but, I am listening."

"If not you, a high-level delegation from you might do the trick and solidify their support. They want to hear from a combat commander, not some low-level staff officer or an intelligence agent. There is little doubt in our analysis that the French officers are caught in a very fragile state—national loyalty versus alignment with us against the Germans. None of them, with the exception of perhaps Giraud, wants to be caught in the open supporting us against the government."

"They want cover."

"Yes, precisely, sir."

"Let me give that some thought. How long are you going to be here?"

"Eddy and I were planning to leave tomorrow morning for Algeria and Morocco. We can remain if you would prefer we do so. Phillips is stationed here, of course; he is always available."

"Not necessary. Proceed with your plan. Before we adjourn this little meeting, and while I have you all here, I have a couple of points of curiosity before you go." Murphy nodded his consent. "I understand Colonel Eddy's status and position in all this, but I am still a little confused regarding your position," he said, looking at Murphy and Phillips.

"The easiest is Bill," Murphy answered and looked at Phillips to respond.

"General Donovan personally asked me to be his chief of station here in London."

"I understand that part, but to my knowledge, you are or were a career diplomat in the State Department. What changed?"

"I resigned from State a year ago. Bill Donovan and I have known each other since before the Great War, and he is very persuasive," Phillips responded.

Everyone laughed.

Eisenhower was the first to regain control. "Indeed, he can be."

"He felt my years of diplomatic experience would be beneficial in this assignment, and to be direct, General, I am a placeholder, at my request."

"I see," Ike said and looked at Murphy. "So, do you work for State or the OSS?"

"Technically, State, General, but in my current capacity, I suppose practically I work for Secretary Hull and Director Donovan."

"That is a rather precarious arrangement, it seems to me," Eisenhower commented.

"Oh my, General. My predicament is nowhere near as precarious or complicated as yours, working for six military chiefs in two countries, a prime minister and a president," observed Murphy.

"*Touché*," chuckled Ike.

"While I must respond to and keep two masters informed, Bill Donovan is far more engaged in the affairs of French North Africa and Operation TORCH. To be brutally blunt, General, the director has made it crystal clear to all of us. Operation TORCH is far more the inaugural test of the OSS and the concept of strategic intelligence than it is a vital military action. Not only must we contribute to the success of TORCH, but we must prove that the OSS is an essential element of that success."

"Well, now, when you put it like that," responded the supreme commander with a smile, "I must do my part. I have told General Donovan directly several times, and I will continue to do so, I am a supporter of his mission. I have faith in the contributions of the OSS and the ultimate success of Operation TORCH. Thank you all for your contributions. Keep up the great work, gentlemen."

The three intelligence officers paid their respects, excused themselves, and departed.

———

Tuesday, 8.September.1942
No.10 Downing Street
Whitehall, London, England
United Kingdom
20:30 hours

The renovations induced by the bomb damage of The Blitz were still ongoing, but Prime Minister Churchill insisted upon small gestures in their gradual return to normalcy even as the global war continued to boil around them.

The prime minister's guests for dinner this particular Tuesday evening were only the Supreme Commander Allied Forces and his deputy.

The meal had been simple but delicious as usual with Mrs. Landemere's food preparation. The dinner conversation had been light and social in tone and content, rather than business. The business portion of the evening waited until they retired to the prime minister's study. As soon as the brandy and cigars had been distributed, and the door closed, the prime minister handed the supreme commander a small, single sheet, yellow paper message for his review.

Eisenhower read the message, then handed it to Clark.

TELEGRAM

SEP 8 1942

TO PM UK
OK FULL BLAST

FDR

"That was simple and direct," quipped Clark.

"There is no subject, and it was sent via conventional means," Eisenhower added. "Are we sure this is real? What does it mean?"

Churchill smiled broadly. "It is rather succinct and cryptic, isn't it? I think you can recognize the telegram is from the president to me. It means Operation TORCH is approved in full without reservation or conditions. God bless you and your troops on your noble crusade."

"Thank you very much, Prime Minister."

"I do have a few minor queries if you will permit me?"

"Of course, sir."

"Tell me about your relief valve?"

"Relief valve, sir?"

"Yes. When the pressure of combat exceeds your threshold of tolerance, how will you relieve the pressure?"

Eisenhower smiled and opened his mouth to answer but stopped when the prime minister held his right hand up, palm out.

"It was a rhetorical question, General. As I indicated during our last review, I agreed with your assessment. You have insufficient forces should TORCH encounter the full defense of the French Territorial Army of North Africa. As President Roosevelt and I have agreed, we are intrigued by the potential of your compartmented initiative to nullify French resistance in Northwest Africa. It is one thing to consider the theoretical or notional. It is altogether another thing to turn the hypothetical into the practical. My concern lies in the application of that initiative."

"There are far too many likely twists and turns in the supplement. The bottom line is and will remain, we must respond and utilize what appears before us. I am absolutely convinced the OSS has the correct mindset and initiatives in play to realize the benefits. A few days ago, I met with the OSS leaders in the region to get the latest progress. The key appears to be General Giraud."

"Henri Giraud is a good man, an accomplished general, and a respected leader in the French military."

"Yes sir, and he wears an Army uniform. Admiral Darlan is the most senior, the titular head of the French joint chiefs of staff. We are working to engage both."

"Admirals Pike and Pound might be of assistance with the Darlan path," offered Churchill.

"Yes sir, we are continuing to consult both."

"I believe we are also agreed that the U.S. must lead here. Our standing with the French, at present, is not so high."

Eisenhower chuckled. "Yes, we understand that point of reality." He paused. No one spoke. "The three paths of approach and engagement specified in the supplement remain the same, although we continue to collect relevant intelligence and refine the plans contained in the supplement. What is new from my most recent meeting with the OSS is what we should call a fourth path, not yet contained in the supplement. The OSS requested that I, or a high-level delegation representing my position, meet with senior generals in Algeria, to convince them of our sincerity regarding potential operations in Northwest Africa."

"That is new, but surely you are not considering such a meeting," Churchill said.

"Actually, yes . . . ."

"No!" Churchill interrupted and proclaimed. "You are the supreme commander of this armada. The risk is simply too great."

"You mean like your visits to France in June of 1940," Eisenhower said and smiled, "when the battle was not going well."

Churchill smiled as well. "Oh, dear, well done, General. Excuse me and my impertinence here. I need to listen with anxious anticipation, pray tell me what you are proposing."

Eisenhower nodded. "Mark and I have discussed the OSS proposal. We both agree it has merit. I certainly understand and support the rationale for the OSS proposal."

"Ike, I cannot support your undertaking such a mission."

"I appreciate your concern, Prime Minister, and I respect your wise counsel." Eisenhower glanced at Clark and nodded.

"We are considering sending the deputy commander for this important mission," Clark said.

"You?"

"Yes sir."

Churchill stared at Clark, with an occasional glance at Eisenhower. "How do you think that would work?"

"We are still considering the details," Clark responded, "and the OSS is still fleshing out an agenda, attendees, and itinerary, but the notional concept involves a submarine insertion to a remote clandestine meeting sight on the Algerian coast." Churchill nodded his head.

"We should have a workable, functional plan in a couple of weeks," added Eisenhower.

"I eagerly anticipate the reading of your plan. *Prima facie*, I am not against such a gesture. My appreciation of the French, I suspect they will respond favorably. We . . . you must decide whether the benefit outweighs the risks."

"Of course," Churchill answered. "As you well know, part of the purpose in any plan is that particular analysis. We must consider our actions if the supplement is not successful."

Eisenhower chuckled in a very awkward, uneasy manner. "Oh, my dear prime minister, I have certainly done that. This is going to be a close-run thing, no matter how we cut it. I have directed the development of another secret supplement—a withdrawal plan."

"I am not an advocate of negative thoughts in such endeavors . . . however, one of my painful lessons learned from the debacle of Gallipoli, the worst time to prepare a withdrawal plan is when it is needed."

Eisenhower chose to move onto the prime minister's original queries. "You have other concerns, Prime Minister?"

Prime Minister Churchill stared at General Eisenhower like an angry bulldog about to charge. "I appreciate your sense of propriety." He continued to stare at Eisenhower. "Very well. As you know, I recently returned from my first meeting with Stalin." Eisenhower nodded. "Let it suffice to say, he does not believe TORCH will satisfy his concerns."

"To be rather direct, Prime Minister, that is a political matter and outside my domain."

"Quite so. I report this for awareness. The president and I are under considerable pressure from Chairman Stalin to execute SLEDGEHAMMER."

"I understand that dimension and reality, but I'm not sure of your purpose with such a declaration."

Churchill smiled. "We are committed to TORCH. I believe it is the best we can do at this stage of BOLERO. We must ensure TORCH is successful, if for no other reason than to prove Stalin wrong. We are going to have difficulty with the Soviets once this is done. My point is, failure and withdrawal are not available options."

"I appreciate the observation, Prime Minister. Respectfully, I do not disagree. We are doing everything we can to make the most of the resources we have. There are no guarantees in combat." This time Eisenhower stared at Churchill. "If there is anything you think we have failed to explore or address, I trust you will inform us."

Again, Churchill displayed his bulldog expression. A smile eventually bloomed on Winston's face and eyes. "Please excuse my nervousness, General. I believe you appreciate the political dimension. But, as you note, those burdens belong to the president and me. I suppose I just wanted you to be aware."

"I can assure you, Prime Minister, I am keenly aware of the political dimensions, but my focus must be on winning the battle ahead."

"As right it should be," Churchill announced. "Now, for lighter fare, we have an advance copy of the new movie *Flying Tigers* with John Wayne."

"Well," said Clark, "this should be interesting. We get to watch how it should be done."

All of them laughed. The prime minister led the way to the mansion's room converted to a home theatre. The remainder of the evening was occupied by the new movie and lighter discussions before the host and his guests retired well after midnight.

———

Tuesday, 15.September.1942
Headquarters, European Theater of Operations, United States Army
20 Grosvenor Square
Mayfair, London
United Kingdom
13:00 hours

The second anniversary of the Battle of Britain Day seemed like a most auspicious time for this moment in history. *I'll take the positive sign, but why am I the only one recalled to headquarters? I do not like being the only one, especially in this instance.* The corporal at the reception desk in the small lobby stood and saluted.

"May I help you, sir?"

"I have been ordered to report to General Hunter."

"Your name, sir?"

"Drummond . . . Flight Lieutenant Brian Drummond with Seventy-One Squadron."

The reception corporal checked his clipboard, presumably to validate the appointment. He gestured toward one of a half dozen privates sitting along an adjacent wall. "Please escort Flight Lieutenant Drummond to General Hunter's office."

The private nodded his head and said to Brian, "Please come with me, sir."

They ascended the stairway to the second floor and proceeded down the left hallway to a specific door. The gold lettering on the half, frosted glass door said,

COMMANDING GENERAL
VIII FIGHTER COMMAND
BGEN HUNTER

The private opened the door without knocking and gestured for Brian to enter. He heard the door close behind him. The only occupant of the anteroom was a snappy sergeant, sitting at a modest desk. "May I help you, sir?"

"Flight Lieutenant Drummond to see General Hunter," Brian answered.

"One moment, sir." The sergeant stood, went to the inner door, and announced Brian's arrival. "Let's have him," Brian heard from the inner office. The sergeant turned back to Brian and said, "The General will see you now."

Brian entered the general's office and recognized him as the chairman of his evaluation board. He marched to a spot one pace in front of the desk, saluted crisply, and said in a strong voice, "Flight Lieutenant Drummond reporting as ordered, sir."

"At ease, Captain," he said. *Doesn't he recognize an RAF flight lieutenant's uniform when he sees one?* "Please be seated." Brian looked around, saw a simple, straight-back, wooden chair, and sat down. "If I understand correctly, your callsign is Hunter. What a coincidence! We share a common name."

"I don't think that was the intent, sir," Brian responded.

"No. I'm certain it was not, since you acquired your combat callsign by your hunting skills in the air, long before the United States entered this war, and I became your commander." Brian sat very still, in total silence, and as devoid of expression as he could manage. "I know our last meeting was not so encouraging to a highly accomplished fighter pilot such as yourself. Brian, first, I want to tell you directly, emphatically, and without the slightest equivocation, as well as the best research the War Department or myself can do, you are the most experienced and accomplished American pilot short of Eddie Rickenbacker . . . and he holds the Medal of Honor for his exploits." *That's a bit of an exaggeration, I do believe.* Brian did not twitch or blink. "It is my duty to inform you that the War Department has granted your college degree waiver and approved your transfer to the Army Air Forces."

"Damn!"

Hunter chuckled a couple of times. "That was not quite the response I expected."

"I'm sorry, sir. Thank you, sir."

General Hunter held up his right hand to stop. "Thank you, Brian, for wanting to join us. Let's get the first order of business out of the way." He opened a folder in front of him and removed what looked like three pieces of paper, clipped together, with a dark sheet between two white sheets. The General held up the papers. "This is your commissioning letter. You need to read it carefully, then sign it." Hunter extended the paper to Brian, who had to stand to retrieve the letter.

Brian read every word twice.

Headquarters
European Theater of Operations
United States Army

September 15, 1942

Brian Arthur Drummond.
London, United Kingdom,

    1. The Secretary of War has directed the Theater Commander to inform you that the President has appointed and commissioned you a temporary captain in the Army of the United States effective September 15, 1942. This appointment may be vacated at any time by the President and, unless sooner terminated, is for the duration of the present emergency and six months thereafter. Your serial number is O-713446, and you will hold rank from December 8, 1941.

    2. This letter should be retained by you as evidence of your appointment as no commissions will be issued during the duration of the war.

    By command of Lieutenant General EISENHOWER

Brian D. Hathaway
Brigadier General
Adjutant

Accepted: _____
        Brian A. Drummond
        Captain, USAAF

"Do you have any questions or concerns?"

"Only one . . . do you have a pen, sir?"

Hunter chuckled and handed Brian his pen. Brian signed the letter and returned the pen and papers to General Hunter. The General removed the paperclip and carbon sheet. He placed the top copy back in the folder, but did not close it, and then pushed the carbon copy across the desk to Brian.

"Retain this copy on your person, at least until we complete the transfer of the Eagle squadrons."

"Yes sir."

"Now," General Hunter paused, "to the real purpose of this moment." *What the hell is he talking about?* "I wanted to meet with you face-to-face. To be direct, you are a unique case due to a variety of timing issues. I must remind you . . . you are sworn to secrecy since you are gaining a preview. First, you are going to be in an odd position of being in two worlds simultaneously. Seventy-One Squadron will be officially transferred from the Royal Air Force, Fighter Command, to become the 334th Fighter Squadron, 4th Fighter Group, 8th Fighter Command, 8th Air Force, effective on the 29th of this month. However, the War Department, by direction of the president, has ordered you to return to the States before the official transfer, in direct support of the 1st National War Bond Drive. It seems you are a bit of a celebrity, Captain Drummond, and you are considered essential to the bond drive.

"Although you will technically still be a flight lieutenant in the Royal Air Force, you will depart England as a captain in the United States Army Air Forces. You will remain in RAF uniform until you appear at your transfer base, where you will become an Army captain. You will need appropriate coaching to make sure you perform properly. You will receive more specific information next week. I have personally briefed Squadron Leader Meares and Air Chief Marshal Douglas. They have concurred. You are granted leave pending your transportation to the States. I presume you will enjoy your furlough at Standing Oak Farm."

Wow! His intelligence staff work is pretty good. "Yes sir . . . with my wife Charlotte and our infant son."

"I will instruct my staff to contact you there."

"Thank you, sir. May I ask a question, sir?"

"Shoot."

"Why don't I just travel in my current uniform? I know how to act the part."

General Hunter chuckled softly. "Because, Captain, you will officially transfer during your stint in support of the bond drive, and the War Department would rather not distract the proceedings explaining your transformation in the middle of the tour. You will also be aboard an Army B-17 heavy bomber en route to New York."

General Hunter passed Brian's orders to him for him to read.

Headquarters
VIII Fighter Command

September 15, 1942

Captain Brian A. Drummond, USAAF
334th Fighter Squadron
4th Fighter Group, 8th Fighter Command,
8th Air Force
USAAF Station F-356

    1. You have been selected by the War Department to represent the Army Air Forces in the upcoming first national war bond drive for the present conflict. This is a distinct and unique honor, as well as recognition of your contributions to the war effort. This assignment is expected to remain in effect for three (3) months duration.

    2. You are ordered to stand detached from your present unit, proceed by the fastest available means to New York City, New York, and report to Bond Drive Coordinator Colonel Harold Q. Peters, GS, no later than September 29, 1942 for the first national war bond drive.

    3. Subsequent assignment will be determined at the conclusion of these orders.

    4. You are granted leave immediately until appropriate transportation can be arranged. Your transportation coordinator within this command is Major John H. Smith, TC.

    5. This letter should be retained by you until this assignment is completed.

    6. You are assigned Travel Priority: AAAABB-1, under these orders.

Frank O. Hunter

Brigadier General
Commanding General
VIII Fighter Command

"May I ask another question, sir?" Brian said.

General Hunter seemed to squint at him as if he was irritated by Brian's request. "Let's have it," the general responded.

"New York City is a very big place. How am I supposed to find Colonel Peters?"

General Hunter chuckled as if Brian had told an immodest joke. "With orders like these Captain, I dare say a representative of the colonel will be waiting for you when you land. If anything goes wrong, seek the assistance of any officer at your location and show them these orders."

"Yes sir. What will I be doing?"

"The best I know is that you will most likely stand as one of the nation's military heroes at various public appearances to encourage our citizens to buy war bonds."

"What does that mean, sir? I'm no hero, and I'm certainly no salesman."

"Just stand tall, look pretty, and do what the coordinators say."

The response struck Brian in a not so good manner. They had been show ponies since the squadron had been formed two years ago. It sounded like this new assignment was just another version of the very same frustration he had endured since joining Seventy-One Squadron. The notion of giving up his seat in a front line fighter in combat for a vaudeville exercise actually produced sensations of anger. *I cannot react to this. I've got to change the subject.* "These orders," Brian said, holding up the second page, "do not say I'm coming back to the squadron."

Hunter laughed more heartily this time. "Captain, you are in the Army now. You serve at the pleasure of the President, and you will perform duties assigned to you by the Army to meet the Army's objectives to the best of your ability. The Army will decide what the Army needs you to do next. Do you understand this reality, Captain?"

"Yes sir. I would like to return to my squadron. Flying is the only thing I know . . . the only thing I want to do."

"You are not alone in that wish, Captain. I wish I had the seat you are giving up. However, as I said earlier, you are in the Army now. Unfortunately, Air Commodore Spencer or Prime Minister Churchill himself can't help you now, Captain Drummond."

I do not like the sound of that statement, but I am not asking for special treatment . . . just a request . . . or perhaps an appeal. "Yes sir."

"Any other questions?" the general asked.

"No sir. Thank you for your time and patience," Brian said as calmly as he could muster up.

"Very well, Captain Drummond. God be with you! You are dismissed."

Brian stood, came to attention, and saluted General Hunter. The General returned Brian's salute and turned his attention to the papers in front of him. Brian did an about-face and departed. He left the headquarters building in somewhat of a daze. A million thoughts flooded his consciousness as he walked without focus to the Bond Street Underground Station for the trip back to Debden. Checking his watch, Brian thought he could make it back to the base before the CO secured for the evening. *Based on these orders, I need to close things out with the squadron, and then get home to Charlotte and Ian.*

Tuesday, 15.September.1942
RAF Debden
Saffron Walden, Essex, England
United Kingdom
16:30 hours

Rain had been falling all day long, off and on, from the overcast sky. Brian returned to the squadron just in time to be released. Half the pilots were walking out as Hunter walked in. Within seconds, Brian was alone with Corporal Harris and Squadron Leader Meares.

"Mister Drummond, welcome back . . . a word, if you please. Corporal Harris, no reason to wait around. You are dismissed."

"Yes sir. See you in the morning."

The sound of the Dispersal Hut door closing punctuated the transition.

"So, how was your meeting?"

"Good, sir," Brian announced.

"Congratulations," Meares said. "You have your orders?"

"Yes sir. You know?"

"Yes, I do. I was informed last Friday. You were the last to receive the board's decision and the first to be ordered away from the squadron. We will surely miss your skills, experience, and leadership, Brian. As I understand your orders, you will be on this temporary assignment for three months or so, which in turn means the squadron will be under different command, if you return."

"I do not know what happens after this assignment, but I most assuredly want to return . . . to finish what the Germans started."

"Quite understandable, but to be frank and honest, Brian, you have served for three years in combat. You are entitled to a no less contributory but less intense assignment."

"I appreciate that, sir, but my family is here. I need to be here to do my part to win the war."

"There is little I can do, but you certainly have my vote. All air forces, including ours, need pilots like you, Brian. I could sing your praises for the rest of the evening and then some. However, the gears of the machine continue to turn. The squadron, actually all three American volunteer squadrons, is scheduled to officially transfer from the Royal Air Force to the U.S. Army Air Forces on the 29th of September. We are both sworn to secrecy regarding your orders, and so we both shall respect that requirement. You are being granted extended leave from this moment until your report-for-transport date next week. To avoid any difficulty or awkwardness, I would suggest you gather up your personal belongings and quietly check out. That way, you can avoid the inevitable questions."

"I would prefer to say good-bye to me mates," Brian said with his best Cockney accent.

Meares laughed heartily. "Well done, Hunter. You have my counsel. What are you going to do?"

"I will heed your advice, sir. I need to call Charlotte since I will arrive home rather late."

"We can take care of that."

"Please pass along my gratitude to the squadron, especially Dusty and Frog, and my crew: Jacobs, Hawking, and Easton."

"I will take care of it personally, Hunter. Do you want to take your flight equipment . . . well, except your pistol?"

"May I?"

"Yes, of course." Meares stood, came around the desk, shook Brian's hand, and then hugged him.

Brian followed Meares counsel, quietly packed his belongings, paid his remaining mess bill, checked out, and took the proffered car to the railway station for the trip home.

The next phase of Brian Drummond's career began.

Chapter 14

The alteration of motion is ever proportional
to the motive force impressed,
and is made in the direction of the right line
in which that force is impressed.

-- Sir Isaac Newton

Thursday, 17. September.1942
Office of the Secretary of War
Pentagon Building
Arlington, Virginia
United States of America
09:00 hours

Secretary of War Stimson reviewed his notes for the scheduled meeting. Neither the president nor the secretary had been impressed with the performance of Colonel Marshall in just the first month of his appointment. Virtually the entire scientific and engineering teams had voiced concerns from modest to serious that Colonel Marshall was blocking or resisting actions nearly to the point of stopping development. The technical folks had lost confidence in Marshall's ability to appreciate the significance of the Manhattan Project. The chief of staff agreed with the immediate need for change, and the president concurred.

Stimson had been very impressed with the stern, aggressive supervision of Pentagon Building construction, and although the full structure was a year from completion, Stimson wanted that manager to take over the Manhattan Project management.

The knock at the door interrupted the secretary's thoughts and reading of the report in front of him. He held up his left index finger. His long-term secretary and administrative assistant Cynthia Hammond entered, saw the finger, closed the door behind her, and waited for her boss. Miss Hammond had been directly supporting Henry Stimson since he had been secretary of state under President Hoover.

Stimson looked up. "Sorry, Cynthia. I needed to finish that report. I presume Colonel Groves is here."

"Yes sir. Do you need anyone else here for this meeting?"

"No. Please show Colonel Groves to the inner sanctum."

Cynthia smiled, nodded her head, opened the door, and nodded to an unseen person. "Colonel Groves, sir."

Stimson came around his desk and extended his right hand to a serious-looking colonel in pink and green uniform with castle lapel insignia of a member of the Corps of Engineers.

Colonel Leslie Richard Groves Jr., USA, CE [USMA 1918], had been the chief of the Construction Division's Design and Engineering Section with direct supervisory responsibility for the massive construction of the Pentagon Building. He had a well-earned reputation for being a relentless, unforgiving taskmaster.

"Welcome, Colonel Groves."

"Thank you, sir."

"Please," Stimson said, gesturing to the facing couches. "Would you care for some coffee?"

"No, thank you, sir."

Stimson shook his head to Miss Hammond, who left the two men alone and closed the door behind her.

"I know you are extraordinarily busy, and I must say at the outset that you are doing a masterful job with this building," Stimson said and swung his arm around the office. "The chief and I are quite grateful you have been able to finish the front of the building and allow us to move into these spacious offices."

"Glad to be of service, sir."

"Do you know why I have asked to see you?" asked the secretary.

"I presume there is a problem with the building construction."

Stimson chuckled. "My apologies for being so abrupt and cryptic, but no. The building construction is going incredibly well from my perspective." Stimson paused and smiled. "From this moment on, the project we are about to discuss is classified Top Secret – Paramount. You are not to discuss anything said in any form with anyone not previously cleared for Paramount access authorized by the president or me, only. I need to know you understand this restriction and will comply precisely and strictly. And, before you answer, you need to know that just one deviation from this restriction in any form at any time will send you into isolation incommunicado for the duration of the war. Do you understand this restriction?"

"Yes sir."

"Will you comply with this restriction?"

"Absolutely, sir."

"Very well. The restriction starts now. President Roosevelt designated me as the Cabinet overseer of this project on behalf of the president, the American people, and our Allies. The president initiated with Prime Minister Churchill a joint development project to produce an extraordinary explosive device designed to release the unimaginable energy of nuclear fission."

"Excuse me, sir. I do not know what that means. I am not familiar with the term, nuclear fission."

"I was only marginally aware before this project began."

Stimson explained the genesis of the nuclear fission research that came to fruition in Germany in 1938, the more robust confirmatory experiments in England the following year, and the development of the theoretical calculations by British physicists in 1940. He summarized the various supporting documents for the project. Stimson went to his desk, retrieved a red binder, and pushed it across the desk to Groves. Stimson indicated the background materials were contained in the binder, boldly marked TOP SECRET-PARAMOUNT. He also noted the collective intelligence estimate that the Germans might well be ahead of the Allies in the development of a nuclear device. The project's objective was to deliver a functional atomic bomb before the Germans.

"I have coordinated with OSS Director Donovan for you to receive a detailed briefing on the intelligence collected to date as well as on-going operations to gather more information and potentially interfere with German nuclear development. I have taken the liberty of scheduling you to meet with Director Donovan tomorrow morning at eight at his E-Street Complex headquarters." Groves' puzzled expression coaxed out more information. "My secretary Cynthia Hammond will give you the address and directions for entry."

"Yes sir. Thank you, sir. I'm sure I have an awful lot to digest and swallow," Groves said, patting the red binder on the desk.

"For now, as you get up on step, bring your questions to me directly until you get more immersed in this effort." Groves nodded. "Now, to the crux of this meeting and to be brutally blunt, your predecessor as chief of the Manhattan Project has been relieved of duty in less than a month from his assuming command. He was relieved because he resisted the directions of the scientific and engineering teams growing to fulfill the objectives of this project. Your job, Colonel, is to carry out the necessary land acquisitions, construction projects, testing and such, as required, by the physicists to achieve the objective as soon as humanly possible . . . and, emphatically, before the Germans. You are not and will not be a filter, regulator or throttle; you are an enabler, period. We cannot tolerate a learning curve. You are also scheduled to meet with the physics team tomorrow afternoon. You have through the weekend to assess the task at hand and decide whether you are up to the management of this project."

"Yes sir."

"If you decide it is too much for you, for whatever reason matters to you, then no harm, no foul, and you will return to your current assignment. If you agree to take this mammoth project on, then Katie bar the door. The president has designated the Manhattan Project, and I do mean THE, highest national defense priority effort in the entire war effort. There is no option for failure here."

"That is rather direct, Mister Secretary."

"We do not have time for a dance, General." Groves started to protest the error but stopped with the secretary's raised hand. "As of this moment, by order of the president, you are hereby promoted to the temporary rank of brigadier general."

A broad smile bloomed across Groves' otherwise stern face. "Thank you, sir."

"No need to thank me. This is not going to be easy, no matter how we cut it. You are also scheduled to be back here at nine o'clock on Monday morning to deliver your decision. Use these next few days wisely. I await your decision."

Groves grabbed the red binder, stood, came to attention, and saluted the secretary. Stimson returned his salute. Groves departed the secretary's office.

General Groves would agree to manage and ramrod the massive Manhattan Project development and manufacturing effort. He would successfully lead the unprecedented effort to its ultimate conclusion, three years later.

—

Wednesday, 23.September.1942
Standing Oak Farm
Winchester, Hampshire, England
United Kingdom
09:00 hours

The morning milking had gone quite well. Charlotte had done such a good job expanding their dairy business, using the excess grass from the acquired farms that were now theirs. Brian really liked Charlotte's plans and fully supported her ideas. The crew had been fed, and Mom had taken care of Ian, whom she had insisted on still allowing him to breastfeed when he sought it. Charlotte still referred to Edith's contribution to raising their son as a godsend.

Horace had taken the Bedford delivery truck with yesterday evening's and this morning's milk yield and cheese products. After breakfast, Lionel had gone over to the Brownfield parcel to help with an equipment problem. Charlotte worried about both of her elderly farmhands, since Lionel was 63 years old, and Horace was now 67 years old. Jacob, who had just turned 14 years old a few months ago, was off to school for the day and would be back for the evening chores.

Charlotte clasped her husband's hand, led him outside and down the gravel path to their bench under the oak tree. "Thank you for all you have done while you were home. Even a few days are a huge contribution."

Brian looked at Charlotte as they sat. "Surely, you did not think I was going to lay about for four days."

Charlotte giggled softly. "No, but you have every right to do so. I just felt the urge to acknowledge your contributions."

"Thank you." Brian was not content to wait for Charlotte to get to her point. "What is on your mind?"

"Directly to the point as always, my darling." She looked into Brian's eyes and smiled modestly. "I am not eager for your departure tomorrow morning."

"That is a positive sign," Brian chuckled.

"I think the arrangements you set in place before your pending deployment to Russia last July have been working well."

"I agree."

"I feel more confident with these arrangements, and I think your people in Kansas . . . ."

"Our people."

"OK, yes, our people in Kansas have transitioned smoothly to my involvement. I feel good about that part. I am not too keen on you being so far away."

"Likewise, my sweet. But my country says it needs me to do this for the war effort. And, on the plus side, at least I won't be strapped into a fighter cockpit in combat."

"Thank goodness for small blessings and thank you for showing me how to send telegrams. The post will just take too long."

"More expensive than the mail, but worth it; I do believe it will be worth it. I am told we will be moving every few days. They tell me that we will be authorized to tell you where we are and where we have been, but not where we are going. My guess is, we will work our way across the country from east to west. I will try to keep you informed so we can communicate. I am not sure what address to use, but hopefully, they will tell us what address to use, and I will let you know as soon as I can."

"I can ask no more," Charlotte said, smiled demurely, held her smile, and looked deeply into Brian's eyes. "I have no idea of what to expect with this pending assignment, but my imagination urges caution."

Brian listened intently without responding with words or expression.

Charlotte continued, "From what you have told me, you are going to be in close proximity to and working with many beautiful women—actresses who are publicly known for their appearance and acting skills. I want to assure you that I trust your love for me and for Ian. No matter what might happen, I need you to believe that I love you very much and nothing will interfere with that love." Brian opened his mouth to respond but stopped when Charlotte raised her right hand and placed her index finger to his lips. "There is no need for you to protest, object and assuage my imagination. I say this to put your mind to rest. If anything happens, please do not tell me by telegram or letter. I would like you to tell me once we are eye-to-eye again. What is most important to me is honesty and truthfulness. I do not want anything hidden between us." Charlotte paused and stared into Brian's eyes. "What say you?"

"I understand. I never cease to be amazed and gobsmacked by your enlightenment, concern, and love. I am not going into this with any thoughts of transgressions or dalliances. I truly appreciate your wisdom. So, I must say in response, what is good for the goose is good for the gander."

Charlotte smiled. "Agreed."

Brian kissed his wife, but she had broader desires. She wrapped her arms around him, and he joined her. They kissed passionately.

Holding him close, Charlotte whispered, as if someone might hear, "Now, take me to bed and make me a mother again."

"What?" said Brian, in shocked protestation.

Charlotte smiled and gave him a peck on the lips. "I am at that point in my cycle that I am the most fertile."

"Good to know, but I thought you said you did not want any more children until the war and danger were behind us."

Again, she smiled and gave him a brief kiss. "A woman can change her mind. To be frank, Edith is a large contributor to my change of mind. I am not as afraid of motherhood in our circumstances as I once was. I believe in you and in us."

"Well, thank God for Edith." Brian stood. Charlotte followed. They embraced, side-by-side, and slowly walked in synch to the house. Edith was upstairs with Ian. The two lovers went to the master bedroom and leaped into their lover's endeavor with enthusiasm and gusto. They remained ensconced in their intimacy for several hours and repeated couplings. The sound of one of the vehicles crunching on the gravel driveway ended their morning session.

They picked up the daily chores, beginning with a mid-day meal for themselves and their crew. Both of them would return to their intimacy once they retired for the evening. They only had hours remaining, and they intended to use those hours fully. Rest could come later.

———

Friday, 25.September.1942
USAAF Station B-110
Oundle, Northamptonshire, England
United Kingdom
07:30 hours

Brian had reported to the transportation office at the new U.S. Army Air Force base at the former RAF Polebrook station yesterday, just after midday.

After his paperwork had been checked, he was informed that he would be outfitted with two complete pinks & greens service uniforms replete with the appropriate insignia. He was entitled to wear his RAF wings and decorations over his right breast pocket. Those unique ribbons and insignia took several hours to resolve. For the time being, he would have only his silver Army aviator's wing above his left breast pocket. An Army Air Forces captain spent hours that afternoon teaching Brian the minor differences between American Army and British Air Force customs and conduct. Brian's escort, Captain Johnny Holcomb, joined him for supper at the mess hall, where they extended their meal to talk and continue Brian's fire hose indoctrination, and then settle him in the Visiting Officer's Quarters. His scheduled transportation was an Army B-17E, specifically tasked with flying Brian to New York City. Brian was issued cold weather flight gear that he would travel in and packed his bag.

The escort captain picked him up, ate breakfast with Brian, and delivered his charge to a new, combat green, B-17 heavy bomber. As Brian and his escort walked toward the aircraft, another captain in cold weather flight gear noticed them approaching and came to them.

"You must be Captain Drummond," he said.

"Yes, I am."

"I'm Charlie Parker, the aircraft commander of this beast," he said. "Your carriage awaits."

"Thank you, Charlie. I've never been in a B-17 before, so I'll need a little coaching."

"Not a problem. To be proper, before we board, may I see your orders," Parker asked.

Brian retrieved the travel copy of his orders and handed the paper to Captain Parker. Charlie examined the orders, nodded his head, and handed the paper back to Brian.

"Also, may I see your ID?"

Brian complied. Again, after Parker was satisfied, he handed the laminated card back to Brian.

Parker turned to Brian's escort. "I've got him, Johnny. He's ours now."

"OK, Charlie." Holcomb turned to Brian. "It was an honor to help you, Brian. Good luck and raise lots of money for the cause."

"I'll do my best, Johnny. Thanks for the rushed education and your expertise."

"You betcha. I'll leave you boys to it."

Parker declared, "Let's get this show on the road. We've got a long way to go, and I've got a deadline to meet." Charlie Parker led Brian to the starboard side of the empennage, just forward of the horizontal stabilizer. "Normally, we would board at the nose, but this is a special event. We'll start at the tail. We will take off with full fuel, no bombs, and minimal crew. Our crew bombardier and the four rear gunners will remain here." Parker gestured to the small boarding hatch that was locked open. Brian tossed his travel bag into the tail and preceded Charlie into the aircraft's tail section. "The waist guns have been removed, and the gun portals covered with plexiglass panels to make it a little less drafty back there," he said, pointing up. Patting the top of a large, green sphere poking up through the deck, Charlie continued, "The ball turret will remain stowed." Forward of the ball turret was an open compartment with a small desk and medium-size black box with a bunch of knobs, a few switches, and a dial window. "This is Sergeant Bob Henderson, our radio operator and hump gunner if we need it." Brian shook hands with Henderson, who was a good foot shorter and looked like a high school student in uniform. *But, who am I to be talking? That's what they say about me.* "This is the bomb bay." Empty bomb racks hung on both sides with a very narrow walkway in the middle, barely six inches wide at the bottom. Two puffy, pea-green, suspended sleeping bags were suspended, fore and aft, in the bomb bay. "We've rigged a couple of thermal hammocks," he added. "They have electric heating elements that help with the cold. The heating system is not perfect. The bags will help."

"Well, that is reassuring, isn't it?"

Parker laughed. "Welcome to Bomber Command. You fighter jockeys have it nice." Parker led Brian across the narrow walkway. Just forward of the bomb bay was the flight engineer's station, who also manned the twin 50-caliber machine guns of the top turret. "This is Technical Sergeant Jeff Bridges." The two men shook hands. "Jeff knows more about this beast," Charlie banged his fist on the fuselage aluminum skin, "than anyone in Bomber Command."

"He's fibbing," Bridges spoke with a smile.

"Good to know," Brian said.

Just in front of the top turret was clearly the cockpit, pilot's seat on the left and copilot's seat on the right. "This is where the magic happens. The hole in the deck leads to the nose, and we'll get to that part shortly. My cohort for today's show is Lieutenant Ted Holcomb, no relation to Johnny." Ted waved from the right seat. Another first lieutenant poked his head up through the deck hole. "This is our illustrious navigator Lieutenant Bill Masterson. He'll take you into his domain, while I strap into the king's throne and bring this beast alive. Bill will show you around, and get you strapped into the best seat in the house."

"Thanks, Charlie."

Masterson motioned for Brian to follow him. Brian descended through the short passageway and emerged in the nose compartment. "Welcome aboard,

Captain Drummond. Not often we get a mission to transport a single Army captain."

"Changing times, I suppose."

"Yeah. Anyway, this is my station. They give me a nice little desk. This is my celestial sextant and dome," Holcomb said, pointing to the circular, shallow dome directly overhead. "This is your seat," Bill said patting the simple seat at the transparent nose. "It's not the most comfortable seat in the house, but it certainly has the best view."

The sound of the No.1 engine starting made talking a little more problematic. Bill gave Brian a leather helmet, oxygen mask, and throat microphone—equipment that was similar, although not the same, as he was used to in the RAF. The navigator showed Brian the oxygen regulator and method of operation, as well as intercom controls. The No.2 engine started. Brian plugged in his helmet cord and immediately was listening to the pilots going through the start checklist. No.3 engine started, and shortly thereafter the No.4 engine was up and running smoothly. The bombsight had been removed. Brian examined the bombardier's control panel through which he controlled everything from the bomb bay doors to the individual or salvo release of the bomb load. He also noticed they had removed the nose machine-guns and plugged the ports.

When the pilots were ready to taxi for takeoff, Charlie said, "Bob, get us up on Tower."

"You're up, Chief."

Ted called for taxi and takeoff. They were cleared for takeoff. Bill had been quite correct. It was fantastic watching the English countryside fall away beneath the nose of the bomber. The aircraft passed directly over the ruins of Fotheringhay Castle.

"That is where the English executed Mary, Queen of Scots, in 1587," Bill said, pointing out the nose transparency at a pile of rubble.

"Wow!" was all Brian could muster up to say.

"Nasty business back then. Lots of killing by all sorts of despicable means," Bill mused out loud rather than for any particular directed conversation with Brian. "The worst was being drawn and quartered . . . nasty, nasty stuff. Mary was simply and swiftly beheaded with the blade of a battle-ax. Nasty, nasty, nasty," he kept repeating.

In less than an hour, the green of England and Ireland gave way to the expansive blue of the Atlantic Ocean. They donned their oxygen masks as they climbed through 10,000 feet on their way to their initial cruising altitude of 18,000 feet, well below condensation trail altitude and into decidedly colder air. Bill explained that they want to get to a point about 200 miles out to sea before they completed their climb to their final cruising altitude of 28,000 feet.

A little over four hours into their transit flight, Charlie Parker said over the intercom, "Brian, things are fairly calm and quiet, humming right along, why don't you come on up here and trade seats with Ted, if you would like to get a feel for one of these beasts."

"Sure. On the way," Brian responded.

"Don't dally! You don't want to be off oxygen too long."

Ted was out of his right seat and standing behind Charlie Parker's left seat. Brian noticed the Ted was already attached to a walking bottle of oxygen. He maneuvered into the right seat. Ted made sure he plugged in Brian's oxygen hose, and the flow was good before he assisted Brian with the remainder of strapping into the seat and completing the connection of his headphones and microphone jacks.

Charlie flipped a switch on the center console that caused a slight jerk. He adjusted the trim wheels to his satisfaction. "We're off autopilot," Charlie announced to Brian and the crew. "She's all yours, Brian."

Brian placed his feet on the rudder pedals and grasped the control wheel. He initially focused on making flight control adjustments to maintain altitude and airspeed.

"We're ahead of our fuel consumption schedule, so you can maneuver her around a little to get a feel for the difference between your Spitfire and a Flying Fortress."

Brian responded by making small roll and pitch inputs to gauge the responsiveness. The bomber was decidedly less agile than his fighter. The aircraft felt more responsive in pitch than in roll—a trait that seemed to be common to large aircraft. Once he felt he had played enough, Brian returned the aircraft to the original altitude, airspeed, and course.

"Had enough?" Charlie asked.

"Hey, I'll fly this monster as long as you will let me."

"Your machine."

Brian maintained the controls and manually flew the aircraft as he familiarized himself with the instrumentation. The aircraft obviously had more space, and the various flight instruments like attitude indicator, airspeed indicator, altimeter, turn & slip indicator, and such were not the same but similar to those in the Spitfire and other fighters he had flown. The engine instruments were well laid out with four of everything.

"New heading, two six seven," Bill Masterson called out.

"Turning to two six seven," Brian answered and adjusted his heading accordingly. Brian located the trim wheels and tweaked the trim to maintain zero force on the controls. As Brian continued his instrument scan and control adjustments to maintain their state, he asked Charlie, "Have you flown any combat missions, yet."

"Nope, not yet, only training missions, so far. But, combat is coming, and we'll be ready."

"Bomber Command has had a helluva time of it. They used to fly night and daylight missions, but not anymore. They concentrate on all, night missions now."

"We need daylight for our bombsight and accuracy."

"The Norden?"

"Yeah, but we don't call it that. We call it the box or the gadget. You probably noticed they removed the sight from the aircraft for this mission—too secret for a transport job, they say."

"Yeah, I noticed."

"The Brass get all freaky about the damn thing, so we try to minimize its importance. That sight is going to relegate us to daylight bombing, though, which we all feel is going to be rough for us. We will be dependent upon our guns and you fighter jockeys to survive."

"We've already done some bomber escort missions for the RAF. I believe we escorted a squadron from up here on their first combat bombing mission last August."

"That was Major Tibbets' 340th Bombardment Squadron, not us, and so the reports said, you fellas kept the enemy fighters at bay."

"I'm sure we will do a lot more before this ordeal is done."

"Yeah, but those Spitfires of yours don't have the range to stay with us once we start going into Germany."

"We won't be flying Spitfires for much longer, they tell us. They'll be switching us to some American fighter aircraft."

"Whatever you get, we sure hope it has more range to stay with us and keep the enemy fighters away. The flak will be bad enough, but it is the fighters we worry about the most—far more accurate."

"We'll do our best."

Brian continued to fly the big aircraft for another hour. Ted Holcomb checked on the rest of the crew, and then descended into the nose compartment, presumably to take Brian's bombardier's seat and plug into the ship's oxygen system. The ride remained smooth and easy. Clouds were predominantly below their altitude, although they had to deviate slightly around several cumulous build-ups to avoid penetrating the clouds with the concomitant turbulence.

Once back on track, Charlie asked Brian, "Have you had enough hand-flying?"

"Do you need the controls back?"

"No, no. I just don't want to wear out our guest," Charlie said into his oxygen mask and integral intercom.

"I'm kind of enjoying this, as long as you don't mind."

"We can engage the autopilot anytime . . . when you've had enough."

"I have no experience with autopilots," Brian added. "I'm only used to flying."

"Yeah, well, we fly for a really long time. It wears a body out."

Brian simply nodded his head in acknowledgment. He made the recommended course changes, as stated by Bill Masterson, to maintain their great circle route transit over the North Atlantic Ocean. The hourly position reports were provided by the navigator and broadcast over the HF radio by Sergeant Henderson.

Eleven plus hours flying time had elapsed from takeoff to the descent for landing at Gander, Newfoundland. As Charlie informed Brian and the crew, they would spend the night here for some rest, and then proceed to New York City tomorrow morning. Arrangements had already been made.

"Do you think you can handle this beast for landing?" asked Charlie Parker.

"With a little help on procedures, I think I can manage."

"Gander's got a big runway, so you should be fine."

With the assistance of Jeff Bridges, Charlie Parker stepped through the pre-landing and landing checklist. Brian manipulated the controls to establish the conditions Charlie directed. They were cleared to land at Gander, Newfoundland, with the wind ten degrees off the nose at 13 knots. Charlie talked Brian through the approach, flare, and not quite perfect three-point landing and rollout. As Brian gently applied the wheel brake to slow the aircraft, Jeff raised the flaps, opened the engine cowl flaps, and prepared the aircraft for shutdown. The aircraft felt so much heavier than his fighters but handled essentially the same. Once off the runway and taxing at a modest speed, Charlie took the controls back to maneuver the four-engine bomber to their designated parking spot in front of what looked like the terminal building and control tower.

Charlie and Jeff stepped through the shutdown procedures, switched everything off that needed to be off, and secured the engines. Brian checked his watch. They crossed the North Atlantic without incident or difficulty in 12 hours and 14 minutes.

They secured the aircraft for the night, ordered the fuel load for the next leg to New York, and gave the ground crew their planned time of departure. The ground crew was American, assisted by a couple of Canadian civilians, who had become quite proficient with the care of transiting aircraft and their crews. Once the necessary paperwork was complete, the enlisted men were dropped off at their transit barracks, and the officers were taken to the Visiting Officers Quarters. They were fed, had one quick drink, and went directly to bed for a good night's sleep.

———

Saturday, 26. September. 1942
Newfoundland Airport
Gander, Newfoundland
Dominion of Newfoundland
07:30 hours

The same truck and driver picked the crew up in reverse order from their drop-off last night. Everyone seemed to be satisfied with their meals, overnight stay, and rest. Their clearance into U.S. airspace had been received. Brian joined Charlie and Ted for their walkaround pre-flight check, and Jeff Bridges confirmed the required fuel load, and engines and systems were ready for flight. Charlie was a little more apprehensive about the U.S. air defense procedures and what they might find in New York, so Ted would remain in the right seat for this leg.

They started all four engines nicely, made sure everything was operating correctly, and taxied for takeoff. The aircraft was airborne in comparatively no time at all and headed 246° on a direct course for New York City. The view out the nose glass was truly extraordinary. Brian challenged his geography knowledge to identify the sights he saw en route to New York.

The flight took just over four hours and again was fairly smooth and easy. They arrived at New York Municipal Airport among other commercial and military traffic, and taxied to the Military Terminal at the north end of the field. *I've been here before.* Several officers, drivers and staff cars appeared to be waiting for them.

———

Saturday, 26. September. 1942
Headquarters, No. 11 Group
Uxbridge, Middlesex, England
United Kingdom
16:30 hours

"What do we know?" asked Air Commodore John Spencer to the Kenley wing commander and the No. 11 Group intelligence officer.

Wing Commander Brian Kingcome, DSO, DFC with bar, had been the Kenley Wing commander since June. He was also an ace and an accomplished fighter pilot as well as a member of The Few.

Wing Commander Jason Hudson was a career RAF intelligence officer, who had just taken his current position the previous month.

The day's CIRCUS mission had been a daylight-bombing raid on the fighter airfield and support facilities near the Brittany coastal community and port of Morlaix, in occupied France. A USAAF B-17E bomber squadron was to be escorted by the Kenley Wing of three Spitfire fighter squadrons—the British No.64 Squadron, the American No.133 Squadron, and the Canadian No.401 Squadron.

Kingcome and Hudson looked at each other without expression. Kingcome took the initiative. "First, foremost and at the bottom line, only one aircraft of 133 Squadron made it back to England, and he crashed his aircraft in a farm field near Kingsbridge, Devon, having exhausted his petrol. We know by radio traffic and the lone returning pilot that the mission had gone dreadfully wrong, largely due to worse than forecast weather conditions."

Spencer looked directly at Hudson, who took the cue. "We agree, sir, the Met office missed this one. From our debriefing of our surviving fighter pilots and as well as direct collaboration with the American 97th Bombardment Group intelligence officer, we can confirm Wing Commander Kingcome's observation. The cloud cover turned out to be multi-layered with several levels of 10/10ths overcast that seriously complicated the rendezvous process. Worse, the winds proved to be stronger than forecast as a pure tailwind on the outbound leg that became headwinds on the return." Hudson looked back at Kingcome, who picked up the report.

"The weather conditions and other factors negated the rendezvous planned for mid-Channel. The bombers and fighters never made the join-up. The bomber squadron commander reported only fleeting sightings of the fighters. Not one of the fighter squadrons actually made it to the join-up. From the information provided by the lone returning 133 pilot, who was seriously injured in the crash, they tried to find the bomber squadron and kept trying too long. The maintenance folks will recover the aircraft and evaluate whether it can be repaired. We believe this has been a comedy of errors."

"Comedy!" protested Spencer. "Don't you mean a tragedy?" Kingcome started to answer but stopped when John held up his right hand in a stop signal. "Were you supposed to lead the fighter wing on this mission?"

"Yes sir. I was. But, ..." Again, Kingcome stopped with Spencer's signal.

"Do I understand correctly that the commanding officer of 133 Squadron was missing from this action as well?"

"Yes sir, you are correctly informed. Squadron Leader McColpin was in London, receiving his commission as a major in the U.S Army Air Forces in preparation for the transfer of the Eagles Squadrons to the Americans next week."

"Isn't that just grand . . . a comedy, so you say."

"Sir, my apologies for the poor choice of words. Many things went wrong today."

"I dare say, wing commander, that is a bit of an understatement. We lost an entire fighter squadron today. That has never happened before, even during the worst days of the summer battle of 1940. And, they just completed their transition to the Mark Nines."

"Yes sir, they did. This event was their first mission after they completed their transition training period."

"Dear God above," John stopped himself and collected his thoughts. Spencer nodded his head several times. "Back to my original query, what happened?"

"They had trouble with the rendezvous. They pressed on in their attempt to fulfill their mission. According to Pilot Officer Beaty, Richard Norton Beaty, the only returning pilot, he developed engine trouble, like a misfiring cylinder, and turned back. By the time the rest of the squadron aborted, the wind apparently had blown them too far south. They were well beyond the range of Chain Home, so they had no help. Beaty heard broken radio transmissions that suggest they found a hole in the overcast, believed it was England, and descended through the hole.

"Beaty pressed on. Chain Home picked him up over the Channel and vectored him through the clouds to the closest aerodrome, but he could not quite make it to the landing area."

"Nearly an entire squadron," muttered Air Commodore Spencer.

"Yes sir . . . a genuine tragedy."

Spencer grimaced in a quasi-smile. "Do we know anything about those who dove for the hole?"

"No sir, other than they did not return. However, based on our back-calculations from the few facts we do have, we suspect that the hole the squadron went through was somewhere over Brittany. We must assume at the very best they were captured, and at the worst, shot down and killed. If the former, as you know, it will take weeks before we should receive notification from the Germans or the Red Cross."

"And, it will likely be even longer before we can acquire the testimony of any of those who might have survived. Do you have anything else to add?"

"No sir. Those are the facts we have so far."

"Very well. By this coming Wednesday, I want your after-action report in full along with your recommendations regarding preventative measures to avoid a tragedy of this nature again. We are not going to win this war with such tragic losses."

"Yes sir. You shall have it.

Air Commodore Spencer dismissed the two officers and considered what he was going to tell his superiors.

On that fateful Saturday, three days prior to their official transfer to the U.S. Army Air Forces, No.133 Squadron lost 11 of their 12, brand new, Spitfire Mark IXs; Beaty's aircraft was recovered, repaired and returned to service. As happenstance would have it, the hole in the cloud had been virtually over Brest, a heavily defended, Atlantic port city in German-occupied France. Four of the American Eagle Squadron pilots had been shot down and killed, six became POWs, and one, Pilot Officer Robert E Smith, bailed out and evaded capture, eventually returning to England via Spain. The leader of the squadron that day, Flight Lieutenant Gordon Brettell was one of those captured; he later took part in the 'Great Escape' from *Stalag Luft III* in March 1944. Brettell was also one of the 'Great Escape' men re-captured and subsequently shot by the Gestapo upon direct orders from Hitler. Three of the No.401 Squadron Spitfires also failed to return, but the remainder of the Wing, including all of the No.64 Squadron Spitfires, reached England safely, but in many cases only just barely made it back.

———

Monday, 28.September.1942
Allied Forces Headquarters
Norfolk House
No.31 St James's Square
St. James's, London, England
United Kingdom
13:45 hours

Only a few weeks earlier, Supreme Commander General Eisenhower separated the administrative staff of HQETO from the combat command to execute Operation TORCH. The Norfolk House mansion had been loaned to the newly formed, joint Allied Forces Headquarters (AFHQ) for the duration of the war. The European Theater of Operations headquarters remained separate and distinct from the Allied Forces headquarters to handle the administrative workload of Operation BOLERO—the build-up of the armed forces of the United States in Great Britain. AFHQ was specifically tasked to perform the planning for and execution of Operation TORCH—the Allied amphibious landings and combat operations in Northwest Africa and the link up with the British 8th Army, now driving Rommel's *Afrikakorps* back across the desert of Cyrenaica.

The room's ceiling and walls remained festooned with the ornate, gilded, detail scrollwork and imbedded fresco artwork that defied military austerity but remained representative of an 18th century, London mansion, in this particular instance, for the 8th Duke of Norfolk.

Captain Juli Calhoun announced the arrival of OSS Director, General Bill Donovan. The two generals shook hands, then sat in comfortable chairs opposite each other. Calhoun closed the door for privacy.

"Thank you for making time for me, Ike."

"My door is always open to the OSS director."

"I am on my way home from an extended tour of Asia, Australia, and South Asia. I wanted to pay my respects and personally convey my gratitude for your support and listening to my guys in my stead."

Eisenhower chuckled. "I appreciate the recognition, Bill, but it's strictly business. We have the best plan we can produce for the forces we have, but the plan and resources are insufficient for the potential resistance we may face. We have been through all the options we had available. A third of our TORCH landing forces are coming directly from the States because there is insufficient time and lift capacity in the European Theater to deploy from England. To be candid, Bill, I am enormously grateful and guardedly optimistic that the efforts of your Northwest Africa agents will neutralize or significantly reduce the opposition we will face from the French Territorial Army."

"That is the second reason I chose to visit directly. We have confirmed the location of General Giraud. We have also confirmed that Laval has repeatedly tried to convince Giraud to return to confinement. So far, Laval has not engaged the Gestapo or the Milice, but that potential and threat is only a telephone call away."

"Are you suggesting we move sooner than planned to extract Giraud?" asked Eisenhower.

Donovan smiled. "I am not a gambler, General, but I do understand, and appreciate risk and reward. The safe bet would be to move now while we have him, but that would risk diminishing his influence over Mast and the others, and probably amplify the time the Germans and Vichy government would have to negate whatever influence he might have. My counsel, sir, let us stay to plan. It minimized the time the enemy has to counter our efforts. I will add that I asked Bob Murphy to take steps to surreptitiously protect Giraud as well as keep track of him until the execution date arrives, as an insurance policy."

"Which brings me to an enduring question. I asked Bill Buxton and others during the July meeting about Murphy's relationship with the OSS."

"And, he said?"

"That he technically works for State, but practically works for you."

Donovan smiled. "He is being generous, Ike, but I would not correct that impression in your thoughts. Bob and I have been friends, beyond this business, for many years well beyond both world wars. He understands the world of diplomacy and intelligence. I trust him explicitly."

"That is reassuring. Buxton also indicated that you have placed priority on TORCH support."

"Ned stated it precisely. I like the supplement. I believe we will deliver, Ike. I cannot say we will achieve negation with the whole of the French Territorial Forces of North Africa; however, we are confident that one or more of the paths contained in the supplement will yield the necessary advantage to the Allied landing forces. The French Navy remains the most problematic, although we continue to look for cracks."

Eisenhower lapsed into contemplation.

Donovan sat patiently and examined the artwork still on the walls around them. It was an elegant building and unlike any military headquarters outside wartime England.

"Wise counsel, Bill," Eisenhower finally responded. "The plan supplement is sound, well thought out, and reasoned. It matches up well with the assault plan. Unless your folks see changes in the foundational assumptions, we will stick to the plan. I discussed all this and the supplemental plan with the joint chiefs last month, including the additional support mission. We are preparing to send Mark Clark and several staff officers to meet with Mast and other French officers."

"I had my doubts when I heard Bill Eddy's proposal. It is a rather bold move," Donovan commented.

"Yes, it is . . . and very risky. Perhaps a sign of our desperation, but truth is, we need a force multiplier to shift the balance of forces equation in our favor."

Wild Bill Donovan nodded his head in agreement. "I certainly understand that requirement. If there is anything else we can do to support you, please do not hesitate to ask."

"Thank you, Bill. I have sung your praises to the chiefs. The OSS activities in support of TORCH are essential to the overall success of the operations. I have high hopes for the contributions of the OSS to this and the entire war effort."

"As do I, Ike."

"I recognize and acknowledge the uphill grind you face against the traditional intelligence personnel and their desire to maintain the status quo, but I am on your side and a supporter, as best I am able." Eisenhower checked his wristwatch. "Now, I'm afraid I must be on my way."

Donovan stood. "Thank you for carving out some time for me, General." He took Eisenhower's proffered hand.

The two men departed the supreme commander's office. Donovan departed the building and headed to OSS London Station before heading to the airport for his return to the United States. Eisenhower went to a conference room for another meeting.

———

Tuesday, 29.September.1942
USAAF Station F-356
Saffron Walden, Essex, England
United Kingdom
11:00 hours

All three of the RAF American volunteer fighter squadrons were assembled in formation before the dignitary platform—No.71 Squadron in the center, No.121 Squadron on the left, and what was left of No.133 Squadron on the right. The overcast blotted out the sun into a diffuse illumination with a light breeze from the northwest. Air Chief Marshal Douglas represented RAF Fighter Command, and Brigadier General Hunter represented the U.S. Army's 8th Fighter Command in the rapidly building 8th Air Force.

The ceremony was short, direct, and to the point. Speeches were given about the British gratitude for the courage, sacrifice and commitment of the American volunteer pilots, and the respect the American Army had for their commitment to freedom for all. All three squadrons were formally transferred to the U.S. Army Air Forces.

At this moment in history, the three Royal Air Force American volunteer squadrons became the 4th Fighter Group. RAF Nos.71, 121, and 133 Squadrons became the 334th, 335th, and 336th Fighter Squadrons, respectively. The Air Ministry had already begun reconstructing the decimated No.133 Fighter Squadron with new replacement Mark IX Spitfires. Several young Army aviators in the audience were actually replacement pilots, who would take their place after the transfer was officially complete.

The rest of the day would be devoted to changing their uniforms and going through indoctrination instructions regarding the Army's conduct and flight procedures rather than those of the Royal Air Force.

American enlisted mechanics and service personnel would spend the next few days completing the transfer of the aircraft, the stock parts, and the tools to maintain the aircraft. All of the aircraft had to be repainted with American star roundel insignia and marking. For the time being, the squadrons would retain their flight equipment and such, until replacement aircraft could be delivered. The decision had been made from on high that switching the formerly British aircraft over to American flight equipment was not worth the effort in the short term since the three squadrons possessed capable, functional machines and equipment. The pilots had been informed they would not continue to fly Spitfires for the duration of the war, and eventually American aircraft of an, as yet, unspecified type would be delivered to complete their integration into the U.S. Army, in a few months or so.

The American volunteer pilots, some of whom had served in the Royal Air Force for years, were in the Army, now.

———

Wednesday, 30.September.1942
Madison Square Garden
Eighth Avenue and West 50ᵗʰ Street
Manhattan, New York City, New York
United States of America
20:00 hours

Captain Brian 'Hunter' Drummond, USAAF, had been met and escorted at each transport change, and installed at the Washington-Jefferson Hotel on West 51ˢᵗ Street in Manhattan. He felt he was being treated like a celebrity far beyond his rank. The generousness and opulence of his treatment produced a dramatic contrast with the rather austere condition in which he had lived for the last three years. Every minute was scheduled and orchestrated by the minders.

The marquee over the main entrance of the famous Madison Square Garden boldly announced:

STARS OVER AMERICA
NATIONAL WAR BONDS DRIVE

What on God's little green earth am I doing here? I do not belong here. My place is in the cockpit.

Brian tried mightily to contain and mask his amazement with the city, the arena, virtually everything about New York City. The contrast between the devastation and darkness of wartime London, and New York City with its lights, and hustle and bustle, defied the imagination. Even though the United States was at war as well, the authorities had issued orders for what became popularly referred to as "dimout" conditions rather than the hard blackout strictly enforced in England. The marquee and lights of Madison Square Garden were all below the 15-story boundary, above which lights were required to be out and window shades required. The United States learned an immediate and powerful lesson when several American merchant ships were sunk by German U-boats, shortly after war was declared last December—silhouetted against the city lights.

Brian sent his first telegram to Charlotte for notification of his safe arrival in New York City.

The evening's celebratory event was planned as an acknowledgment of the stage and cinematic stars who had performed so many public appearances since January in support of the war effort. The military "heroes" were not planned to participate until the beginning of the first national war bond drive in early October.

Brian recognized some of the movie stars who passed in front of him and were introduced to the cheering crowd—James Cagney, Ginger Rogers, and Fred Astaire. Seven groups of stars came together at this place on this evening to be recognized nationally for their efforts; 40 plus stars were the center and focus of the evening's celebration. Several company-grade officers disappeared among the sea of flag-grade and senior field-grade officers, glad-handing with the stars.

"Guess you feel out of place like I do," came a voice from beside him—a U.S. Navy lieutenant with a distinctive light blue ribbon with an inverted gold star around his neck.

"You got that right," Brian responded and extended his right hand. "Brian Drummond."

"'Butch' O'Hare."

The two men shook hands. Brian would later learn that his new comrade was Lieutenant Edward Henry 'Butch' O'Hare, USN [USNA 1937], who had just received the Medal of Honor from President Roosevelt last April. He had been assigned to VF-3 fighter squadron aboard the USS *Lexington* fleet aircraft carrier, operating north of New Ireland Island in the Bismarck Archipelago, last February. O'Hare and his wingman were the only fighters airborne when the carrier detected an inbound second wave of Japanese bombers. Flying their Grumman F4F-3A Wildcat fighters, they engaged the flight of Japanese bombers, who were flying without fighter escort. O'Hare shot down five Betty medium bombers and damaged a sixth during the engagement that afternoon. None of the bombers reached their target.

"Were you ordered to do this public relations stuff like I was?" asked Butch.

"Yep. This is not what I wanted to be doing."

"Where you comin' from?"

"I just arrived from England a few days ago."

"Are you scheduled to do the War Bond Tour?"

"Yes, unfortunately. I am no salesman. I've done the show pony routine before, and I was given no choice in this one."

"You've done this stuff before?" O'Hare asked.

"Well, kinda. I was flying with 609 Squadron when the Air Ministry formed up 71 Squadron with American volunteer pilots like me. They kept us out of combat operations for months and paraded us in front of journalists like we were some precious circus animals. I was not a fan then, and I am certainly not a fan, now."

"Me either. Ever since they hung this around my neck," he said, flicking the star hanging below his throat, "they told me I cannot go back to my squadron. After I raised a stink, they eventually assigned me to a training squadron in Hawaii, and then again, pulled me off for this dog-and-pony show."

'I don't have one of those,' Brian said, looking at O'Hare's Medal of Honor, "but there is doubt about whether they will return me to my squadron."

The two men watched in silence from the wings as the show played out in front of them on the stage. Eventually, they were introduced to the audience along with four other decorated enlisted men. They waved and waited for the applause to end. When the show was over, Butch and Brian decided to walk back to the hotel, even though a ride was offered. They enjoyed a couple of beers in the hotel bar before calling it a night.

—

Thursday, 1.October.1942
Hampshire House
150 Central Park South, Apartment 2301
Manhattan, New York City, New York
United States of America
10:30 hours

Brian was pleasantly surprised to see a four-hour free period at mid-day, only to learn from his minder that the time was spoken for by unspecified authorities. He checked the address on the note to confirm that he was at the correct place. This was indeed an odd place for some undescribed meeting. Brian used the brass knocker to announce his arrival.

A small-ish, balding man a good foot shorter than Brian answered the door. "Welcome to my residence, Captain Drummond. I am Bill Stephenson," he said with a unique accent—not British, not American.

I've seen this guy before.

"Right on time. The others are here," Stephenson continued.

"Others?"

"Yes, this is a planned and coordinated meeting with you. I will introduce the others. Please, please, come in." Four older men were standing in a quasi-reception line.

"Gentlemen, may I introduce our guest of honor, Captain Brian Drummond."

First in line was a handsome, brigadier general dressed in Army pink & green service uniform with no branch insignia on his lapels. "This is General Bill Donovan, Director of the OSS," Stephenson said. The two men shook hands. *I have seen those eyes before.* The next in line was a distinguished-looking man in RAF uniform. "This is Air Marshal Billy Bishop of the Royal Canadian

Air Force." They shook hands. Stephenson gestured to a jovial rotund man in a business suit. "This is Mayor Fiorello La Guardia of the Great City of New York." They also shook hands. "And, last but certainly not least, this is Clayton Knight, who, along with Air Marshal Bishop, has been instrumental in the recruitment of American volunteer pilots for service with you in the Royal Air Force, before the U.S. entered the war."

What the hell am I doing here? What is going on?

Brian's puzzled, if not shocked, expression caused Stephenson to chuckle softly. "This may be a bit much for you, but give us a few minutes, it will all become clear. Let's go into the living room for some comfortable seating."

Brian nodded his head and followed the older gentlemen into a surprisingly spacious living room with large glass windows overlooking the whole of Central Park. Brian could not believe the awesome view of the city, looking north across the park. By the time he realized he was the only person still standing, Brian shuffled around and must have appeared quite awkward. The only seats remaining were single, overstuffed, armchairs at either end between the two long couches. Brian chose the one facing the interior to avoid being distracted by the view.

"It is quite a view, isn't it?" said Stephenson.

"That's an understatement," Brian mumbled.

"That's quite all right, young man," added Bishop, "we were all struck in such fashion when we first saw this scene."

"This rather eclectic group has been assembled at the behest of General Donovan," announced Little Bill. "I play a minor part in this drama, beyond my function as host. So, Bill, if you will, please assuage the apprehension of our young guest."

Donovan smiled and nodded to Stephenson before looking directly at Brian. His stunning, ice blue eyes penetrated deeply. "Great to see you again, Brian."

Yes, I have seen him before.

"We, Bill and I, met with you more than two years ago. You showed us around your Spitfire fighter at RAF Northolt, during my fact-finding visit that summer. You were an ace already at that point, and now you are an ace four times over, and decorated by King George the Sixth, no less."

Ah, yes, that's it. I knew I'd seen them before. "Yes sir."

"Those were the opening weeks of the Battle of Britain. You have accomplished a great deal in those two years." Brian only nodded his head. "As Bill said," Donovan nodded to Stephenson, "we are a rather diverse group, but we do have one thing in common. You may not know these gentlemen, but I can assure you, they know you. I have known all of them for many years, well before this war began. I asked them to join me for this meeting, as I believe each of them has a potential contribution to make toward my proposal."

Proposal? To me?

"Are you familiar with the OSS—the Office of Strategic Services?"

"No sir."

"It is a new strategic intelligence and special operations organization that President Roosevelt asked me to stand up. In that capacity, I require highly skilled pilots for a host of related aviation tasks. Do you recall our conversation of two years ago?"

"Vaguely, sir."

"It is not important. My primary objective in this conversation is to convince you to join the OSS."

Brian shook his head.

"Before you reject my proposal, please hear me out."

Brian nodded his agreement reluctantly.

"It is too much to explain the depth and breadth of air operations we will be involved with, but let it suffice to say that we will be doing some rather extraordinary things involving special aircraft."

"Fighters?"

"No. We are not a combat arm. We are an intelligence organization. However, a facet of that mission involves special operations, inserting and extracting special teams behind enemy lines. I also envision you, or someone with your skills, periodically serving as my pilot with a dual purpose of transportation and being a direct advisor during field visits regarding aviation matters."

"General, excuse me, sir, but I am a fighter pilot—a shooter and a hunter. There are far more capable transport pilots out there or bomber pilots for that matter. I have flown with a few of them. They have skills I do not." *Bishop is smiling; he must know what I'm talking about.* "I am told that the Army will send me wherever they believe I can best serve. As for me, I want to return to my squadron. I am good at what I do, and I want to keep doing it until this war is won."

"Bless you for that focus," Knight added.

Donovan smiled eventually. "This august group is on your side, Brian, and so advised me before this meeting. Let us leave this element open, for now. Although I have the authority to request your services from the War Department, I can assure you I will not do so. In fact, I will see what I can do to help you with your professed objective. I was a little older than you in the Great War, so I certainly appreciate your sense of commitment." Donovan paused but did not take his eyes off of Brian. No one spoke. "Failing the long shot element of my proposal, I have a secondary objective to offer for your consideration."

My consideration? I am just a fighter pilot. I have nothing else to offer.

"To that end," began Donovan, "please accept my . . . our condolences for the loss of your parents—very tragic—a year and nine months ago." Brian simply nodded his concurrence. "It is my understanding that you became a man of considerable means with your inheritance."

Oh, oh, where is this going?

"It is my understanding that you also inherited some aviation assets from your mentor and benefactor, Malcolm Bainbridge. As a side note, I never had the pleasure of meeting him while we served in France, but I certainly knew who he was, along with some of his exploits." Brian did not respond. "I also understand you have formed a fledgling aviation company—Bainbridge Air Service, Incorporated—under the management of Mister Bobby Joe Sales." Donovan stopped and waited for Brian's response.

He knows a lot more about my life than he should. I wonder what else he knows. And where did he get his information? Brian set aside his curiosity and simply answered, "Correct."

"Would you be amenable to government contract support services?"

What the hell? We only have a few planes, and they are certainly not modern. "We do not have much, General. I have no idea what kind of services we might be able to provide, given our limited assets and range."

"Ah, yes, therein lies the reason for these other gentlemen to be in attendance. If you are agreeable, we," he said gesturing to the others, "will assist you, or rather your company, in acquiring state of the art aircraft as well as the flight and maintenance crews to operate them for special contract work in support of the OSS and SOE."

"SOE?"

"Special Operations Executive, the British sister service to the OSS. We will utilize a portion of your operational capacity, say 30 to 40%, and you will be able to utilize the remainder of that capacity for other commercial purposes, such as passenger or cargo transport."

"The devil is in the details, General."

"Yes, quite so, and those details are beyond us this morning. All I seek at this juncture is your concurrence to flesh out the details. Do you have confidence in Mister Sales that he can do that for you?"

"I will need to confer with him, but on its face, yes, I believe he can handle the negotiations."

"So, you are agreeable to take the next step or two?"

"Yes sir."

"Excellent. Then, I know you will be very busy for the next few months with this War Bonds Tour, but if I could ask you to let me know directly, in a few days, or a week or two at the outside, whether this proposal is agreeable to you. With the assumption you agree, I will task my deputy, Colonel Ned Buxton, to mark out the details to our mutual satisfaction."

"That seems reasonable, General."

"Good show," Bill Stephenson said. "We have all signed onto General Donovan's vision. Each of us has something to contribute to the success of this venture. If you do agree to proceed, we will each do our part to ensure your success. Now, lunch is soon to be served," Stephenson said and stood. The others followed.

Mayor La Guardia was the first to approach Brian. "I look forward to working with you, my boy."

"Thank you, sir."

Fiorello Henry La Guardia had been mayor of New York City since Roosevelt had become president. He also saw combat service during the First World War with the U.S. Army Air Service toward the end of the war. He explained, "I cannot tell you my involvement in this enterprise, until proper security arrangements have solidified, but rest assured, I am ready, willing, and able to help. Wild Bill and I go back quite a way in New York politics and in the law."

Knight shook Brian's hand and said, "You joined up before I got involved. Nonetheless, I feel some kinship. I served in the same wing as your mentor and instructor. I was so sorry to hear we lost Malcolm Bainbridge two years ago. He was a great man."

"Yes, he was. Everything I know, I learned from him. I inherited his aircraft that became the foundation for the Bainbridge Air Service."

Clayton Knight was a New York native and also saw service with the Royal Flying Corps during the last war. After his service, he became an accomplished author and artist. As the clouds of war darkened, he formed the Clayton Knight Committee and joined with Billy Bishop in defiance of the Neutrality Act to recruit, train, and transport American pilots to Europe for service with the French and British.

Air Marshal Bishop extended his hand, which Brian took. "I have been an admirer of yours since you arrived in Windsor, Ontario, in June 1939. You have been and I am certain you will continue to be an inspiration to all of us."

"Sir, pardon me, but I recognize the purple ribbon on your tunic."

Bishop glanced down, as if to check the ribbons on his chest. Air Marshal William Avery 'Billy' Bishop, RCAF, VC, CB, DSO & Bar, MC, DFC, had been awarded the Victoria Cross for extraordinary valor in aerial combat during the Great War. He also tallied up 72 aerial victories in combat. Since 1936, Bishop had been an essential player in the build-up of the Royal Canadian Air

Force for Commonwealth service in the approaching war. On the eve of war in Europe, Bishop joined Knight in the illegal and clandestine recruitment of American pilots for service with the Royal Air Force. He also worked with the more mysterious Colonel Charles Sweeny for the same purpose.

The luncheon proceeded smoothly in casual form. They avoided the proposal, preferring not to press Brian, and give him space. To his surprise, they wanted to hear details of Brian's flying experience. Even Wild Bill Donovan, the only non-aviator in the bunch, asked very knowledgeable and finessed questions about combat flying. Brian was impressed by how much these older men knew about his flying. *They clearly have done their homework.*

—

Chapter 15

Life is a maze in which we take the wrong turning
before we have learnt to walk.
-- Cyril Connolly

Friday, 2. October. 1942
USAAF Station F-356
Saffron Walden, Essex, England
United Kingdom
08:15 hours

The 4th Fighter Group operated for the first time as a group on its first combat mission. The primary target of the CIRCUS mission was several railroad and paved road bridges, as well as ammunition and supply storage facilities in the Calais-Dunkirk area. Assigning three fighter squadrons to escort one bomber squadron seemed like overkill until they encountered several waves of German fighters. This particular mission had been the first engagement when the 334th Fighter Squadron pilots faced a squadron of the new German Fw190 fighters.

The squadron had reorganized quickly, expanding from the British model. The Americans adopted the German combat element. Each section had four fighters—the finger four, or *schwarm*, as the Germans called a flight of four, rather than the three aircraft per section in the British structure. Pete Peterson had been promoted to major and selected as the commanding officer. Dusty Langford had been promoted to captain and made 'B' Division Leader—leading both Red and Yellow Sections. The squadron received the four additional Spitfires plus two spares, along with the replacement pilots to fill the open seats. Brian was listed as on temporary assignment, which was probably wishful thinking due to the ambiguity of Brian's orders.

The 336th Fighter Squadron, the former RAF No.133 Squadron, had been fully reconstituted and brought up to full strength before the day's mission.

The group had been assigned as top cover for the mission with the other two squadrons on each flank. Oddly, the flankers got most of the business. The 334th FS shifted above the formation to cover. The bombers experienced some damage from flak bursts, but they got all the bombers home, and they hit the targets . . . well, at least as far as the fighter guys could tell when they were not busy.

Two fighters with the 335th Fighter Squadron had received battle damage sufficient enough for them to land at the nearest airfield en route back to Debden. Both pilots received minor wounds, but all the fighter pilots returned as well.

Friday, 16.October.1942
Allied Forces Headquarters (AFHQ)
Norfolk House
No.31 St James's Square
St. James's, London, England
United Kingdom
10:15 hours

Solemnity blanketed the commander's conference room—a converted bedroom adjacent to General Eisenhower's spacious office. The assembled, closed group stood silently behind their chairs around the oak conference table in the center of the room.

The limited attendees in the large room came to attention when General Eisenhower entered the room. He gestured for everyone to be seated as he took the single seat at the head of the table. Ike nodded to his friend from West Point and the leader of this highly classified, limited access, risky mission to support the upcoming Operation TORCH invasion of Northwest Africa.

General Clark nodded his head. He introduced the other members of the FLAGPOLE team.

-- Rear Admiral Bernard H. Bieri, USN [USNA 1911] – senior U.S. naval representative to AFHQ (Deputy Chief of Staff, U.S. Atlantic Fleet).

-- Brigadier General Lyman Louis Lemnitzer, USA [USMA 1920] – head of the allied forces planning section for Operation TORCH.

-- Colonel Archelaus L. Hamblen, USA – staff logistics expert on shipping and supply.

-- Colonel Julius C. Holmes, USA – head of the civil affairs branch for TORCH.

-- Captain Jerauld 'Jerry' Wright, USN [USNA 1918] – liaison officer with the Royal Navy.

Clark continued, "The intelligence associated with Operation FLAGPOLE remains unchanged as of this morning—an hour ago. We can dispense with regurgitation of what we know and what we are trying to accomplish."

"Yes, I agree," Eisenhower responded. "At this stage, I am far more concerned about the safety of you and your team, and thus the operational plan for this mission."

"I will cut to the chase," Clark said. Eisenhower nodded his consent. "The assigned flight leader informed us the flight from Polebrook to Gibraltar will take eight hours. We depart at fifteen hundred hours on Sunday in two B-17 heavy bombers with three British commandos to land prior to midnight at Gibraltar. The British submarine HMS *Seraph* will be waiting for us, and we will board as soon as possible under cover of darkness and blackout conditions. We expect to put to sea shortly after we board. The transit to our rendezvous will take two days. The British commandos of the Special Boat Service will help us paddle into shore in inflatable boats. Two OSS men will be onshore with two French resistance men to periodically signal our landing spot within our agreed time window. Once we are safely ashore, they will also guide us to the meeting location in the basement of a nearby farmhouse.

"We expect to meet with General Mast of the Vichy French Territorial Army of North Africa. Captain Wright will meet privately and personally with French Navy Commander Barjot."

"This is the first I've heard of Barjot. What do we know about him?" asked Eisenhower.

Clark nodded to Wright. "Pierre Barjot was XO of the battleship *Richelieu*," explained Wright. "He has been active in the informal resistance network. Barjot got crosswise with the Vichy government, was arrested, and was retired to Algeria earlier this year. He has been very helpful as the middleman with the active Navy commanders."

Eisenhower nodded his head, then looked back to Clark.

"According to Bob Murphy, all of the groundwork has been completed. This mission is as much to show the French we are serious about their liberation from the German yoke as it is about encouraging their support, or at least neutrality during the TORCH landings."

"I see a whole lot of risk in all that Mark," Ike commented.

"Yes sir. There is definitely risk. So many things could go wrong, not least of which the French could be setting us up. However, Bob Murphy and Bill Donovan's Bill Eddy have assured us they are as confident as one can be in situations like this."

"Yeah, I know. I've heard the arguments from all three—Murphy, Eddy, and Wild Bill Donovan—together and on separate occasions. They know our objectives. They have done their part to set this up. Even if the French forces in North Africa decide to resist our efforts, I believe we have sufficient forces to overcome them. Bill Donovan feels, and I agree, the Vichy French forces in North Africa are not likely to gain reinforcements from France, or Germany for that matter. The risk that causes me the most hesitation is the potential of losing any one of you," Eisenhower said, as he looked at each man in the eyes, "at this critical stage of planning. We will land substantial Allied forces in three weeks' time. Heck, the forces coming from the States are loading as we speak."

"But, the reward, Ike, is the potential elimination of any resistance to our landings and build-up of forces."

"Oh, I understand all that. Do any of the rest of you have something to add?"

"No sir," came the chorus of replies.

"We're as ready as we can be. We think we can deliver the French to our side," Clark added.

"Quite true. That is the carrot." The room sat in silence as their commander contemplated the final decision. "General Marshal and Admiral King have agreed, and support FLAGPOLE. They believe the rewards outweigh the risks. This is my last opportunity, and I wanted to hear directly from you and your team. I also wanted each of you to hear me. Be careful. Do not take any unnecessary risks. If something does not look right or feel right abort the mission. I want that clearly understood by each of you." Again, a chorus of acknowledgments came. Once more, Eisenhower looked at each man in the eyes, as if to judge the veracity of this consent. "Very well, then. We are a go for FLAGPOLE. Good luck, and may God bless you and protect you all."

Eisenhower stood, followed by the others. He made a point of shaking each man's hand, offering a word of encouragement, and thanking each man for his service to the country and the cause. Eisenhower saved Mark Clark for last. "Do good work down there, Mark. And remember, I want you back here safely. I am most serious, do not take any unnecessary risks."

"I got it, Ike. We'll be back in a week to debrief the mission with you."

"I eagerly await your debriefing."

With that, Eisenhower departed the conference room, and the FLAGPOLE team left the building to complete their final preparations for their top-secret mission.

—

Sunday, 18.October.1942
North Front Airfield
British Overseas Territory Gibraltar
23:30 hours

The weather had been cooperative with minimal turbulence. The B-17E heavy bomber, known as Red Gremlin by its nose art, touched down smoothly on the dimly lit runway. The lights from Spain offer just enough illumination to see the north face granite mountain known simply as The Rock. As soon as the bomber decelerated to taxi speed, the runway lights were extinguished and a "follow me" truck with a highly directional set of dim lights to lead the bomber to its pre-assigned, designated, parking spot.

Major Paul Tibbets, as the commanding officer of the 340th Bombardment Squadron, had been personally selected by Major General Spaatz as the most experienced pilot in the 8ᵗʰ Air Force for this special mission. Tibbets left the shutdown to his copilot and made his way past the flight engineer's station and top turret, through the bomb bay, and radio operator's station and ball turret to the makeshift passenger compartment. General Clark and the five members of his team used small, dimmed flashlights to gather their things in the darkened interior of the bomber's waist gunner section of the tail.

"We have arrived, General."

"Thank you, Major. Well done."

Tibbets opened the rear hatch stepped out, followed closely by Clark and his team. The cool night air was markedly warmer and more humid than they had at departure. Only a single, Royal Navy lieutenant greeted them.

The lieutenant saluted. All of the senior officers returned his salute."

"Bill Jewel, sir," he said extending his hand to General Clark. "I am the commanding officer of *Seraph*. We have two vehicles handy to move your team to the dock. We will cast off and set sail as soon as your team is aboard."

Royal Navy Lieutenant Norman Limbury Auchinleck 'Bill' Jewell had been the commanding officer of HMS *Seraph* since May. The 29-year-old officer was young, strikingly handsome and clearly held the confidence of the Admiralty. The S-Class submarine he commanded was equivalent to the German Type VIIC submarine.

"Very well, Captain," Clark responded, and then looked back at Tibbets. "Thank you for delivering us safely and on time, Major. See you in a few days."

Tibbets saluted and said, "We'll be here with bells and whistles on, General. Good luck on your mission."

The FLAGPOLE group split in half to each, covered bed, small, military truck. The ride to the dock and submarine took all of five minutes. Jewell had several sailors on the pier to assist the senior officers and get their gear aboard. Jewell stood beside General Clark as they watched the loading process.

"Are the commandos aboard already?" Clark asked.

"Yes sir, two Royal Marine commando officers and three Special Boat Service troopers boarded with the inflatable boats and their gear to get your team ashore. They also are well-versed on our infiltration and exfiltration procedures. They will brief your team during our transit, just in case you need to extract yourselves for some reason."

"Very good. That should work well."

"You are welcome to join me on the conning tower for our departure, if you wish, General."

"Thank you. I think I will accept your invitation. This is the first time for us soldiers to be aboard a submarine."

"Fine way to get your virgin mission, sir," Jewell chuckled. "We plan to run at full speed on the surface until morning twilight unless we encounter any potential threats. We will run submerged during daylight hours. The Med can get crazy in short order, so best we avoid the risk. Our transit plan accounts for the speed changes."

"Excellent, Captain. We are in good hands."

The team was all completely aboard. The command to single up the mooring lines indicated the preparations for departure. Clark followed Jewell aboard the submarine and climbed the small built-in ladder on the aft end of the island. The general stood back in the small space of the conning tower and observed the process. The submarine separated from the pier and moved slowly forward. Clark looked back at the brilliant contrast between the nearly invisible Gibraltar hidden by the wartime blackout and the blaring electric lights of La Línea de la Concepción, Cádiz, Andalucía, España, just across the fence to the north. Spain remained notionally neutral in the war, but the fascist government was far more closely aligned with Germany and Italy. German spies were permanently present in La Línea and kept a very close eye on the isolated British protectorate.

Jewell ordered an increase in speed when they were well into the bay heading south. Clark was fascinated by the occultation of Spanish lights by the dark mass of Gibraltar. Clark noted the uneasiness of Jewell as they left the bay and entered the Strait of Gibraltar. He repeatedly cautioned the two lookouts to report the slightest disturbance to the sea. The lights of Spanish Morocco first appeared as a glow on the southern horizon and came into direct sight when Jewell changed their heading to due east. Their transit would take three days with margin for diversions or actions due to enemy activity, weather or anything else.

The mission plan called for the submarine to approach the Algerian coastline submerged, aided by highly directional, intermittent, alignment lights operated by OSS field agents near the small fishing village of Cherchell, 55 miles west of Algiers. The submarine would partially surface at midnight on the 21st. The FLAGPOLE team would be paddled ashore by the SBS personnel. The farmhouse for their initial meeting with the French had already been secured by the OSS. They would spend three days talking with French officers. The team would re-board the *Seraph* near midnight on the 24th.

———

Monday, 26. October. 1942
Allied Forces Headquarters (AFHQ)
Norfolk House
No.31 St James's Square
St. James's, London, England
United Kingdom
14:20 hours

The Top-Secret FLAGPOLE mission plan had been executed as close to perfect as any military plan can be. The team paddled back out to their rendezvous point. The *Seraph* submerged as soon as the team was aboard, and the hatches secured. The submarine moved to another specified rendezvous point, as best as they could determine. When Captain Jewell brought the submarine to periscope depth, he raised the search periscope partially, just enough for the optics to break the surface. He had quickly completed a full circle scan in a crouched position, then raised the telescope fully. They were several miles from a Consolidated PBY-5 Catalina Mark I in RAF livery. Jewell maneuvered the submarine to a point roughly 100 meters off the port wing of the seaplane, stopped the vessel, ordered the FLAGPOLE team to be ready for debarkation, and then surfaced the ship. The team was met by three inflatable rafts. They made their way to and boarded the Catalina, and as soon as everything was secure. They took off as the *Seraph* submerged.

Major Tibbets and his B-17 were waiting for the team as the Catalina extended its landing gear and landed on the runway. The seaplane taxied to the B-17 with the Red Gremlin painted on the nose. The transfer of the team and their gear from the Catalina to the Flying Fortress had been accomplished in a swift and smooth manner. As soon as everyone and everything was aboard, the bomber took off for the eight-hour flight back to England, arriving well after dark.

General Clark met with General Eisenhower in the supreme commander's office an hour before the whole team would debrief this mission with the Allied Forces staff.

"Welcome back, Mark," Eisenhower said and extended his right hand, as Clark entered his office.

"Thanks, Ike. Great to be back. Nice to have this one behind us."

Eisenhower gestured to the comfortable chairs. They both sat facing each other. "I do not want to go over stuff you will cover in detail during your pending debriefing with the staff. Let me start from the bottom line. Did you accomplish your mission?"

"Short answer, yes. There will always be glitches, but General Mast asked me directly to convey his genuine appreciation for your approval of FLAGPOLE. I, well, the whole team believes General Mast wants to and will support our TORCH operations. He was very careful to caution us that local commanders have wide latitude to respond to perceived threats, and as commanding general of the Algiers Division, for him to issue orders of cooperation would be a death warrant, since both the Milice and Gestapo were prevalent in Algiers and Algeria at large. He proposed to take action once the invasion has begun."

Eisenhower nodded his agreement.

"We also met separately with other resistance or potential resistance officers as well as selective civilians, predominantly civil servants on assignment in Algiers. Among those, the most closely aligned with our objective is Colonel Germain Jousse, who is currently assigned as garrison major in Algiers, roughly the equivalent of a base commander. Jousse has been surprisingly open in his opposition to the Vichy government collaboration with the Germans. He narrowly escaped arrest and certain execution, as other officers around him suffered. Much to our surprise, Jousse has been caching weapons in anticipation of an active resistance as soon as a viable opportunity presents. While we could not be specific with him or any of the French officers, I believe he is ready to take the TORCH opportunity.

"We also met with several civilian members of an active resistance network headed by cousins José Aboulker and Roger Carcassonne-Leduc. Another cousin, Bernard Karsenty, is a former soldier who barely escaped incarceration after the armistice, and now serves as deputy to Aboulker and is the leading spokesman for the network. I must say at this juncture that Bob Murphy and Bill Eddy have been extraordinarily effective in connecting with and protection of both the military and civilian resistance networks. They see more potential for cooperation than even the French may be aware of at present. Jousse and Karsenty were the most vociferous and adamant about the potential for French cooperation when the invasion has begun.

"I wanted you to be aware of these men so that you are aware of the extent of connections Murphy and Eddy have been able to generate. Further, I want to add my compliments to you for taking the risk of sending us to Algeria. The gesture alone has stiffened the French. Through our contacts, I think we can move quickly and effectively against those commanders who do resist. We should expect resistance in various forms.

"Lastly, Ike, I have directed my team not to raise the names of those we met with on this mission during the staff debriefing, since most of the staff officers are not read into FLAGPOLE. It is my opinion and recommendation that we should protect the identity of those individuals who came forward at considerable risk to their safety to speak with us. They were exceptionally candid with us. We tried within our constraints to encourage them that liberation was close at hand."

"Agreed," responded Eisenhower. "For now, we shall keep FLAGPOLE closed. I will further add that none of the team should refer to their position or location in addition to their identity, if you would so instruct your team before the briefing."

"Absolutely, I will see to it before the debriefing."

"Thank you. While you were away and based on your preliminary report message of the 23rd, we pulled the trigger on the extraction of General Giraud. The process is proceeding as planned, so far. The "your son is ill" message to Admiral Darlan is prepared and approved and will be sent on the morning of the 5th. The whole of the compartmented supplement is or will shortly be in play."

"Excellent. With all that, I think we are ready, Ike. Let's execute TORCH."

"Everything does seem to be lining up. The Western Task Force has departed the States. We move our forward headquarters in accordance with the plan on the 5th. In a few days, it will be up to the sergeants."

Clark smiled broadly. "As it always is." Clark checked his wristwatch. "I've got 15 minutes to the debriefing. I need to get your instructions to the team before the meeting."

"Thanks, Mark. Well done. You and your team may well have saved thousands of lives . . . on both sides. I'll see you in the conference room."

"Thanks, Ike." Clark stood and left the office.

Eisenhower remained in his chair and contemplated the information he had just received. No general felt comfortable before a major operation, because every general knew the plan was only the plan until the first bullet was fired. Eisenhower nodded his head to no one but himself, and then stood and went to his desk. The incessant stack of papers, documents, reports, requests, and assorted paperwork was always a distraction that got his mind off worrying.

—

Wednesday, 28. October. 1942
East Room
The White House
Washington, District of Columbia
United States of America
20:00 hours

Captain Brian Drummond had joined other military participants in the upcoming First War Bonds Tour to have dinner at the hotel before the White House reception, as they had been advised by their minders since there would only be light finger food and drinks at the reception. He had enjoyed a simple but satisfying meal with Butch O'Hare, and another air ace, who had just arrived from duty in the Pacific Theater, fresh from Guadalcanal.

Captain Marion Eugene 'Slim' Carl, USMC, deployed with Marine Fighter Squadron 221 (VMF-221) aboard USS *Saratoga* initially to Wake Island, but diverted to Midway Island. He achieved his first aerial victory during the Battle of Midway in June, in which 15 of 25 squadron aircraft did not return. Carl received the Navy Cross for that action. After a short rest, he deployed with VMF-223, the first fighter squadron ashore with the Cactus Air Force, so called for the Cactus code name for combat forces during the Battle of Guadalcanal, where he became the first Marine ace and received his second Navy Cross. Like Brian and Butch, Marion was not pleased with being pulled out of his combat fighter seat for the public relations tour, but he did his duty.

After supper, the three pilots joined the other military personnel for a short bus ride to the White House. Before they debarked from the bus, their duty minder, an Army major, stressed that all military personnel attending the reception were expected to mingle and socialize with the celebrities, politicians and guests for the occasion. They could partake in drinks and snacks with moderation. Any sign of drunkenness would be dealt with severely. Further, everyone was expected to remain engaged in the purpose of the reception until the conclusion.

They apparently arrived early since there were very few other people in the large banquet room of the White House. Very few straight-back chairs were scattered around the periphery of the room, which indicated they would be standing for the evening. For the lack of anyone else to talk to, the pilots continued their discussions from dinner.

"After I met you last night," said Carl, "I did some asking around. The rumor is, you ran away from home to join the RAF in '39?"

Brian laughed heartily. "I've heard a lot of nonsense in my short life, but that's a topper, as the British like to say."

Marion Carl joined Brian in the laugh. "That is a common problem. So . . . ?"

"I was 18 years old, so by legal definition, as I am told, I did not run away. I went by train to Windsor, Ontario, and joined the RAF in June 1939."

"What? Did you have some premonition about the approaching war?"

"Not really . . . but kinda. My mentor and flight instructor was a Great War ace with the Royal Flying Corps. We talked about the growing signs of war, especially after the Munich Accord."

"Well, that explains a lot," interjected Butch.

All three of the pilots laughed this time as if some inside joke had been delivered. Before they could return to their conversation, many other men and women became a steady stream of people arriving in the East Room. Politicians of various forms recognized Slim Carl and Butch O'Hare, and pulled them away for introductions to others. Brian quietly made his way to the back corner of the large room, content to watch the people gathering in the room. He recognized many of the movie stars from the Madison Square Garden event. There were so many people around them. Waiters in formal attire circulated among the people with *hors d'œuvrés* and drinks. There was the temptation to meet a few of the celebrities he knew from the few movies he had seen, but it was a fleeting urge.

A thin, rather frail appearing, bespectacled man nearly Brian's height approached him. "Excuse me for intruding young man, but I cannot ignore the distinctive ribbons above the right breast pocket of your uniform tunic and the RAF pilot's wing," the man said in a distinctive British accent. Brian nodded his head. "I am Cecil Smith," he said and extended his right hand. The two men shook hands.

"Brian Drummond, sir."

"The Brian Drummond?"

Brian was puzzled as to what that query could mean. Reluctantly, Brian responded, "Last time I checked."

Smith chuckled softly at the flippant answer. "If I am correctly informed, you are one of The Few, and the third-highest scoring ace in the whole of the RAF."

Brian slightly and briefly smiled. "So, they say."

"If I am not mistaken, those are ribbons that represent your CBE, Military Cross, and Distinguished Flying Cross. That is quite an array for a young man."

"I did not ask for any of them," Brian said softly.

Smith smiled. "One does not ask for any of those medals. They are awarded to you for distinguished or heroic action. I appreciate your humility, Mister Drummond, but from everything I have heard, read and understand from knowledgeable individuals, those awards on your tunic are justly deserved, and more to come, I must say."

"Thank you very much, sir."

"Since you are now in an American Army uniform rather than your RAF uniform you wore for the last three years, I assume that the transfer of the Eagle Squadrons has taken place?"

This is making me nervous. Why is he asking me all this? "I am not sure I should be talking about those details, Mister Smith. May I ask, why are you here?"

Smith chuckled softly. "My apologies for making you uncomfortable, Captain Drummond. I do not know why I am here either, other than I suppose I may be considered somewhat of a celebrity by a few of your fellow citizens. I am a novelist. I am more commonly known by my pen name—C.S. Forester."

"Hornblower!" exclaimed Brian with a demonstrably brightened expression.

Smith smiled broadly. "Yes, I am the creator of Horatio Hornblower. Do I presume correctly that you have read one or more of my books?"

"Oh, dear God above, yes. I read *Beat to Quarters*, what . . . six years ago. I was fascinated by everything: Horatio, HMS *Lydia*, square-rigged sailing ships, and the Napoleonic War—everything. I waited in antsy anxiety and pestered Mister Henricks at our local bookstore until *Ship of the Line* came out."

"If you were so enamored with sailing, why not the Navy rather than the Air Force?" asked Smith.

Brian smiled broadly. "No 36-gun frigates in Wichita, Kansas."

Smith laughed. "Indeed, but there are aeroplanes on the Great Plains."

"Exactly. And, I had the best teacher."

"You are most fortunate, young man, and we are blessed to have enjoyed your service in this dreadful affair. So, you have read only two of my books?"

"I regret to say I have not had time to read *Flying Colours*, yet, but I will as soon as I have more time when the war is over."

"Quite understandable, I have not written much fiction since the war started."

"Oh, please, tell me it is not the end," Brian said.

Smith smiled and shook his head in the negative. "There is so much more to Hornblower's story, but like you, I am too busy supporting the war effort."

"Over here?"

"Yes. I am embarrassed to confess I left England as the Battle of Britain was about to begin. I work for the Ministry of Information, and split my time between New York and Washington."

Brian noticed Mister Smith's eyes glance over his left shoulder. Brian looked over his left shoulder as well, to see General Donovan and Bill Stephenson walking purposefully toward them.

"Big Bill and Little Bill," Smith said boldly.

"Evening, Cecil. I see you found our hero," responded Stephenson.

Brian saluted. Donovan returned the salute. All four men shook hands.

"First, to allay any concerns Brian might have," Donovan said and looked at Smith, "Mister Smith is one of us." Brian nodded his head. Donovan looked back at Brian. "Thank you for arranging the meeting between Bobby Sales and Ned Buxton. I trust you received a comparable report from Mister Sales. Ned felt the initial meeting was very productive."

"As I heard the same, General."

"Please, Brian. In these circles, I prefer the familiar. In military situations, we should maintain decorum, but in this business, we are partners, or soon will be, once Mister Sales presents the expansion and operating plan."

"Excuse me, General. I respect your preference, so I only ask for your patience with me to see past your rank. That aside, I have had a number of conversations with Bobby without discussing the details over public telephone lines. I think he has a good grasp of the task and requirements. I look forward to seeing his proposal, as well. I can assure you, Bobby is enthusiastic about helping, as am I, and we will do our best to meet your needs."

"Agreed, Brian," Donovan said. "I hold out hope that you will change your mind about joining us, but I emphatically respect your choice. I would like to meet with you, on occasion, when I am in London, or wherever you are stationed.'

"Sure . . . as I am able. I cannot predict combat operations, and that must take priority."

"Quite so. I am grateful for your support, Brian, and I truly look forward to working with you. Bill," Donovan said glancing at Stephenson, "will manage supplemental support to the SOE and others through our contract with you."

"I see no problems with any of that, as long as we are satisfying the conditions of any contract, which you and your folks will judge."

"That is fair." Donovan extended his right hand to Brian.

Donovan looked off behind Brian's right shoulder. "Marlene," he said strongly, then gestured to someone to join their small group. Brian looked over his right shoulder this time to see a strikingly beautiful, curly blond-haired woman dressed in a low-cut, form-fitting, shimmering gold, floor-length dress walking toward them. "Please allow me to introduce Captain Brian Drummond, a decorated, ace, fighter pilot."

Brian turned to face an actress he recognized. "An honor to meet you, Miss Dietrich. I've not seen all your movies, but I loved you in *The Blue Angel.*"

The 41-year-old, Marie Magdalene 'Marlene' Dietrich left her native Germany in 1930, condemned Hitler and the Nazis, and renounced her German citizenship and became an American citizen in 1939. She began her film acting career at the height of the silent film era and successfully made the transition to "talkies" in 1930 with her breakout role as Lola-Lola in *The Blue Angel.*

Dietrich giggled softly. "You were one of the few, then."

"He is indeed one of The Few," interjected Stephenson.

"So, I hear, Bill."

"Marlene has continued to be most helpful," said Donovan, "to the OSS, MI6 and the SOE in the war effort."

"Thank you very much, Bill—a gentleman as always," Marlene said with her distinctive, German-accented voice. She turned and looked directly, deeply and seductively into Brian's eyes. "I know all of these gentlemen," she said with a dismissive hand gesture and without breaking eye contact with Brian, "some more than others," she added, glancing and winking at Donovan, and to Brian, "but I want to know more about you. I have heard stories, but I want to know if they are true."

"Ma'am, I have no idea what you've heard. I'm just a simple pilot who has been pulled from the cockpit to perform this duty."

Dietrich smiled alluringly. "Humility is an admirable trait, Brian . . . may I call you by your given name?"

"Of course, ma'am."

"I heard your name the first time on the radio two years ago, and I have become more curious about you since then. What do you fly, Brian?"

"Anything they let me."

Everyone including Marlene laughed. "Very well done. I should be more precise. What were you flying before you came here?"

"The Spitfire mark five 'B,' ma'am."

"Please, Brian. I may be a few years older than you," she said and smiled, "but, I do not feel old, or look like a matron. Please called me Marlene. I insist."

"Certainly ma . . . Marlene."

"So, you have flown other aircraft?"

"Yes . . . a few."

"Which aircraft do you like the mo . . ." A bell interrupted Dietrich. They all faced the dais. Brian felt a small, delicate hand slip inside his left arm and gently grasp his elbow. She raised up on her tiptoes and leaned in close to his left ear and said, "I want to continue our discussion. I really must know more about you."

What the hell does such a famous woman want with me? Brian nodded his head in agreement.

The distinctive musical notes of ruffles and flourishes preceded "Hail to the Chief." They could see only fleeting glimpses of the president in his wheelchair being pushed by an Army major general. Brian felt Marlene slowly and gently stroking the inside of his left elbow. Such a simple touch, but it seems so intimate. The president was pushed up a side ramp onto the dais. His iconic face grinning broadly, slightly above the crowd. He raised and waved his hands in gratitude for the applause, and then gestured for quiet.

"Thank you very much," President Roosevelt said in a commanding and familiar voice. "Good evening and welcome to the White House. With so many celebrities, movie stars, political and military leaders, and especially our military heroes," Dietrich squeezed Brian's elbow several times, "coming together to begin our first War Bonds tour, I felt compelled to recognize all of you for your personal and individual contributions in helping the war effort. Together, we shall overcome." Enthusiastic applause punctuated the president's words. Roosevelt raised his hand and the cheers stopped. "As I have urgent affairs of state to attend to on your behalf, I have limited time with you tonight, unfortunately, but I would have failed as your host to not appear personally, and convey my deepest and sincerest gratitude to each of you from the bottom of my heart for the work you have done and will do on behalf of the war effort."

President Roosevelt applauded demonstrably. The assemblage joined in. "Please enjoy the delicious *hors d'œuvrés* and libations. Now, I must say please excuse me for not meeting with each of you serving in the War Bonds tour. I truly wish I could, but I must leave you to enjoy this *soirée*."

The audience applauded as the general pushed the president's wheelchair out of the East Room.

"Not quite what I expected," Marlene said, and then she turned to face Brian.

Brian turned around to find that Donovan, Stephenson and Smith had vanished, leaving him alone with Dietrich.

"As much as I would like to pick up where we left off, I am afraid I must be going as well," Marlene said. She rose on her toes and kissed Brian on the cheek, lingering just a little longer than most folks would consider appropriate.

"It was an honor to meet you, Marlene."

"The honor was mine, Brian. It is quite rare for a woman to meet a fighter pilot with 21 aerial victories, five short of Eddie Rickenbacker."

Brian smiled. "I am surprised you know such details, Marlene."

Dietrich smiled demurely, leaned in and kissed Brian on the cheek, again, and then turned and walked away. Brian could not help but marvel at the movement of her dress until she disappeared from view.

As soon as Brian took his eyes off the East Room entryway portal, he noticed Butch O'Hare's Cheshire Cat grin coming toward him.

"Well, well, well," Butch said with reverie, "you move in fast circles, Brian. Marlene Dietrich . . . really?"

"I just met her," Brian protested.

"Sure didn't look like it to me."

"I don't know what that was all about, but hey," Brian said and smiled, "she is a beautiful woman."

"Yes, she is. If I may ask, who were the men you were talking to when she joined you?"

"The brigadier is Bill Donovan, Director of the OSS."

"OSS?"

"Office of Strategic Services. The shortest fellow is Bill Stephenson, who apparently heads the British Passport Control Office in New York City. The taller, thin man is author C.S. Forester."

"Horatio Hornblower?"

"Yes, exactly how I reacted on meeting him."

"Love those books. I've read all three."

"I've only been able to read the first two, but they were captivating. He says there are more, but they will likely have to wait until after the war.

He is too busy writing for the Ministry of Information. I never got to ask him why he was based in this country, but he did say he left England just before the Battle of Britain began."

The three pilots rejoined as the reception event ended, and the people dispersed. They continued to exchange their stories of the evening's interactions, as they moved from the East Room of the White House to the hotel bar. They were scheduled for a full-dress rehearsal of the routine they would use for each of their public events as they made their way across the United States over the next two months. The primary purpose of the War Bonds Tour was to encourage all Americans to buy war bonds and support the war effort.

—

Monday, 2. November. 1942
No. 10 Downing Street
Whitehall, London, England
United Kingdom

Chief of the Imperial General Staff General Sir Alan Brooke entered the prime minister's refurbished office with a courier—an armed Army sergeant with a metallic case manacled to his left wrist. The visit was unannounced but accommodated by the prime minister's duty private secretary.

"'C' sent this to me first," he gestured to the courier.

The sergeant placed the case on the prime minister's desk. Churchill retrieved his key, opened the case, and removed a single sheet of paper.

MOST SECRET - ULTRA

```
SECRET
DATE: 2 NOV 1942
TO: SUPREME COMMANDER NORTH AFRICA XX CORPS
ARMORED AFRICA GROUP
FROM: CMDR DAK
COPY: ARMED FORCES HIGH COMMAND
BREAK
FUEL SUPPLIES NEARLY EXHAUSTED BREAK TWO DAYS
COMBAT OPERATIONS REMAINING BREAK TWO WEEKS
REDUCED OPERATION AT THE OUTSIDE BREAK TROOPS
EXHAUSTED BREAK AS A CONSEQUENCE WITHDRAWING
BREAK NEED SPECIFIED REINFORCEMENTS AND
SUPPLIES SOONEST BREAK HAIL VICTORY BREAK HAIL
HITLER END
SECRET
```

MOST SECRET - ULTRA

"DAK? That is a term with which I am not familiar."

"Translated as sent. DAK stands for *Deutsches Afrikakorps*, or German Africa Corps in English. The crew at Station X analysis section sometimes interpret rather than just translate."

"So, Rommel is on the ropes, as the boxers like to say."

Brooke extended his hand for the message. Churchill gave it to the general, who, in turn, returned the paper to the case and closed it. "Thank you, sergeant. Please convey our gratitude to 'C.'"

"Yes sir." The sergeant departed.

Brooke waited for the door to close and latch. "The information has been sanitized and sent to Middle East Command and 8th Army. Since Montgomery's offensive began, Rommel has counter-attacked five times and has been repulsed. Montgomery suspected Rommel might be losing his edge, but now we know why."

"He must press the attack," Churchill mused.

"Yes, exactly. I wanted to confer with you first. I will send an appropriate follow-on message as soon as I get back to the office."

"Appropriate?"

Brooke smiled. "We agree. Attack!"

Churchill chuckled. "A man of few words."

"Yes sir, short and sweet. Rommel and his vaunted Africa Corps are spent. The Navy has been progressively more successful at interdicting the enemy's convoys. The 8th Army independently reported more than a few instances of abandoned armored vehicles, purposefully destroyed or disabled. We now know why. There is still fight and bite in that dog, but I think we may have turned the corner."

"I agree, Brookie, but the advantage articulated in the Boniface message will only last and be exploitable with constant pressure. Monty must not give the Desert Fox an opportunity to catch his breath."

"I will convey your concerns to General Montgomery."

"We cannot and must not sacrifice this opportunity. We have worked too long with great cost in blood and steel to let this moment slip through our fingers. General Eisenhower intends to depart for his forward headquarters in three days. Unless some unforeseen difficulty arrives, the TORCH landing will take place in the early morning hours this coming Saturday. The compartmented supplement continues to play out per the plan. By the way, I meant to ask you a few days ago, have you had the opportunity to talk to General Clark about his visit to Algeria?"

"Yes, I have. He met with the joint chiefs once he completed his debriefing with the supreme commander. We were universally encouraged by the outcome of FLAGPOLE. I must say, Prime Minister, the Americans have stood up to the mark in fine fashion as our front with the French. We have not seen or detected any French reaction or resistance. Things seem to be lining up well with the Army and Air Force, but the Navy persists with their resistance. The first sea lord suggests we should be prepared for full engagement of French naval units in the region."

"Yes, yes, but I also understand from the first sea lord that the ships of the line are sufficient to deal with the French even if they do engage fully."

"Yes sir. That is the first sea lord's position and the supreme commander concurs. We will deal with the Navy, if they decide to fight. Our concern remains on the ground forces. As I mentioned earlier, the supplemental plan appears to be on track to reduce or negate ground resistance. And, if General Clark's assessment of General Mast is correct, we will likely encounter token resistance to save face with the government. Further, if the Allies can quickly establish themselves firmly ashore, the French Territorial Army may well join the Allies in North African operations. I think that is a bit tenuous at this stage, but the potential clearly exists."

"I know enough from experience to avoid predicting how the French will respond in any given situation. What I do know is, we need TORCH to make a bold statement to the Germans that the other side of the vice is ashore and moving to close with the 8th Army."

"Allied Forces Headquarters are about to execute an excellent plan to achieve that objective. We are in good . . . ." Brooke stopped with the knock on the prime minister's door.

The prime minister's duty private secretary opened the door just enough to partially enter. "Excuse me, Prime Minister, it is time for your scheduled War Cabinet meeting."

Churchill waved to his secretary dismissively. The door closed. "You were saying, Brookie."

"We are in a good position. We have an excellent plan. I also believe we will satisfy the Mast threshold within days, not weeks."

Churchill stood. General Brooke followed. "I genuinely pray your assessment is correct. Now, I must get on to the War Cabinet. Thank you for the discussion, General. We shall pray for success."

The two leaders left the office and went in opposite directions.

—

Wednesday, 4.November.1942
USAAF Station F-356
Saffron Walden, Essex, England
United Kingdom
14:00 hours

The unspecified dignitary visit had been scheduled for several weeks. Only this morning did the men of the 4th Fighter Group learn their visitor was none other than First Lady of the United States Anna Eleanor Roosevelt— fifth cousin and wife of President Roosevelt. Brigadier General Hunter and Air Marshall Leigh-Mallory accompanied Eleanor Roosevelt on her tour of the base, the three American fighter squadrons, and especially the men who served on the now U.S. Army Air Forces base. She chatted with officers and enlisted personnel in all three squadrons. The first lady was attentive and asked well-informed questions as she was shown the differences between the now American Spitfire Mark V and Mark IX fighters, all distinctively marked with white star roundels of the U.S. Army Air Forces. She also made it very clear that she knew the history of the three squadrons, including their contributions to the war effort before and after the U.S. entered the war. Everyone who had the opportunity to interact with her was impressed by her warmth, openness and knowledge. She knew where she was and whom she was talking to on the chilly but dry autumn afternoon.

——

Thursday, 5.November.1942
USAAF Station B-110
Oundle, Northamptonshire, England
United Kingdom
15:00 hours

Major Paul Tibbets shuffled from foot to foot in a failing effort to hold off the autumn chill, as he waited for his primary passenger and his entourage. The four B-17E heavy bombers assigned to this mission were all preflighted and ready for takeoff. His crew and the Red Gremlin bomber were in position.

The olive drab, Chevrolet staff car with a red front bumper plate with three white stars stopped 10 meters from the Red Gremlin. General Eisenhower stepped out of the car. Tibbets saluted. "Major Tibbets, sir. I am the commanding officer of the 340th Bombardment Squadron and your pilot for this mission."

Eisenhower returned the salute and extended his right hand to Tibbets. Both men shook hands, then turned to watch the personnel and baggage being loaded on the other three bombers. After several minutes, Eisenhower turned to face Tibbets. "If I am informed properly, Major, you flew General Clark and his group to Gibraltar a few weeks ago."

"Yes sir, we did. We've made the trip a few times now, FLAGPOLE being one of those missions."

"And, the journey will take eight hours?"

"Yes sir, notwithstanding any interference from the enemy. We have to head out into the Atlantic a couple of hundred miles to avoid German radar and minimize fighter intercept potential. We are not too worried about Condors; we can outrun them."

"The weather forecast?"

"Should be smooth for the most part, but we should expect a couple of spots with light to moderate turbulence."

"Good. We lost a whole squadron of fighters a few months back due to weather."

"Yes sir. We all heard about that one—133 Squadron."

"That's it. They are now the 336th Fighter Squadron. They have been fully reconstituted and returned to combat service. We just do not want that kind of loss to happen again. It was sadly preventable."

"We will ensure it does not happen to us."

"Excellent." Eisenhower glanced at the other bombers. "It looks like the others are loaded. Shall we get this show on the road?"

Tibbets gestured for the general to board first. He made sure his principal was properly seated and strapped in, and then made his way to the cockpit. He patted his radio operator on the shoulder and winked at his flight engineer as he passed them. Tibbets quickly strapped into his seat and made the necessary connections. He simply signaled the ground crew and his copilot by holding up his left index finger, first out his side window, and then to the right seat. They smoothly stepped through the process of starting the other engines and making sure all of their systems were operating normally.

The four bombers took off without incident, joined up, and headed southwest. They would hold that heading until they were well out into the Atlantic, and then they turned due south.

—

Chapter 16

Who asks whether bravery or
cunning beat the enemy?

-- Virgil

Thursday, 5.November.1942
North Front Airfield
British Overseas Territory Gibraltar
23:20 hours

General Eisenhower's luminous dial wristwatch in the dark interior of the Red Gremlin bomber told him they landed just 20 minutes late to plan after an eight-hour flight from England. It took only a few minutes to taxi to their assigned parking spot. Not but seconds after they came to a complete stop, Major Tibbets appeared and gestured to the hatch, as the engines were shut down one at a time in the order of their start sequence. The last engine wound down as Tibbets opened the hatch.

Governor of Gibraltar Lieutenant General Sir Noel 'Mac' Mason-MacFarlane advanced toward the bomber, as Tibbets latched the door open, and Eisenhower emerged.

"Welcome to Gibraltar, General," MacFarlane said.

"Thank you, Sir Noel."

As the two generals conversed on the darkened tarmac, the other bombers parked, shutdown, and disgorged their passengers and baggage into waiting trucks.

"We have transport waiting for you and your entourage. Your advance team has established your communications center and continues to work with our personnel to serve your needs. We have prepared a suite at the Governor's Residence for your personal use."

"Thank you. May I call you Mac? I prefer Ike."

"By all means."

"I truly appreciate your hospitality, Mac, but please excuse me. I really must get to my headquarters."

"Very well. We shall go their directly. We have set aside and secured the Admiralty Tunnel for your sole use for as long as you need the space. My orders are to ensure you have everything you need and I'm able to provide."

Eisenhower, and then Mason-MacFarlane, looked to the other aircraft. The transfer from the aircraft to the trucks appeared to have been swiftly completed. "Looks like we're ready to go. If you do not object, may we go directly to the Admiralty Tunnel."

"Absolutely," MacFarlane responded and gestured to the standing limousine.

MacFarlane gave Eisenhower a quick tour of the arrangements and facilities of the Admiralty Tunnel as well as the provisions for Allied Forces Headquarters Forward. The accommodations were rudimentary compared to Norfolk House in London, but their purpose here was not comfort. It was after midnight by the time the administrative arrangements had been concluded. The invasion of Northwest Africa was planned to occur in two days. General MacFarlane left Eisenhower in his office. The dank, dimly lit, back half of a carved-out cubbyhole in the rock would serve as the supreme commander's office for as long as they remained.

The office was furnished with a modest desk and cushioned chair, a large map of the Mediterranean Sea, a small table with four, wooden, straight back chairs, a small cot, and a washbasin with no plumbing and a pitcher of water. After his quick survey, his chief of staff appeared.

Brigadier General Walter Bedell 'Beetle' Smith, USA, arrived in the European Theater of Operations and assumed his position as chief of staff to the supreme commander, Allied Forces, on 15.September.1942. He promptly and effectively took control of the Allied Forces Headquarters staff. He had been in Gibraltar with the advance team for two days.

"Welcome to Gibraltar, General."

"Thanks, Beetle. Rather humble," Eisenhower said and quickly glanced around the room. "Tell me we are up and running."

"We are. We are functional in all divisions. Most importantly, the communications center is fully functional, including the crypto room. All are secured by U.S. MPs."

"Good."

"That said, while you were en route, you received an ULTRA from Churchill. It is rather telling if you ask me." Eisenhower held out his hand and gestured for the message. Smith opened a locked case. Before he handed the message to Eisenhower, he said, "This references Rommel's November 2nd ULTRA. Do you need the prior message?"

"No."

"I can retrieve it quickly for you."

"No, not necessary. I remember that one."

Smith handed the red, candy-stripe border, single sheet message to Eisenhower.

MOST SECRET - ULTRA

```
MOST SECRET - ULTRA
DATE: 1610 5 NOV 1942
TO: SUPREME COMMANDER AFHQ
```

```
FROM: PM UK
SUBJECT: MESSAGE YOUR DOMAIN
SECRET
DATE: 5 NOV 1942
TO: CMDR DAK
FROM: OFFICE CHANCELLOR
COPY: ARMED FORCES HIGH COMMAND SUPREME
COMMANDER NORTH AFRICA XX CORPS ARMORED AFRICA
GROUP
BREAK I HEREBY COUNTERMAND YOUR 2 NOV 1942
MESSAGE BREAK MY ORDERS ARE SIMPLE AND DIRECT
FOR YOUR COMMAND VICTORY OR DEATH BREAK THE
LEADER END
SECRET
DECYPHERED 0341 5 NOV 1942
MOST SECRET - ULTRA
```

MOST SECRET - ULTRA

"Well, well, well . . . .victory or death, ay."

"That's what got me," Beetle said. "Hitler is telling one of his most accomplished generals that he must die."

"That's the way I read it. On top of Rommel's fuel supplies exhausted message, this," he said, shaking the message, "has to really stick in his craw."

"A delicate understatement, sir."

Eisenhower nodded. "I've been out of the loop for eight hours. What is our status?"

"I can arrange an immediate staff meeting if you wish."

"No, no, not necessary. We can take our regular staff meeting at nine. I just wanted your quick, summary assessment."

Smith nodded. "Very well. The headquarters forward is functional, although not yet fully staffed. All of the initial assault forces are at sea. Their latest situation reports, as of eight hours ago, all indicate they are progressing to plan."

"And, what of the supplemental?"

"The *Seraph* is in position. The extraction should be going on right now, or shortly. The Darlan message was sent," Smith checked his wristwatch, "three hours ago. By the way, Bill Eddy arrived yesterday morning to serve as the direct OSS/SOE liaison for the landings. According to Eddy earlier this evening, Darlan was assured his son was in good health and agreed to cooperate under the cover message. He is arranging a flight from Toulon to Algiers under the pretense of visiting his son. I made direct calls to both air commanders to ensure they do not intercept or interfere with Darlan's plane. Eddy believes Darlan will do his part to thwart major naval resistance. That said, the supplement appears to be proceeding to plan as well."

"Excellent. Is there any urgent business that can't wait until the morning?"

"No sir. So far, so good."

"Very well, then. Go get some sleep, Beetle. I will try to do the same."

"Here, or at the governor's residence?"

"I think showing up on his doorstep after midnight is not good form. I'll probably read a little and try out the cot."

"My office is just next door. I'll be there if you need me."

"Thanks, Beetle. I'll see you in a few hours."

Smith nodded and departed. Eisenhower considered returning to the reading, actually re-reading, of the scholarly English translation of *De Origine et situ Germanorum* (Concerning the Origin and Situation of the Germanics) by Gaius Cornelius Tacitus, chronicling the decimation of three Roman legions under the command of Consul Publius Quinctilius Varus in the Teutoberg Forest in 9 AD. He turned instead to his briefcase and burdensome logistics status reports, hoping they would aid early sleep or at least some sleep.

———

Friday, 6.November.1942
43° 7' 19" North – 6° 23' 49" East
Off the coast of Lavandou, Vichy France
01:15 hours

Lieutenant Jewell, Captain of HMS *Seraph*, submarine P219, was performing his third 360° scan of the area with the submarine search periscope. The only person in the small control compartment of the submarine, who was not a member of the vessel's duty section, was U.S. Navy Captain 'Jerry' Wright—the only American on board was a surface warfare officer with no submarine experience.

"I've got 'em," announced Jewell. "They sent the approach light code. Mark!"

"Zero nine seven relative," announced the chief of the boat.

"Chief of the Boat, prepare to surface to boarding depth. Seas are essentially calm. One-foot swells."

"Aye, Captain."

Jewell stood back from the periscope eyepiece with both hands still on the handgrips. He looked at Wright. "Are you ready, Captain?"

"Yes, Captain."

The plan called for Captain Wright to "act" as the submarine's skipper, including raising the U.S. ensign on the conning tower to soothe

the sensitivities of French General Giraud. They would also deploy the full gun crew, in addition to the boarding team, including the 76mm deck gun and the 20mm anti-aircraft gun, just in case any shooting started. Jewell remained in command of the submarine from the control room.

Jewell considered maneuvering the submarine from a broadside position to the shoreline to a stern-to-the-shore position, just in case they needed to make a quick get-away. He abandoned the thought in order to ensure the guns of the submarine could be brought to bear on any potential threat. Jewell kept watch on the approaching small craft and increased the frequency of his periscope search as it neared the decision threshold.

"Bring the boat to boarding depth," commanded Jewell.

The surface crew deployed and helped the small craft party aboard the submarine. No sign of any threat was detected. The two lookouts and chief of the boat slid down the ladder from the conning tower. "Hatches secured, Skipper," the chief announced.

"Very well, Chief. Submerge to periscope depth," commanded Jewell.

The crew carried out the order. Jewell searched, again. Satisfied they were clear, he commanded, "Down periscope. All ahead five turns. Come to heading one eight zero." Both of the submarine's propellers turned at five revolutions per minute and the vessel slowly moved away from the shoreline and turned south. By prior agreement, Jewell and Wright wanted the general and his party to remain in the wardroom compartment until the submarine was far enough away from the shore to dive for the higher pressure of deeper water to safely allow greater speed without risk of cavitating the propellers and making detectable sound in the water. Once the submarine reached a depth of 200 feet and increased speed to five knots, not quite full speed submerged, Jewell passed control of the submarine to his executive officer and departed the control room for the wardroom.

Jerry Wright and four men dressed in civilian attire—three young men, one older gentleman—were enjoying a glass of the wardroom's wine. Wright introduced their newly arrived guests.

-- General Henri Giraud.
-- Captain of infantry André Beaufre, who was an active Army resistance officer and notional aide-de-camp to the general.
-- Ship-of-the-Line Lieutenant Hubert Viret, naval liaison to General Giraud.
-- Aspirant Bernard Giraud, General Giraud's youngest son and an Army officer designate.

"We are safely away and at depth, sir," Jewell said to his "acting" commander in his best imitation of an American accent.

Wright smiled. Giraud stared intently at Jewell. Jerry said, "Bill, I took the liberty of informing the general on deck of our accommodations for this mission. The façade is no longer required. Please send to Allied Forces Headquarters and the Admiralty, Kingpin aboard."

"Aye aye, sir," Jewell acknowledged, again, in his best American form.

"Excellent effort on the lingo, Bill. No need. Please inform the crew. For the general's and my benefit, what is our ETA at the rendezvous?"

Reverting to his native British accent, Jewell responded, "About 34 hours, sir. We expect to arrive at eleven tomorrow morning."

"Thank you, Lieutenant."

Jewell turned to leave and tend to the mission message. General Giraud said in heavily accented English, looking intently at Jewell, "Thank you as well, Captain. I appreciate your gesture to respect my honor. Perhaps later today, when an appropriate time permits, my party and I would appreciate a tour of your vessel. This is the first time any of us have been aboard a submarine, any submarine."

"It would be my honor, sir. Captain Wright will show you to your bunks. Please accept my apologies, General, this is a small warship and we do not have flag accommodations appropriate for your rank. We shall do our utmost to ensure you are as comfortable as we can possibly make this transit. If there is anything we can do to that end, please do not hesitate to let us know."

General Giraud nodded. Lieutenant Jewell left the compartment. Wright gave their guests a short briefing on the remainder of the plan.

—

Friday, 6.November.1942
Admiralty Tunnel
British Overseas Territory Gibraltar
00:45 hours

General Smith knocked on the doorjamb and entered General Eisenhower's rudimentary office inside The Rock. "Two messages, just received, Ike."

Eisenhower gestured for the messages.

SECRET

```
SECRET
DATE: 1610 5 NOV 1942
TO: AFHQ ADMIRALTY
```

```
FROM: P219
SUBJECT: OPERATION KINGPIN
BREAK
KINGPIN SAFELY ABOARD BREAK ON PLAN END
SECRET
```

SECRET

Eisenhower gestured again for Beetle Smith to take a seat across his desk. "So, we've got Giraud in hand. It sure would be helpful to chat with Jerry Wright on his initial impressions."

"Non-starter, as you know. We're not going to be able to communicate with them until we get the delivered message from *Seraph*."

"Yeah, but still . . . . I just hope this outreach to Giraud does not backfire on us."

"Too late for that, Ike. As Caesar pronounced, 'The die is cast.'"

"Quite so. We will deal with whatever comes. I am disappointed recent intelligence from Eddy and Murphy is not more positive regarding Giraud. Mast has assured us of the support of the Algiers Division, but he is clearly backing away from broader support for Giraud."

"All valid, it seems to me. We need to be prepared for the best to the worst."

"What do you see as those two extremes?" asked Eisenhower.

"The best is he agrees to serve as commander of the Free French Forces and all three services accept his command. The worst is Giraud used us to escape Vichy France and refuses to cooperate."

"My view as well, with myriad combinations in between those two outcomes. He is due to arrive here tomorrow afternoon. I'll meet him at the airfield and bring him back here for the substantive discussions. We'll play from there. By the way, interesting that you quoted Caesar. I'm about halfway through my third reading of Tacitus' *Germania*. I have tried to avoid and expunge the arrogance of Varus in our planning, but this whole uncertainty with Giraud leaves me apprehensive. I always fear the Teutoberg Forest ambush that destroyed the legions of Varus."

"You have done everything you can, Ike. Giraud is just one egg, and he remains in a separate basket for now."

"I want you in my discussions with Giraud."

"Sure. No problem."

Eisenhower nodded his head, smiled briefly and slightly, and shuffled to the second message.

TELEGRAM

NOV 6 1942

TO BEETLE
BBC BROADCAST AT MIDNIGHT ALLO ROBERT FRANKLIN
ARRIVE STOP GOOD LUCK END
                    HENRY

Eisenhower nodded. "We will know in a couple of days whether this works," he said, holding up both messages.

"OK. Everything is in play."

The BBC broadcast periodic sets of random, single sentence messages at scheduled times. Some words were meaningless. Others, like the 'Allo Robert' words, were meant for a very discreet audience in the worldwide public broadcast. The 'Allo Robert' words notified the Northwest Africa resistance that the TORCH invasion was a go, and Allied forces would land at dawn on Sunday the 8ᵗʰ in Morocco and Algeria. The resistance fighters would execute the planned sabotage of telephone lines, bridges, railroad lines and paved roadways as part of the overall invasion plan. The generals had done their part; it would soon be up to the sergeants.

—

Saturday, 7.November.1942
40° 04' North – 02° 37' East
Mediterranean Sea
10:45 hours

"**B**ring the boat to periscope depth," commanded Lieutenant Jewell.

The chief of the boat issued the appropriate orders to achieve the captain's command and reported the attainment of the desired condition.

"Up periscope to broach." Jewell crouched and shuffled in his initial minimum exposure search. The tops of the swells lapped over the optics. "Up periscope." Jewell kept his hands on the grips and stood with the periscope as it raised to full extension. He scanned, again. "We are about a mile away. Right standard rudder. Maintain your turns. Come to heading three two seven." The captain's commands were acknowledged and achieved. Jewell continued to scan the surface and the airspace above them. He maneuvered the submarine to the proper position off the port wing of the RAF Catalina Mark I seaplane. "Rudder amidships. All stop. Surface the boat."

Captain Wright and General Giraud entered the control room.

"Thank you for your expertise, Lieutenant Jewell. My compliments to the crew," Giraud said in English.

"Thanks, Bill. Well done," added Wright.

The senior officers departed forward to the forward hatch for their debarkation. Jewell followed the lookout up the ladder to the conning tower. Jewell watched from the tower as the anti-aircraft gun crew manned the 20mm cannon, just in case. The transfer of the four Frenchmen, one American, and their baggage was routinely accomplished. Jewell kept the submarine on the surface to observe the seaplane's takeoff and climb out. Satisfied their contribution to Operation KINGPIN had been successfully completed, he ordered Radio to send the "Kingpin delivered" message to Allied Forces Headquarters and the Admiralty. The warmth of the sun and the fresh air felt so good, as they always did to submariners, but he still had a boat to protect and a mission to perform. Jewell ordered the boat to prepare to submerge, gestured for the lookouts and gun crew to go below, and descended into the submarine, closing and locking the hatch above him. The *Seraph* proceeded to the east and the Axis sea lanes to search for targets.

———

Saturday, 7.November.1942
Admiralty Tunnel
British Overseas Territory Gibraltar
15:30 hours

General Giraud sat in the center chair of the large conference room table, facing the large, covered, wall map. Eisenhower and Smith sat across from the French general with their backs to the map.

"General Giraud," Eisenhower began, "we brought you here to help the French people regain their freedom and self-determination."

"A worthy objective," Giraud responded. "How may I help?"

"I want to share with you our plans to accomplish the objective."

"Surely, the liberation of France is not your ultimate objective."

Eisenhower grinned as he studied Giraud's eyes. "Before I continue, I need your word of honor as a general officer of the French Army that you will respect the sensitive material we are about to discuss, and you will not discuss any of this conversation with anyone else." Giraud nodded. "Do I have your word of honor?"

"Yes, General Eisenhower, you have my word of honor. I shall respect the privacy of this discussion in full."

"Very well. We are on the verge of beginning the defeat of Italy and Germany. The first step in that process will be the invasion of French Colonial Northwest Africa."

"That is a very aggressive move, like the British very aggressive action against the Republic of France in 1940. We did not look favorably on that action, General. Surely, the United States is not intent on joining the British in offending the sovereignty of France."

"General Giraud, I am not going to waste your time and mine by rehashing history."

"Rehashing? I am not familiar with that term."

"It means to go back over or re-analyze something in the past."

Giraud frowned, looked sternly at Eisenhower, and did not respond, presumably thinking about how he wanted to reply.

Eisenhower did not wait. "The British 8th Army has broken the German advance to the east. The Germans are in full retreat. The Allied governments have decided to land a substantial force in the west, and to advance quickly on the retreating Germans to prevent their escape and their ability to fight elsewhere. This is the first major Allied offensive to defeat Italy and Germany, and restore peace and sovereignty to the nations of Europe. I cannot discuss the next steps beyond North Africa, but ultimately any of those steps must involve the liberation of France." Giraud nodded his head but did not speak. "To speak plainly, General, you can be a part of the liberation of France and the defeat of Germany, or not. I am not going to twist your arm to join us." Eisenhower stopped and held Giraud's eyes, to let his words sink in.

"What are you proposing?" Giraud asked.

"I am offering you command of the Free French Forces in North Africa."

"Wait! I understood I was to be commander-in-chief of the liberation forces."

Eisenhower smiled politely and calmed his thoughts. "I do not know how or why you understood that. I have been selected and appointed as the supreme commander of Allied Forces for this operation. I have no intention of relinquishing command, even to a figurehead. As the Supreme Commander of the Allied Forces, I am offering you substantive command and the opportunity to join the Allied Forces in the defeat of Germany, and specifically German and Italian forces in North Africa."

"You are asking me to go against my country."

"General, please, let us not dilute ourselves with false pretense. To be blunt, half of your country is occupied and dominated by Nazi forces. We anticipate the Germans will invade and subjugate the remainder of your country once we have established ourselves in Northwest Africa."

"Then, why would you do this to France?"

"Do what?"

"Provoke the Germans. My government has reached an understanding, an equilibrium, with the Germans. Why would you disturb the peace?"

"I am not going to argue the strategic decisions of the Allied governments."

"How much time do I have to consider your proposal?"

Confident Giraud had limited means to communicate with the Vichy French government, Eisenhower answered, "Allied forces will land in Northwest Africa tomorrow at dawn. We will proceed according to our battle plan with or without your participation. We would prefer the French territorial forces not resist and join us immediately. However, while we will show the most restraint we can, we will deal with any resistance as an adversary. Your choice is simple, join us and help us defeat the Germans, or not. You are under no pressure. In fact, if you wish, we will return you to Toulon, if that is what you desire."

"I would like to confer with other military commanders."

"You cannot, General. This is your individual decision. Take whatever time you wish to decide. Again, with or without your decision, we will proceed. The door will likely close in a few days. Until then, you are our guest and will be treated accordingly."

"Thank you, General Eisenhower. By the way, your family name sounds quite German."

Eisenhower chuckled softly. Giraud looked puzzled, unaware of what was funny. "My paternal ancestors migrated from Germany to America before the revolution—1741 to be precise."

Giraud nodded and smiled. "Very much American."

"Yes, I think so. I know you must be very busy with the invasion so close. I have much to consider."

"Thank you, General Giraud. I realize, recognize, and acknowledge how important and sensitive the decision is that I have placed before you. I shall do my utmost to make myself available to you, should you need further discussion. Needless to say, the sooner you decide, the better it will be."

General Giraud stood. Eisenhower gestured with his head and eyes to Beetle Smith to escort the French general to his transportation back to his quarters.

———

Sunday, 8.November.1942
Allied Forces Headquarters Forward
Admiralty Tunnel
British Overseas Territory Gibraltar

The three essentially simultaneous landings were executed according to plan just after dawn, despite initial Vichy French naval and air force resistance in the French Protectorate of Morocco and French Colonial Algeria. Even a casual observer at any one of the three landing beaches would recognize that something big was underway. The landings sparked a number of collateral actions.

While initially resistive, Giraud relented the following morning but refused to leave for Algiers and take command. When the general was asked why he would not depart immediately for Algiers, Giraud replied: "You may have seen something of the large De Gaullist demonstration that was held here last Sunday. Some of the demonstrators sang the 'Marseillaise.' I entirely approve of that! Others sang the '*Chant du Départ.*' Quite satisfactory! Others again shouted '*Vive de Gaulle*!' No objection. But some of them cried 'Death to Giraud!' I don't approve of that at all." Special security arrangements and provisions had to be made to assure his safety.

General Mast was true to his word, the Algiers Division offered no resistance and assisted the rapid deployment of the Eastern Task Force around Algiers. Satisfied with the security provisions, General Giraud was flown to Algiers, connected with General Mast, and assumed command of the Territorial Army North Africa on the 9th of November.

Most notably, two days after the Allied landing in North Africa, the German tolerance of the Vichy French vanished. German forces invaded the Free French Zone and struck out swiftly on a beeline for the French Navy base at Toulon, to neutralize the potential of the warships of *Marine Nationale* reverting to Allied cooperation. The SS, SD, and Gestapo joined the invasion forces to occupy and control the major cities in southern France, and completed the final and full subjugation of the French. The Vichy French formally broke diplomatic relations with the United States, and for all intents and purposes, ceased to exist as a recognized diplomatic entity.

The titular chief of the *Marine Nationale Amiral de la Flotte* Jean Louis Xavier François Darlan ordered from Algiers a ceasefire for French forces in North Africa. *Chef de l'Etat Français Maréchal de France* Henri Philippe Benoni Omer Joseph 'Philippe' Pétain countermanded Darlan's order, and dismissed the venerable admiral and his old friend from service.

By the 13th of November, the North Africa Armistice was signed, ending the Vichy French resistance in Northwest Africa, including Senegal with the important port of Dakar, and terminating Operation TORCH. Combat operations continued as the TORCH forces drove east, and the British 8th Army chased Rommel's *Arikakorps* to the west. The Allies would link-up in Tunisia, completing the encirclement of the remaining Axis forces, and neutralization of German and Italian forces in North Africa.

Operation TORCH successfully concluded on the 13th of November; however, German and Italian forces did not surrender until the following May. Hard fighting lay ahead. The Axis resistance in North Africa would also cause the Allies to delay the final invasion of Continental Europe—Operation ROUNDUP, as the plan was currently known.

Just seven weeks after the Allied invasion, on Christmas Eve, royalist Bonnier de La Chapelle would assassinate Admiral Darlan in Algiers—a terrible loss for France and the Allies.

—

Friday, 13.November.1942
Allied Forces Headquarters Forward
Hôtel Saint George
24 Avenue Souidani Boudjemaâ
Algiers
French Colonial Algeria
15:30 hours

"Well, this is a damn sight better accommodation than that dank tunnel at Gibraltar," opined General Clark.

"We are functional," announced Chief of Staff Smith, "but, just barely. At least the communication center including the code room is up and running with their initial equipment. We have flights scheduled over the next week to move the rest of the Gibraltar staff. With the exception of a basic maintenance staff, the remainder of the Norfolk House staff will deploy to Algiers just after Thanksgiving Day."

"Excellent," Eisenhower responded. "I just received word from London and Washington that our political leaders have put a marker down for a three-powers joint conference to be held in Casablanca in mid-January. They have assigned the code word SYMBOL for the conference. While French resistance has ceased, we have considerable clean-up and consolidation to accomplish before that date."

"Why Casablanca?" Clark asked.

"Neither of them shared their reasoning with me. If I was to guess, I would say to make a statement to the Axis that we are coming for them."

"A worthy statement."

"But, a heads of state visit so close to the fighting does add a serious complication. Will either leader utilize shipping for transit?" asked Sir Andrew.

Allied Expeditionary Force Naval Commander Admiral Sir Andrew Browne 'ABC' Cunningham, Bart, GCB, DSO with two bars, the successful commander of the raids on Mers-el-Kébir and Taranto, and the Battle of Cape Matapan, held the respect of everyone who knew of him and his exploits. He managed and led the vast joint Allied naval force that delivered the TORCH force, all of its equipment, supplies and follow-on forces to the beach, and dealt with French naval resistance until Darlan's ceasefire order.

"I don't know," Eisenhower responded. "I imagine those details are being worked out by No.10 and the White House. We will know when they tell us. Until then, we have a war to fight." Ike made eye contact with Bob Murphy, who was sitting in the background. "This is an appropriate opportunity to acknowledge the invaluable work you, Bill Eddy, and your field agents have accomplished to ensure the success of TORCH. While the world will not know of your deeds for many years, I shall ensure that the powers that be will clearly know what and how the OSS has contributed to our success."

"Thank you, General," responded Murphy.

All of the flag officers looked to Murphy and applauded. Bob nodded his recognition and silently mouthed his gratitude.

"Well deserved, Bob. Please convey our appreciation to Bill Eddy and your involved personnel as well as Secretary Hull and Director Donovan. I will do the same."

"Yes sir, it would be my honor."

"Now, we have a very long way to go to vanquish the Axis in North Africa."

"I will say, General," Sir Andrew added, "we have been progressively more successful at our interdiction of supply flights and convoys from Italy and France to North Africa."

"Excellent. We need to choke them while we close the vice. I requested a commander's conference next week."

"All three, line commanders, as well as the air commanders, have confirmed, sir," interjected Smith. "They will be here Wednesday morning. We are scheduled to convene at 10 that morning."

"Very well."

"Air support has been less than optimum," Clark declared.

"Agreed," Ike said. "I think that responsibility rests upon me. I was too distracted by the ground operations and the French potential. I will say, Sir Andrew, the Navy has set the example for cooperation and joint operations. I regret not insisting upon an overall AEF air commander as you are for the naval forces." Eisenhower looked at his chief of staff. "Beetle, please schedule a private meeting for me with Air Marshal Welsh and General Doolittle after the commanders' conference. Sir Andrew, since you have more than a few carriers and naval aircraft in direct support, I would ask that you, or your carrier task force commander, attend that air meeting."

Air Marshal Sir William Lawrie Welsh, KCB, DSC, AFC, had been appointed Air Officer Commanding-in-Chief Eastern Air Command and assigned to support the TORCH Eastern Task Force.

General Doolittle had been detached from the 8th Air Force in August and given command of the 12th Air Force when the new unit was created in August. The 12th Air Force was assigned to support the Western and Central Task Forces. Doolittle was approved and slated to be promoted to major general next week.

"Will do, General," Sir Andrew responded, "although I am losing half of my assigned carriers before the meeting."

"Understood, Sir Andrew, but your contribution to the air support collaboration matter would be appreciated."

"Of course. It should be no problem, barring some operational emergency."

"Thank you for your time, gentlemen. Let's get this place settled quickly. We are likely to be here for a while. I will keep you posted on the progress and details of the SYMBOL conference as we get them. Good day, gentlemen."

The men left Eisenhower alone in his spacious office in the converted conference room.

—

Saturday, 14.November.1942
Chequers Court
Ellenborough, Buckinghamshire, England
United Kingdom
16:00 hours

Among the prime minister's guests for the informal weekend conference were the British joint chiefs— Admiral Pound, General Brooke, and Air Chief Marshal Portal—along with Admiral Mountbatten and General Ismay. Foreign Minister Eden had remained in London to accompany Field Marshal Smuts to the prime minister's country retreat upon his arrival at RAF Northolt. They were due to arrive at Chequers before supper.

Field Marshal Jan Christiaan Smuts, PC, OM, CH, FRS, had been Prime Minister of South Africa since 1939 and was made a field marshal in the British Army in 1941. Like Australia and Canada, the Union of South Africa had been a self-governing dominion of the British Commonwealth since 1926, and Smuts had been prime minister for his country for years before and after independence. Churchill and Smuts had been close personal friends since serving together in the War Cabinet of Prime Minister David Lloyd George in the Great War, and the South African leader remained a touchstone counsel to the British prime minister.

"We have reason for optimism, gentlemen," Churchill declared, then held his champagne glass above his head. "Let us toast the British Empire. We are finally witness to the brilliant rays of sunshine through the clouds of war."

"To the Empire," the senior officers said in unison. They clinked glasses before raising their glasses one more time and taking a sip.

"Tomorrow, the church bells shall ring across the nation to acknowledge Montgomery's triumph at El Alamein. The 8th Army has Rommel on the run. While we are not going to declare victory, just yet, this is a major turning point in the war. Further, Operation TORCH has been successfully executed and concluded. Allied armies are grounded and driving east to join the 8th Army in crushing the *Afrikakorps*. We have reason and just cause for a moment of rejoicing."

"No argument, Prime Minister," interjected General Brooke. "However, I caution against exaggerating the successes of the 8th Army and Allied Expeditionary Force. Formidable German forces remain in Tunisia, and Rommel has terrain for several defensive lines. The fighting in North Africa is not over. We have no basis for declaring victory in North Africa."

"I think the rest of us would agree with Alan's caution, Prime Minister," Portal added.

"The bells will ring, nonetheless, but I promise to dampen my public words of joy." Churchill gestured to the circle of couches and chairs the group had used more than a few times over the years. "Now, I have a couple of discussion items. President Roosevelt has agreed to SYMBOL and Casablanca in mid-January. So, we must prepare. While we have not secured North Africa, I think the primary topic will be what next. The American chiefs will likely renew their insistence on SLEDGEHAMMER or ROUNDUP."

"Excuse me for the intrusion," said Lord Mountbatten, "I'm afraid it is not my place . . . ."

"Nonsense," Churchill interrupted. "Speak up, Admiral. We are military men here, and we speak frankly with one another."

"You have articulated quite clearly your 'soft underbelly' concept, Prime Minister," Mountbatten continued. "That sounds far more reasonable than the hard shell of the Atlantic Wall. As we all know, we took a stab at penetration, and we all know the consequences of JUBILEE. We paid a very heavy price for that test. Both SLEDGEHAMMER and ROUNDUP are direct assaults on that hardback shell. From my perspective, SLEDGEHAMMER is a non-starter at the precept stage since it is closer to JUBILEE than ROUNDUP. An assault on the soft underbelly looks like Italy."

"Thank you for that, Lord Mountbatten. So, what say the rest of you?"

"Admiral Mountbatten has offered reasoning we have all agreed to since shortly after ARCADIA," said General Brooke. "But the question is how to convince the Americans."

"Before we get to that aspect," Churchill began, "I have one other, well, actually, two other suggestions that are relevant. One is the south of France. While the Germans have invaded Vichy France as a consequence of TORCH, they have not yet fortified the coastline as they have on the Atlantic and Channel coasts. Perhaps a strike to the South of France before they have time to build would require fewer forces. And two, which we have not discussed previously, is the Balkans." Churchill paused to allow comment, but none came. "After my meeting with Stalin in August, I have become more sensitive to what the Communist dictator intends after this sordid affair is done. Striking north through the Balkans to the Baltic countries might secure Poland and perhaps even Ukraine from Soviet domination." Churchill paused to listen.

"A worthy notional objective," Portal responded, "however, just the thought of supporting a Balkan operation, especially one directly threatening the enemy's line of communications. The threat of cutting off several army groups would surely precipitate a maximum response that might overwhelm such a force. From the air support perspective, our current force structure is woefully inadequate for such an enormous long-range operation."

"There is that aspect," said the prime minister. "We must be prepared to discuss such options, a range of options, to flush out the best choice."

"And, what do you see as that best choice?" asked the first sea lord.

"Since you asked," several chuckles punctuated the prime minister's words, "I cannot foresee taking the next step until North Africa is liberated, secured and stable. Those forces are required for the next step. Once North Africa is secured, based on what we know today, I see the next step as Italy, and the gateway to Italy is Sicily. Knocking out one of the three major members of the Axis powers, albeit perhaps the weakest one, would go a long way to placating Stalin and his second front rants and offer a serious threat on Germany's doorstep. The thought of fighting through the Alps is rather daunting, but the Germans could not ignore the potential."

"Then what?" Mountbatten asked.

"The next logical step is France—ROUNDUP in some form. The question that sits at the forefront of all this discussion is logistics. When can we gather, train, and stage sufficient assault, reserve, and support forces to ensure success, or at least give us an acceptable likelihood of success? Shorter lines of communications enhance our logistical support. As we learned on TORCH, we currently hold insufficient shipping to move such forces. The American industrial mobilization is well underway, but it has yet to hit their production capacity. All of the next steps require closing operations in North Africa. January or February would be helpful."

"Although unlikely unless the Germans surrender," commented Brooke.

"Indeed. Thus, we must focus on combined operations."

"Intelligence, as of yesterday afternoon, indicates Rommel's first defense attempt is materializing just east of El Agheila. Monty has the intelligence. He is moving as fast as he considers prudent to keep the pressure on the retreating Germans without plunging into an ambush. Rommel must buy time in hopes of obtaining supplies."

"ABC is doing his best part to close that door," Pound said.

"Of that, there is no doubt. He has been one of our most accomplished commanders in using Boniface to advantage," said Churchill, referring to the special intelligence provided by ULTRA. "Rommel must recognize his supplies are tenuous at best, and the potential to evacuate and save his forces in North Africa has nearly vanished. It must be a very sinking feeling."

"So long as we do not repeat Hitler's mistake in allowing DYNAMO," Brooke muttered.

Churchill grinned broadly, and then the smile disappeared, and he lowered his chin like a bull preparing to charge. "This is a social occasion, Brookie, so there is more latitude. Surely, you are not comparing me to that little corporal?"

"Of course not, Prime Minister," General Brooke responded. "I am only acknowledging history. Guderian and Rommel had us surrounded with our backs to the sea. Those three days enabled us to prepare sufficient defense and recover a third of a million men."

"I do not need a history lesson, General Brooke."

"Perhaps we should change the subject," offered Admiral Mountbatten.

"Good idea," added Admiral Pound.

"Let us enjoy the bells of celebration tomorrow," Air Chief Marshall Portal suggested.

"Gentlemen, I appreciate your sensitivity," Churchill said, "but as I said, this is a social evening. We can argue things out here. We can disagree. We should argue things out. Yet, I trust each of you can recognize that if the Americans see division, it will dilute our argument. Let me assure you all, my apprehension is that I will press too hard rather than hold up once we have them at our mercy."

The prime minister's duty private secretary John Peck entered the study and announced, "Foreign Minister Eden and Field Marshal Smuts have arrived, Prime Minister."

"Please show them in, Mister Peck. We still have an hour until supper will be served."

'Very well, sir."

In short order, Eden and Smuts entered the study. Introductions were not necessary since they had all known each other for years. Prime Minister Churchill summarized the afternoon's discussion with the best humor he could render.

"I am old enough and wise enough not to immerse myself in this internal debate," commented Smuts.

"Yes, yes, Jan, but this is just an opinion. What would you favor?"

"Do we have a movie after supper tonight?" Smuts asked. Everyone laughed at the blatant attempt to avoid the answer.

"Very well, then . . . at least for now," Churchill said and chuckled. "Yes, we do. I thought it quite apropos that tonight's selection is a new release, just released actually, *Road to Morocco*, an American comedy starring Bob Hope, Bing Crosby, and Dorothy Lamour."

The rest of the evening was filled with laughter and light-hearted conversation. The movie was enjoyed by all, even though the characters spoke in the American form and accent.

—

Chapter 17

But true love is a durable fire,
In the mind ever burning,
Never sick, never old, never dead,
From itself never turning.

-- Sir Walter Raleigh

Sunday, 22.November.1942
Chequers Court
Ellenborough,Buckinghamshire, England
United Kingdom
17:00 hours

An early snow was falling gently from the very low overcast and fog. The prime minister's library remained warm with the modest fire that had been maintained all afternoon. They had just been served ample flutes of Churchill's favorite champagne—Pol Roger 1928. His supply was dwindling, but this was a special occasion with a special guest.

"This seems a bit unusual, Prime Minister," observed 'C'—Secret Intelligence Service Director General Brigadier Stewart Menzies.

"How so?"

"Am I your only guest for the evening meal?"

Churchill chuckled. "Well, I guess that is a bit unusual, isn't it? I like people. I like the contrast of ideas, opinions, experience, and life lessons."

"I am not a particularly social person, Prime Minister."

Winston laughed more robustly this time. "I did not invite you out to the country for chit-chat, Stewart. I do confess to my desire for a less formal or official setting for the discussion I had in mind." 'C' nodded his acknowledgment. "Winter is setting in across Russia. I was encouraged by the Red Army's offensive Operation URANUS that began three days ago. What is the latest information?"

"Marshal Zhukov initiated the two-pronged offensive, and as of a few hours ago, before I left London, the field reports have been very positive. They appear to have caught the Germans napping, which suggests they obtained particularly good intelligence regarding German weaknesses in their uncharacteristic focus on Stalingrad."

"The Boniface messages from last June indicated that Hitler had personally directed the formation of Army Group B from elements of Army Group Center and Army Group South, and then order the new army group to strike out directly to Stalingrad, presumably to choke off a major supply line to Moscow and the preponderance of Soviet forces."

"Correct. That is precisely what our field intelligence indicates," answered 'C.'

"How is URANUS progressing?"

"Remarkably well from all of our field sources. It appears quite likely the two-prongs will link up in the next few days and complete the encirclement of the entire German 6th Army, which is fully engaged in urban warfare in Stalingrad."

"Who commands the 6th Army?"

"Paulus, Friedrich Paulus, an odd duck, at least by contemporary standards. He has never commanded more than a battalion, but he is the protégée of and staff officer to his predecessor Field Marshall Walter von Reichenau, who took command of Army Group South, only to die a month later from the effect of an apparent stroke, or the crash of his aircraft transporting him to Leipzig for medical treatment. From what we know, Paulus has performed quite well under what would otherwise be called tragic conditions."

"Never heard of the man."

"He was not high on the list of accomplished field commanders."

"If history and the Soviet encirclement hold, Paulus will soon receive his victory or die message from that damned little corporal."

"If he does, we should receive it promptly. We are in a productive cycle with ULTRA at the moment," announced 'C.'

"Keep a close eye out. Do you have anyone inside the 6th Army?"

"No sir. And now, the risk is simply too great. I'm afraid for the moment we shall be relegated to bearing witness from afar. The 6th Army appears to be doomed." Menzies paused, but the prime minister did not speak. "By the way, Prime Minister, we have somewhat of a Red Army celebrity among us on a goodwill tour. Lieutenant Lyudmila Mykhailivna Pavlichenko is in Coventry at the moment. She is credited with 300 plus kills in combat operations at Odessa and Sevastopol as a rifle sniper."

"Quite the marksman."

"I do believe that is a fair statement, Prime Minister."

"The Red Army could use more like her."

"The Soviets have made good use of women. They formed three all-female night fighter and bomber squadrons. The Germans call them the 'Night Witches.' From what we can see in their message traffic, the title is justly deserved."

"Maybe we should give our women the same opportunities."

Menzies smiled. "That is a political matter and entirely in your domain, Prime Minister."

"Our women have been performing exceptionally well in the Air Transport Auxiliary. Several have petitioned the air minister for transfer to Fighter Command."

"Why not? The Russian women have done exceptionally well in the 586th Regiment, flying Yak-1 night fighters. Why not give our ladies a shot? They can clearly fly Spitfires, Hurricanes, Beaufighters, and all the rest. By Jove, they also fly Lancaster heavy bombers."

"I appreciate the sentiment, 'C,' but there is a significant difference between flying and getting shot at while flying."

"Whether you choose to give the women a chance to prove themselves is entirely your choice, Prime Minister. Nonetheless, we shall keep a close watch on the Stalingrad enclave. This might well be the turning point of the war in the east."

"As El Alamein and TORCH appear to be in North Africa."

"Rommel is going to defend the El Agheila line. Aerial photography confirms they have taken defensive positions. The 8th Army will make its first assault tomorrow."

"Fingers crossed. Elsewhere, the Germans are on the outskirts of Toulon."

"What of the French fleet?"

"Nothing, yet. The French have consistently reassured us they will not allow their warships to reach the hands of the Germans."

"So, here we are. This is Mers-el-Kébir all over again."

"So, it would seem."

"Our state is not the same as it was in the summer of 1940. Do Admiral Cunningham and General Eisenhower have your latest intelligence?"

"Yes sir . . . to both."

"The first sea lord has conferred with ABC. The fleet is prepared to take aggressive action should the French fail to take the necessary steps to prevent compromise. That is another situation we must keep a very close watch on until it is resolved."

"We have quite a bit to keep watch on in the world."

"Yes, you do, as we all do."

The remainder of the evening's conversation entailed less serious topics.

———

Wednesday, 2.December.1942
Amos Alonzo Stagg Field
University of Chicago
East 55th Street
Chicago, Cook County, Illinois
United States of America
09:54 hours

Underneath the west grandstands, an old squash court had been converted to a rudimentary, clapboard workshop and served as the laboratory that had been assigned to Noble Laureate, Italian refugee-immigrant physicist, Professor Enrico Fermi for his nuclear reaction experiment. The intent of the elaborate construction of what they called Chicago Pile Number 1 (CP1) was essentially a larger scale, more elaborate version of the German Hahn-Strassman experiment in 1938, and the confirmatory experiment in Great Britain the following year by refugee German scientists Lise Meitner and her nephew Otto Robert Frisch. It was Frisch and his colleague Rudolf 'Rudi' Peierls, who mathematically proved the theory that a critical mass of high neutron-flux material like uranium 235 (^{235}U) or plutonium 239 (^{239}Pu) could produce an unimaginable spontaneous release of energy in what chemists and physicists called an explosion. The Frisch-Peierls Memorandum to Marcus Oliphant in early 1940 was the singular document that convinced the British and Americans to attempt building such a device.

The objective of the Fermi experiment was a controlled fission reaction and measurement of the neutron-flux generated by a sub-critical mass of uranium. To accomplish the scientific objective, they constructed a pile of graphite blocks as high absorptive matter with control rods to absorb the natural radiation until they were ready to initiate the reaction. The uranium enrichment facility being constructed at the highly secret Site X at Oak Ridge, Tennessee, was months away from producing sufficient enriched ^{235}U for the experiment. The physicists calculated they could use natural uranium, but they would need a lot of the metal. The resultant construction of Chicago Pile Number 1 contained five tons of uranium (^{238}U) metal along with 40 tons of uranium oxide (UO_2), surrounded by 45,000 ultra-pure graphite (^{12}C) blocks weighing 330 tons. The design used super-neutron-absorbent cadmium (^{48}Cd) control rods that could be withdrawn and reinserted to regulate the free neutrons emitted during the reaction, and thus control the intensity of the reaction. The pile had no shielding or coolant system to dissipate the heat generated, so they agreed to operate the reactor at very low power levels to avoid heat damage to the structure, or worse losing control of the reactor.

Professor Fermi checked for the umpteenth time to ensure everyone was at their assigned stations to respond appropriately no matter what they encountered. The instrumentation had been checked and rechecked numerous times, including the strip recorders needed to save the historical record of what they produced. The key was the measurement, as precisely as possible, of the neutron flux at each stage of control rod withdrawal from the core.

With nearly four-dozen physicists, engineers, technicians, and dignitaries, including Arthur Compton representing the S-1 Uranium Committee present to witness the experiment, Fermi queried in his distinctive Italian accent, "Is everyone ready?" He received affirmative answers from each key person in verbal or gesture form. "George, if you would, please withdraw control rod 17 to 10 percent."

"Control rod 17 has been withdrawn to 10 percent."

They waited and only detected an ever-so-slight increase in neutron flux within the interior of the pile, but within the scatter value. Several more control rods were pulled out slightly. They continued the process until a significant rise in neutron flux registered on the gauges.

"Insert all control rods," commanded Fermi to stop the reaction. The technicians performed as they were commanded. The flux dropped quickly to the base level. Professor Fermi smiled but did not speak. He looked over the shoulder of his instrumentation team to confirm what he saw and heard. Satisfied, Fermi directed the test procedure to be repeated several more times, increasing the flux level each time. They paid particular attention to the thermocouples imbedded in the pile since they had no cooling system to dissipate the heat generated by the nuclear reaction.

Enrico Fermi's experiment had not only confirmed the Hahn-Strassman and the Meitner-Frisch experiments, but had more importantly gone much farther on a larger scale to establish the likelihood that the Frisch-Peierls Memorandum prediction was achievable. The Manhattan Project scientists and engineers were another significant step closer to their objective, having collected essential data to refine their calculations and guide their engineering. The process was repeated several more times that afternoon with the same results—the experiment was repeatable and consistent.

Once Fermi and the other physicists agreed with the preliminary analysis of the results, Compton placed an open-circuit telephone call to his boss, Jim Conant, on the S-1 Uranium Committee of the National Defense Research Committee in Washington, DC, to inform the supervisory committee about the experiment's results.

"The Italian navigator has landed in the New World," Compton simply stated without salutation.

"How were the natives?" asked Conant.

"Very friendly," Compton responded, and then the call was terminated.

The simple, open-circuit, coded, telephonic message indicated the Fermi experiment had safely achieved all of its technical objectives and recorded the data the Project physicists needed.

Over the following months, the Chicago Pile Number 1 reactor was progressively raised to higher power levels until they reached the agreed to threshold of heat generation tolerance, then stepped back to lower acceptable power levels to refine the data quality. Two months after the team's initial success, the Chicago Pile Number 1 reactor was shut down, carefully disassembled and moved to Site A—Argonne National Laboratory, Argonne Forest, Cook County, Illinois. The CP1 reactor was reassembled and would continue to carry out experimental operations for another year until it would be shut down permanently.

Of particular note from the Fermi experiment, some scientists and engineers inside the Manhattan Project spied for and were exploited by the Soviet Union. They stole the design and results of the Fermi carbon pile setup that became the basis of the reactor design used throughout the Soviet Union, including the infamous Unit Number 4 at the Chernobyl Electrical Power Station. The United States, Great Britain, and their allies abandoned the carbon pile construction in favor of a pressurized water system for more precise control of the heat generated by the nuclear reaction, with containment vessels to limit the damage of any accidents.

—

Sunday, 6.December.1942
Chequers Court
Ellenborough,Buckinghamshire, England
United Kingdom
13:30 hours

Winter had set into Southeast England. Everyone adjusted to the change of seasons. The mansion staff always did a magnificent job maintaining the interior temperature in a comfortable range that made the winter scene out the windows appear more like a picture.

"That was a delightful luncheon as always," declared Ambassador Winant. "My compliments to Mrs. Landemare. She managed to work her magic with sparse ingredients."

"Quite so," added Foreign Minister Eden. "I assume you have been briefed on the events at Toulon."

"You have been traveling, Anthony," responded Churchill, "so, you have missed last week's War Cabinet meetings. Yes, we have discussed the events. Have you been briefed on Toulon, Gil?"

"Only that the Germans were advancing on the French naval base."

"The Germans reached the famous naval base on the 27th of last month, a week and a half ago. As they entered the gates, the Navy scuttled their entire in port fleet, 73 ships in total including all of their capital ships at Toulon, a very heroic act."

"Dear God!" exclaimed Winant.

"If they had only done that in Algeria two years ago, Admiral Somerville would not have had to open fire on our one-time ally. They have done their duty," Churchill pronounced.

"The sinkings have been confirmed by multiple independent sources," said Eden. "We have some indications of reprisals against the officers, especially the senior ones, but Pike and 'C' are still working to confirm the status of the naval officers."

"Is there anything we can do to help those officers?"

"Win the war," Eden said flippantly.

"We are working on that. Monty is pounding on the El Agheila line. Anderson is engaged in heavy fighting in Eastern Algeria, while Fredendall and Patton are advancing swiftly to join, and aid the Eastern Task Force. We are in the planning and coordination stage in advance of our Casablanca conference next month."

"Is Stalin invited?" Winant asked.

"Invited, yes, but not attending." Churchill stood, went to his desk, retrieved the message he sought, and handed it to Ambassador Winant.

SECRET

```
SECRET
DATE 1610 5 DEC 1942
TO PM FM UK
FROM GS CC AUCP USSR
BREAK
THANK YOU FOR INVITATION TO SYMBOL STOP UNABLE
TO ATTEND STOP BATTLE OF STALINGRAD AT CRITICAL
STAGE STOP GOOD LUCK BEST WISHES END
SECRET
```

SECRET

Winant handed the message back to Churchill. "Well, from everything I've heard, Stalingrad is quite the fevered battle."

"Yes, it certainly is, and the Red Army has the German 6th Army surrounded in the battered city. The German Air Force is using all of its available lift capacity to supply the 6th Army despite the strangulation of the encirclement. From everything we can see, the aerial supply is woefully inadequate, and the 6th Army appears doomed."

"But that is only one army among many. As I understand the situation, the Germans have multiple army groups, each comprised of multiple armies on the eastern front."

"You are accurately informed, Gil. But, do not underestimate the power of imagery. The Germans repeatedly surrounded massive Soviet forces with devastating consequences. This time, the shoe is on the other foot, and an entire German army is facing a slow and tortuous death. History may well record Stalingrad was the inflection point that turned the German advance into a long, slow, painful withdrawal."

"Conscious that I may be stepping over the line, North Africa is not yet won, but the signs are positive. The obvious question is, what next?"

"Gil, we have been together for a sufficient time now, and you have been a part of our effort. I understand your place in the political and diplomatic processes of war. I trust you, and I trust that you will be worthy of my trust."

"Absolutely, without qualification, Winston."

"Beyond assessing our current situation, the primary task of the Casablanca Conference is precisely that question. We have evaluated a range of possibilities. It is the position of His Majesty's Government that the next step should be Sicily as the steppingstone to Italy."

"Surely, you are not intending to invade Germany across the Alps?"

Churchill chuckled. "No, although the threat should hold divisions against the potential. Are you familiar with Operation ROUNDUP?"

"Yes."

"Some version of ROUNDUP will begin the final push to Berlin."

"When?"

"That is too far ahead to know the answer. To our current thinking, our subsequent actions are dependent upon the swift conclusion of our North African operations. There are many chess pieces still on the board. We have a notional objective of the late summer of next year, which will be none too soon for Uncle Joe. An awful lot of numbers must fall our way between now and then."

"Thank you for sharing that, Winston," said Winant. "We shall pray for Allied success. Back to Stalingrad, I recognize that the battle is important, but I would think a joint summit to map out the rest of the war would be more important."

"We think alike, Gil. This is the second leaders' conference he has skipped. He was invited to ARCADIA as well. For whatever reason he chooses not to attend, we will continue to invite him. Have you met Stalin?"

"No, I haven't."

"Both Anthony and I have . . . on different occasions."

"What was your impression?" Winant asked.

"Anthony," Churchill said and looked at Eden.

"My impression . . . he charming when he wants to be, but in fact, he is devoid of ethics and oblivious to any common decency that is not in his immediate best interest. He is truly a ruthless brute. He leads by fear. I mean real fear. I sense there is no one who is not afraid of him, no general or admiral, not even the chairman of the NKGB."

Churchill looked at Eden and smiled, and then back at Winant. "That is my impression as well. He is quite charming, when he wishes to be, but his mood can turn foul in an instant. Regardless, he is the leader we must deal with in this war." Churchill glanced at the clock on the bookshelf. "Now, if you gentlemen will excuse me, it is my nap time. You are both quite familiar with the offerings of Chequers. I will see you again in a few hours."

Both Eden and Winant were familiar with and understood Winston Churchill's peculiarities. The prime minister had been taking an afternoon nap, even during the height of the Battle of Britain, for many years. It was part of his coping mechanism. His afternoon naps kept him stable and balanced.

———

Thursday, 10.December.1942
No.10 Downing Street
Whitehall, London, England
United Kingdom
11:15 hours

Prime Minister Churchill shifted his calendar when Foreign Minister Eden's secretary called for an urgent meeting.

Duty Private Secretary John Martin stood in the door and announced, "Foreign Minister Eden, sir."

"Yes, yes, show him in."

"Thank you for making time for me on such short notice."

"By all means, Anthony. You said urgent. I take you at your word."

"We just received a 16-page report from the Polish government-in-exile on the Jewish situation in Poland. The contents are nauseatingly detailed and delineate the brutality of the Nazi regime."

"Do you have a copy of the report for me to read?"

"Yes," Eden responded and handed over the professionally printed document.

Churchill held the cream-colored pamphlet with bold red lettering on the cover and stared at the title. "The title speaks volumes—*The mass extermination of Jews in German-occupied Poland.* Can you quickly summarize the contents?"

"As you will note in your reading, the report claims that many of the three million-plus Jews in Poland before the war have already been murdered."

"So, *Mein Kampf* has come to life."

"Yes," Eden responded with muted solemnity.

"The Americans have the report?"

"Yes. The report was simultaneously delivered to Secretary Hull, to Minister Molotov in Moscow, and to me. They are recommending a joint declaration of condemnation regarding the Nazi actions. It is our intention to fulfill the recommendation with a joint Allied declaration. We will coordinate with our allies to achieve the result. I should say that Foreign Minister Raczyński has done an exemplary job in compiling the information in the report and in focusing our attention on the Nazi conduct in Poland. While the report constrains itself with the activities in Poland, we have direct evidence that similar actions are being carried out in Germany itself as well as the occupied territories to the east. MI6 has indications, mostly second and third-hand information, that those special units of the SS are conducting this genocidal annihilation, using industrial-scale techniques. We are working to corroborate these reports as well as the identification of those involved. Further, this horrific campaign extends beyond those of the Jewish faith in the occupied territories to include gypsies, cripples, mentally ill, homosexuals, and anyone else they declare undesirable to their notion of Aryan supremacy."

"When you say industrial scale, what do you mean?"

"As we have discussed last year, the SS special action squads in the Baltic countries have shot hundreds, if not thousands, of those they have classified as undesirables, and dumped them into mass graves. In the case of the Baltics and now the other occupied territories in the east, they have employed sympathetic local nationals to do their dirty work under the supervision of the SS. We have bits and pieces at the evidentiary level that give us the picture that they are building large buildings and crematoria at what they concentration camps. The smoke from the ovens spreads the foul odor over a wide area. We have not been able to get reliable agents close enough to the facilities to photograph them."

"Task the Air Ministry to conduct aerial photography missions over the sites you specify to see what they can turn up," commanded Churchill.

"I will do that. I must add that we have sketchy indications, not yet verified or validated, that the SS is using toxic gas, quite possibly a high concentration of insecticide—a nerve agent. We have photographic evidence that railcar loads of large containers from the chemical company I.G. Farben, labeled as Zyklon B, are moving east. We have been working with Porton Down to identify the agent. We know that people go into those facilities, and very few come out. Other than the guards, those who come out are males who are transported to other sites for forced labor, which is actually slow death by labor. We have evidence of the forced labor at several construction sites, and indications of forced labor being used in remote defense sites."

The British Chemical Defense Experimental Station (CDES) at Porton Down, Wiltshire, was created in the aftermath of the first use of chemical weapons by the Germans on the Western Front in 1915. The British scrambled to catch up with the production and use of chemical weapons on the battlefield. The United States took similar action to develop chemical weapons and formed the Chemical Warfare Service (CWS) in 1918, which eventually became the Chemical Corps, a formal service branch of the Army.

"That does sound like an industrial scale, indeed. Do we have any collateral information from the Russians or the Americans?"

"Not yet, but they are both looking."

"Our allies have this information?"

"Most of it but not all of it."

"Why?"

"We are sensitive to the security of our sources and too much of this is circumstantial."

"As you negotiate the language for the declaration with our allies, I think it would be appropriate for us to share and compare notes on the subject. We need as clear of a picture as we can collectively generate."

"Very well."

"Keep good, secure records. It is becoming quite apparent that this information will be useful in the post-war prosecution of those involved in this abomination. I suspect when we see the physical evidence, as we most assuredly will, the dimensions of this tragedy will be far worse than we know today—the tip of the iceberg."

———

Thursday, 17.December.1942
Oval Office
The White House
Washington, District of Columbia
United States of America
16:00 hours

The President sat at his desk reading through his incessant stack of reports, memoranda, and correspondence, and occasionally making handwritten notes in the margins for further staff action or just simple comments for the record.

The knock at the door did not need an answer, since Roosevelt recognized the distinctive tap of his trusted aide Harry Hopkins. The conformal door opened, Hopkins stepped in and closed the door behind him. "Cordell is here for his scheduled meeting at his request."

"This must be the public announcement."

"I do believe you are correct, Franklin."

"Please show him in and join us, if you would. I think this may be an interesting conversation."

"No problem."

As Hopkins went to retrieve Secretary of State Hull, Roosevelt laid down his pen and wheeled himself to his usual spot between the two long couches.

They quickly dispensed with the usual cordialities. Hull sat on the right-hand couch and closest to the President. Hopkins took his usual seat behind and to the left of the President. The Secretary of State extracted a single piece of printed-paper from his brown leather briefcase. "Here is the declaration for the Jews," he announced matter-of-factly and handed the paper to the President.

A Joint Declaration
by Members of the United Nations
Against Extermination of the Jews

The attention of the Governments of Belgium, Czechoslovakia, Greece, Luxembourg, the Netherlands, Norway, Poland, the United States of America, the United Kingdom of Great Britain and Northern Ireland, the Union of Soviet Socialist Republics and Yugoslavia, and the French Committee of National Liberation, has been drawn to numerous reports from Europe that the German authorities, not content with denying to persons of Jewish race in all the territories over which their barbarous rule has been extended the most elementary human rights, are now carrying into effect Hitler's often repeated intention to exterminate the Jewish people in Europe. From all the occupied countries Jews are being transported, in conditions of appalling horror and brutality, to Eastern Europe. In Poland, which has been made the principal Nazi slaughterhouse, the ghettoes established by the Nazi invaders are being systematically emptied of all Jews except a few highly skilled workers required for war industries. None of those taken away are ever heard of again. The able-bodied are slowly worked to death in labor camps. The infirm are left to die of exposure and starvation or are deliberately massacred in mass executions.

The number of victims of these bloody cruelties is reckoned in many hundreds of thousands of entirely innocent men, women and children.

The above-mentioned Governments and the French National Committee condemn in the strongest possible terms this bestial policy of cold-blooded extermination. They declare that such events can only strengthen the resolve of all freedom-loving people to overthrow the barbarous Hitlerite tyranny. They reaffirm their solemn resolution to ensure that those responsible for these crimes shall not escape retribution and to press on with the necessary practical measures to this end.

Done at Washington and London
December 17, 1942

"That is the official print version of the joint declaration that has been issued in London and here," Hull continued, as the President read the document.

"Foreign Minister Eden read the declaration this morning our time in Commons as Lord Simon read it in Lords. The *New York Times* published the declaration on the front page this morning. Now, the world knows."

Roosevelt handed the paper back to Hull. "We have to do something about this," the president declared. "It is one thing to condemn what is going on in Poland, and elsewhere I suspect, but our condemnation does not translate to actions that might help these innocent people."

"I do not see that we can do much more other than defeating the Germans."

"You could lighten up a little on accepting refugees."

"I understand and appreciate your sentiment, Mister President, but there is a limit to all good deeds. We cannot possibly accept all those people who are fleeing German tyranny, whether they are Jewish or not."

"And, I understand your concern, Cordell; however, as our declaration properly states, the Germans have focused their genocide on the Jewish, primarily. They deserve extra care and support."

"Where do we draw the line?"

"I do not know. That is the essence of our conundrum, is it not? My inclination is somewhere more absorptive than our present conduct."

"Easier said than done, I'm afraid," Hull said with an air of solemnity. "You have stated more than a few times since you and Churchill first discussed the matter at Placentia Bay a year and a half ago that the best way to end this crisis is to defeat the Germans. We should stick to that policy."

"Aren't you troubled by what is written on that paper?" the president asked.

"Yes, of course, I am. But the Jews have brought this one on themselves in part."

"Surely, you jest, Cordell. You cannot be serious here. Who would seek or induce genocide?"

"We have discussed this before, Mister President. On this matter, we do not agree. However, I continue to endeavor with vigor to implement the nation's policies. This declaration is one of those efforts."

"Are you suggesting you do not agree with the declaration?" asked the president.

"No, Mister President. As a matter of policy, we stated what needed to be and had to be stated. What the Nazis are doing is wrong, as we so state. We managed to gain concurrence from most of the governments in exile as well. We all know it is wrong. This declaration," Hull said, holding up the paper, "makes that fact quite clear. The Poles were the first to alert Britain and us that something untoward was happening in their country." Roosevelt chose not to correct the Secretary of State. The very first reports came from MI6—the British Secret Intelligence Service. "They are satisfied with this declaration."

"I don't think that is correct, Cordell. The Poles want us to take action to stop the disaster. They want us to bomb the railway lines the Nazis use for transportation. They want us to bomb and break-up the perimeter confinement fences to allow the internees to escape. They want us to take offensive action."

"All of that is fine. I just do not think it is appropriate to ask Americans to open their homes and communities to millions of . . . of . . . of people, who are trying to escape Nazi tyranny."

"You mean Jews," Roosevelt said with a distinct growl to his voice.

The Secretary of State shook his head. "Please don't try to paint me as a bigot, please, Mister President. I am only trying to offer you the best State counsel I can. There are limits to what we can absorb."

President Roosevelt retained a stern, almost angry expression in his eyes and on his face. He stared intently at Secretary of State Hull. "You know Henry Morgenthau is advocating forcefully for more offensive action to enforce this declaration, including the humanitarian acceptance of refugees."

"Yes, I do, and he's a Jew. Of course, he wants us to accept far more Je . . . refugees."

"That is quite unbecoming, Cordell. Enough! I will ask you to review our immigration policy, especially regarding refugees from the occupied countries. I want the results of your review and your recommendations by the first of the New Year. Is that understood?"

"Yes sir."

"Very well. Then, we are concluded here. Thank you for the extra effort in releasing the joint declaration. At least we have that."

"Thank you, Mister President," Hull said and stood.

"Good day."

Franklin Roosevelt was not happy at the moment but contained his irritation. He had to get his mind onto other topics to help dissipate his anger. He did not wait for Harry. Roosevelt pushed himself back to his desk before Cordell Hull had left the office.

———

Wednesday, 23.December.1942
Office of the Director, Office of Strategic Services
National Institutes of Health Building
2430 E Street Northwest
Washington, District of Columbia
United States of America
09:15 hours

"I received this personal note this morning from General Marshall," announced Bill Donovan and handed the note to his deputy.

General George C. Marshall

December 23, 1942

Dear Bill,

    I cannot let the holiday season pass without expressing my gratitude to you for the cooperation and assistance you have given me personally in the trying times of the past year.

    The quickly growing list of accomplishments achieved by the Office of Strategic Services is the opening chapter of what I am certain will be a glorious history. Please convey my gratitude to your troops. With great respect,

George

"Well, how about that!" exclaimed Ned Buxton. "We are making headway."

Donovan smiled. "Progress by jerks, as the physicists like to say. While we still have obstructionist detractors, we do have some powerful supporters, the most obvious being Ike Eisenhower. I am making some progress with Nimitz, and MacArthur remains problematic. The fragmented nature of the Pacific war makes our ability to help much more tortuous."

"Do you think MacArthur will eventually come around?"

"Not likely on his own. His ego is too prideful to accept help, especially from an organization of which he does not approve. Our best opportunity with him is in China and the Philippines. I am becoming convinced that we simply must seize the day—*carpe diem quam minimum credula postero.*"

"I recognize the seize the day part, what is the rest of it?" asked Ned.

"It comes from the Roman poet Quintus Horatius Flaccus and book 1, number 11, of his work *Odes*, written around 23 BC. Roughly translated, it means seize the day, trusting as little as possible in tomorrow."

"I learn something every day from you, Bill. I do not know how you keep all of these little tidbits in your brain. Nonetheless, how does that apply to us?"

"We are going to have to accept the risk of going alone without cover into his areas of operations to do what we are chartered to do. The facts, valuable evidence that MacArthur can use, will help him come around. Unfortunately, our field agents will be taking all of the real, physical risks."

"They are up to it; of that, I am confident."

"Yes, they are. We also received word, confirmed by MI6, that Manstein has abandoned his counterattack to save the German 6th Army at Stalingrad."

"An entire field army, that is a helluva loss, even for the Germans."

"You got that right. And, it is not looking much better for the Germans in North Africa. The British 8th Army broke the El Agheila Line, and once again, the Germans are in full retreat west across the desert. It looks like they are going to make another delaying defense at Buerot, to buy time for their engineers, who are feverishly building robust defenses at Mareth, just across the border in Southeast Tunisia. Eisenhower is approaching the mountains in Western Tunisia. They will soon have Rommel in the vice, and that can't feel well for the Germans."

"There is still a lot of fight in that dog."

"Yes, there is, just as the Germans still hold massive forces in Russia. This war is long from over, and we have much to do."

The two OSS leaders split and returned to their respective paperwork.

———

Wednesday, 23.December.1942
Ambassador Hotel
3400 Wilshire Boulevard
Los Angeles, Los Angeles County, California
United States of America
21:30 hours

Many, if not most or all, of the movie stars had homes close by. Butch, Slim and Hunter had rooms in the luxury Ambassador Hotel along with the other military and civilian personnel supporting the tour. Their final event of the tour had been completed earlier this evening. The pilots did not have to go far for the after-tour farewell party. The champagne and platters of delicious *hors d'œuvrés* as well as the contemporary background big band music gave the party a very lavish and extravagant feeling. *I wonder who is paying for all this?*

"Hey bud, we'd better mingle before we're ordered to do so," announced Slim Carl.

"Yeah, good point," added Butch O'Hare. "See ya later, Hunter."

I'll take my chances. Brian remained at the back of the room, out of the way of the large and growing crowd. He was not much of a crowd person and not particularly comfortable with social chit-chat. Brian did note a wave, at least he thought the gesture was to him, from James Cagney, Fred Astaire and Ralph Bellamy, and a nice wink or blown kiss from Hedy Lamarr and Dorothy Lamour. Each of the stars had small groups around them. He was perfectly content to stand back for good people-watching in a target-rich environment.

The Army colonel, whose name Brian could not remember and who was their titular leader for the First War Bonds Drive, used the band's microphone. He achieved silence in quick time when he clinked his champagne flute glass several times near the microphone. The colonel thanked everyone from the movie stars to the active military personnel, both enlisted men and officers, with punctuating applause. Then, the colonel answered the question on many of their minds. "The federal government initiated this first War Bonds Drive to engage the American people in the war effort. Not all of our citizens can serve in uniform, but all citizens can help win the war by their labor and by giving their hard-earned money. To that latter method, the Treasury Department's accountants have just informed me that through your collective efforts, we have raised over $13 billion." Cheers, applause and shouts interrupted the colonel. "That's billion with a 'B.'" More cheers filled the room. "The goal for this First War Bonds Drive was $9 billion. The early assessment has established that approximately $1.6 billion of the total came from individual citizens—one dollar to hundreds of dollars. We, especially those of us serving in uniform, greatly appreciate the contributions, and I am authorized by President Roosevelt to convey his enormous gratitude for everyone's participation. Thank you and enjoy your evening."

Brian refreshed his champagne from the tray of a passing waiter. The cacophony of the large banquet hall made conversation unintelligible except at close proximity. Butch and Slim were probably buried in the mass of human beings filling the hall, but he could not see them. Brian snatched glimpses of faces he recognized—famous and not so much—but they were only flashes that surfaced in the sea and disappeared. *Damn, I've not seen so many generals and admirals ever. Did all these guys just come here for the party?*

His peripheral vision detected a head above the ocean of people working his way along the back wall. Brian thought the face looked familiar, but it was not someone he remembered meeting. People seemed to recognize him and move out of his way. The man appeared to be moving toward Brian. He tried not to look, but Brian was very much aware of the tall man's approach. Brian was tall by the standards of the people in the banquet hall, but the guy was a few inches taller than Brian. When the man reached a point a few yards away, and the last people between them parted, Brian turned to face the man's intense stare.

The man extended his right hand as he closed the last few feet. "Brian, I have been looking for you." They shook hands firmly and vigorously. "I am Howard Hughes."

Now I recognize the tall, thin, mustachioed man. "Nice to meet you, sir." Hughes released Brian's hand. Brian noticed people around them moving away, opening space around them, as if there was some undetected contagion. They kept looking over their shoulder at the pair of aviators, now focused on each other.

"We have mutual friends and interests. One of our common friends encouraged me to seek you out. I am not much of a party or crowd person, but when Bill Donovan speaks, I listen."

Brian nodded his head, not sure why Hughes was bringing up Wild Bill Donovan. "I have met General Donovan several times, sir, but I cannot claim him as a friend."

Hughes chuckled. "You may not, but he sure does. He has been singing your praises for weeks now." Hughes looked around them, and Brian followed suit. "You are a famous pilot, Brian."

"I do not hold any world speed records, Mister Hughes."

Howard chuckled again. "Those are just numbers and pieces of paper. You have 21 aerial victories in combat. You have been decorated by the King no less," he said, tapping the ribbons over the right breast pocket of his Army tunic. "You are a genuine hero and a rare member of The Few, as my friend Winston so eloquently proclaimed two and a half years ago." Brian could only nod his head. "Bill has informed me of your little endeavor." Once again, Hughes looked at the people nearby. "We cannot talk here. I would invite you up to my suite in the hotel, but given our conversation, I think it would be more appropriate to chat in private at my aircraft company in Culver City. I know it is Christmas, but could you spare a day or two and meet me at the plant tomorrow evening?"

This sounds intriguing and might actually be interesting. "I think I can delay my departure until Saturday. My family is in England, and my parents have passed."

"I am so sorry for your loss, Brian. I lost my parents, as well. I know how it feels. Tragic accident. How are Charlotte and Ian?"

He knows way too much about me. "They are healthy and as safe as they can be with the Germans so close."

"*Guten Abend mein Liebchen,*" came the familiar, soft German voice. Brian looked behind Hughes to see the exquisitely coiffed and dressed, blond Marlene Dietrich. She did not acknowledge Hughes and raised up on her toes to kiss Brian on the lips. He felt his face flush. She smiled seductively and mischievously. "No need to be embarrassed, my darling. We are friends." Marlene looked over her right shoulder. "Always a pleasure to see you again, Howard."

"The pleasure is mine, Marlene. You are extraordinarily gorgeous this evening. And I see you know our hero."

Dietrich looked back at Brian, stared deeply into his eyes, and smiled. "Yes, we know each other."

Brian felt his face flush again. *Is she going to tell all to Howard Hughes and everyone within earshot? Why does she have this effect on me?*

Hughes smiled knowingly. "It's OK, Brian. I know what she is capable of in life. I shall leave you two." He looked at Brian. "I will see you tomorrow evening, Brian."

"Yes sir."

"Just tell any cabbie or driver you need to go to Hughes Aircraft in Culver City. You should have no problem getting over there. Have a good evening," Hughes said, turned smartly and walked away through the parting in the sea of people.

"What did Howard want with you?" Marlene asked, "if I may ask."

"To meet me, I guess, and as you heard, he wants me to meet him at his aircraft company for more private discussions."

Dietrich waved her delicate hand dismissively. "None of my business." She smiled again. "I was not invited to this party, but I knew you would be here. I do not know if I will get to see you again, or when." Marlene leaned in and up to whisper in Brian's right ear. "I want, no, I need one more romp with you, my darling, at least until we meet again."

Brian felt his jaw drop. He tried to regain control of his emotions. "I don't thi . . ." His reply was terminated when she grasped his hand and literally led him out of the hall. Dozens of previously unseen flashbulbs burst from the parting crowd. He had not seen any photographers until just this moment.

Dietrich did not speak and continued to lead Brian to the elevator. Several other people on the elevator prevented any discussion. They went to the fourth floor and down the long hallway to a corner suite. The two lovers renewed their intimacy in between short talks of the past, present and future. Beyond the pleasures of the flesh, Brian noted Marlene's explicit desire to meet

Charlotte and Ian the next time she made it to London. Brian waffled but did not reject her request. He could not predict how Charlotte would respond to everything that had happened in the last two months, but he had to tell her, to give her the right of refusal.

———

Thursday, 24.December.1942
Hughes Aircraft Company
5865 Campus Center Drive
Culver City, Los Angeles County, California
United States of America
22:45 hours

Sure enough, the taxi driver knew precisely where to go and had delivered Brian to what looked like the main gate in a high cyclone fence topped with barbed wire. A large, professional sign stated:

Hughes Aircraft Company
Culver City Campus
This is a designated U.S. defense facility.
Unauthorized entrance is strictly prohibited
and will be enforced.

The guard had his full name and rank on a clipboard for access. As he completed the sign-in process, a small truck drove up and stopped on the other side of the gate. The electrical locks were audibly opened from inside the guard shack. Brian passed through the gate. The driver stood by the open passenger door.

"Welcome to Hughes Aircraft," the man said. "Mister Hughes is expected here shortly."

"Thank you."

The driver knew precisely where he was going. They passed several large buildings, external storage areas, forklifts, and other equipment common to a manufacturing facility. The truck stopped in front of a smaller hangar at the far end of the facility. The driver parked by a side door, shut off the truck, and gestured to the door. Brian got out and followed the driver to the door.

The interior of the well-maintained medium size hangar was very well lighted with a couple of immaculate aircraft parked inside. Immediately inside the door was what looked like a card table with a brilliant white, spotless tablecloth, glasses, bottles of liquor and wine, and a large platter of sandwich triangles, cookies and other snacks in the middle. Only two chairs were placed at the table.

"Help yourself if you wish. Mister Hughes should be here in a few minutes."

"Thank you very much."

The driver departed, leaving Brian alone in the hangar. Two aircraft and a large model partially filled the space. Brian examined both aircraft. The closest was a very sleek, single radial engine, monoplane with unusually long retractable landing gear with a retractable tailskid. The aircraft had very smooth, highly polished aluminum skin. The aircraft's skin was like a curved mirror. The machine was clearly built for speed. The low-profile canopy-cockpit was not a practical design for combat. The other, much larger aircraft was a twin-boom, twin radial engine machine with a single-seat, centerline cockpit. The twin-engine airplane looked similar to the Lockheed P-38 fighter. The model sat on a long table and obviously reflected what was intended to be a very large flying boat with eight engines on a high wing. The wingspan of the model was at least six feet. Brian was still trying to imagine the actual size of the aircraft when he heard the metal door open and close.

Howard Hughes appeared more like a workingman than he did in his black-tie tuxedo last night. He had a brownish-gray fedora, brown leather flight jacket, and khaki trousers. As Brian started to move toward Hughes, Howard gestured for Brian to stop.

"What do you think of this beast?" Hughes asked, pointing to the model.

"The thing looks really large."

"It will be the largest aircraft ever built. We have a government contract to build a prototype we have designated the HK-1. We are in the detailed design phase and expect to fly it in one to two years. The requirement calls for it to carry an entire fully equipped battalion, or two, M-4 Sherman main battle tanks. We had a model DC-3 to show the size." Hughes looked around the table, then underneath the table skirt. "Ah, there it is," Howard said, pulled out the model and placed the diminutive model under the left-wing.

"Damn!" Brian exclaimed. "That is huge."

Hughes did not respond and then turned to face the two flying machines. "That's the H-1 Racer," he said, pointing to the single-engine machine. "The other one is our D-2 prototype. She's going through a re-design at the moment. I did not like the control forces."

"Impressive, I must say, Mister Hughes," Brian said.

"Please, Brian, it's Howard between us."

"Yes sir."

Hughes gestured to the table by the door. "Help yourself, all specially prepared." Brian sat across from Hughes and nodded his head, but he did not take anything. "This place is quite private and more appropriate for the discussion I wanted to have with you, or rather Bill Donovan asked me to have with you." Brian nodded but did not speak. "Bill thought I might be helpful to you and your new endeavor."

Brian just looked at Howard with no reaction or response. *I do not know what he knows, and General Donovan never mentioned anything about assistance from Hughes.*

"Bill briefed me on his contract with your Bainbridge Air Services company. He indicated he is financing your acquisition of Beech Model 18s and Lockheed Lodestars. Bill knows about our working with Lockheed to produce the fastest, highest-flying transport airliner for my airline."

"Your airline?"

"Yeah. I am the majority shareholder of TWA—Transcontinental & Western Airlines. You are going to provide air transport services for his OSS. He really wants you to be successful and wants to help you grow into the work. As I understand things, your man at Bainbridge is Bobby Joe Sales."

"Correct."

"If you have no objection, I would like to contact Sales to make certain skills available to him. Your tasking is quite different from TWA, but there are similarities, and it is in those similarities that we can be of assistance. Things like route selection surveys, load factor control, and such might be useful."

"Sure. That would be great. Thank you very much, Howard. That is most generous."

"What I really wanted to talk to you about is your flying."

Hughes showed genuine and earnest curiosity about Brian's flying history. He clearly knew a fair amount from Bill Donovan. He also shared some of his similar flying experiences interlaced among questions. They discussed details of the Spitfire airplane. Howard's genuine fascination impressed and encouraged Brian. More significantly, Howard probed Brian's combat experience to glean out characteristics that would help his company build better fighter aircraft. For someone who had never flown in combat, Howard displayed a keen appreciation for the raw, brute traits as well as the distinguishing subtleties.

"I could listen to you all night," Howard said, "but, there is one more topic we must discuss. TWA has ordered 40 new airliners from Lockheed. Hughes Tool is fronting a goodly chunk of the developmental funding for this aircraft. I have agreed with Bill Donovan to give up six production slots of our 40 for Bainbridge Air Services. I wanted to tell you a little about the design." Brian nodded his head in agreement. "The Lockheed Model 44 just wasn't bold enough, so I injected myself in the design process. I have been working with Lockheed's chief research engineer, Kelly Johnson, and their chief line engineer, Hall Hibbard." Hughes looked around the hangar. "I really need to get a scale model of the 'L' Forty-Nine, the new designation for our aircraft. The sleek fuselage will carry 40 passengers at least 3,500 miles with all the appropriate services for a modern airliner. I will state here, I think the design will do much better than that, but first things first. The aircraft will cruise at 340 miles an hour at 24,000 feet with a pressurized cabin. The aircraft will be powered by four 3350 supercharged radial engines. Lockheed is preparing the first prototype for its first flight in two weeks from its Burbank plant. We expect the aircraft to enter low-rate production and enter service with TWA later next year. The second prototype is a military configuration. The Air Force has ordered 20 of that configuration."

"I am still a little concerned that the Air Force is such a large organization with all kinds of aircraft for virtually every purpose. Heck, TWA is an established airline like Pan Am, American, United, and all the others. Why does the OSS need Bainbridge? Until this contract, we had a hodge-podge of old aircraft, the oldest being a pristine Sopwith F.1 Camel, the newest being a Beech Staggerwing that is now about five years old and not even remotely as capable as the Model 49 you described."

"A Camel, damn, Brian! How the hell did you get a Camel?"

"I inherited it along with the other aircraft when my mentor and flight instructor passed."

"Malcolm Bainbridge?"

"Yes, precisely. He flew Camels in the Great War, a personal acquisition for him."

"You are an amazing young man with surprisingly brilliant facets. Have you flown it?"

"Yes. I've flown them all."

"Could I impose upon you to fly your Camel? I've flown them during the filming of *Hell's Angels* but flying yours is a good excuse to visit Wichita."

"Sure. We can arrange that."

"Excellent." Hughes looked at the clock on the hangar wall. "It's after one o'clock in the morning. I've kept you here much longer than I expected. We have covered everything Bill Donovan asked me to discuss with you and much more. I should answer your previous question, as best I am able. Donovan wants his own transportation service for his personnel to avoid questions from anyone. I have encouraged him to do this. You are the chosen one, and I, for one, think Bill made a brilliant selection. I truly look forward to working with you and getting to know you better. Now, before we go our separate ways tonight, I must tell you, Brian, you are blessed to know Marlene." Brian felt his face flush, again, with the memories of last night. "She is an incredible woman, and I have known a few. I will urge you to cherish her friendship. I hope and trust your relationship with Marlene will not interfere with Charlotte and your family."

"I hope so, too, but that is yet to be determined."

"I cannot say when I will be in England, again, or when you will return to the States, but I would be honored to meet Charlotte. If she is even a fraction of your accomplishments, she is a very impressive woman as well."

I would love to ask him how well he knows Marlene, but I can't. "She would love to meet you as well, Howard. We also need to watch some of your movies. I was too young for the early ones, and now, I have no access to theaters."

"If you had more time, I would gladly set up a separate screening for you. Perhaps another time."

"That would be great. I'm going to be in Wichita, checking on things before I am scheduled to head back across the pond. You are welcome to visit if you have the time. We keep all of the aircraft, including the Camel, in fine flying fashion."

"Outstanding!" Howard exclaimed. "For an opportunity to fly a genuine Camel, I will make the time. What works for you?"

"I should be back there in a couple of days. I am traveling by rail. Give me a few days to make sure things are ready. What about right after the New Year? Say mid-week, something like the 6th plus or minus a day. Not the best time to be flying in Kansas, so bring your cold weather gear. I've got a Mystery S Malcolm modified with Walter Beech for my flying competition work before the war. I can fly with you if that is alright."

"That would be perfect. You have a date, my friend," Howard responded with genuine enthusiasm.

"Thank you very much for your time, Howard, and especially for your help."

"It is my pleasure, Brian. So, until two weeks' time, safe journey home."

Hughes gave Brian a printed card with his private contact information—postal, telephone, and telegraph. The two men shook hands outside the hangar. Two black Cadillac limousines stood ready with the drivers. They said good-bye. Brian was returned to the Ambassador Hotel.

———

Wednesday, 30.December.1942
Bainbridge Ranch
Rural Route 14
Wichita, Sedgwick County, Kansas
United States of America
13:30 hours

With the War Bonds Tour complete, Brian used his travel priority to take the train home. The journey took not quite two days with all the stops to embark and debark passengers, mail, and, some cargo in places.

He had also gratefully received his orders to return to the squadron and his family. He had been granted one to two weeks of leave before reporting at an as yet unidentified location and time for his transport back to England. Brian took one day to do nothing but sleep and lay around his childhood home with the memories of his parents. The housekeeper Mister Braddock hired to tend the house continued to take very good care of everything, including plenty of cold bottled beer in the refrigerator. Yesterday had been the first day all to himself, without any commitments, in many months. Brian found the first two Hornblower books and surprisingly discovered a copy of the third published C.S. Forester Hornblower book—*Flying Colours*. The books remained fascinating to him. It had been years since he took the time to read for pleasure. He jumped well into the story, but only made it a quarter in before sleep had claimed his consciousness last night.

To Brian's surprise, the blue 1938 Ford pickup truck Gertrude Bainbridge had given him during his last visit in February 1941, had started up promptly and robustly. *Someone had been maintaining the truck as well. I had not thought of that. I need to find out who and thank them.* Brian chose a simple T-shirt, Levi's, and his winter coat, rather than the mandated uniform of wartime.

The drive out to Bainbridge Ranch had been equally pleasant in the cold, clear, winter day. Gerty appeared on the porch despite the cold air as Brian drove up and parked in the gravel area to the right of the house.

"Welcome home, Brian," Gerty Bainbridge shouted.

"Thank you. It's great to be home, even for a short time, and great to see you, again."

The house was warm, and the aroma of freshly baked cookies filled the house. *If my sniffer is calibrated, she's baked her delicious chocolate-chip cookies.* Brian was not bold enough to ask.

"Bobby had to make a run into town," Gerty announced and gestured to the living room couch. "He should be here shortly."

"No problem. How have you been?" asked Brian.

Gerty sat in the single chair to the right of the couch. "Thanks to you, Brian, I am about as near perfect as life can get. Your generosity has vanquished my worries."

"I am glad I could help."

"Bobby has been very busy, especially in the last few months. Something is going on. Do you know?"

"Yes, but I'm afraid I cannot talk much about the details. We gained an important government contract for aircraft transportation services."

"That seems rather odd, Brian. The government has far more and bigger aircraft than you do."

Brian smiled. "It is for special air services not otherwise regularly provided by the Army Air Forces."

"That sounds rather mysterious."

"Part of the contract requires secrecy, so yes, I suppose it is rather mysterious."

"Are you OK with all this?" Gerty asked. "I mean I don't want you to get into any sensitive matters."

"Well, I suppose that risk will always be present, especially in wartime."

The crunch of gravel outside probably announced the arrival of Bobby Joe Sales.

Gertrude stood and said, "Do you want to talk in here or in the kitchen?"

"The kitchen will be just fine," Brian responded, as he stood and went to the front door.

"I've prepared sandwiches, coffee, tea for you, and a nice platter of fresh cookies."

"Thank you, Gerty. Bobby and I will join you shortly."

After Gertrude went to the kitchen, Bobby entered the house. "Great to see you, boss." The two men shook hands. Gertrude had everything on the table. They all sat. Each of them helped themselves to a ham and cheese sandwich on homemade bread.

"How long are you in town for?" asked Sales.

"A couple of days to maybe a week. I was granted leave pending transportation back to England."

"They're sending you back? I would have thought you have had enough combat."

"I requested it. I do not want the safety of some desk job in Washington. I want to fly. My squadron is at the forefront."

"They've transferred you and your squadron to the Army Air Forces?"

"Yes, actually, all three of the American volunteer Eagle Squadrons have been transferred. We are now the 334th Fighter Squadron in the 4th Fighter Wing."

"Why aren't you in uniform like everyone else?"

"I'm here on private business during leave."

"We saw photographs of you in your Army uniform when you stopped in Kansas City," observed Gerty. "You are so handsome in that uniform."

"Thank you."

"We also saw a photograph or two, somewhere—I can't remember where—with Marlene Dietrich."

I need to avoid that one. "The whole point of the tour was to encourage all of our citizens to buy war bonds, to support the war effort. We worked with many Hollywood stars, like James Cagney, Ginger Rogers, Fred Astaire, and many others."

"Sure looked like you were pretty chummy," observed Bobby.

"We worked with them every day. We traveled with many of them on the train. It was a very busy couple of months."

"Were you successful?" asked Gerty.

"They told us we were, but they are still totaling things up. Now, enough questions for the moment. Let's get our business done, and then I would be happy to answer all your questions. I know you are curious." Neither Bobby nor Gerty answered and only nodded their consent. "So, Bobby, at the summary level, where are we?"

"We have a signed contract. Our customer is working very fast. I need more help, Brian."

"I don't know if I will have time on this visit to talk to Jonas Braddock. Start with him. You need legal and contract support services. Jonas should know the right people for you to hire."

"You want me to talk to him?"

"Yes. You are the chief of operations, Bobby. Get the professional help you need. Jonas can help you find the correct people to help."

"OK. I was just in town meeting with city and airport management personnel. Our customer has obtained approval for three large hangars and a large two-story office building to be built on the east side of the municipal airport, on the other side of the field from the Boeing plant. They are still building the Boeing facility, but they have also begun assembling aircraft over there. Things are moving so fast. Boeing flew the prototype of a massive heavy bomber, much bigger and more powerful than the B-17, earlier this year. The second prototype flew this morning. Boeing Wichita will be a major assembly line for the B-29. They flew the first one in here a couple of weeks ago for a kind of a fit check. Damn thing is massive."

"What has that got to do with us?"

"Boeing is going to dominate operations at Municipal Airport. They are under contract to deliver the first production bombers next spring. I can't imagine, but that is what the plan is. We have to compete with their incredible building process."

"Why do they want us at Municipal Airport?"

"A variety of reasons, not least of which is to blend with the Boeing building effort. Our customer has very ambitious plans, and I must say, they have ponied up."

"What about the aircraft?" Brian asked.

"That is a whole other story. We have ordered and received priority placement six Beech Model 18s—the Army calls them a C-45 Expeditor; but, we will get a civilian version. We will keep the markings to a bare minimum, so they can be quickly painted black when required. I'm not sure why, but that is the requirement.

I am in the process of closing a contract with Lockheed for the civilian version of their Model 18 Lodestar."

"How many?"

"The initial buy is 12."

"Where is the money coming from?"

"Incredibly, the government's deposits in a separate company bank account have already been made. We have the money, Brian. We have to account for it all, but the money is there."

Just as Bill Donovan said it would be. "Good. Lockheed is working on the design of their Model 49, an advanced derivative of their Model 44. I met with Howard Hughes a week ago."

"The Howard Hughes . . . the movie producer?"

"Yes, but he is very much the aviator and owns an aircraft company. He is also the majority shareholder of Transcontinental & Western Airlines. TWA has ordered 40 of the Model 49s, and one of Hughes' other companies, Hughes Tool, the drill bit company, is paying for the development. Hughes agreed to allocate six of the TWA buy for us."

"Well, that explains a lot."

"How so?"

"The contract requires us to form and operate a for-profit air transport company to specific sites as well as other open sites of our choosing."

"Have they specified their sites?"

"Yes, but we will need to talk about them later."

"OK."

"Can I ask a question?" Gerty interjected.

"Yes, of course," Brian answered.

"So, we have a government contract to build an airline for the transportation of people and cargo."

"Yes."

"But, they, the government, is going to utilize a portion of the seats we have."

"Yes," answered Brian. He looked at Bobby. "Does the contract specify a portion of our lift capacity?"

"Yes," Bobby said. "The contract says 30% of our lift capacity with an option for an additional 10% with coordination, and their dedicated capacity may be utilized in whole or in part with prior notification and coordination."

"Does that seem right?" Gerty asked.

"It is a bit odd," responded Brian, "but, I think our customer sees a unique need to move personnel and equipment without being dependent on other transportation services."

"So, both of you are comfortable with the federal government giving this business to little old Bainbridge Air Services for such monumental air transport support."

"I am," answered Brian, "but, I am not directly involved at the moment. Bobby is. So, his voice counts more. Bobby, what say you?"

"For whatever reason, this opportunity has come to us, it is here. As long as Brian supports what we are doing, I am eager to see where this goes."

"Very well," said Gerty. "One last question, if I may, you two keep referring to our primary customer in rather distant, misty terms. Is this really legal?"

Brian chuckled softly. "I appreciate your concern here, Gerty. I acknowledge that this is a bit unusual, but I can assure you there are very good and logical reasons for the strange setup. Bobby needs to confer with the customer's administrator to clear you for access. As a director on the board of Bainbridge Air Services, I think you are entitled to know the details of the arrangements, but the customer must clear you and authorize access."

"I will take care of it tomorrow," Bobby responded.

Brian smiled and nodded to Gerty, who nodded and smiled back at him. He looked directly at Bobby Joe Sales. "My root question here is, do you think you can manage this monster?"

"To be candid, Brian, the scope of this thing is rather daunting. We need full-time accountants and contract administrators."

"Does the contract allow for administrative staff?"

"Yes, several million dollars in the initial allotment."

"Hire what you need. Unless you have a better suggestion, I recommend we start with their routes and their schedule. That traffic is known and dependable. You need to do a market assessment and add in what makes sense from a profitability standpoint. Hughes is going to contact you soon, probably after the holidays, to offer TWA technical support to us. Let's make this work."

"We have a long way to go," Bobby said.

"Long journeys begin with small steps," added Brian

"Do you want to fly while you are here?" Gerty asked.

"Ah yes, thank you for reminding me." Both Gerty and Bobby displayed puzzled expressions like something strange had just been spoken. "We are going to have a distinguished visitor next week."

"The hell you say!" Bobby exclaimed.

"Yep, we are," Brian answered. "Howard Hughes is going to fly in on Wednesday next week. He wants to fly the Camel. I will fly the Mystery S with him."

"Oh wow! That should be fun. Can I take up one of the other planes with you guys? Maybe one of the FF-1s I still have . . . both here now?"

"Sure, I don't see why not," responded Brian.

"Excellent. I'll make sure Charlie has all the aircraft in pristine condition."

Charles 'Charlie' Rogers had been their chief and only mechanic since they formed Bainbridge Air Services.

"By the way," Bobby added, "Charlie has done a great job, but we are going to need more of him. I talked to him about supervising . . . being our chief of maintenance."

"Fine by me."

"So, what next?"

"I'll probably get my travel information soon after New Year's Day, so we can settle things out once we know that."

"It is so great to have you home, Brian," Gerty added. "I hope you can get some rest while you are here before you head back to the war."

"I will. I found a copy of C.S. Forester's *Flying Colours* that I started reading last night, and I will probably take it with me for the journey back."

The rest of the day was spent in laughter and reminiscence, as they shared stories of the recent months. *This feels good and right with the world. But I really need to get back to Charlotte and Ian. I am ready to go home, and home is where Charlotte and Ian are.*

—

Cap Parlier

Author

——

Cap and his wife, Jeanne, live in Fountain Hills, Arizona, along with their precious dogs. Their four grown children have begun their families, raising seven exceptional grandchildren. He is a graduate of the U.S. Naval Academy, a retired Marine aviator, Vietnam veteran and experimental test pilot, and has finally retired from the corporate world to devote his full time to his passion for writing a good story. Cap has numerous other projects completed and in the works including screenplays, historical novels and a couple of history books.

——

Interested readers may wish to visit his website at <http://www.parlier.com> for his essays and other items, or subscribe to his weekly Blog: "*Update from the Sunland*." Cap can be reached at: cap@SaintGaudensPress.com.

——